VEIL OF THE DIVINE

Book One of the Veiled Trilogy

Jana Jimenez

Copyright © 2025 by Jana Jimenez
All rights reserved.

No part of this book may be reproduced, distributed, or transmitted in any form or by any means, including photocopying, recording, or other electronic or mechanical methods, without the prior written permission of the publisher, except in the case of brief quotations used in critical reviews or scholarly works.

This is a work of fiction. Names, characters, places, and events are either products of the author's imagination or used fictitiously. Any resemblance to actual persons, living or dead, or actual events is purely coincidental.

For inquiries, contact:
www.janajimenez.com
or **janajimenezauthor@gmail.com**

First Edition, May 2025
ISBN: 979-8-218-67619-3

Cover photography by Jana Jimenez
Cover model: Aly Kerley
Published in the United States of America

To the one who carried too much,
said too little,
and still protected everyone else.
You were never weak.
You were never invisible.
Your big heart is showing.
I remember you.
This is your reckoning.
This is your redemption.

Protect the Ember – Arianna

The room is too quiet.

I know before they say it.

I know by the way the midwife lowers the bundle in her arms, her face pale and drawn. By the way the priest grips his holy symbol a little too tightly. By the way the room—so full of frantic voices only moments ago—has settled into suffocating silence.

I know because I cannot hear my child cry.

A breath shudders from my lips, and I don't need to ask.

Stillborn.

A daughter who never took a breath.

A princess who never got to be.

A queen who never rose.

The grief is distant at first, buried beneath the fire in my veins, beneath the unbearable pull of my body tearing itself apart. Blood soaks the sheets beneath me, too much, too fast. I am slipping.

Somewhere above me, Alexey is shouting.

I don't hear his words at first. His voice sounds all wrong—unsteady, broken.

I blink sluggishly, my head tilting toward him. He's gripping my hand too tightly, his face tight with barely restrained panic.

Alexey.

Always so calm. Always so in control.

But not now.

Not for me.

For me, he breaks.

I try to smile. It doesn't work.

He shakes his head, his hand tightening around mine. "Stay with me, Arianna."

I swallow, trying to focus on his face, on the sharp, clean lines of him, the unwavering blue of his eyes. I want to look upon his handsome face, chiseled by the Gods themselves. He has always been my anchor, my greatest shield.

But even he cannot stop this.

I know he sees it.

I see it too.

Still, he refuses to accept it.

"Just hold on," he says, his voice raw. "You're going to make it."

"Liar." I exhale weakly. "Alexey—"

"Don't." His jaw locks, his fingers tightening around mine like he can keep me here by brute force. "Just—don't. Stay."

I try to squeeze his hand, but I have no strength left.

"I lost them," I whisper. "Both of them. I have no reason to stay."

Alexey flinches, like the words are a dagger to his heart.

"This is the sum of my choices, Alexey. You know that."

I do not have much time left.

I can feel it, the weight of it pressing into my bones, dragging me toward something I cannot fight. The world tilts, the candlelight flickering, the voices around me beginning to fade.

My fingers brush the Eternum Relic still suspended around my neck.

I say a prayer.

I am not sure what I am praying for.

And then—

The Vision Takes Me.

Fire.

It rises against the night sky, devouring the ruins of a once-great castle.

Elarion Castle.

The scent of smoke and blood lingers in the air, a battlefield lost to time.

And she stands in the wreckage.

A girl.

Not my daughter.

But she should have been.

Her hair is red as flame, just like Odin's.

Her blue eyes fierce, unyielding.

She is not afraid.

She is not broken.

She stands strong, the ember that has risen from the ashes of the kingdom I failed to save.

I know her.

Not by name, not by sight.

But by destiny.

She is wrapped divinely in the veil that shrouds this world.

This girl—this future queen—was never meant to be mine.

But she will be everything I wanted my daughter to be.

She will be fire.

She will be the reckoning I never lived to see.

And she will not kneel.

I Am Back.

The pain rushes in all at once.

The weight in my limbs, the fire in my veins, the unbearable emptiness in my arms.

Alexey is still holding me.

I swallow, my throat raw, and force the words out. "There is still hope."

His brow furrows, his breath unsteady. "Arianna—"

"Listen to me." My voice is weak, but I pour what little strength I have left into it. "You will find her."

His expression tightens. "Who?"

I blink slowly. The room is fading. "The ember that rose from the ashes of Lorna."

His fingers dig into my hand, his jaw clenching. "You need to stop talking and hold on."

I try to smile again. This time, it works. Just barely.

"You'll protect her," I whisper. "Like you always do."

His grip shakes. "No. Arianna. Stay with me."

I wish I could.

But fate is cruel.

The warmth fades from my limbs. The world tilts, slipping away from me.

The last thing I hear is his voice, low and rough, a whispered plea against my skin.

"Arianna, please."

I exhale slowly.

The world softens.
And I let go.

Почему блестящие звёзды над нами позволили нам мечтать, что мы могли быть вместе?

Why did the shining stars above us allow us to dream that we could be together?

The Funeral – Alexey

The first time I held a sword, I was too young to understand what war meant.

The first time I saw a woman die in childbirth, I understood too much.

Now, I stand in the cold morning air, watching as the last shovelful of dirt seals her beneath the earth.

Arianna is gone.

The grave is fresh, the ground damp from yesterday's rain. Even the clouds mourn her loss. The scent of turned soil lingers, mixing with the incense burned by the priests. The ceremony is over. The nobles have left. The priests have finished their rites.

But I cannot make myself move.

I have seen too much death to grieve like other men.

This—this should not be different.

But it is.

Murphy stands beside me, unusually quiet. His arms are crossed, his gaze unreadable. He has always been better with words than I am, but even he has nothing to say.

Odin isn't here.

I do not know if that makes it better or worse.

I exhale slowly, my breath curling in the crisp morning air. The north is always cold, even in summer. Even in June.

I never got used to it.

I was not born beneath the violet-crowned mountains, where the air is sharp and the winters stretch long and unforgiving. I was not raised in the shadows of stone, in a land where strength is survival and red-haired warriors carve their names into history with steel and blood.

I come from the south—where the air is warm, the roads are lined with citrus groves, the scent of sun-ripened oranges and salt carried on the breeze. The land of golden light and easy laughter, where people dance before they march to war, where their hands were meant for harvesting, not fighting.

They not belong in the war.

But the war did not care.

Five years ago, Lorna burned.

The royal family, the lineage that had ruled for centuries, was wiped from existence. Not just the king and queen. Every heir, every cousin, every branch of the bloodline, cut down before they had a chance to beg for their lives.

Their deaths were not enough.

The rebellion began in the northeast, in the bitter lands where the mountains flatten into rocky plateaus. They had spent decades resenting the crown, waiting for the moment they could turn against it.

And when that moment came, they did not hesitate.

But the war did not stay in the north.

It spread. It bled into the valleys, into the riverlands, into the golden groves of the south, where the air is warm and thick with the scent of citrus.

The southerners—olive-skinned, sun-kissed, carrying the light of life itself—were never meant for war. Their hands were made for picking oranges, for crafting music, for making love under the orchard trees, for carving art into the walls of their city squares.

And yet, war found them anyway.

I remember standing in those burning groves, watching the trees shrivel to ash, the sweet scent of oranges turning acrid in the air.

The people of the south had never wanted this war.

But war does not care who wants it.

The west, with its cliffside villages and the treacherous Channel of Lorna, was the last to suffer.

The war came late to those shores, but when it did, it came with fire and steel. Ships burned in the harbors, the wind carrying embers out to sea like the ashes of a kingdom long past saving.

Beyond the waves, across the channel, Zavros lingered, untouched and golden in the sun, its people watching from their painted streets and temple steps. They had never known war like we had.

Perhaps that is why we have always looked at each other with curiosity but never understanding.

They do not bleed for their land the way we do.

They do not rise from the ashes because they have never had to.

But Lorna?

Lorna was made for suffering.

And still, we endure.

I look at the freshly turned earth, at the simple stone marking Arianna's resting place.

I remember her fire, her sharp wit, the way she held herself like she was already wearing a crown, even before Odin placed one on her head. I remember Odin's obsession with her, how he wanted her from the moment he saw her.

And now, she is gone.

Her daughter, gone with her.

A mother and child, buried before they ever had a chance to see the potential of what we created.

Murphy exhales beside me, shattering the silence. "Did we make the right choice, Alexey?"

We've asked the question before. But this time, it feels like a regret, not a doubt.

I can no longer ignore what Odin has become. And I can no longer deny that I helped make him.

I swallow the truth like poison. Because it doesn't matter.

It should. Gods, it should. But it doesn't.

Not anymore.

"We put Odin on the throne," I say instead. "Now we live with it."

Murphy doesn't argue. He never does.

But the silence between us isn't agreement. It's a wound left open, festering.

It lingers, thick with the weight of every wrong we ignored, every excuse we made.

I look at Arianna's grave one last time.

And for the first time since we crowned him, I wonder—

Did we save Lorna?

Or did we damn it, delaying its fall?

The wind shifts, whispering through the trees, and for one cruel moment—I hear her.

"Oh, Alexey."

Soft. Amused. As if she's standing right behind me, close enough to touch.

"You always did take things too seriously."

A ghost of a laugh—bright, careless, untamed.

The kind of laugh that made the world feel smaller, safer, like nothing could ever touch her.

But something did.

And I couldn't stop it.

I see her as she was—a storm in silk, head held high, eyes alight with fire.

A woman who belonged to no one, not by birthright, not by conquest—only by choice.
A woman who refused to be caged—
Until the day she was.

The wind dies. The moment is gone.
And I am left with nothing.
Just the silence.
Just the weight of what I failed to protect.
Just the truth that she was never mine to save.

The Anomaly - Arianna

I have always been practical.

Logical.

Never one to be swept away by sentiment.

That isn't to say I don't feel deeply—I do. But I have never let my emotions rule me.

Unlike my sisters—Alisa, Anya, and Anastasia—I was the anomaly, the black swan among women who dreamed of love, marriage, and children.

They longed for hearth and home, for the warmth of a husband's embrace, for the quiet joys of motherhood.

I longed for something else.

Even as a child, I was different.

While my sisters swaddled dolls and whispered about courtships, I climbed trees and studied maps.

While they spoke of romance, I spoke of war.

I traced the shifting borders of Lorna's history, reading about men who bent fate to their will—not with love, but with ambition, with strategy, with sheer, unrelenting force.

I watched my sisters find beauty in the domestic, in the gentle rhythm of a life spent within safe walls.

I never envied them.

I was meant for more.

But in a world where women's futures were written in wedding contracts and dowries, I had only two choices:

Accept the role assigned to me.

Forge my own.

So I chose the temple.

Not because I lacked love in my heart—
But because I refused to let love be my only purpose.

My sisters were insufferable.

Of course, my sisters had their own opinions about my choices.

"Honestly, Ari," Alisa sighed, flicking a stray curl from her shoulder. "You have a perfectly good face and a noble name. Why waste them?"

I rolled my eyes. "You speak as if I'm throwing myself into exile."

"You might as well be," Anya sniffed. "At least in exile, you could have some sort of scandal."

"She's right," Anastasia agreed. "A noblewoman joining the temple? No intrigue, no romance, no excitement? You're going to be so boring."

"She'll be smug about it, though," Alisa muttered. "Priestess Arianna, better than all of us."

"I do not think I'm better than you," I said patiently.

"You do," Anya argued. "And you know what? That's fine. But at least admit it. You'll be sitting in your temple while I'm out wearing imported gowns and dripping in emeralds."

"Are we supposed to be impressed by that?" Anastasia asked dryly.

"Yes," Anya said simply.

Alisa sighed dramatically, shaking her head. "You could be at court, Ari. The Queen of Lorna, even."

"Yes, because that's exactly what I want," I deadpanned.

"You don't know what you want," Alisa said breezily. "One day, you'll meet a man who makes you forget all this temple nonsense."

"If a man makes me forget my entire life's purpose, I'll be gravely concerned for my own intelligence."

That earned a snort from Anastasia.

Anya smirked. "I give her a year before she realizes she made a mistake."

Alisa, ever dramatic, placed a hand over her heart. "Oh, I'm so generous—I give her two."

"Five," Anastasia said.

"Ten," I countered.

The three of them turned to me with identical mischievous grins.

"Fine," Alisa said. "You say ten. I say one. Bet?"

"Bet?" I repeated, amused.

"If you stay a priestess forever, you win," she said. "If you leave the temple for a man, I win."

"And what exactly do you win?"

Alisa considered. "Your firstborn child."

Anya laughed. "She won't have one."

"Fine. Then her pride."

I rolled my eyes. "You're all ridiculous."

"You love it," Anya said smugly.

And I did.

Because for all their teasing, for all their rivalry—they were my sisters.

And despite everything, I would miss them.

My Father's Legacy – Arianna

Baron Maxim Vasiliev was not born noble—he became one.

His textiles flowed through Lorna like lifeblood, his name whispered in the halls of Elarion alongside trueborn lords. But it wasn't wealth that defined him. It wasn't even power, though men twice his stature deferred to his judgment in matters of trade, eager to secure a place in his orbit.

He was warmth, charisma, and wit—a man who could sell the same bolt of silk twice, not by deceit, but by charm alone.

His laughter was a melody that filled our home, bright and effortless, woven between the scent of fresh linen and sea air. He turned every evening into a story, his voice rising and falling with the tide, teaching me that joy was not something given, nor something owed.

It was something we created.

From him, I learned one of life's greatest lessons: Expectation is the thief of joy.

And so, we did not dwell on what could be. We did not mourn what had yet to come.

Except for my mother.

Where my father saw fortune, she saw risk. Where he embraced the unknown, she braced for catastrophe.

She loved him with a devotion so fierce it burned, and yet, beneath it lay a quiet terror—an unspoken certainty that happiness, once acknowledged, could be stolen.

She was right.

The Merchant Who Became a Baron – Arianna

The nobility of Lorna had long prided themselves on their bloodlines—ancient houses stretching back centuries, their names carved into the pillars of history.

Maxim Vasiliev was an outsider.

A merchant's son from the southern coast, a man who built his fortune on trade, not inheritance. He was granted his title, not born to it.

And the old lords never let him forget it.

But my father had timing, and timing was everything.

With the new king on the throne, the nobility was in a state of upheaval.

King Odin had claimed his crown by conquest, not blood—his legitimacy balanced on a blade's edge, and even his most devoted allies knew that Lorna was still settling beneath the weight of his rule.

Where some lords lost their titles for siding against Odin in the war, others rose in their place.

My father saw opportunity.

Trade along the Sunfire River and the Channel of Lorna had long been a lifeline of the kingdom, but war had left it unstable, vulnerable to raiders and smuggling.

It was a problem.

And my father?

He had always been very good at solving problems.

His network along the ports and trade routes was unmatched, his expertise in logistics and supply chains indispensable. When Odin looked to rebuild his economy, he turned to men who understood commerce, not court games.

Maxim Vasiliev secured his title not through war, nor through family ties—
But through gold, ships, and the promise of prosperity.

And yet, despite his service to the throne, despite the wealth he funneled into Lorna's war-torn coffers, despite the fact that half the noble houses owed him favors—

The old lords still looked at him and saw a merchant.

I remember the first time I saw them try to humiliate him.

It was at one of my mother's wretched dinner parties, where the wine flowed too freely and the laughter always carried an edge. The lords of Elarion were there, resplendent in their deep crimson coats and gold-trimmed collars, their voices dripping with false courtesy.

And my father?

Dressed in simple navy silk, sleeves rolled up at the cuffs as if he had come straight from the docks.

The insult was subtle.

"Tell me, Baron Vasiliev," one of the older lords said, swirling his goblet lazily. "How does it feel to sit among men whose grandfathers would have called yours… what was the word? Ah—tradesmen."

A hush fell over the table.

My mother went rigid, her knuckles white against the tablecloth.

I clenched my hands beneath the table, waiting for my father to snap, to frown, to defend himself.

He did none of those things.

Instead, he took a slow sip of wine, as if truly considering the question.

Then, with an easy smile, he leaned forward. "Oh, I don't have to imagine. Your grandfather did call mine a tradesman."

The lord's lips pressed into a thin line.

My father grinned.

"Of course," he added, "that was before he went bankrupt and had to beg my father for credit. My grandfather called him a debtor."

Anastasia choked on her wine.

Anya covered her smirk with her goblet.

Alisa gasped—not in horror, but in delight.

The insult was delivered with such flawless charm that no one could call it what it was.

The lord cleared his throat, muttering something about old times.

And my father?

He simply lifted his goblet. "To old times, then."

The tension shattered with laughter.

But I noticed something else.

The other nobles at the table—the ones who had been ready to sneer at him—were now laughing with him.

That was my father's gift.

He didn't fight to be respected.

He expected it.

And somehow, that made it impossible to deny him.

But not everyone at that table laughed.

And not everyone ever would.

A Mother's Disappointment – Arianna

Where my father thrived in the present, my mother was consumed by the future.

She saw it so clearly, as if it had already come to pass—a house bursting with warmth, filled with the echo of grandchildren's laughter, tiny feet pattering across polished floors.

She envisioned quiet mornings spent braiding her daughters' hair, evenings teaching them to mend torn seams, whispering secrets over candlelight.

A legacy not of wealth or power, but of family, of love passed down through generations like an heirloom.

I was no help in that department.

If I had been born with a different heart, a softer spirit, perhaps I could have given her what she wanted.

Perhaps I could have folded myself neatly into the life she imagined, let it shape me into something gentler, something familiar.

But I was not made for lullabies and cradle songs.

My hands were not meant to rock cradles.

They were meant for something else.

"You did something wrong when you were pregnant with her," my mother announced about herself, waving a delicate hand in my general direction.

I stared at her. "I'm literally right here."

She ignored me.

"She barely played with dolls. I gave her a perfectly good set when she was three, and do you know what she did?" My mother turned dramatically to my sisters. "She lined them up like soldiers and made them march into battle."

"I see nothing wrong with that," I muttered.

Anya, reclining on the settee, smirked. "I remember that. Alisa cried."

Alisa huffed, crossing her arms. "They were hand-painted porcelain dolls! She made them fight in the mud."

I shrugged. "Soldiers don't get to choose their battlefield."

My mother let out an exasperated sigh, pressing a hand to her forehead. "And now, instead of a husband, she chooses the temple. What am I supposed to tell people? That my eldest daughter has married prayer?"

Anastasia, lounging beside Anya, sipped her tea and offered, "You could just say she's dramatically pious."

"That doesn't make it better," my mother snapped.

Alisa shook her head. "You know what's even worse? She's going to look so smug about it."

"I do not look smug."

"You do," Anya said. "It's the way you purse your lips."

"I don't purse my lips."

Anya immediately pursed her lips in an exaggerated imitation of me, lifting her chin as if she were assessing the morality of the room.

Anastasia burst out laughing.

My mother groaned. "See? This is what I mean! She's going to be sitting in that temple, watching us like we're sinning degenerates."

"Well," Anastasia mused, "to be fair, Alisa is a little bit of a degenerate."

Alisa gasped. “I am not!”

Anya arched a brow. "You let Lord Mikhail kiss you in the gardens."

Alisa scowled. “That was one time.”

"And it was scandalous," Anya added.

I sighed, rubbing my temples. "This is getting wildly off topic."

My mother ignored me again, pacing now, fully in her dramatic spiral.

“I wanted just one daughter who would carry on our legacy—”

“You have three,” I pointed out.

“—but no,” she continued, as if I hadn’t spoken, “my eldest decides she is above marriage! What next? Will you renounce wearing silk and walk around in sackcloth?”

Anastasia tapped a finger to her lips. “Sackcloth would be a bold fashion statement.”

“I hate all of you,” I muttered.

My mother wheeled on me.

“You’ll regret this,” she declared. “Mark my words. One day, you’ll wake up, and you’ll realize you want a husband and a home and children, and it will be too late!"

Anya nodded sagely. “She does love to be dramatic. Maybe she’ll have some big, tortured romance one day.”

I scoffed. “Not likely.”

Alisa leaned forward, grinning. “Ooooh, imagine—a handsome, brooding man.”

Anastasia smirked. “One with piercing eyes and a dark past.”

Anya’s eyes gleamed. “One who will ruin you.”

My mother shrieked in horror.

I pinched the bridge of my nose.

"You are all insufferable."

Anastasia sighed, dramatically placing a hand over her chest. “She says that now, but wait until she falls in love with some forbidden man of mystery.”

“That won’t happen.”

Alisa shrugged. “You’re right. No romance for Ari. Just the temple.”

“Yes,” I said firmly.

“Alone,” Anya added.

“Yes.”

“Forever.”

“Yes.”

My sisters exchanged looks.

“Well,” Anastasia said, barely suppressing her smirk, “this will age poorly.”

And of course—

It did.

The Protest – Arianna

I expected resistance. Protests. Dramatic weeping.

I was not disappointed.

My mother was outraged.

"The best place for a woman to serve her community," she snapped, "is within her own household."

She paced like a caged tiger, her silken skirts snapping at her heels, her voice sharp enough to cut glass. Frustration rolled off her in waves, thick with the weight of expectation—generations of women who had obeyed, who had stayed, who had built their legacies within the gilded confines of a home.

"I will never understand you, Arianna," she said, her eyes dark with disbelief. "What kind of future is this? No husband, no children, no home of your own?"

I met her gaze, steady and unflinching. "I will have a home, Mother," I said evenly. "The temple will be my home. The people will be my family."

Her nostrils flared. "That is not the same!"

But beneath the outrage, beneath the anger, I saw something else—fear.

She had spent her life weaving the perfect futures for her daughters, each one neatly wrapped in tradition, tied with the ribbon of noble obligation. She had stitched their fates with careful hands, ensuring not a single thread was out of place.

And now, I stood before her, knife to the ribbon, ready to cut myself free.

She did not know what to do with that.

But she was not the only one whose opinion mattered.

I braced myself for my father's resistance.

I had prepared for it, steeled myself against the weight of his disapproval, expecting the same fierce objections my mother had unleashed upon me.

Instead, he studied me in silence.

There was no anger in his eyes, no frustration—only contemplation, his mind moving like the tide, slow and steady, shaping itself around the truth of me.

"Ari, is this truly what pleases you?"

"Yes, Papa. Very much."

A pause, long and measured. A moment stretched between us, filled with the unspoken.

Then—

"Then it is done."

No argument.

No protests.

No sorrow.

I blinked, uncertain. "That easily?" I whispered.

He chuckled, low and familiar, the sound wrapping around me like a beloved old story.

"My Ari always gets what she wants."

And that was that.

The first time my father took me to the temple, I was four years old, wrapped in a woolen cloak too big for my small frame, my hand swallowed in his as we stepped onto the grand white steps.

I still remember the way the world changed when we crossed the threshold.

The air smelled of sandalwood and beeswax, the flickering candlelight casting golden halos along the marble floor. I had never seen anything so beautiful, so endless.

A priest greeted us, bending down to my level with a kind smile.

"Is this your first time in the High Temple, little one?"

I nodded, suddenly shy, pressing myself against my father's leg.

"Would you like to light a candle for the Divine?"

I don't know why it mattered so much to me, but I remember how deeply I nodded, how carefully I took the offered taper, how I held my breath as I reached out toward the holy flame.

I was so small.

But in that moment, I felt big.

I remember how my father watched me, his face unreadable as I lit the candle and whispered a prayer no one had taught me.

I don't remember what I said.

But I remember how he squeezed my shoulder afterward, gentle and steady.

"You liked that, didn't you?" he murmured as we left.

I beamed up at him, my heart feeling too big for my chest.

"Yes, Papa. Very much."

A Funeral in Disguise – Arianna

The next morning, beneath the golden glow of dawn, I took my vows in a quiet ceremony.

The temple was hushed, the air thick with incense and reverence, the flickering candlelight casting long shadows across the marble floors.

My voice was steady as I spoke the sacred words, binding myself to a future of service, of purpose, of a life I had chosen.

And my mother?

You'd think I was being buried instead of blessed.

She arrived at the temple draped in black velvet from throat to toe, a heavy lace veil obscuring her face as she sobbed into an embroidered handkerchief.

A full mourning ensemble.

For an event that was not a funeral.

The temple doors hadn't even closed behind her before she gasped loudly, clutching her chest.

"I have lost my daughter today!"

She declared it so dramatically that even the temple elders—stoic men who had likely seen every kind of grief imaginable—shifted uncomfortably.

A priest tentatively offered her a seat.

She waved him off with a shaking hand, as if her grief was too great for furniture.

"To think," she sighed, tilting her head toward the heavens, "I raised her, fed her, loved her—only for her to throw away her life and marry the Divine."

Alisa sniffled into a handkerchief, though I was fairly certain she wasn't actually crying. "Poor Mama," she whispered to Anastasia.

Anya leaned in. "Poor us. We're never going to hear the end of this."

"Shhh," Anastasia murmured, watching our mother with professional admiration. "This is some of her best work yet."

I shot them a glare.

Meanwhile, my mother continued her flawless performance.

"She was so beautiful before this," she lamented. "Now, she will wear plain robes and live a loveless existence."

"Arianna was always beautiful," my father attempted.

She wheeled on him. "Not the same kind of beautiful, Maxim!"

My father, ever the wise one, simply sighed. "Yes, dear."

Anastasia elbowed me. "Are you sure you don't want to change your mind? This show is really something."

Anya nodded. "It's not too late to run off with a handsome lord and spare us all from another twenty years of this."

I ignored them.

Across the room, a young acolyte whispered to one of the older priests, clearly unnerved.

"Should we… do something?"

The elder priest, who had clearly lived long enough to know better, shook his head.

"Just let it play out."

The ceremony continued, but my mother never wavered.

She sobbed at the appropriate moments, clutched her heart when I kneeled, and when I received the final blessing, she let out a tiny, tragic wail, as if the Divine itself had stolen me away.

At one point, she dropped her handkerchief.

A priestess bent to pick it up.

My mother refused.

"Let it lie," she whispered. "Like my dreams for her."

Alisa choked on suppressed laughter.

Anya pinched the bridge of her nose.

Anastasia muttered, "Incredible. A master at work."

And I?

I stepped forward.

Stepped into the light.

Into the life that was mine alone to choose.

With my mother still sniffling into the void of my indifference.

The Call to Serve – Arianna

The temple—glistening white stone, sapphire-stained glass—stood less than an hour's carriage ride from the capital, Elarion. But to me, it was the center of the universe.

Where I found my purpose in servitude:

Healing the broken.

Warming frozen hands during Lorna's endless winters.

Stitching garments for the poor.

I believed in the Divine, not as some distant, untouchable force, but as something living, something guiding me.

To serve.

To bring light.

To teach others that they were deeply, beautifully, unconditionally loved by the Divine.

And sometimes, that meant listening to absolute nonsense.

The temple was a place of worship, wisdom, and healing.

It was also, apparently, a place where people came to unload all their bizarre, long-winded personal stories, whether we wanted to hear them or not.

I quickly learned that helping the faithful did not always mean tending to the wounded or distributing alms.

Sometimes, it meant listening to a woman named Mistress Lelia recount, in excruciating detail, every moment of her dog's life.

Her dog's name was Biscuit.

Biscuit was "an angel among beasts", and I had to hear about:

His dietary preferences. (He could eat roasted duck, but only if it had been seasoned with precisely one sprig of thyme.)

His sleeping habits. (He required a silken pillow, fluffed three times before bedtime.)

His social life. (He had a longstanding feud with Baron Grigor's cat, which had apparently escalated to a "battle" involving a stolen pheasant leg.)

I had stitched wounds, carried the sick, and mediated arguments over land disputes.

But nothing—nothing—had tested my patience quite like Biscuit.

"Mistress Lelia," I had finally interrupted, "how can the temple help you today?"

She blinked.

"Oh! Right. Biscuit requires a blessing."

I took a long, slow breath.

"A blessing."

"Yes, well," she said with a dramatic sigh, "he is entering his twelfth year, and I simply cannot bear the thought of him aging unprotected from misfortune."

Misfortune.

For the dog.

I glanced at the long line of actual sick and injured people waiting behind her.

"Perhaps Biscuit would enjoy an extra treat instead," I suggested.

She gasped in horror. "You think bribery can replace Divine favor?"

I pinched the bridge of my nose. "Bring him by at sunset."

And that is how I found myself kneeling in the temple garden, solemnly blessing a dog.

Biscuit sneezed on me.

I told myself this was a lesson in humility.

Then there was Old Man Vasily.

Vasily was a retired blacksmith who came to the temple every week to warm himself by the hearth and remind us all that he had "seen war with his own two eyes."

He was very proud of this fact.

There was just one problem.

Vasily had never served a single day in the military.

But that did not stop him from talking about the war as if he had personally carried the crown to victory.

One afternoon, as I was bandaging a farmer's injured hand, Vasily parked himself on a bench nearby and began his weekly speech.

"Ah, the smell of iron!" he declared. "Takes me back to the battlefields."

I sighed. "Which battlefields, exactly?"

"All of them," he said proudly.

I gestured for him to continue, purely for entertainment.

"Did I ever tell you about the time I saved a cavalry unit from certain death?"

"Do go on," I said, utterly deadpan.

"Well," he leaned forward, his voice lowering conspiratorially, "it was during the Siege of Irondale—"

"Vasily," I cut in, "you were a blacksmith in Irondale."

"A frontline blacksmith," he corrected.

"That's not a thing."

"It absolutely is!" Vasily huffed. "Who do you think kept the weapons sharp and the shields mended? Without me, the entire war effort would have crumbled."

I exhaled. "So you provided weapons?"

"More than that! I inspired the soldiers! Do you know what I told the captain before the final push?"

I crossed my arms. "What?"

He clasped his hands together, eyes gleaming with the weight of his own legend.

"Fight bravely, and if you survive, bring your sword back in one piece so I don't have to fix it again."

I stared at him.

"That was it?"

"It was a powerful moment," he insisted.

"Vasily, that was your job."

He sniffed. "Doesn't make it any less heroic."

"And did you ever see actual combat?"

"Not directly. But I heard plenty of swords clashing. I was at least within earshot of glory."

"Within earshot of glory," I repeated.

Vasily nodded sagely. "It still counts."

I let out a long, tired breath. "Would you like some soup, Vasily?"

He beamed. "That would be wonderful, my dear!"

And that is how I ended up serving soup to a man who had single-handedly, allegedly, won a war he never fought in.

Settling In – Arianna

Temple life was everything I had hoped for.

It was also everything I hadn't expected.

Yes, I was a keeper of wisdom, a servant of the Divine, a woman of purpose.

But I was also:

A referee in heated theological debates that somehow always ended in petty wagers.

An unwilling participant in the Great Candle-Lighting Races of morning prayer.

The reigning champion of "Guess Who Fell Asleep in the Library Again?"

I woke before dawn, kneeling in the great hall as golden light spilled through the stained-glass windows.

By all appearances, I was a picture of devotion.

In reality, I was silently counting down to see if Brother Mathis would trip over his robe again.

(Two seconds. A new record.)

I stitched my purpose into every moment.

Quite literally.

Because Sister Elira had made it her personal mission to turn embroidery into a lesson in patience—which meant I was now the reluctant owner of many, many lopsided doves stitched onto cloth.

I did not need wealth.

I did not crave romance.

I craved victory in the silent game of "Who Can Memorize the Most Ancient Texts Before Evening Prayer?" (Currently, I was winning.)

I was exactly where I was meant to be.

And if that place involved a secret, ongoing battle of wits with the other priests to see who could keep me on my toes the longest—

Well.

That just made it all the more fun.

Within a year of meditation and prayer, I was able to use the Eternum Relic.

The Eternum Relic was the key to it all—a sacred artifact said to be imbued with the lingering touch of the Divine.

With it, I could peer beyond the veil, glimpsing echoes of the past and fragments of a future the Gods were willing to reveal.

But the future was not a story written in ink.
It was a shifting thing, a river that carved new paths with each choice, each breath, each step. Usually, the scenario revealed was one that our current path would lead to.

The Gods, in their wisdom, revealed only what was necessary.
Not to control us—
But to guide us.

And guidance came at a cost.

Some days, it was merely exhaustion—a headache pressing behind my eyes, the weight of knowledge settling heavy in my bones.

Other days, it was worse.

The visions came as flashes, scattered glimpses of what had been, what could be, what would be if fate remained unchallenged.

Some paths were inevitable, carved into time like the Sunfire River itself.

Others twisted and shifted, shaped by the choices of those who walked them.

I was trained to interpret, not interfere.

But the more I saw, the more I realized—

Even the Gods could not save everyone.

And that knowledge weighed on me more than anything else.

Maybe this was the will of the Gods.

Not everyone at the temple shared my unyielding faith.

Some priestesses whispered of politics, of alliances, of how the temple itself was a pawn on the board of kings and lords.

Some saw power in prayer, not as a means of guidance, but of influence.

There were rivalries among the priestesses, not all of them holy.

Sister Nadya, older than me by five years, resented my place in the High Temple.

"You think faith alone brought you here?" she once sneered, arms crossed, eyes sharp as cut glass. "No, priestess. It was your father's coin."

I had learned long ago that silence was sometimes the best answer.

But in the temple, silence could be a battlefield.

There were debates in the council, where the eldest priests argued whether charity should be given freely or earned.

I had opinions. Strong ones.

But young priestesses were expected to listen, not speak.

So I listened.

I absorbed.

I waited.

I did not challenge them yet.

But I would.

In good time.

Despite all my discipline, all my study, all my unwavering certainty—

There were moments of doubt.

Moments where I lay awake at night, staring at the vaulted ceiling above my cot, wondering—

If the Gods loved us, why did they allow suffering at all?

Why did children freeze in the streets while kings gorged themselves on feasts?

Why did good men fall while tyrants built golden thrones?

Is there some greater purpose we don't understand at our soul level?

And the greatest question of all—

Why did the Divine Sight show me tragedy I could not stop?

I had glimpsed a child who would not survive the winter.

I had seen a merchant's daughter, bright-eyed and full of laughter, who would not see twenty.

I could not warn them.

I could only watch.

Faith, I reminded myself, was not about certainty. It was about trust.

But some nights, I wasn't certain I trusted the Gods at all.

And I suppose that makes me a hypocrite.

A Glimpse into Madness – Arianna

I should've known better.

No, truly. I do know better. I've lectured acolytes on the dangers of using the Eternum Relic for selfish gain. I've quoted scripture. I've rattled off every warning about fate, choice, and the Divine's disdain for curiosity.

And yet—here I am.

Kneeling alone in the sacred chamber, the air thick with incense and guilt, the Relic warm in my hand.

It hums beneath my fingertips like it knows.

Knows I've grown restless.

Knows that despite all my discipline and faith and blinding certainty—I've begun to wonder.

Not about the Divine.

About me.

Who I'm supposed to be.

What happens if I'm wrong.

What happens if I'm not as steadfast as I pretend to be.

What happens if I've never been.

I close my eyes.

Just a glimpse.

One glimpse won't hurt.

Right?

The Relic flares in my palm—light blooming beneath my eyelids—and then the world falls away.

I stand beneath a sky spun from gold.

The sun filters through a veil of clouds, bathing everything in a soft, holy glow. I'm in a temple, but not this temple. The walls are carved from marble and ivy, the pews lined with noble guests I cannot name.

At the end of the aisle—

I see myself.

Wearing a wedding dress.

A gown is gorgeous, delicate and blasphemously low-cut. My hair flows long and radiant and pinned with golden blooms, my lips painted rose. I look radiant. Confident. Entirely unlike myself.

A priest stands before me.

And beside me… a man.

I cannot see his face.

But his hair—copper, wild, kissed by flame—catches the light like a halo forged from mischief and charm. His hand is in mine, steady and warm.

My heart stutters.

He makes me feel—

Like I'm the only woman in the world.

Like I belong here, in this moment, despite everything I once swore.

There is laughter in his voice. And I feel the heat in his gaze though I cannot see it. And when he leans close, brushing a kiss against my temple like a secret—

I smile.

Gods.

I smile.

It is the most divine feeling I have ever felt in my life.

I want more.

But then—

A crack. A shift.

The vision tilts.

The sky darkens.

The aisle vanishes.

I'm on a beach. I see a horse rearing in panic, hooves slicing the air. A crab scuttles across the sand. A man falls—hard—his head striking stone with a sickening thud. Blood blooms beneath his temple. Copper hair is matted with it.

He looks dead though he still breathes.

I can't move.

I look down at it.

Cracked. Bloodstained. Still warm.

I want to scream. I want to reach for him. I want to run.

But the vision shifts again—

Now I am somewhere else.

Cooler. Quieter. Dim candlelight and a stone corridor lined with banners I don't recognize.

Another version of myself stands beside a man cloaked in shadow.

This one—

He is nothing like the first.

No boyish charm. No wicked grin.

This man is a wall of restraint. Dark hair, cropped short. Shoulders broad enough to carry kingdoms. He says nothing.

But his presence roars.

He emanates power just by existing.

I can feel his restraint crackling in the air.

And I… I lean into it.

Like I've known him forever.

Like the silence between us is safer than any vow I've ever spoken.

I can't see his face.

Only his eyes.

His eyes meet mine.

Blue. Devastating. Knowing.

Oh the depth his eyes held made my knees buckle.

He lifts a hand to brush a lock of hair from my cheek, his thumb grazing my jaw—

And I almost lean in.

We almost kiss.

I flinch.

Then—

I drop the Relic.

The vision shatters.

I gasp, lungs convulsing like I've just surfaced from a deep, forbidden sea. The Relic clatters to the floor, spinning once before stilling.

The silence in the chamber presses in around me.

My hands tremble.

I never tremble.

"What," I whisper, "in the name of the Divine… was that?"

Two men.

One with charm like wildfire. One built like a fortress.

One who made me feel adored.

One who made me feel seen.

I am a priestess.

I do not belong in a gown. I do not crave a kiss. I do not belong to any man.

I don't even want to.

And yet—I saw it.

Felt it.

Wanted it.

Both of them.

I clench my jaw, forcing the thoughts back down where they belong. I will not analyze. I will not dwell. I will not dignify this madness with a response.

Still… I can't stop shaking.

Because I don't know what scares me more—

The vision itself…

Or the terrifying, whispering truth that some part of me wants it to be real.

The Name of a King – Arianna

The summer air was warm that evening, thick with the scent of jasmine and polished stone. The High Temple shimmered in the waning light, its marble columns glowing like honey. I had just finished vespers, my prayers still clinging to the edges of my mind, when I wandered into the gathering hall where the nobles of Elarion congregated.

These twilight gatherings were always the same—robes of silk brushing against gold-tiled floors, laughter that never reached the eyes, and piety worn like jewelry. I had long learned that the Gods were not the reason these people came to temple.

They came for theater.

For politics wrapped in perfumed incense and whispered judgment.

I lingered near the sacred fountain, letting the cool water ripple through my fingers, when I heard his name.

"King Odin," a noblewoman purred, her voice smooth and indulgent, "is quickly running out of excuses."

That caught my ear.

She stood just behind me, speaking to a small circle of overdressed courtiers with the casual sharpness only the privileged could wield. Her gown was crimson, sheer at the sleeves, with gold cuffs that glinted each time she gestured.

"It's been nearly three years," another woman chimed in, older, draped in peacock-blue velvet. "Three years of parades, treaties, and scandal—and still no queen."

"He isn't exactly lacking options," the man beside them drawled. "But Odin has a very... particular palate."

That drew a round of soft laughter.

"Particular?" the crimson-gowned woman echoed. "Please. The man refuses to be seen with anyone less than celestial. The court is starting to call him the King of fire."

"Because of his hair?" someone asked.

"Because he burns through women like wildfire," the man said dryly, "and only ever turns his gaze toward the most breathtaking among them."

"Green eyes," said the older woman, swirling her wine. "He has a weakness for green-eyed girls."

"That explains the twins from Citrigrad," the man said with a grin. "And the grafina from Lilovyn."

"All green-eyed," the crimson woman confirmed, her smile knowing. "And all discarded when he got bored with them."

There was a pause. Then someone muttered, "He doesn't want a wife. He wants a goddess."

"No," the older woman corrected, "he wants a mirror. Something beautiful to reflect his own light."

The laughter turned brittle.

"He's not interested in ruling with someone. He wants to be adored like the Gods themselves."

The man sighed. "Well, the council is growing tired of waiting. The nobles want stability. An heir. Someone to temper him. He needs a woman's touch to settle him."

"Good luck tempering a storm in golden skin," the crimson woman whispered.

There was a silence that felt almost reverent.

And then the older woman said, almost absently, "Let us just hope whoever he chooses... survives him."

That silence returned.

Not devotion. Not awe.

A stillness like something was being mourned before it ever began.

I crossed myself with the holy water and then I turned from the fountain, my hands cool but trembling.

I had not meant to linger.

I had not meant to listen.

But the name stayed with me and I didn't know why.

Odin.

And I, a priestess with no crown and no future beyond holy service, should not have thought of him again.

I should have prayed him from my mind.

I should have.

But I didn't.

A Father's Visit – Arianna

One crisp April afternoon in my twentieth year, my father paid a rare visit to the temple.

This, of course, meant two things:

He missed me (which he would never admit).

He wanted something (which he would also never admit).

We sat in the temple gardens, a sanctuary of fragrant roses, ivy-draped trellises, and the occasional disgruntled squirrel (who, I suspected, had declared Priest Howard as its nemesis).

The world here was a soft place—the scent of earth and blooming jasmine on the breeze, the warmth of afternoon sun dappling the marble benches, the sound of temple bells ringing in the distance.

I loved my life.

Truly.

And I loved my father.

And so, we sat, sipping spiced tea in the golden afternoon light, letting the moment stretch as long as it pleased us.

Then—my father, ever the businessman, cleared his throat with a very suspicious level of purpose.

"It has been wonderful catching up with my eldest and most beautiful daughter."

Ah.

Flattery.

This was a setup.

I arched a brow. "Your eldest and most beautiful daughter, you say? What an oddly specific compliment, Papa."

He chuckled, not even attempting to deny it.

"However," he continued smoothly, his tone shifting into business mode, "there is another reason for my visit."

Here it comes.

He placed a warm hand over mine, his grin widening just enough to confirm my suspicions.

I narrowed my eyes. "I'm bracing myself."

"Would it be possible to borrow the temple's meeting hall this afternoon?" He spoke casually—too casually. "A high-ranking noble client wishes to shop discreetly, away from the hubbub of the court."

I exhaled.

Really?

That was it?

I had braced for an arranged marriage proposal, a business partnership, or some other form of domestic torture.

This?

This was an easy ask.

I rolled my eyes but smiled. "Of course, Papa. It's all yours."

He kissed my cheek, whispering his gratitude, and I should have known then that something unusual was brewing.

I should have paid more attention.

I should have asked who his client was.

But I did not.

And soon, I would regret it.

Spun Silver and Emeralds – Arianna

If the Gods ever deign to hand out second chances, I'd spend mine entirely at the tavern off Hollow Bend. No court etiquette. No temple bells. Just duck so tender it falls off the bone, rosemary potatoes crisped to perfection, and my father's stories—half true, wholly absurd, and better than wine.

"You know," he said between bites, "I once had a client, a grafina from the coast. Wanted a gown spun from silver."

I raised an eyebrow. "Let me guess. She also wanted a crown of starlight and a husband who doesn't drink."

He grinned. "She said she'd pay whatever it cost."

I leaned in, chewing thoughtfully. "And you, dear father, quoted her something utterly reasonable, I'm sure."

"Oh, absolutely. Told her it would take three years and a hundred enchanted spiders. Highly temperamental ones, mind you. You have to whisper to them in lullabies or they refuse to spin."

I snorted so hard I nearly inhaled a potato.

"She believed me—right up until I offered her a spider egg as a deposit bonus."

"Father," I said, dabbing at my lips, "you are what the temple would call 'a menace.'"

He shrugged with exaggerated innocence. "A harmless one."

But not harmless, not really. My father is a textile merchant by trade, a magician with thread, a trickster with clients, and the only man on this earth who's ever looked at me like I hung the stars instead of just naming them in prayer. Sometimes, I miss him while he's still sitting across from me. I don't know what that says about me—only that the moments we get like this feel both too small and too rare.

The tavern buzzed with the usual din—dice games clattering, a bard in the corner attempting something heroic and just a touch flat, and the occasional waft of mead, sweat, and spilt gravy. Somehow, it all felt more honest than the hush of temple stone or the syrupy flattery of court.

That's the thing about the temple. Everything is quiet, reverent. Even when it shouldn't be. Court, on the other hand? Everyone's loud while pretending not to be. I used to try and make sense of it—wonder why some lives are cloaked in scripture and others in scandal—but now I just chalk it up to the sheer absurdity of being alive.

Some people pray. Others gamble. Most of us just pick a mask and wear it until it sticks.

We wandered back toward the temple under the warm haze of dusk, my belly full and my soul lighter than it had been in weeks. And then, of course, it happened. I saw it.

An emerald necklace in a merchant's cart—rough-cut but vibrant, glinting like moss after rain. The sort of thing a sensible temple girl would walk right past. So naturally, I stopped like I'd been hexed.

My father followed my gaze and raised a brow. "Ah."

"No," I said, before he could speak.

"I didn't say anything."

"You were about to. I saw the look."

"What look?"

"The 'you deserve nice things' look. Don't give me that look."

"I was going to say," he said mildly, "that you're still my daughter. Even if you're married to the temple first."

"I'm not married to the temple."

"You're betrothed. Emotionally."

I huffed. "It's not practical. I don't need it."

"You also don't need half the books you hoard like a squirrel with scrolls," he replied. "But here we are."

He bought it before I could protest again. Handed it to me like it was a flower he'd picked himself.

"I won't get to walk you down an aisle," he said, voice quieter now. "No wedding dress. No feast. But I can give you this. Something small. Something green. A token of joy—for my eldest daughter, who makes the world a little brighter even when she's being a brat."

I swallowed. The chain felt warm in my palm.

"Well," I said, slipping it over my neck with a practiced little smirk, "you're lucky I'm a brat with excellent taste. Thank you, Papa."

He laughed, and the sound tucked itself into my ribs like a keepsake.

And maybe the temple will call it vanity. Maybe the court would scoff at the cut. But I'm still a woman. I like pretty things. Especially when they come wrapped in love.

A Meeting Written in Fire – Arianna

Years of diligent study, grueling discipline, and enough prayer to fill an entire library of holy texts had shaped me into the model priestess—dedicated, wise, and deeply committed to my Divine Sight.

A gift? Yes.

A nuisance? Also yes.

It meant I could often see the consequences of my actions before I even acted, allowing me to gracefully sidestep disaster, minimize damage, and maintain my dignity.

…Well. Most of the time.

Apparently, today was not going to be one of those days.

By the time we returned to the Temple, the meeting hall had transformed.

Gone was its usual simplicity. Instead, luxurious fabrics—velvets, silks, brocades—lay spread across the tables, glimmering like treasures stolen from royal vaults.

I ran my fingers over the rich material, curiosity bubbling over.

"Who are we entertaining, Papa? The King himself?"

I laughed, shaking my head as I arranged the bolts.

Silence.

My father said nothing.

Not even a smirk.

Just kept working.

Suspicious.

I narrowed my eyes but, rather than push for an answer, I went about my duties, sweeping through the temple, preparing the chapel for morning prayers, definitely not thinking about the fact that my father had ignored me—

Until I heard it.

A laugh.

A low, velvety laugh—rich, unguarded, echoing through the halls like a melody played on the strings of fate.

It was too deep, too full of mischief to belong to any of the usual merchants or priests.

I froze.

My stomach flipped.

Something about that laugh tickled my spine, like the first hint of a storm rolling over the sea—unpredictable, electric, full of dangerous possibilities.

Curiosity struck me like a lightning bolt.

Like a cat drawn to a particularly fascinating mystery, I found myself peeking into the meeting room.

Stealthy. Discreet. A shadow in the night.

Or at least, that's what I told myself.

In reality, I was one poorly placed footstep away from full-blown catastrophe.

And then I saw him.

A storm in human form, a presence that sucked the air from the room and set it on fire all at once.

He lounged in one of the temple chairs like a King upon his throne, exuding effortless confidence—the kind that didn't have to be forced, the kind that settled in a man's bones when he knew he had the world at his feet.

And by the Gods, he was beautiful.

Tall. Broad-shouldered. A mess of dark copper curls that caught the light like wildfire.

But it was his golden eyes that undid me.

The color of golden hour, so bright they glowed like twilight over the Sunfire River. They laughed even as he smiled, danced even as he remained utterly still, filled with a kind of reckless energy that made you want to lean closer—just to see if you could keep up.

His grin was the kind that made you question your own intelligence.

Sharp, knowing, with the slightest tilt of amusement—like he could read the thoughts you didn't even dare admit to yourself.

And then—

He looked at me.

Dead in the eye.

Like he had been waiting for me.

Like he had somehow known I was there before I even did.

Oh.

Oh no.

My breath caught in my throat.

I should leave. I should absolutely leave.

Priestesses do not gawk at men.

Priestesses do not stare at warriors who lounge like kings.

Priestesses do not—

He arched a brow, his lips curling into something just shy of a smirk.

And then, with the unshaken confidence of a man who had never once known rejection,

He winked.

He. Winked.

At me.

Oh, for the love of the Gods.

Like a Fairytale

His voice dripped through the air like honey warmed over fire.

"Excuse me, miss?"

I just stared.

That voice was a problem.

Smooth.

Too smooth.

Deep, warm, laced with the kind of arrogance that only belonged to men who had never once heard the word 'no.'

"Please, if you may." His tone dipped, teasing, coaxing, like we were already in on some kind of private joke.

And then, as if he were bestowing a favor upon the Gods themselves, he released me from his grasp.

"You can help me. I require a woman's opinion. I would be indebted."

I hesitated, every instinct screaming at me to retreat, but my gaze flickered instinctively to my father for permission.

His expression? Blank. Unreadable.

Which, in my experience, was never a good sign.

Oh.

The Gods were howling with laughter.

Because as I stepped into the room, I saw him standing there—drenched in golden candlelight, drowning in silks and brocades, like he had just stepped out of a forbidden dream.

Golden-brown eyes, gleaming with mischief.

Fiery copper hair, untamed, boyish and roguish—so effortlessly wild that even the wind would be jealous.

Lean but strong, a warrior's build wrapped in noble silk, the kind of man who was equally at home in a throne room or a battlefield.

And Gods, he was grinning.

Not just any grin.

The grin.

The kind of grin that should come with a warning label.

The kind that ruined lives, wrecked dignities, and made smart women make catastrophically dumb decisions.

And I?

I was staring.

Not subtly.

Not in a quick, polite glance, oh, what a nice tunic, moving on kind of way.

No.

This was full-on, mouth-parted, might-have-forgotten-how-blinking-works, brain-evacuated-the-premises staring.

His brows lifted slightly, his amusement sharpening like a blade.

Oh no.

He knew.

"Do I pass inspection, Priestess?" he asked, and the teasing lilt in his voice was criminal.

I inhaled sharply, my fingers darting to my necklace—a desperate attempt to ground myself—brushing over the cool emerald my father had gifted me just hours before.

His gaze followed the motion.

No.

No, no, do not—

"For any woman who adorns herself with such a jewel," he mused, "must have the fashion sense of an angel."

His voice was so smooth, so deep and velvety, it could have been poured from a golden goblet and served in a palace.

I short-circuited.

"Th-thank you, Milord?" I managed, as if I had forgotten the basics of human speech.

His grin deepened.

Like a fox in a hen house.

My father cleared his throat loudly.

"Your Majesty, Arianna."

He corrected.

"This is King Odin."

My polite, faint smile contorted into a silent, panic-stricken "O."

I snapped my head back toward the man—no, the King—the absolute most powerful man in the kingdom, the very same man whose eyes I had just likened to golden sunlight in my head like some love-drunk poet.

On all that is holy.

I had called it.

No. No, no, no, no.

"King Odin?" I choked.

And then—because I was apparently on a mission to ruin myself—I dropped into the most aggressively overdone curtsy known to mankind, nearly toppling over in the process.

His hand shot out instantly, catching me.

Warmth.

That was the first thing I registered.

The second?

His fingers curled just enough to steady me, but not nearly enough to let go.

I was perilously close to his chest now, and he had the audacity—THE AUDACITY— to glance down at the narrow space between us with the most insufferable smirk I had ever seen.

"Careful, little priestess," he murmured. "I'd hate for you to fall too hard."

I was going to combust.

I regained my composure and put as much distance between us as I could.

His laughter followed me.

Low, rich, wickedly amused.

I was so in trouble.

The next few minutes were a blur of fabric samples and measured breathing, desperately trying to rein in the utter catastrophe that was my dignity.

But Odin?

Odin was having the time of his life.

He twirled a lock of his own copper hair, his voice playful.

"I need a new outfit for the ball I'm hosting in a fortnight. The third anniversary of the end of the Civil War," he sighed dramatically. "Graf Nikolai Belov will be there, and he is always the best dressed. I cannot allow him to outdo me this year. He is smug and pretentious."

He turned to me, as if we were already conspirators in some grand fashion coup.

"Tell me, Arianna. Should I drown myself in gold? Or should I attempt the impossible and be even more devastating in green?"

I blinked rapidly, my brain struggling to reboot.

He said my name.

Like he had been saying it all his life.

I cleared my throat, grasping for composure.

"Green suits you."

The moment the words left my mouth, I knew.

I had doomed myself.

Odin's brow lifted, his amusement sharpening.

Oh, fantastic.

If I had been digging a hole, I had just thrown down my shovel and started hacking at the earth with my bare hands.

I pressed on, horrified at my own loose tongue. I stepped forward, brushing my fingertips over the green brocade, desperately trying to salvage what was left of my dignity.

"You—you would look dashing in green," I stammered. "You'd look nice in gold too! But the green makes your eyes shine like—like the sun at golden hour."

...The sun at golden hour.

THE SUN AT GOLDEN HOUR?!

Odin's grin turned absolutely lethal.

My father ran a hand down his face.

I had lost.

I had lost the game, and I didn't even know I was playing.

And Odin?

He knew.

Odin let the silence stretch, let the moment sit between us, knowing—knowing—I was still drowning in the sheer audacity of my own words.

The sun at high noon.

I wanted to launch myself into the nearest fireplace and never return.

But Odin?

Odin was thriving.

He tapped his chin, as if pondering something of great importance. Then, with the ease of a man who had never once questioned his own perfection, he exhaled a mock-suffering sigh and murmured,

"Then green it shall be. If it makes my eyes shine so… poetically, how could I deny the people such a spectacle?"

I clenched my jaw so tightly I nearly shattered my molars.

Smug. Insufferable. Unbearably handsome.

Odin turned to my father, his tone all business, though the golden gleam in his eyes betrayed his amusement.

"Maxim, have a matching gown made for your daughter in this very fabric."

My father blinked. "I… what?"

“A gown,” Odin repeated smoothly, as if ordering silk and lace for the daughter of a Baron was the most natural thing in the world.

“Bill it to the royal treasury.”

The air vanished from my lungs.

I snapped my head toward him so fast I nearly gave myself whiplash. “What?”

Odin smiled. Slow. Languid. Devastating.

“You’ll need something to wear to the ball.”

The ball.

The ball.

The grand, glittering event celebrating the third anniversary of Odin’s reign.

The event attended by nobles, warriors, foreign dignitaries—by every important person in the kingdom.

I stared at him, horrified and speechless in equal measure.

Odin tilted his head slightly, his curls tumbling across his forehead in a way that was infuriatingly perfect.

“I assume you do dance, Lady Arianna?”

His voice dripped with playful mischief, but beneath it… something else.

Something intentional.

He was playing a game, and I had just been swept onto the board.

I forced my spine to straighten, tried to gather what was left of my shattered dignity.

“I—yes, Your Majesty. I was taught.”

Taught, yes. Practiced? That was another matter entirely.

His grin curved sharper.

"Good."

He took my hand—just my fingers, barely more than a brush of contact, but it burned.

His thumb ghosted over my knuckles in a touch so light, so deliberate that my breath hitched before I could stop it.

The corner of his mouth twitched, like he had caught it.

Of course, he had.

He lifted my hand to his lips and—

Oh no. No, no, no.

His mouth barely grazed my skin, but it was enough.

Enough to send a shockwave of warmth up my arm. Enough to make my pulse betray me.

"Then I shall see you on the dance floor, little priestess."

And with that, he released me.

I did not move.

I could not move.

Odin turned, adjusting his cuffs like he hadn't just upended the very foundation of my existence.

"Maxim, I leave your daughter in your capable hands. Ensure she is well prepared for the ball."

Then, as casually as if he were discussing the weather, he strode toward the doors—pausing just long enough to glance back at me over his shoulder.

"I expect a dance, Lady Arianna. Try not to leave me waiting."

Then he was gone.

The doors swung shut, and the room exhaled.

I remained rooted to the spot, struggling to comprehend reality.

For a moment, the only sound was the distant echo of Odin's boots against the temple floors.

Then—

"…What just happened?"

My voice sounded foreign to my own ears.

My father just stared at me.

Still. Silent. Expression caught somewhere between awe and sheer disbelief.

Finally, after a long, heavy pause, he ran a hand down his face and exhaled a slow breath.

Then—

"The King is courting you."

I stopped breathing.

I blinked.

And then—

"Oh no."

My father blinked back at me. "Oh no?"

"Oh no."

Oh no.

Oh no, no, no, no.

The room spun.

The King—the most powerful man in the kingdom, the golden boy of Lorna, the warrior crowned in victory—was courting me.

Me.

A priestess.

A woman of faith.

A woman who had, until five minutes ago, considered herself entirely immune to the follies of reckless men with too much charm and far too much confidence.

A fool.

I was a fool.

And Odin knew it.

But Gods help me—I wanted to see just how dangerous this could get.

A Masterclass in Suffering – Arianna

The days leading up to the ball were nothing short of excruciating.

Pure, unfiltered agony.

The kind of suffering one might experience if trapped in a tavern while a half-drunk bard wailed endlessly about lost love, except somehow worse.

Because the tragic love story?

Was mine.

And the bard?

Also me.

My mind had become a battlefield, and the only warrior in the fight was King Odin—in all his copper-haired, mischief-eyed, smirking glory.

One man.

Five minutes.

And somehow, I was completely, irrevocably ruined.

How is he doing this to me?!

I had spent years sculpting myself into a pillar of self-discipline, an unwavering beacon of poise and faith—and yet here I was, a hopelessly smitten mess over a man I had met for less time than it took to brew a pot of tea.

I was above this nonsense.

…Or so I had once foolishly believed.

Because now?

Now, I was spiraling.

I tried—*tried*—to focus on my prayers, my duties, literally anything that wasn't him.

It was hopeless.

Every time I closed my eyes, I saw his lips on my hand.

Every time I breathed in, I swore I could still smell the faint traces of lavender and rosemary—teasing me, haunting me, as though the universe itself had decided to turn against me.

And his laugh.

Oh, his laugh.

The moment my mind drifted, I heard it—

Deep. Rich. Entirely too confident.

The kind of laugh that curled around my spine like a promise, the kind that whispered, I am trouble, and you are already in too deep.

A moment.

A single moment that had lasted mere seconds—

Yet somehow shattered my entire existence.

And my treacherous brain, as if determined to torment me, had decided that one replay was not enough.

No.

It had to be played on an endless, merciless loop, over and over again, like a song that refused to end.

Did I really tell the king that green made his eyes sparkle?

Yes. Yes, I did.

Did he really laugh, as though he found my ridiculous, undignified slip charming?

Oh, most certainly.

And did my heart, in a spectacular display of betrayal, decide that his laugh was somehow the most beautiful sound ever to exist?

Absolutely.

Oh. I was doomed, wasn't I?

And the worst part?

My body—once a bastion of discipline, a temple of self-control—was now completely out of my jurisdiction.

My pulse quickened at the mere thought of him. My skin tingled at the memory of his touch.

And my lips—those treacherous, insubordinate things—

Oh, they had the audacity to wonder. To fantasize. To ache.

Would his lips be soft? Firm? Mischievous, like the rest of him?

Could I feel his heart in them, his rapture, his ruin?

Would my own heart survive, or would it simply explode on impact, leaving me as nothing more than a tragic, lovesick puddle on the ballroom floor?

Here lies Arianna—just as ridiculous as her sisters.

I had spent years laughing at my sisters.

Years rolling my eyes at their lovesick sighs, their dreamy stares, their complete and total inability to form a coherent sentence whenever a handsome man so much as looked in their direction.

I had called them fools.

I had mocked their weakness.

I had sworn—with absolute certainty—that I would never, never succumb to such foolishness.

And yet—

Here I was.

Neck deep in nonsense.

Utterly ruined.

So. Not. Above. This.

Oh, I was worse.

So much worse.

At least they had taken months to fall apart.

It had taken me five minutes.

And one man.

With golden eyes and a smirk that had single-handedly rewritten the entire course of my existence.

I was useless.

Hopeless.

Reduced to nothing but a walking, talking, feverishly blushing disaster.

And the worst part?

I understood now.

I understood it all.

The dazed sighs.

The mindless giggles.

The maddening way they would cling to the tiniest details—a glance, a touch, a fleeting word—like it was the most important thing in the world.

Because it was.

Because when a man like the King of Lorna turns his attention to you, you don't just walk away unscathed.

You fall.

Hard.

And you don't even have the good sense to stop yourself.

Goodness.

I owed my sisters a massive, groveling apology.

And if they ever found out?

I would never hear the end of it.

How I Fell Face-First into Destiny – Arianna

The day of the ball finally arrived, and I was one shaky breath away from a full-blown nervous collapse.

And naturally, Anastasia—my youngest sister, my lifelong nuisance, and demon sent specifically to torment me—arrived at the Temple to do my hair.

Or, more accurately, she arrived to bask in my misery.

And she was having a marvelous time.

"I don't know who's more excited—you or me," she teased, weaving delicate baby's breath into the intricate braid she had meticulously arranged.

She met my gaze in the mirror, her sly, knowing smile the exact expression of a younger sibling reveling in the downfall of their elder.

I pursed my lips, feigning indifference even as my stomach threatened to start a full-scale rebellion.

"It's just a ball, Ana."

Anastasia snorted.

Snorted.

Like a barn animal, right into my ear.

"Oh yes, just a ball," she mocked, eyes twinkling with mischief. "With the King. The King who is clearly, utterly, helplessly enchanted by you."

She let out a dreamy sigh before collapsing onto my shoulder dramatically, clutching at my sleeve like some love-struck maiden in a tragic romance.

"Oh, Arianna," she sighed. "My heart burns for you like the dying embers of a once-great fire!"

I groaned. Loudly.

"You are impossible."

Anastasia giggled, returning to my hair with an entirely too smug expression.

"You're in love," she singsonged, twirling a strand of my hair around her fingers before pinning the final flower into place. "You can deny it all you want, but I see it. We all see it."

I nearly snapped my own neck whipping my head toward her, my eyes wide with horror.

"Excuse me?!"

Anastasia ducked just in time to avoid being smacked by a stray curl, her smirk widening.

"Oh, nothing," she said in the most infuriatingly innocent tone I had ever heard. "Just saying what everyone else is thinking. Maybe a little love will make you more fun. Less… you know."

She waved her hand vaguely.

I gasped.

"Less what?"

"Rigid. Uptight. Entirely too serious for your own good. Like a very beautiful, but very stressed-out statue."

I scowled.

She winked.

I huffed, spinning back toward the mirror, pointedly ignoring the way my cheeks had betrayed me by flushing a humiliating shade of pink.

I wanted to argue. I truly did.

I wanted to huff and puff and make some grand speech about how I was a woman of discipline, of faith, of unwavering dedication to my path.

But then—

I saw my reflection.

And for a moment, I stared.

Because I barely recognized the woman in the mirror.

The woman staring back at me was gorgeous.

She was regal and refined.

The green velvet gown draped over me like liquid emeralds, the intricate brocade shimmering beneath the flickering candlelight.

My auburn curls had been woven into a half-up braid, delicate blossoms crowning my head as if I had wandered straight out of some fairytale.

I had spent so long being practical, focused, devout.

And yet, staring back at me was a woman who looked like she belonged at a ball.

Not a priestess.

Not just a daughter of faith.

A woman.

A woman who, for the first time, wondered if she was allowed to want something for herself.

Just because she wanted it.

And then—

I saw it.

Resting right above my collarbone.

The emerald necklace my father had given me.

The very same emerald necklace that had, somehow, completely unraveled my life in a matter of days.

A shiny little beacon of my inevitable downfall.

The symbol of my fashion sense, according to King Odin.

My doom, in gemstone form.

Anastasia, noticing my horrified expression, propped her elbows on my shoulders and rested her chin on my head.

“Thinking about him again?” she hummed.

“No.”

“Liar.”

“I’m not.”

“Liar.”

“Anastasia—”

“Just admit it. He smiled at you, and your heart turned into pudding.”

“My heart is perfectly intact, thank you very much.”

“For now.”

I exhaled through my nose, hands clenching at my skirts, desperately trying not to let her get the best of me.

And then, because the Gods delight in my suffering, a knock echoed through the chamber.

“The King is preparing for your arrival, Priestess Arianna,” the driver announced from the other side of the door. “Let’s not keep him waiting.”

Oh, Gods.

It was time.

There was no turning back now.

I swallowed hard, my heart somehow hammering both too fast and too slow at the same time.

What was going to be left of me by the end of the night?

Anastasia let out a soft gasp, clapping her hands together in giddy delight.

"Oh, it's happening. It's happening. You're about to see him again."

I shot her a glare.

"Anastasia."

She wriggled her eyebrows.

"You're about to see your future husband."

"ANASTASIA."

And with one last, entirely too smug giggle, she gave me a shove toward the door, sealing my fate once and for all.

How I Lost My Entire Sense of Self in One Night – Arianna

The opulent white carriage carried me toward my inevitable ruin, its golden floral designs shimmering under the treacherously romantic glow of the moonlight.

Inside, the luxurious red velvet seats were far too soft, far too indulgent—

Exactly like the man responsible for my current descent into madness.

My stomach? A disaster.

My pulse? Tragic.

My mind? Nowhere to be found.

I had spent years sculpting myself into a paragon of discipline, of faith, of divine purpose.

And yet, one smirking man, five minutes, and an utterly ridiculous fabric shopping incident later—

I had been reduced to a hopeless, lovesick mess, fantasizing about a King's hands, his mouth, his—

No. No. Absolutely not.

I squeezed my eyes shut. I had to stop.

I was not the kind of woman who swooned over a man.

I was not the kind of woman who let a pretty face unravel her.

And yet—

Here I was.

A woman of faith, wisdom, and discipline, who had just spent an entire week wondering how it would feel if King Odin whispered something outrageous into her ear.

The worst part?

I had never felt this way before.

I had never been this way before.

Men had always been distant, irrelevant in my world of duty and divinity. I had spent my life devoted to a higher calling, untouched by temptation, unshaken by longing. Until now. Until him.

And I was actively walking into the fire of my own free will.

As we approached the castle gates, I peered out the window, desperately seeking a distraction.

Instead, I found the entire city waiting for me.

They lined the street to witness my arrival.

Torches lined the streets, casting golden halos over a sea of people, all cheering, clapping, celebrating.

A city-wide spectacle.

For me?

For this?

What is happening here?

This cannot be real.

All this for me, before I stepped into that ballroom and sealed my fate.

Because apparently, the entire kingdom had decided I was doomed before I had.

Oh, fantastic.

So not only was I falling at an alarming rate, but so was everyone else.

No pressure, Arianna, no pressure.

Was no one concerned that I had only met him once?!

Had we, as a people, collectively decided that I was to be

offered up on a silver platter to a man with a dangerous smile and no regard for my emotional stability?!

I was caught in his web.

A web of charm, desire, and sheer, unrelenting magnetism.

And the worst part?

I was walking into it willingly.

I couldn't stop myself.

I wanted to know where this road ended.

Priestess Arianna, once the pinnacle of self-restraint, now hopelessly lost to a man who had winked at her while shopping for fabric.

Absolutely tragic.

The bards will sing of my downfall for generations.

The carriage rolled to a stop.

The doors opened.

My legs—usually reliable, strong, competent—decided to take a sabbatical.

I steadied myself and took a deep breath.

This was it.

I was led through the grand palace entrance, my fate all but sealed.

And then, the doors slammed shut behind me.

A decisive, final thud.

I inhaled sharply.

It was fine.

I was fine.

I could survive this.

I was a woman of dignity, self-control, and—

Then—

A knock.

I whipped around, heart hammering so hard it was probably considering a career change.

No. No, not yet—

The doors swung open.

And there he was.

King Odin.

Dripping in silk and sin, wreathed in candlelight like something out of a dream designed to ruin me.

His presence stole the air, filled the space, commanded every last drop of attention.

His golden-brown eyes, warm and wicked, locked onto mine like they had been waiting.

And worse?

He smiled.

Not just any smile.

A devastating, slow-spreading, life-ruining smirk.

The kind that should come with a warning label.

The kind that said,

I know exactly what you're thinking, and I intend to make it worse.

Oh, and he did.

Because the moment his gaze swept over me, slowly, deliberately—

It was like being touched without being touched.

A burn ignited low in my stomach, spreading like wildfire.

I was not surviving this slow-burning night.

Rest in peace, Arianna, you're not coming back from this.

He extended a hand.

"My lady," he murmured, voice dark velvet, rich with amusement. "Shall we?"

I hesitated.

I should hesitate.

I shouldn't give in so willingly.

But his fingers brushed mine, a brief graze of warmth, and my breath hitched.

The weight of expectation pressed against me, the cheers still echoing beyond the palace doors, the fire in his gaze promising things I wasn't ready to name.

I placed my hand in his.

Helpless.

Defeated.

His grip was firm, sure. His thumb traced the back of my knuckles, deliberate, fleeting, a ghost of a touch that left embers in its wake.

And then, with a smirk that sealed my fate, he led me into the ballroom.

This could not be real.

How to Lose Your Heart in Thirty Seconds – Arianna

As we walked, he spoke—"Priestess Arianna."

My knees nearly buckled.

Because why—why—did my name sound like a sin when he said it? Why did it feel like a vow?

I cleared my throat, scrambling for dignity. Sanity. Anything to tether myself to reality.

"Your Majesty," I managed, my voice miraculously steady despite the riot in my chest.

His eyes sparked.

How was he so calm? So composed? How was I the trembling one?

He looked devastating tonight. That green brocade—my father's green brocade—clung to him like temptation made tangible. I'd chosen it on a whim, insisting to Odin that it would suit him. I hadn't been wrong. The deep, silken green brought out the gold in his hair, the sharpness in his jaw, the quiet cruelty in his smile. It was as if the fabric had been spun just to drape over his arrogance.

He was every inch the monarch he was, regal, untouchable. And yet, somehow, he'd made himself mine in that moment. My choice of fabric on his body. My prediction made manifest.

He was beautiful.

He was dangerous.

He was mine to lose.

"Tell me, little priestess," he drawled, stepping closer—too close. "Did you enjoy your grand welcome?"

My grand welcome. The city-wide parade announcing the unraveling of everything I'd ever believed.

"Oh, immensely," I said, summoning every ounce of wit I had left. "Though I do wonder—did you orchestrate the entire spectacle, or was it simply divine coincidence?"

His lips curved, slow and wicked. "Would you believe me if I said I had nothing to do with it?"

I crossed my arms. "Not even slightly."

A wolfish grin. "Good. I'd be disappointed if you did."

He was infuriating.

He was magnetic.

He was a fire I couldn't stop reaching for.

And I was already falling.

We stepped into the ballroom. He led me to the center without a word. The crowd parted like silk. The music halted.

Then, with theatrical ease, he stepped back and raised his voice.

"The Gods have willed many things, my dear Arianna."

I stiffened. A current shifted beneath the air. Conversations quieted. All eyes turned.

My stomach coiled, but something else curled with it—heat, thrill, anticipation.

"Today, the people of Lorna did not gather merely to celebrate their king's third year on the throne," Odin declared. "They gathered to witness a divine moment."

His voice was rich, sure. Not a man proposing. A king delivering prophecy.

My breath caught. Was this happening?

"I have seen beauty," he said, pacing slowly. "I have seen grace. But never have I stood in the presence of a woman who embodies the will of the Gods so completely."

The hush was complete. Reverent.

"A woman of faith," he continued, "chosen not only by the Divine, but by destiny itself."

I could feel the weight of their eyes. The collective breath of a room being held hostage by his charisma.

I was used to reverence. But not like this. Not in a way that made me feel like an offering.

"Tell me, my sweet priestess," Odin said, his voice gentling, reverent. "Would you deny the path the Gods have set before us?"

I opened my mouth. Closed it.

This wasn't a question. This was coronation. In front of everyone.

He reached into his coat and withdrew a ring—an emerald the color of spring valleys, encased in gold.

"Stand beside me, Arianna," he murmured, the intimacy in his tone making my spine shiver. "As my queen."

My heart slammed against my ribs. The moment stretched—too tight, too fragile. I couldn't breathe.

He stepped closer, lifted the ring, and whispered where only I could hear:

"You wouldn't defy the path the Gods led you to, would you?"

His gaze held mine. A dare. A promise. A trap wrapped in silk.

And I saw it.

I saw the bait. The teeth just beneath the velvet.

But oh, how it gleamed.
How it whispered to every fractured, hungry part of me.
The priestess in me recoiled. The girl in me reached.

Silence fell.

I could say no. I could.
But the way he was looking at me—like I was already his—unraveled something in me.

'Shut up', I told the priestess. 'Just shut up.'
Because the woman in me wanted to be chosen.
Wanted the fire, the hunger, the wicked promise behind his smile.
Wanted him.

More than I have ever wanted anything in my life.

"I would never defy the Gods," I said, stepping into the trap with eyes wide open.

The fire in my chest burned too bright.

I swallowed. "I..." I exhaled. "Yes."

The applause roared before the word had fully left my lips.

He smiled, victorious. And as he slid the ring onto my trembling hand, I thought—

Maybe this wasn't defeat. Maybe this was what I'd been waiting for all along.

But as he led me through the ballroom, reality returned—cold and biting.

The whispers came next:

"She's too plain." "A priestess? How desperate must he be?" "Let her have her moment. It won't last."

Each word struck like a blade. Still, I smiled. I raised my chin. I clutched Odin's hand like it meant something.

Because they were wrong. They had to be wrong.

Meeting the Shadows of War – Arianna

Odin was beaming, which meant I should have been wary.

A man only smiled like that when he was about to introduce you to the best and worst decisions he'd ever made.

"Come, my love," he said, dragging me through the torchlit courtyard, his excitement overriding any attempt at grace or dignity. "You must meet my oldest friends—the men who made me king!"

That caught my attention.

Two figures stood in the shadows of the castle columns.

One leaned with practiced ease, a goblet in hand, smirking like he'd been waiting for this moment all night.

The other stood utterly still. Not the stillness of nobility, but of a man who'd been forged in war—and never quite stepped out of it.

Odin strode forward with the flair of a man in love with his own voice, sweeping his arm toward me like a performer unveiling his final act.

"Allow me to introduce you to my queen-to-be—Lady Arianna Maximovna Vasilieva, Priestess of the High Temple."

The leaning man snorted before Odin could finish, shaking his head with a grin that suggested he wasn't impressed by titles, only by what people did with them.

Odin turned to him next, gesturing with a dramatic flourish, as if presenting some rare artifact pulled from a chest of war medals and forgotten wine.

"My queen, this is Baron Matvei Theodoric Sergeyev von Lorne, Warden of the Eastern Isles, First Knight of the Royal Guard."

The poor man groaned and rolled his eyes. "Gods, Odin, not the full thing."

He looked like he'd been carved straight out of the lumber province of Velkhaven—broad-shouldered, tall, and stocky in a way that spoke of strength, not softness. A man who loved life. Slightly chubby, but not fat. More like someone who could chop down a tree with one swing, haul the timber back, build you a house, and bake you bread inside it—all before noon.

His long, reddish dirty blonde hair brushed his shoulders, and his beard and mustache were streaked with copper, like fire hiding in flax. Rugged. A little scruffy. Handsome in a boy-next-door sort of way. The kind of man your aunt would try to set you up with after temple.

And those cheeks? Absolutely pinchable. I had to fold my hands behind my back to resist the temptation. I must have restraint, after all.

But it was his eyes that caught me. Sea-glass blue-green, open and unguarded, full of mischief and warmth. Kindness, even.

All the things you wouldn't expect from the First Knight of the Royal Guard, second in command.

Then he looked at me and dipped his head—not a bow, not some formal display of obedience, but something quieter. A gesture of acknowledgment.

That was all.

And somehow, it was far more charming than if he'd kissed my hand. He was effortlessly charming.

"Just call me Murphy," he said, his voice edged with a lopsided amusement. Then, with a slow sip of wine and a sideways glance at Odin, he added, "A priestess, hmm? What in the Gods' names are you doing tangled up with him?"

It was a joke, but only mostly.

Odin's smile didn't waver—but his hand settled on the small of my back. Light as a whisper. Firm as a claim.

"Mind your tongue, Murphy," he said, all warmth and velvet charm—with just a flicker of steel beneath. "She's already mine. She just doesn't know it yet."

Murphy exhaled long-sufferingly, tilting his goblet toward me. "She's still here. That alone is a miracle."

I smiled despite myself.

I liked him immediately.

Then Odin turned to the second figure. His tone puffed up with theatrical pride, as if invoking a myth.

"Commander Graf Alexander Volkov, Lord of the Sunfire River Valley, Commander of the Royal Guard."

I blinked.

I turned to the man. Then back to Odin.

Then back to the man.

Slowly, I let out a long, contemplative hum. "Impressive," I mused. "Though I'm not sure which will end first—your title or this ball."

Murphy choked on his wine.

The man, however, didn't so much as blink.

He gave a bow—not deep, not performative. A soldier's bow.

Precise. Measured. Given because it was meant, not because I expected it.

"Alexey," he said simply.

Voice like stone—quiet, grounded, and devoid of flair.

No smirk. No flash of ego. No reaction to my jab.

Which, for some reason, only made him more interesting.

I arched a brow.

He was handsome. Devastatingly so.

Not like Murphy's warm, boyish charm—but something colder. Sharper.

Black hair fell loose around his brow, unruly but purposeful. His jaw was cut like marble, edged in stubble that only made him look more severe. And those eyes—pale blue, like a blade catching light in a snowfield.

Piercing. Merciless. Beautiful.

He looked like he could win a war with the sharp edge of his stare alone.

A man carved from command.

And he wasn't from here. That much was clear.

Not with that dark hair, or the olive skin kissed by a sun that never shows itself in Elarion.

He was southern. A Velvodan, perhaps. An outsider among our red-haired frost-born nobility.

He didn't look like he belonged in this court.

He looked like he'd survived it.

He saw everything—and offered nothing.

There was no hunger in his presence. No desire to impress.

Just silence. Restraint. Power held tightly in hand.

He was the kind of man you didn't look at too long.
Not because he might catch you—
But because some part of you might want him to.

Unnerving.

"So," I said lightly, "as Commander of the Royal Guard, is it your job to keep Odin alive?"

Murphy snorted. "And Gods help him."

Then, with mock severity, he raised his goblet toward Alexey. "To the poor bastard who has to keep His Majesty here breathing."

Alexey did not acknowledge his comment.

We all sat at the banquet table before us.

"A queen, hmm?" Murphy took another slow sip of wine. "Doesn't seem fair, does it, Alexey? We fought the same battles, saved his insufferable ass more times than I can count—and Odin gets the crown, the credit, and the most beautiful woman in the kingdom. Some men have all the luck."

Odin threw an arm around Murphy's shoulder, grinning like a fox who'd devoured the whole coop.

"Luck? You mean charm, skill, and undeniable handsomeness."

Murphy didn't blink. "I meant luck."

I laughed.

There was something disarming about Murphy—easy, bright, but with the eyes of a man who'd seen too much to be fooled by anything.

And then, there was Alexey.
Still silent. Still watching me.
But not like a man watching a queen-to-be.

No desire. No envy. No indulgence.

Just a calm, piercing kind of scrutiny that made my spine straighten on instinct—

like I was being evaluated for weaknesses.

I met his gaze and lifted my chin.

He didn't flinch.

He didn't soften, didn't blink, didn't offer so much as a diplomatic nod.

I got the sense he didn't approve of our union—

and didn't care if I noticed.

Odin clapped him on the back.

"Alexey here is Commander of the Royal Guard now—but before that, he was the reason I didn't die in the war. The reason any of us made it out alive."

Alexey didn't straighten. Didn't even blink.

"Odin exaggerates," he said.

Odin barked a laugh. "Odin does no such thing! You dragged me, bleeding and raving, across enemy lines because you were too damn stubborn to leave me behind."

He turned to me with a grin. "And now look at us! A kingdom. A queen. A golden age of peace."

Murphy sighed. "Yes, Odin. We bled, we fought, we suffered… so you could sit on a throne and marry a woman far too good for you."

Odin smirked, unbothered. "And I appreciate every moment of it."

I turned to Alexey.

"Do you hate balls, Alexey?"

His gaze met mine again. Still unreadable. Still sharp.

"They aren't my thing."

“And what is your thing?” I asked, leaning in slightly.

His voice didn’t change. But the weight behind it did.

“Surviving,” he said.

Then, after a beat, added—quietly, deliberately, without breaking eye contact—

“And making sure the right people do too.”

Then—without needing to move—he shifted the air between us.

And looked at Odin.

Not long. Not obviously.

But it was enough.

Enough to make my spine straighten and my breath catch.

Enough to tell me that this man was not what he seemed.

Enough to leave me wondering—

If he saw something I didn’t.

Or if he knew something I should.

A Night of Fire and Devotion – Arianna

The night of the ball was one of the best nights of my life.

The kind of night that stories were written about, that poets ached to capture, that left the air thick with something intoxicating and unnameable.

Odin and I danced until my feet ached, until the world blurred into nothing but the press of his hand against my waist, the heat of his breath against my skin, the golden flicker of candlelight reflecting in his devastating, soul-stealing eyes.

He introduced me to everyone—nobles, generals, dignitaries—his presence at my side a silent, undeniable declaration.

And to my astonishment, most of them welcomed me warmly.

Some did have an edge of disapproval or tension, but I suppose that is to be expected.

I won't be able to win everyone over.

Maybe my piety will be enough to put them at ease.

Perhaps it was the sheer certainty in Odin's posture, the way his hand never left me for too long, the way he gazed at me as if I were the most beautiful, impossible thing to ever grace the earth.

Or perhaps it was simply that the people adored their king.

And Odin?

He adored me.

The music swelled, and he twirled me on the dance floor, guiding me with an effortless grace that should have been impossible for a man so powerful, so commanding.

Yet he moved like the night had been made for him.

Like he had been made for me.

The moon above bathed us in its glow, seeping through the windows, its silver light a silent witness to my undoing.

Then—

His lips brushed the shell of my ear, his husky voice thick with something far too dangerous to name.

"Ari, my Queen," he murmured, his breath warm against my skin, sending a delicious, forbidden shiver racing down my spine.

"Tell me how you have enchanted me so."

His voice was low, indulgent, as if he were tasting each word before offering them to me, wrapping them in silk and seduction.

"If we could bottle up your charm," he continued, his tone rich with amusement and something darker beneath, "we would be as rich as the King and Queen themselves."

I giggled, a soft, breathless sound, my fingers tightening slightly against the fabric of his tunic.

Oh, he was good.

He always knew exactly how to make me smile, how to make me feel like I was the only woman in the entire kingdom.

"Oh, no can do, Your Majesty."

I tilted my chin up, feigning innocence, my lips curving into something dangerously close to a smirk.

"A lady never shares her secrets."

His low chuckle reverberated through me, rattling through my ribs, down my spine, curling into a slow-burning ache that settled low in my stomach.

Odin was a man who devoured life whole.
And that night—
I thought he might devour me, too.

Then, just as my head was spinning with warmth, with excitement, with the heady, dangerous thrill of it all—his hand tightened slightly against my waist.

"Arianna," he murmured, softer this time, his tone shifting into something almost reverent. "Do you know what this night is?"

I blinked up at him. "A celebration?"

He smiled, but there was something behind it—something deeper, something knowing.

"A devotion," he corrected, twirling me once more, pulling me effortlessly back into his embrace. "A night where we do not merely celebrate the blessings of the Gods—but honor them. A night where we listen, where we follow the paths laid before us."

The air seemed to still. The laughter, the music, the revelry—it was still there, but suddenly, I felt apart from it. Removed.
Because Odin was looking at me with something heavier than adoration now. Something more than desire.

Something fated.

"You were meant for me, Arianna." His voice was a whisper of silk and steel. "The Gods willed it. Can you not feel it?"

My lips parted, but no words came.
Because in that moment, I did feel it.
Or maybe I wanted to.

Maybe that was more dangerous.

He leaned in, brushing the softest kiss against my temple.

"If you deny this," he murmured, barely more than a breath, "if you deny me—do you not deny them as well?"

The world seemed to tilt beneath my feet.

Odin only smiled.

Because he knew.

I had already given in.

The Garden of Almost – Arianna

The air in the palace garden smelled like jasmine and secrets.

I shouldn't have followed him.

Not after the announcement.

Not after the kiss on the back of my hand, the dancing, the sweet nothings, the divine declarations, the emerald ring. Not after he told the entire court I would be his queen.

But when Odin offered me his arm and said, "Walk with me, little flame,"

I obeyed without hesitation.

Like it was a prayer.

We moved through the hedges under moonlight, his coat brushing my arm with every single step, his silence thick with something I couldn't name. Anticipation? Arrogance? Lust?

Maybe all three.

I should've said something clever. Something sharp enough to remind him I still had teeth beneath all this perfectly poised submission.

But I was too warm.

Too breathless.

Too busy pretending I wasn't already leaning in.

He led me into a marble alcove, half-hidden behind ivy and stone. Candlelight from the ballroom flickered across the stones like it, too, was peeking in on something it shouldn't see. The world beyond fell silent, like even the air held its breath for what came next.

Then he turned.

And I was against the wall before I could blink.

One arm caught above my head. His body crowding mine—close, not crushing. Not rushed. Just there. Like he'd always belonged in my space and was merely reclaiming it.

My pulse stuttered.

My spine tried to straighten, but my body betrayed me—arching instead, greedy for him.

"Odin—" I started, half protest, half prayer.

He tilted his head, that boyish smile blooming slow and wicked.

"I like the way you say my name," he murmured, lips just a breath from mine. "Like you're afraid to say anything else.

His fingers found my waist, then slid upward with a reverence that felt rehearsed.

Measured.

Dangerous.

"But I could do without the tone."

I opened my mouth to retort—too late. He kissed me.

Soft at first. Just a test.

Then deeper. Like he knew he'd passed.

His tongue teased mine, coaxing and patient, like seduction was a sacred language only he was fluent in. My breath hitched. My grip on reality dissolved.

He kissed me like he already owned me—like he'd forged the deed in fire and tucked it behind my ribs. And worst of all, I kissed him back like I didn't want it returned.

When I moaned—Gods help me—his smile deepened.

"I knew you'd taste like honey and rebellion," he whispered, lips brushing mine, tasting the words.

"Tell me—was this what you wanted when you left the temple?"

His mouth grazed the shell of my ear. "Or are you still pretending you came for the Gods?"

I hated how my body arched into him.

How my skin prickled under his breath.

How his words wrapped around my spine like silk, smooth and binding.

My knees already ached to fall.

His hand trailed slowly down the curve of my thigh, fingers exploring the bare skin beneath my gown with maddening care—like he was mapping out a kingdom he intended to conquer one inch at a time.

Then he stopped. Just shy of where I needed him most.

I whimpered. A sound I'd never made for any man.

A sound I didn't know I could make.

And he grinned like I'd just confirmed everything he already believed about me.

"You're trembling," he said softly, almost kindly. "As if I've touched you."

"You have," I managed, barely.

His brows lifted, that wicked amusement glinting behind his lashes.

"Oh, love," he murmured. "You haven't seen anything yet."

He cupped the inside of my thigh, palm hot and possessive, and I nearly cried out.

But again—he didn't move. Didn't press.

Just held me there.

Fully aware of the pressure. Of the fire he'd stoked and refused to extinguish.

"You don't know what you're doing to me," I whispered.

He dragged his lips along my jaw.

"Oh, I do," he murmured. "And you'll be screaming my name—and thanking me—by the time I'm finished.

"Then he leaned in, brushing his lips down my neck—one slow drag that made my pulse riot and my breath shatter.

"But not here," he said, voice low and thick with restraint. He pulled back just before my world tilted completely.

"Not like this. You should be savored… properly."

His eyes flicked over me, dark with promise. "And I don't like to rush what's mine."

And then, he stopped.

He stepped away. Just like that. Like nothing had happened at all.

Like he hadn't just undone me with a kiss and a promise he had no intention of keeping.

I stared at him, dazed. Wanting.

"Odin…" I breathed, my voice barely tethered to my body.

He reached for my hand and kissed my palm, slow and deliberate.

"You're divine, Arianna."

His thumb brushed over the frantic pulse in my wrist.

"But divinity should be unwrapped slowly."

My breath caught. I wanted to speak. Wanted to scream, to curse him, to fall at his feet and demand he finish what he started.

"You're…" I swallowed, cheeks flushed, lips still tingling.

"You can't be real," I whispered.

He grinned.

"And yet you followed me here."

I hated him.

I adored him.

I wanted to slap him.

I wanted to kneel.

But I stayed frozen in place, skin still buzzing, thighs still shaking.

Because his kiss still lingered.

Because his touch still haunted.

Because my knees were still weak from a pleasure that never arrived.

And somehow, I was the one left thanking him for the ache.

This had to be love.

Because surely no one could make me feel like this… and not love me.

Right?

A Dance with a King – Arianna

When the ache in my belly dulled and my thighs steadies, I returned to the ball.

The ballroom shimmered with gold and candlelight, but it was nothing compared to him. He was instantly intoxicating. He took my hand. I acquiesced control.

Odin's hands were fire and certainty, his touch both possessive and reverent as he led me across the ballroom floor.

And Gods, I could still feel it.

The ghost of his fingers against my inner thigh.

The phantom press of his lips just beneath my jaw.

The ache he left behind when he stepped away in the garden and didn't finish what he started.

That moment haunted me.

Where he brought me to the edge and left me there—breathless, flushed, and burning.

He knew what he'd done.

Knew I was still trembling from it.

And now, here in front of the entire court, he held me like I was his victory. His muse. His fire-bride waiting to be crowned.

I had never been twirled, dipped, and swept away before.

Never with a man who moved like the world belonged to him—who held me like I was the reason it did.

He smiled down at me, his golden eyes burning with something deeper than desire—something inevitable.

"I thought I couldn't be any happier than I was," he murmured, his fingers tightening around mine as he led me

into another spin.
"But you have proven me wrong, Arianna.
My fire in the darkest of nights."

I stumbled.

Not physically—his sure grip on my waist never faltered—but internally, my world tilted.

The words crashed into me like a tidal wave, sweeping me off my feet before I could catch my breath.

This was not a passing flirtation.

This was not a fleeting attraction that would fade like candlelight come morning.

This was something more.

Something terrifying.

Something inevitable.

And the best way to fall—
Was headfirst.

I inhaled sharply, bracing myself for what I already knew was coming.

I rose onto my toes, my hands sliding up the broad expanse of his chest, fingers curling into the rich fabric of his coat as I tilted my face up toward his.

His eyes darkened.

A storm brewing.

I closed my eyes—
And surrendered.

I let go and jumped.

His fingers found my cheek, cupping it gently, but there was nothing gentle about the way he pulled me in.

Nothing hesitant about the way he claimed me.

His lips met mine, strong yet deliberate, as if he had been waiting his entire life for this moment and had no intention of rushing it.

I forgot how to stand.

My knees buckled instantly, but before I could even begin to fall, his arm curled around my waist, anchoring me against him, steadying me as if he had known I would melt for him before I even did.

Oh, he knew.

He knew exactly what he was doing to me.

And he took his time.

It was slow. Devastatingly slow.

A lesson.

A promise.

A conquest.

He kissed me like a man who knew his own power—who knew he could command, take, consume—but chose instead to savor.

To teach.

To savor.

And Gods help me, I let him.

I wanted to drown in him, in the heat of his lips, in the way he tasted of wine and something heady and unmistakably Odin.

I wanted to memorize him, to devour him the way he was devouring me, but he wouldn't let me.

And when he finally—finally—pulled away, I realized something terrifying.

I had already memorized him.

I was never going to forget this.

I blinked slowly, my senses drunk on him, the edges of the world slowly coming back into focus.

But there was one thing that remained crystal clear.

Him.

The way he looked at me—

Like I was something precious.

Something treasured.

Something his.

A moment of pure, unadulterated reverence crackled between us, stretched so taut that it might snap and unravel us both.

And then—

The moment shattered.

Clapping.

Laughing.

Roaring applause, loud and unabashedly delighted.

Oh, Gods.

I ripped myself away from his embrace, mortification crashing into me at full force.

I whipped my head around, only to find that—

The entire ballroom had been watching.

I let out a horrified squeak, immediately burying my face in his chest.

His chest.

Which was still warm from our kiss, still heaving slightly from the remnants of desire, still pressed against me like I belonged there.

His low, rich chuckle rumbled against my cheek.

Smug. Infuriating. Insufferable.

I loved it.

I smacked his chest, glaring up at him.

He laughed harder.

Oh, I was never going to live this down.

But somehow—as his arms curled around me, as I let out a deep, shuddering breath, as I finally allowed myself to breathe normally for the first time since I had met him—

I realized something else.

I didn't care.

Because in his arms, I felt something I had never felt before.

I felt home.

We married one month later.

The Queen's Mother – Arianna

My mother screamed.

Not a delicate gasp. Not a quiet, dignified sniffle.

A full-bodied, hands-flung-in-the-air, the-Gods-have-finally-heard-my-prayers scream.

I barely had time to react before she lunged, gathering me into an embrace so tight I briefly feared for my ribs.

"My beautiful girl!" she sobbed into my hair, rocking us slightly as if I were a child again. "I always knew you would find someone special!"

I swallowed the urge to remind her that she had, in fact, not always believed that.

That she had once sighed wistfully at my disinterest in courtship, lamenting that I was too strong-willed, too particular, too impossible to ever let a man in.

And yet, here I was.

Betrothed to the most eligible man in the kingdom.

She pulled back just enough to cradle my face, her eyes shining with dramatic, unfettered joy.

"And not just anyone," she breathed, as if she could barely believe it. "But him. The hero. The king."

Her lips trembled. "A love story fit for the Gods."

I forced a smile. "It is, isn't it? I'm blessed."

Across the room, Anastasia practically vibrated with excitement, clasping her hands together.

"You have to introduce me to all the handsome nobles at court," she gushed, her hazel eyes gleaming. "Think of all the eligible men, all the potential suitors—"

"I would prefer not to think about that," my father muttered dryly.

Unlike my mother, he had not moved from his seat. He watched me with quiet, thoughtful eyes, his expression unreadable.

Anastasia ignored him entirely.

"Oh, Ari, can you imagine? The gowns, the jewelry, the attention—"

"Yes, Anastasia," I sighed. "I can imagine."

I didn't need to, really. I had already lived it—the glittering ball, the whispered envy of women who watched as Odin swept me into his orbit.

And I had loved it.

Alisa, sitting in the corner with her arms crossed, barely spared me a glance.

"I don't see what the fuss is about."

My mother gasped in offense. "Must you always be so indifferent?"

Alisa shrugged, unfazed.

I nearly laughed. It was so like her—unbothered, uninterested.

And then, there was Anya.

She stood near the window, her back stiff, her hands clasped in front of her skirts. She had said nothing since I announced my engagement.

But I saw the way her fingers curled against the fabric. The way her lips pressed into a thin line.

I knew that look.

It was the look she gave me whenever I won.

And now?

Now I had won something that she had wanted, too.

"I suppose I should congratulate you," she said finally, her voice pleasant but empty. "A queen. Imagine that."

She turned to me with a smile that didn't reach her eyes.

"I suppose some people are simply lucky."

Before I could respond, my father sighed, running a hand down his face.

"Enough," he muttered, before shifting his gaze to me.

His expression was different than the others. Softer. Wiser.

"You don't have to rush into this," he said. "You could take time to think."

I blinked. "I don't need time to think."

His brows pulled together. "Are you certain?"

"Of course I am," I said quickly. "I love him."

He studied me for a long moment, his face unreadable.

Then, finally, he nodded.

"If that's what your heart tells you," he murmured. "Then I hope it's right. Sometimes, love isn't enough."

A strange, uneasy feeling settled in my stomach.

And I would wonder, for the first time, if my father had seen something that I had not.

But in that moment, standing in the warmth of my family's home, basking in the attention, the excitement, the envy… I ignored it.

I was in love.
And I had already leapt.
What is done is done.
I was past the point of no return.

The Things I Refused to See – Arianna

Suddenly, I was a queen.

I wore it like a birthright.

The gown clung to me like molten emeralds—silk so fine it shimmered like breath in moonlight. Tiny glass beads kissed the sleeves, catching every flicker of light like the stars themselves had stitched them into place. My hair was woven into a braided crown, pinned with gold and quiet authority.

I looked radiant.

More than that—I looked powerful.

I stood before a mirror taller than any door, framed in dark iron. My reflection gazed back with sharp eyes and a knowing smile. A queen. A wife to a king whose hands never trembled.

And then I saw it.

My belly.

Rounded. Heavy.

Pregnant.

Soon to be mother.

I reached for the swell, cupping it with reverent hands. I should've felt joy. Awe. Peace.

But my heart kicked violently against my ribs.

The crown atop my head gleamed brighter—too bright. The shimmer turned red.

Deep, angry red.

Blood.

It began to drip.

Slow at first. Then faster—thicker—until crimson ran down

my temples, over my cheeks, staining the neckline of that perfect green gown.

I stumbled back, gasping, clawing at the crown.

It burned cold.

So cold it seared.

I screamed and ripped it from my head.

It hit the mirror—

And the glass shattered.

The world cracked with it.

Now I was somewhere else.

Snow.

Thick, endless snow.

The Myroska Tundra? Maybe.

I couldn't tell.

It blanketed everything—rooftops, trees, broken fences—softening the world into something that should've been peaceful. Magical.

But it wasn't.

Ash choked the air, fighting the snow for dominance.

Smoke clawed at my throat.

Before me lay a village I didn't recognize—half-buried in flame, its houses split open like overripe fruit. The snow hissed where fire touched it. Blackened water pooled in frozen gutters.

The ground was littered with the dead.

A man slumped over a wagon.

A child crushed beneath a beam.

A woman curled around something that had already stopped breathing.

So much blood, steaming in the cold.

Then he came.

Odin.

Walking through the wreckage like a god who had grown bored with mercy.

Unburned. Unbothered.

And in his arms… a baby.

Wrapped in cloth too clean for this place.

He cradled it like a prize. A symbol. A declaration.

When he reached me, he smiled.

“A gift,” he said.

And offered the child into my arms.

I took it—reflexively, stupidly—and looked down.

My belly was flat.

Empty.

Gone.

The child wasn’t mine.

My arms trembled.

The village burned on.

Odin stood there, watching me.

And behind him, through the smoke and snow—

Her.

She didn’t run. Didn’t scream. Didn’t beg.

She just stood there.

Watching.

Like she’d already lived through the worst of the world, and this?

This was just the ash that followed.

Her eyes were blue.

Not soft. Not sad.

But clear. Unyielding.

The eyes of someone who had been broken open—then reforged.

Golden curls clung to her face, streaked with blood and soot.

They looked like a crown too stubborn to fall.

Freckles scattered across her skin like constellations smeared by warpaint.

Her hands hung at her sides—bloody, shaking, but capable.

Her dress was torn. Clinging in pieces.

A ghost of modesty draped over a woman who had already been claimed by fire and survived it.

She was magnificent.

Not in the way of queens or courtesans.

But in the way of myth.

The kind of creature whispered about in places too old for books.

The kind of woman prayers don't reach, because she no longer asks for salvation.

She was iron, cooled in blood.

Sacred.

And furious.

The snow did not touch her.

The flames bowed away, as if they feared to burn her twice.

She was ruin and resurrection.

And when she looked at me—

I felt it.

A weight. A knowing. An accusation that didn't need words.

I didn't understand.

But she did.

She saw Odin hand me the child—her child—and said nothing.

Not with her mouth.

But with her silence.

With her stillness.

With the terrible, holy defiance in her eyes.

She didn't scream.

Didn't kneel.

Didn't give him the satisfaction.

She burned brighter than the fires behind her.

Even hollowed out.

Even bleeding.

And she was watching me.

Not him.

Me.

And I—

I couldn't look away.

I didn't know who she was.

But I felt it in my marrow.

She was something ancient.

A mirror forged in ash and aftermath.

A soul bound to mine by thread I couldn't see but couldn't deny.

She was stronger than me.

And I hated that I could feel it.

Where was the child's father?

Where were her people?

Why was she alone?

Why had he handed me her child like a token?

What had I just accepted?

I had so many questions.

I looked down at the baby in my arms, swaddled in perfect cloth that did not belong in this frozen hell. The child was a girl. Copper curls. Rose-petal cheeks.

The snow kept falling.
The fire kept burning.
And the woman in the ash did not move.

Not for me.
Not for him.
Not even for the child.

Because she knew—
Her time would come.
She just had to bide it.

I woke gasping, fingers clutching the edge of my pillow like I was still holding the child.

The sheets were soaked with sweat.
The room was dark.
Silent.

My heart wouldn't settle. It beat like I was still running from something—
Or toward it.

I sat up slowly, pressing my palm to my chest.
The dream clung to me like ash.
The fire. The snow. Her.

She wasn't real.
Of course she wasn't.

Just a figment. A feeling. Some strange echo conjured from too much wine and too little sleep.

I'd been thinking too much. Wanting too much.
That was all.

I let out a shaky breath.

The room didn't answer.

It was just a dream.

Just a dream.

Just…

A strange one.

Again.

Leaving the Temple, Embracing the Future – Arianna

The temple smelled of warm candle wax and aged parchment, a scent so familiar it had become part of me.

For three years, I had woken before the sun, bathed in the hush of morning prayers, and walked these halls with purpose. I had learned discipline, patience, devotion—not just to the Gods, but to the people who came here seeking solace.

And now, I was leaving it all behind.

I ran my fingers along the worn wooden desk in my chamber, tracing the grooves carved into its surface over the years. My packed satchel sat beside it, filled with what little I owned—a few personal books, my priestess robes, a collection of handwritten letters from the women I had counseled.

I had expected to feel sadness.

But instead, all I felt was excitement.

I had given three years to the temple. Three years of quiet service, of tending the sick, of feeding the hungry with whatever scraps we could afford, of holding the hands of grieving mothers as they whispered to the Gods for mercy.

But now, I would have power.

Real power.

Not just to offer comfort but to change things.
To build something lasting.
To make a difference beyond these stone walls.

I pressed my palm flat against my chest, feeling the rapid thrum of my own heartbeat.

The temple had taught me how to help people survive.
But the castle? The throne? That would teach me how to help them live, thrive.

A knock at my chamber door pulled me from my thoughts.

Sister Elira stood in the doorway, her kind eyes full of quiet wisdom.

"It feels strange, doesn't it?" she said softly. "Leaving behind the only life you've known."

I smiled. "It doesn't feel like an ending. It feels like a beginning."

She tilted her head, studying me for a long moment before stepping inside. "I hear you have plans already."

Excitement flickered through me.

"Yes," I said, my voice gaining strength. "Shelters—not just places for food and rest, but places for rehabilitation. People don't just need a meal. They need purpose. A way to get back on their feet."

I could already see it so clearly—stone halls filled with bakers, weavers, blacksmiths, and scribes, all teaching the forgotten people of the city how to work, how to reclaim their lives, how to move forward.

No more endless cycles of hunger, of begging, of despair.

Not just charity.

Opportunity.

Sister Elira nodded slowly, the corners of her lips curving in approval. "A noble vision."

A vision that I would make real.

I had no illusions—I knew the court would sneer, the nobility would scoff at the idea of giving common beggars a place to work, a future to build.

But I had spent three years looking into their eyes, seeing the hopelessness, the hunger, the quiet surrender to fate.

If no one else would fight for them, I would.

I turned one last time, gazing at my chamber—the simple wooden bed, the stack of books beside it, the single window where I had watched countless sunrises.

I had once thought my life would always be here.

That I would serve until my hair turned white, that I would remain in these halls, praying and guiding and hoping that the world outside would somehow change on its own.

But now, I had a king who loved me.

A future brighter than I had ever dared dream.

And the power to finally make that change myself.

I reached into my satchel and felt the smooth, cool weight of the Eternum Relic in my palm.

A glimpse into the future.

The thought sent a shiver down my spine.

It would be so easy. Just one look. One vision. One certainty.

Would Odin and I be happy? Would the court ever accept me? Would I make the change I dreamed of?

I traced my fingers along the intricate engravings, the ancient runes that shimmered faintly beneath the candlelight.

Did I want to know?

For a fleeting moment, I almost did.

But then, I exhaled, steady, sure.

The Gods had led me here. To this moment. To this path.

And if they had guided my steps this far, who was I to second-guess them now?

My faith was not built on certainty. It did not demand guarantees.

I had spent years teaching others to trust in the divine plan—it was time to practice what I preached.

With quiet reverence, I placed the relic back into my satchel, untouched.

Lifting my satchel over my shoulder, I stepped into the corridor.

It was time to begin.

The Wedding of the Century – Arianna

The wedding was nothing short of legendary.

Not just an event, but an epoch—the kind of spectacle that would be whispered about in reverent awe for generations.

Poets would compose verses about it.
Artists would paint sweeping murals.
Bards would likely never shut up about it.

And, of course, Odin insisted on making it as theatrical as humanly possible.

Because he lived for this.

Elarion Castle glowed with splendor, draped in gold and the rarest floral garlands, blooms imported from every corner of Lorna. The grand temple on the castle grounds, where our vows were to be exchanged, was awash in candlelight, each flickering flame a whispered promise of forever.

The castle had been a whirlwind of preparations, every corridor buzzing with the weight of expectation. But now, as I stood at the grand entrance of the temple, the world beyond its towering doors seemed to fade.

Here, in this sacred place, beneath the watchful eyes of Gods and men, we would make our vows.

I barely recognized myself.

My gown, a masterpiece of silk and embroidery, shimmered like molten sunlight, each delicate stitch of gold and silver thread catching the light as I moved. My father had overseen the creation of my gown, his love woven into every single thread.

Odin had commissioned the diadem himself—an intricate crown of emeralds set in twisted gold, designed to highlight the rich auburn copper of my hair, the fair glow of my skin, the depth of my eyes, so he said.

"To make you look like the goddess you are," he smiled.

And now?

Now he was utterly undone.

The King of Lorna.
The Victor of the Lorinian Civil War.
The unshakable warrior-king…

Frozen in place by my mere presence.

I saw it before I even reached him.

His throat bobbed, hard, like he'd forgotten how to breathe. His fingers flexed at his sides—curling, uncurling—like he was physically restraining himself from pulling me into his arms right then and there. He looked at me like I was some celestial vision, some miracle forged just for him, and for a fleeting, breathless moment… I believed it.

The way he devoured me with his eyes should've been forbidden. Especially here. Especially now.

As I stepped beside him at the altar, he leaned in—his voice a hushed, aching whisper only I could hear. "Gods help me, Arianna," he murmured, voice trembling with such practiced wonder, "you are more beautiful than I deserve."

I opened my mouth to respond, but I couldn't. Not yet. He had already taken my hands—gentle, reverent—lifting them to his lips like they were relics meant for worship. His gaze flickered up to mine again, golden and molten, glinting with something deeper than adoration—something theatrical. Something hungry.

"You are…" He trailed off, shaking his head slowly, jaw tight with what looked like awe. "There are no words to describe a celestial being such as yourself."

I laughed despite myself, heart fluttering, senses sparking. "That's unfortunate, Your Majesty," I teased. "Because we're about to take vows. I need your words, oh mighty King of gab."

He gave a low, helpless laugh and bowed his head, pressing his forehead against my knuckles like a man overcome.

Just for a second.

Just long enough to make the crowd sigh.

Then he looked up, and the fire in his eyes nearly burned through me.

"Then let me swear the greatest vow of all, my fire in the darkest of nights."

The room quieted. Even the High Priest seemed to vanish beneath the weight of that moment.

But Odin? Odin didn't blink.

His gaze never left mine, not even to nod to the priest. He was entirely, obsessively focused—like I was the only thing anchoring him to this realm. And when he spoke his vows, his voice did not shake from nerves or doubt—it swelled, brimming with a depth I was certain only I could inspire.

"Arianna," he said, gripping my hands tighter, "from the moment you stepped into my life, I have been a man undone."

I felt my lips part, my heart thudding in protest. He meant it. He had to.

"I do not care what fate has written," he continued. "I do not care for time, or logic, or reason. You are mine, and I am yours, and that is the only truth I need. We will overcome anything thrown at us, together."

Then, lower—soft, raw, meant only for me—
"Say yes, my love. End my misery and say yes. Be my queen. My heart. My home."

Everything in me twisted.

It was reckless. It was madness.
It was the truest thing I had ever known.

"Yes, Odin," I breathed. "I accept you—mind, body, and spirit… forever."

The priest hadn't even finished the rites. The sacred words still hovered, half-formed, between us.

But none of that mattered.

Because Odin broke.

His patience, his decorum, his restraint—all of it shattered in an instant. I barely had time to breathe before he seized me, pulling me flush against him. His hands dug into my waist like he was afraid I might vanish, gripping with a desperation that felt almost... practiced.

His mouth crashed onto mine before I could speak.

And the temple disappeared.

The guests? Gone. The priest? Forgotten. The ceremony itself became irrelevant. All I could feel was him—his lips, his touch, the sheer need pouring off of him like fire.

It wasn't gentle. It wasn't sweet.
It was feral. Possessive. Like he had waited a lifetime to

claim me—and now, finally, the curtain had lifted and the scene was his to devour.

And Gods help me… I let him.

The temple exploded around us.

Applause like thunder. Cheers. Laughter. Whistles.

Somewhere in the din, I swore I heard my father groan in exasperation and my sisters dissolve into giggles—but it all felt like background noise. Blurred, distant.

None of it mattered.

Because this… this was our moment.

And we didn't care who saw.

Gods, we wanted them to see.

Odin pulled back—just enough for air to rush into my lungs, just enough for my world to spin—but not nearly enough to free me from him. Not really.

His forehead pressed to mine, breath ragged, golden eyes darkened with something that looked like worship but felt like possession.

"You're mine now," he whispered, voice thick with emotion, cracked and trembling like he could barely hold it together.

A shiver ran through me—sharp and sweet and overwhelming. I was still breathless, still trembling, still wrapped in the gravity of him.

"Always," I whispered back.

And then he smiled.

That slow, wicked smile—the one that curled like a promise at the edge of a blade.

The kind of smile that made the room disappear and my

knees threaten betrayal.

"Let's get out of here," he said, and it was less a request than a command whispered like a secret.

Oh.

Oh, Gods.

Yes.

He took my hand, leading me down the steps of the altar like we were fleeing something sacred and heavy and old. And I followed without hesitation—

Drunk on the moment.

On him.

On the reckless, delicious heat that pulsed between us like a second heartbeat.

But just as we passed the pews, something flickered at the edge of my joy.

I turned. Just for a second. Just long enough to catch a glimpse—

Murphy, still grinning like he always did… but it didn't quite reach his eyes. There was something else there. Something I couldn't name.

And Alexey—

Stone-still.

Expression unreadable.

Gaze fixed straight ahead like a statue carved from quiet disapproval.

My smile faltered. Only slightly.

Were they… not happy for us?

But then Odin's fingers tightened around mine, anchoring me back to him, back to the moment, back to the high.

And truly?

I didn't care.
Not right now.
Not when I had him.
Not when the whole temple had just watched him choose me.

Let them watch.
Let them whisper.
Let the world feel what it means to burn.

Desperate to Begin – Arianna

The ceremony had ended in a blaze of gold and thunder.

Crowds roared. Petals rained. The air dripped with wine and triumph and forever.

And him.

Odin.

My husband.

My king.

My every fantasy made flesh.

He didn't wait. Not for the procession. Not for the crowd. Not for permission.

His hand seized mine—tight, scorching, possessive—like I was the final piece of his empire to click into place. I barely had time to breathe before we were running. Down the steps. Past the nobles. Past every rule and expectation.

Straight into the carriage.

Straight into the evening glow.

Straight into the kind of hunger that made me dizzy.

He swept me into his arms like I was made of petals, not bone. I gasped, laughing, my hands clinging to him as he carried me like I was precious cargo. Like I was his prize.

"Odin—"

"Mine."

One word. Spoken like a vow. Growled like a threat. Branded like fire.

Then he tossed me inside—literally tossed me—onto the velvet cushions, slamming the door behind us with a finality that felt of holy desire.

The air thickened.

Lanternlight flickered over his face, painting him in gold and shadow. He looked like a god. My god. I melted.

He stared down at me, molten eyes drinking me in.

And I saw it.

I saw hunger in his eyes.

I felt his urgency.

Every move he made, every whisper, every kiss—it all felt like so thrilling.

I never once questioned it.

Why would I?

He was my husband. My king.

And I… I was his.

"Oh, my queen," he murmured, voice dark silk over steel. "The things I'm going to do to you... and all the things you'll beg me to do again."

My thighs clenched. My lips parted. My whole body leaned into him, every nerve on fire.

"No spoilers," I whispered, voice trembling with want. "Surprise me."

That grin—

Gods help me.

It was devastating.

"Your wish," he said, slipping off his gloves with maddening precision, "is my obsession."

Then he pounced.

His mouth crashed into mine—hot, wicked, relentless. His kiss wasn't gentle—it was a promise. A threat. A claim. My thoughts scattered like birds as his hands tore into the laces of my gown, dragging it off one shoulder, then the other, baring skin like he was unwrapping treasure he'd fought wars for.

I moaned into his mouth as his lips dragged down my throat, over my collarbone, lower. And when his path hit the corset, he snarled—low and furious.

"Oh no," I gasped, breathless and aching. "Is something in your way?"

His eyes flared—lit from within. "You enjoy testing me."

"Maybe a little."

A dangerous smirk curved his mouth. "Then let's raise the stakes."

I heard it before I felt it. The metallic whisper of a blade unsheathing.

Snip.

My corset loosened.

"Odin!" I gasped, half laughing, half scandalized. "That was custom made!"

He leaned in, lips brushing the shell of my ear. "You won't need it where I'm taking you."

Before I could respond, he was back on me—his hands sliding beneath the fabric, pulling it away like silk between his fingers. My skin pebbled at the rush of cool air… then his mouth replaced it.

Hot. Open. Devouring.

His voice rasped against my ribs. "So beautiful. So perfect. So damn mine."

Then he hauled me into his lap—his chest heaving beneath my hands, his arousal hard and demanding against my thigh. One arm locked around my waist. The other slid between my legs, slow and sure, knuckles grazing heat.

"Odin—"

"Shhh." His lips grazed my neck. "I want you dripping before I even fill you."

My head fell back, a moan slipping from my lips as his fingers moved with devastating expertise—slow, then firmer, curling just right. I clenched around nothing, aching for everything. He knew exactly what he was doing. Every move was calculated chaos, coaxing pleasure with the precision of a king who never missed his mark.

"I want you," I gasped.

He stilled, exhaling hard against my neck. "Say it again."

"I want to feel you inside me. Right now."

He growled—low and savage—and in a blink, I was beneath him.

My gown hiked up to my waist, his mouth stealing my cries as he spread my thighs wide and—

Slid into me.

I lost my senses.

A cry tore from me—sharp and helpless—as he filled me to the hilt, stretching me so perfectly it bordered on pain. My nails scraped down his back, legs locking around him.

"Oh—Oh, please don't stop."

He didn't.

He moved—long, deep thrusts that lit my nerves on fire. Each one harder, hungrier, until the rhythm was raw, primal. His hand gripped my thigh. The other slid into my hair, tugging just enough to make me gasp with submission.

"You feel like you were made for me," he growled. "So tight. So perfect. So fucking mine."

I didn't answer.

I couldn't think.

I could barely breathe.

I couldn't do anything but obey.

He kissed me like he wanted to ruin me, and I let him. My whole body arched into him, chasing that edge, falling toward it with every thrust. I felt the tension building in my lower belly. I felt the cord of my desire pull taut, on the verge of snapping free.

"I'm so close—"

"Then come for me, my queen."

The words shattered something in me.

The cord snapped.

I unraveled for him on his command.

Pleasure ripped through me, violent and endless. I cried out, pulsating around him. My toes curled. I arched into him. My eyes slammed shut, and I threw my head back.

I forgot how to breathe.

Through the haze, I heard him moan like a god made flesh, drunk on devotion—his or mine, I couldn't tell. He slammed into me one last time before I felt every muscle in his body tremble with release.

He collapsed over me, breath ragged, lips pressed to my throat.

"I love you," he said, voice low, almost reverent. "You are the crown I fought for. My world. My flame. The only woman holy enough to stand beside me—because you see me. All of me."

I smiled, drunk on him. On us. On this perfect, breathless, blazing moment.

And I believed him.

Of course I did.

Because this was love.

It felt like forever.

I closed my eyes as the carriage rumbled toward the castle,
grateful the Gods had led me here.

When we arrived at the castle, Odin carried me from the carriage like a hero stepping out of legend—his arms strong, effortless, as though I weighed nothing at all. A king, yes, but more than that. A god bearing his goddess. His prize. His fire. My chemise the only thing standing between me and impropriety. The thunderous cheers of the crowd only fueled him, and he basked in it—eyes blazing, mouth curved into that wicked, perfect grin that made my knees forget how to function.

We changed in a flurry of silk and gold, trading sacred white for something darker, more opulent. His tunic was emerald, threaded with gold so fine it looked alive. A living deity draped in power. And me? My gown clung like prophecy, like every thread had been spun by the Gods themselves. We were no longer bride and groom.

We were myth.

We were legend.

And tonight, the kingdom would bear witness.

We walked hand in hand toward the grand ballroom, the air around us humming with awe. No one dared approach. No one even breathed too loud. It felt sacred—a hush reserved for miracles.

We moved like celestial bodies caught in orbit, drawn together by something older than fate. His pulse thudded against my fingertips, steady and sure.

I looked up at him, my chest tightening with reverence. How had I been chosen? How had I won him?

He looked over at me and smirked. "Do you like what you see, my Queen?"

My breath caught. That voice—velvet wrapped in danger. He already knew the answer.

"You couldn't please me more," I said sweetly, smiling like I wasn't about to combust.

He laughed. Low. Dark. Exquisite. That sound slithered down my spine like a silk ribbon set aflame.

The doors to the ballroom opened before us like gates of heaven parting open for us, and the roar of applause rose like a tide. It hit me then—the sheer scope of it. The spectacle. The glory. The power. And all of it tethered to this man who held my hand like a promise.

I was his. He was mine.

The ballroom was ablaze with revelry, music and laughter tumbling through the air like gold-dusted confetti. Odin twirled me through the crowd, effortless, resplendent—a king unveiling his queen.

We passed near the VIP table—just close enough for a few stray words to rise above the music.

Murphy's voice drifted through the din, amused and lazy. "Man knows how to make an entrance."

I caught a flicker of movement beside him—Alexey, unmoving, unreadable.

I didn't mean to eavesdrop. But something in the way they stood—like they were outside the celebration, not part of it—made me glance back.

Then, softly, like a riddle half-swallowed by candlelight: "The sun shines the brightest before it burns out." Alexey murmured.

I missed Murphy's response—Odin dipped me low at that exact moment, his grin radiant, claiming all my attention.

And yet, something in Alexey's tone lingered.

The words pressed against the back of my mind, unwanted and impossible to dislodge. I didn't understand them. But a part of me didn't want to.

Odin spun me again, pulling me close until his lips brushed my ear. "I have never been so utterly ruined by anyone before," he murmured, his voice like wine soaked in smoke.

My heart fluttered in a frenzy. I was dizzy, drunk on him.

"I find that hard to believe." I teased, though my pulse thundered in my throat. "Surely many have tried."

He chuckled, dark and pleased. "Oh, many have tried, Arianna."

Then he leaned in closer, so close I could feel the promise in his breath.

"But only one has ever succeeded."

By the time we returned to our table, the room had blurred into a dream of clinking glasses, lilting music, and candlelight flickering like stars. But Odin wasn't done. Of course he wasn't.

He had arranged a private performance—an entire troupe summoned to reenact his favorite play for our wedding night. Lavish sets. Costumes embroidered with silver thread. A story of impossible love.

A princess and her invisible prince.

Not a warrior. Not a god. Not a man of legend. A shadow. A whisper. A presence no one else could see.

It was romantic. Tragic. Haunting.

But something in me tightened as I watched. The story felt... familiar. A girl giving herself to something she could not name. A love built on belief alone.

No. I was imagining things. It was just a play.

Still, when the princess cried out in the final act—reaching for a lover she could feel but never hold—I thought I heard it.

Laughter.

Soft. Distant. Cruel.

I blinked, and it was gone. Odin squeezed my hand, and I focused on the warmth of his skin, grounding myself in it.

He was real. He was here.

And I was his.

We were untouchable. And I would not let anything spoil the dream we had built.

I waited until the last lantern was doused.

Until the feast ended, and the courtiers bled into drunken oblivion.

Until the guards turned their backs, and the castle fell still.

Then I made my move.

I slipped into our chambers wearing nothing but a robe of silver silk, the neckline open, the hem scandalously high. My hair spilled over my shoulders in waves. My lips were stained the color of crushed pomegranate.

I looked dangerous.

I felt dangerous.

It was exciting.

Tonight, I would set the tone. I'd make him want me—need me—lose himself in me. I'd make him unravel first. I'd be the one in control. He had his fun in the carriage.

I lit the candles myself. Poured the wine. Arranged myself on the edge of the bed, legs crossed, gaze soft, posture open.

I didn't flinch when the door opened.

I smiled.

He paused in the doorway, golden and tall and glowing with just enough wine to be relaxed—but not drunk. His gaze swept over me slowly. Not hungrily. Not in shock.

Like a man admiring his own fortune.

"Well," he said, voice honey-smooth. "Either I married a vision… or my wine was stronger than I thought."

I uncrossed my legs with purpose. "You took a priestess from the temple. Surely you expected some divinity."

He shut the door behind him, never looking away.

"Oh, I expected a great many things," he said, undoing the clasps at his collar, slow and graceful. "But not this."

"Disappointed?"

He laughed—low, warm, almost fond.

"Not even a little." He stepped closer, eyes glittering with that impossible confidence. "Tell me, is this your plan? Seduce me into surrender?"

"Is it working?"

He tilted his head, as if genuinely considering it. Then that smile—dangerous, delighted—curved across his lips.

"You are beautiful, Arianna. Bold. Unignorable." His fingers traced my jaw, light as breath.

"But don't mistake my admiration for surrender."

I blinked. A beat too long.

He leaned in, his mouth brushing just beneath my ear. "You don't have to command me, my queen. I already want to give you everything."

It sent a shiver through me.

Not from fear.

From thrill.

His hand found the tie of my robe, loosening it without ceremony, and it slipped down my shoulders. The air kissed my bare skin. Still, he didn't rush.

He didn't reach for me like a man undone.

He was calm. Collected.

In control.

"I thought you'd be impatient," I said softly.

"I am," he replied, fingers grazing my collarbone, "but I want to remember this."

He kissed me then. Deep and deliberate.

Not like a man who needed. Like a man who knew.

And I—

I melted.

Somewhere in the haze, I stood up, I pushed forward, I tried to flip the moment—push him back, take charge.

But he caught my wrists gently. Amused.

"No," he murmured. "Not yet."

I should've fought it. Should've reclaimed the moment.

But his hands were already at my hips, coaxing me back toward the bed—

He kissed me again.

Slower this time.

Thorough.

His tongue slid over mine, coaxing rather than claiming, but every pass made my spine arch and my knees soften. When I leaned up to deepen it, he chuckled against my mouth and pulled away—just enough to deny me.

"Easy," he murmured, thumb brushing my lower lip. "We've only just begun."

He guided me backward until my calves met the bed. I sat, heart pounding.

He watched me with a look that made my skin burn—like he already knew what I'd sound like when I broke.

With deliberate patience, he sank to his knees.

I froze.

"Odin—"

"Hush," he said, voice silken. "Let me see what's mine."

He pressed a kiss to the inside of my knee, then my thigh, and then higher—his mouth trailing up until he hovered just before the part of me that throbbed in time with every heartbeat.

He didn't dive in like a starving man.

He teased.

He tasted.

The first slow lick of his tongue made me moan outright, my hips jerking before I could stop them.

I felt him smile.

"You're already shaking," he whispered, breath hot against my most sensitive skin. "And I've barely touched you."

Then he went to work.

Long, languid strokes of his tongue, precise flicks over the bundle of nerves I never dared explore, slow sucks that made me curse the Gods I'd once served. He held my thighs wide apart, firm and unrelenting, even as they trembled in his grip.

I wanted to close them.

I wanted to pull away.

I wanted to cry out until the whole castle knew I'd abandoned my vows.

Instead, I whimpered.

And he hummed like that was what he wanted to hear.

When I was soaked and gasping, when I tried to grind against his mouth for more friction, he pulled back and licked his lips like he was savoring something rare.

"You taste like sacrilege," he murmured. "Like something the Gods would punish me for touching—and I'd still go back for more."

I barely had time to process the words before he pushed me back onto the bed and he was on top of me, lifting my hips and sliding his fingers between my legs. Two of them—long, deft, relentless.

My back arched as they curled inside me, finding a place that made me wail.

It was intense.

He swallowed the sound with his mouth on mine.

"You want me to take you," he whispered, his breath skating over my lips. "But you don't want to want it."

I shook my head, barely. A flicker of defiance I wasn't sure I meant.

He smiled.

Gods, that smile.

Slow. Sinful.

Certain.

"Too late," he said, dragging his mouth along my jaw. "Your thighs are already shaking. Your pulse is singing in my hand."

His fingers traced the hollow of my throat.

A phantom claim.

"You're still pretending, aren't you?" he murmured, lips grazing the shell of my ear. "Still trying to play the priestess. Still hoping you'll be the one who stays in control."

I tried to breathe evenly. To hide the tremble that bloomed low in my belly.

He chuckled—low, velvet-dark.

"But we both know who's on the altar tonight."

My breath hitched. I hated how much it thrilled me. He felt it. I know he did.

"I saw the way you looked at me from the moment we met," he said. "Like the Gods had finally answered a prayer you didn't dare speak."

He kissed the side of my throat. Reverent. Possessive. Blasphemous.

"This," he whispered, his fingers ghosting over my pulse, "this is where your power used to live. All those prayers. All those holy little sounds."

He paused—just long enough for me to forget to exhale.

"I think it's time you gave those sounds to me."

And then—

He pushed inside me.

One slow, deliberate thrust.

No warning.

No mercy.

No hesitation.

Just heat. Pressure. Excitement.

I arched. A breathless sound slipped from my mouth—half gasp, half plea.

My hands scrambled for his shoulders, anchoring myself to the only solid thing in a world suddenly unsteady.

He grinned against my throat.

"That's better," he breathed. "That's what I want to hear."

He moved—slow, purposeful, each thrust measured like a sermon spoken through skin.

"I'll make you say it," he whispered, dragging his mouth along mine. "Say you're mine."

"No—" I gasped, but my body betrayed me.

I was trembling. Clinging. Ruined.

He kissed me again—deep, claiming, with just enough control to let me know I had none.

"Say it, little flame," he growled, thrusting harder. "Say you belong to me."

He was inside me—deep and still—his breath warm against my skin, his fingers curled possessively along my thigh.

Then he stopped.

Mid-thrust.

Mid-motion.

Just... still.

I whimpered. I didn't mean to. It escaped me like a prayer I'd forgotten how to silence.

He smiled against my jaw, maddeningly patient.

"Say it."

His voice was calm. Almost gentle. Like we had all the time in the world.

"Odin—" I gasped, trying to roll my hips, to pull him back into motion. "Please—"

Another soft thrust—just enough to tease—then nothing.

"You are so beautiful like this," he murmured, brushing a strand of hair from my cheek. "But you're not mine until you say it."

I gritted my teeth, every nerve ending begging him to move again. To finish.

He didn't.

He hovered. Waiting.

"You can't take what I won't give," I whispered, the last thread of defiance tangled on my tongue.

He chuckled. "Who says I want to take?"

His hips tilted—just enough to make me moan.

"I want to be given."

He kissed my throat.

"I want you to admit what I already know."

Another shift. Another withdrawal.

The tension inside me snapped taut.

I was fire, caught mid-burn.

I clenched around him instinctively—desperate.

He stilled again.

Silent.

Smiling.

My body trembled. My pride screamed.

But my lips—

"I'm yours," I breathed. Barely audible.

He tilted his head. "Say it like you mean it."

Gods. I hated him. I wanted him.

I wanted him to move.

My hands fisted the sheets. My breath shuddered.

"I'm yours," I whispered again—this time with reverence.

And then—

He moved.

Deep. Devastating. Unrelenting.

"Yes," he growled. "Good girl."

His mouth found mine as his rhythm picked up—measured, brutal, perfect.

"You were made to kneel in temples," he whispered against my lips, "but you look so much holier spread beneath me."

A sharp thrust—just enough to draw a cry.

"You think this is sin?" he growled, hands curling around my hips. "This is divinity."

He thrust again—deeper, harder.

"I am your altar now."

His voice, low and sensuous, made the cord in my belly snap.

I shattered with a cry I didn't recognize—clutching him, pulsing around him, unraveling like a flame that had waited too long to be touched.

He followed with a soft curse and a bite to my neck—marking me, claiming me, spilling inside me with a sound that turned my bones to dust.

We collapsed together, breathless.

His fingers laced through mine.

He kissed my temple.

"See?" he whispered. "You never had to fight me for control. All you had to do… was trust me."

And somehow—

That unnerved me more than anything.

Because I had trusted him.

And I hadn't been conquered.

I'd leapt.

I'd surrendered.

And now—I didn't know where I ended and he began.

The Card Game & The Nobles of Lorna – Arianna

Marriage, I was learning, was a world unto itself.

I had spent my first weeks as queen settling into life at court—learning names, untangling alliances, mapping the ever-shifting social terrain that now belonged to me as much as it did Odin.

There were endless ceremonies, traditions, obligations—but at the heart of it all, Odin remained Odin.

And Odin's favorite ritual of all was playing cards with his closest friends at least three times a week.

It wasn't just a game.

It was a battlefield, where strategy and deception reigned, where power was measured in who folded first and who could lie through their teeth with a grin.

And tonight?

I was winning.

Murphy leaned back in his chair, feet kicked up onto the table, a self-satisfied grin stretched across his face as he shuffled the deck at an infuriatingly slow pace.

I studied him, watching the way the cards flicked between his fingers before slipping into a mock pompous tone.

"Tell me about your lands, Baron Matvei Theodoric Sergeyev von Lorne, Warden of the Eastern Isles."

Murphy didn't even glance up. "I assume they're still there." He flicked a card between his fingers, utterly unbothered. "It's not like they can walk off."

I scoffed. "That's all you have to say?"

He exhaled dramatically. "What else is there? They are islands. They exist. They're very good at it. A bit boring, though."

Odin barked a laugh. "Murphy wanted the benefits of nobility without the responsibility, so I gave him uninhabited islands to watch over."

I turned to Murphy, arching a brow. "Are they really uninhabited?"

Murphy smirked. "There may be some goats. But they're very self-sufficient."

I shook my head. "So you are the Warden of Goats?"

Murphy placed a hand over his chest, feigning deep offense. "Goats who respect me, thank you very much."

I rolled my eyes. "A title with no burden. A barony with no people. Odin, you truly are a generous king."

Odin raised his cup. "I do what I can."

But my focus had already shifted.

If Murphy's lands were nothing but an elaborate joke, then Alexey's were surely the exact opposite.

I flicked my gaze toward him, measuring.

Unlike Murphy, Alexey was not reclining, not smirking, not preoccupied with idle talk.

Instead, he was idly rolling a coin over his knuckles, slow and practiced, the flickering candlelight catching the glint of gold as it passed from finger to finger.

He had yet to look at me.

A challenge, then.

I smiled, tilting my head. "And you, Commander Graf Alexander Volkov, Lord of the Sunfire Valley & Commander of the Royal Guard—what of your lands?"

He didn't stop rolling the coin. "They are fertile."

"That's all you have to say?" I pressed, leaning in slightly, letting my voice drop just enough to tease. "The second-largest province in Lorna. A trade hub. An agricultural empire. You rule over one of the richest lands in the kingdom, and yet you sound utterly unimpressed by your own title."

The coin stilled.

Alexey lifted his gaze then, blue eyes sharp as honed steel, locking onto mine with the weight of something too heavy to name.

"It is not the land that matters," he said, voice even, measured. "It is how it is kept."

Gods.

I swallowed, covering my intrigue with a slow, amused smile. "And you keep it well?"

A pause. A flicker of something unreadable in his gaze.

Then, softly—

"It prospers."

Murphy cut in smoothly, grinning like a cat who had just found something entertaining to bat around.

"His chef alone is a woman of unique talents. She once made a stew so rich I briefly considered pledging my undying loyalty to Alexey."

Odin laughed, shaking his head. "Born to farmers, ruling over farmers. I'd say it's poetic."

Murphy leaned toward me conspiratorially. "You should see him in the fields. Watching over the crops. A true man of the people."

Alexey ignored them both.

The coin resumed its slow, methodical roll over his fingers.

I wasn't done with him yet.

I leaned forward, resting my chin on my palm, watching him with the kind of interest that could crack a lesser man.

"And are you a fair lord, Alexey?"

He didn't take the bait.

His gaze flicked to mine, steady as ever.

But this time, there was something else there. A glint. A warning. A game he refused to play.

"I do not seek to be fair," he said. "I seek to be just."

I studied him, my intrigue sharpening. "And the difference?"

Alexey's lips pressed into a faint, unreadable line.

"Fairness is the idea that all are given the same opportunity. Justice is ensuring that opportunity is not squandered by those who already have more than they need."

The words struck deeper than I expected.

I stilled.

That… was not an answer I had anticipated.

Murphy let out a low whistle. "Damn, Alexey. That was almost inspiring."

"Alright, enough of this—I came here to drink and win, not sit around talking about dirt and peasants!" Odin exclaims.

"You never win," Murphy pointed out.

"I win in spirit."

"Do you?"

"Shut up and deal, Murphy."

Murphy laughed, shuffling the deck with practiced ease.

But as the game resumed, my focus remained elsewhere.

Because now, I wanted to know what else Alexey would say if I pressed him hard enough.

And given enough time—

I would.

A Crack in the Crown – Arianna

The castle was unusually quiet as I made my way down the hall, the soft rustle of my gown the only sound against the polished stone floors.

Odin's council meeting had ended nearly an hour ago, and though I had no real reason to seek him out, I found myself drawn to him anyway.

It was still new—being his wife, his queen, his chosen.

Still electric. Still breathless.

And Gods, I wanted him to look at me like he had that night in the ballroom—like I was the most precious thing he had ever touched.

So I would surprise him.

A playful wifely gesture.

Something sweet, something adoring, something worthy of a newly crowned king and his queen.

I smiled at the thought, picking up my pace as I neared his study. The door was slightly ajar, and inside, the warm glow of candlelight spilled across his desk.

He was exactly where I expected him to be—seated at the long oak table, papers spread before him in an endless, meticulous sprawl.

Three of his council members stood nearby, their voices low, the remnants of whatever discussion they'd been having still lingering in the air.

But Odin himself was silent.

Focused.

His eyes flicked across the page before him, his jaw set, his fingers tapping once, twice against the wood before he reached for his goblet and took a slow sip of wine.

Something in his posture gave me pause.

It wasn't cold.

It wasn't unkind.

But it was… distant.

Still, I stepped forward, leaning playfully against the doorframe. "Have you been in here plotting all night, or will you make time for your wife?"

Odin glanced up at me.

A flicker of recognition.

A flicker—and then gone.

His expression remained neutral, composed, as though I were just another guest in his court, just another voice in the room.

Then, after a beat too long, he exhaled, offering me a tired but distracted smile.

"Arianna."

That was all.

Just my name.

No smirk. No wicked glint in his eye. No teasing remark, no arms reaching to pull me onto his lap like I half-expected.

Just a name. A formality.

One of the men cleared his throat, shifting awkwardly. "Shall we continue, Your Majesty?"

Odin gave a small nod, then looked back at me.

"I'll find you later."

Not Come here.

Not Stay.

Not Gods, I've missed you.

Just a promise, tossed carelessly into the air like a gambler rolling dice.

I'll find you later.

Something in my chest tightened, just slightly.

It was nothing.

Nothing.

He was the king. He was busy. He had a kingdom to run, meetings to attend, decisions to make.

I could not expect to always be the center of his gravity.

So I smiled, bright and unbothered, pushing aside the strange, fleeting ache in my ribs.

"Don't take too long, my king," I said lightly, tilting my chin up before stepping back into the hall.

The door shut behind me.

And though I did not let myself dwell on it,

I could not ignore the lingering whisper in the back of my mind.

War Stories – Arianna

The next day the fire in the great hall crackled low, casting long shadows across the room. The scent of aged parchment, spilled wine, and the distant trace of rain from the open windows wove through the air.

Another night, another game of cards.

Odin leaned back in his chair at the head of the table, fingers tapping lazily against the wooden table, a half-drunk smirk playing on his lips. Murphy sat next to him, grinning like a man who thrived on chaos, shuffling the deck with an unnecessary amount of flair.

And Alexey?

Alexey sat to the other side of Murphy, arms crossed, unreadable, already looking like he regretted sitting down.

Which only made me more curious.

I glanced between them, my gaze settling on Odin. “You never did tell me how you three ended up fighting together.”

Murphy snorted, dealing the cards. “Oh, sweetheart, that’s a tale worth telling.”

Odin exhaled dramatically, stretching. “It’s simple, really. There was a war. We fought. I was brilliant.”

Alexey didn’t even blink. “You were reckless.”

Murphy, without missing a beat: “And Alexey was magnificent.”

I arched a brow. “Go on.”

Odin’s grin widened, his eyes glinting with mischief. “Would you like to hear how Alexey saved my life?”

Murphy chuckled, flipping his first card. "Which time?"

Odin waved a hand, dismissive. "The big one."

Alexey sighed, rubbing his temples. "Must we?"

Murphy ignored him, leaning forward. "Picture this, Majesty—a battlefield soaked in blood, swords clashing, arrows darkening the sky. Our forces were outnumbered, the enemy was closing in, and your husband here decided to do something monumentally stupid."

Odin scoffed, but he didn't deny it.

Murphy continued, clearly enjoying himself. "Odin gets himself surrounded, back against the cliffs. And there we were, watching this disaster unfold, when Alexey—who had been busy actually winning the battle—turns, sees Odin about to get skewered, and instead of letting natural selection take its course…"

I covered my mouth to hide my laugh.

Murphy made a dramatic gesture. "…He charges in and cuts down three men before Odin can blink. And then—then!—some bastard tries to take advantage of the distraction, and guess what Alexey does?"

Odin leaned forward, eyes alight with nostalgia. "He threw me off a cliff."

I choked. "I—I'm sorry, he what?"

Alexey, still stone-faced: "It was a short cliff."

Murphy howled. "Arianna, he grabbed Odin by the collar, yanked him backward, and threw him over the ledge into the river below."

I turned to Alexey. "Did you warn him?"

Alexey blinked once. "…There was no time."

Murphy grinned. "Odin screamed like a dying animal the whole way down."

Odin jabbed a finger at him. "It was undignified and unnecessary."

Murphy smirked. "It saved your ass."

Odin grumbled, slouching in his chair. "…I suppose."

I was still reeling. "So Alexey saved you twice in one battle?"

Odin waved a hand. "That was one time. There was also the siege, the ambush, the time he carried me back to camp after I got stabbed—"

Alexey exhaled sharply. "Do we have to recount every time you almost got yourself killed?"

Murphy grinned, eyes flaring. "It's a long list."

Odin sat up, slamming a hand on the table. "That's because Alexey is too good at what he does. He's been saving lives since the day he picked up a sword."

I looked at Alexey. "And yet, you let them talk like this."

Alexey finally met my gaze, expression unreadable, voice calm but edged. "Because they won't stop, even if I tell them to."

Murphy beamed. "Exactly. You understand us perfectly."

Odin laughed, picking up his cards. "You should be proud, Arianna. You married a warrior. But Alexey? He's a legend."

A legend.

I liked the sound of that.

And as I sat there, wine warm on my tongue, the flickering fire casting gold against my skin, I realized I was a legend too.

The gilded queen.

The woman a king chose.

The one they whispered about in hushed voices, wondering if she was the greatest love story ever written—or the beginning of a storm that would consume them all.

So, if Odin would not worship me tonight, then perhaps I would let someone else admire the view. Just for fun.

I leaned forward, tilting my head just so, letting my voice drop like silk against skin.

"You know, Alexey," I mused, "it sounds to me like Odin owes you his life."

Alexey's fingers stopped tapping against the table.

Murphy, ever the menace, smirked. "He does. At least a dozen times over."

Odin waved a dismissive hand. "Details."

I tilted my head, studying Alexey. "If it weren't for you, Lorna wouldn't have its king."

Alexey met my gaze. Held it. Unyielding.

"Correct."

Odin chuckled, oblivious. "And yet, here we are."

But I wasn't looking at Odin anymore.

I was looking at the man who had shaped my husband's fate, who had been there for every moment of his rise, who had carried him off a battlefield more times than I could count.

Alexey wasn't just Odin's right hand.

He was the reason Odin had a throne at all.

A slow smirk curled at my lips.

"You must be a difficult man to impress, Commander Volkov."

Alexey's gaze darkened, unreadable. "And yet, people keep trying."

The room felt smaller. Warmer. The firelight flickered, catching the sharp planes of his face, the quiet steel in his expression.

Murphy was grinning between us, eyes glinting like he'd just been handed a new favorite game.

Odin's smirk didn't fade, but his fingers tapped against the table. Once. Twice. A beat too long.

I lifted my goblet, smiling sweetly.

"To the man who saved a king."

Alexey didn't move, didn't break my gaze.

Then, after a long pause, he lifted his own goblet.

"To the king who keeps making my job harder."

Murphy barked a laugh. Odin rolled his eyes.

I sipped my wine.

And for the first time since the wedding, Odin's attention was exactly where I wanted it.

I had learned many things tonight.

That Murphy talks too much. That Odin talks just as much but pretends he doesn't. That Alexey is an actual legend but refuses to acknowledge it.

And most importantly?

That my husband had almost died too many times for my liking.

"So," I said, resting my chin in my palm, "tell me something else. Why were you three even fighting that war to begin with?"

The table fell silent.

Murphy glanced at Odin. Odin glanced at Alexey. Alexey sighed the sigh of a man who was trapped in a room full of fools.

"Oh," Murphy finally said, taking a sip of his drink. "She's asking the big questions now."

Odin smirked. "What, love? You don't know your history?"

I rolled my eyes. "I know history, husband. I want to know your version."

Murphy grinned. "Oh, this is going to be good."

Odin stretched back in his chair, fingers tapping against the wooden table. "It started with an uprising in the northeast."

I feigned surprise. "Really? I thought you all just wandered into a battlefield for fun."

Murphy snorted into his drink.

Alexey, as expected, looked unimpressed.

Odin gave me a pointed look but continued. "Nobles from the Alenkhyr Heights Province lead a rebellion against the crown. Fast. Brutal. We weren't ready."

Murphy nodded. "They slaughtered the royal family in the first wave. They got past the royal guard easily. Barely an inconvenience."

That made me pause. "All of them?"

Odin's smirk faded slightly. "Down to the last heir."

I sat back. That explained a lot. No succession, no stability. Chaos.

Murphy leaned forward, eyes glinting. “And then there was us.”

I raised an eyebrow. “You?”

Odin grinned, all teeth. “We were soldiers in the Army. Fighters. We had no name, no title—just steel in our hands and blood on our boots.”

Murphy grinned wider. “And an unfortunate habit of surviving.”

Odin chuckled. “The people needed a leader. Someone to push back. Someone to win.”

“And that was you?” I asked.

Odin shrugged with all the false modesty of a man who absolutely believed his own legend. “They didn’t have many options.”

I turned to Alexey. “And you?”

Alexey exhaled slowly. “Someone had to keep him alive.”

Murphy choked on his drink, laughing. “That should’ve been his title”.’”

I grinned. “Savior of reckless kings… mm. Good thing queens don’t need saving.”

Alexey rubbed his temples, exhaled slowly, and said nothing.

But for a moment—just a breath—his gaze met mine before returning to the void.

Odin laughed, waving Murphy off. “The war lasted two years. Bloody. Relentless. But we won. And when it was over…”

He gestured vaguely, like the crown had just appeared on his head by accident.

I leaned in, voice silk. “You took the crown.”

Odin met my gaze. “It wasn’t handed to me, love. The people chose me. The army demanded it.”

He said it like it pained him. Like power was a cross he bore for their sake.

But I knew better. Odin didn’t take the crown out of duty. He took it because no one stopped him.

I tilted my head. “And you? Did you want it?”

Silence.

Murphy glanced at him—but for once, no one had a quip.

Odin’s fingers tapped once. Then again. Then—

“I wanted the war to end,” he said. “I wanted the bloodshed to mean something.”

I didn’t blink. “And power?”

A beat.

Then that slow, serpentine smirk. “That, too.”

I turned to Alexey. “And you followed him.”

Alexey’s jaw tightened. “Someone had to make sure he didn’t get himself killed.”

Murphy grinned. “And how’s that been working out for you?”

Alexey stared into the middle distance like a man questioning every decision he’d ever made. “Poorly.”

I laughed. “So you three saved the kingdom.”

Murphy lifted his drink. “You’re welcome.”

I shook my head. “You went from nameless soldiers to war heroes. And Odin became king.”

Murphy wiggled his fingers. "And I became incredibly handsome and well-loved."

Alexey sighed. "Unbearable at best."

Odin smirked. "And Alexey became the greatest Commander the kingdom has ever seen."

Alexey's jaw tightened again. But he said nothing.

I watched him. "And you still hate hearing that, don't you?"

Alexey didn't look at me. "I did my job."

Odin chuckled. "You did more than that."

Murphy grinned, leaning in. "He did so much more than that."

Alexey pinched the bridge of his nose. "Are we playing cards or not?"

I smirked, placing my bet. "Just one more question."

Odin raised a brow. "You're full of them tonight."

I ignored him, turning to Alexey.

"You fought in a war. You saved a king's life. You shaped the future of this kingdom."

I rested my chin on my palm. "Did you ever want the crown for yourself?"

Silence.

The air shifted.

Murphy's grin faded. Odin went very still.

And Alexey?

Alexey finally met my eyes, his face unreadable.

"...No," he said simply.

I narrowed my gaze. "No?"

His jaw clenched. "I don't want power. I never did."

Odin exhaled sharply. "That's why you were the only one fit to wield it."

I glanced at Odin. Something in his expression was almost… regretful.

Alexey just shook his head. "Power was never mine to take."

Murphy hummed. "And yet, you keep cleaning up after it."

Alexey rubbed his temples. "Are we going to play or what?"

Murphy threw an arm over his shoulder. "You love us."

Odin smirked. "Admit it."

Alexey scoffed. "If I didn't, one of you would've bled out by now."

I smiled to myself as they argued over the next hand.

I had wanted to know why they fought.

But what I learned was something much deeper.

These men had not just won a war.

They had rewritten the fate of an entire kingdom.

And at the center of it all?

A king who was never meant to rule.

A commander who never wanted power.

And a rogue who was far too entertained by it all.

Gods save the kingdom.

It never stood a chance.

When the game ended.

Murphy left first, whistling some out-of-tune melody as he wandered off, undoubtedly searching for more wine or more trouble—or both.

Odin followed soon after, pressing a kiss to my forehead before retreating to our chambers, looking far too pleased with himself.

Which left one person still sitting at the table.

Alexey hadn't moved.

I watched him for a moment, studying the way he sat—rigid, controlled, unreadable. The firelight flickered across his face, highlighting the sharp angles of his jaw, the deep-set focus in his eyes.

He was staring at the cards, but I had the distinct feeling he wasn't seeing them.

I tilted my head, voice like silk.

"You could've asked me to stop."

His jaw flexed. "Would you have listened?"

I smirked. "Not a chance. But I do admire a man willing to try."

A flicker of amusement crossed his face before disappearing into something tired.

I let the silence stretch just long enough to be noticeable before asking, "Did you ever want the throne?"

He exhaled through his nose—not quite a scoff, not quite a sigh. He didn't roll his eyes, didn't dismiss me outright like before.

Instead, he finally looked at me. "No."

I tilted my head. "Not even once?"

His fingers drummed once against the table, slow and deliberate. "What would I do with it?"

I shrugged. “Rule. Change things. Shape the kingdom into something better.”

His lips twitched—not a smile, something darker. “And what if I made it worse?”

That gave me pause.

Alexey looked back at the cards, his voice quieter now, measured. “Power doesn’t change men. It reveals them.”

I studied him. “And what would it have revealed about you?”

Silence.

Then, a barely-there smirk. “That I hate paperwork.”

I scoffed, shaking my head. “And Odin doesn’t?”

Alexey’s fingers brushed against the edge of a card, turning it over slowly.

A beat of silence.

Then, finally—“He never lacked ambition.”

I narrowed my gaze. “But?”

He exhaled through his nose, shaking his head slightly. “But ambition isn’t enough.”

I tapped my fingers on the table. “So, what does it require?”

Alexey’s stare was unreadable, but something settled behind his eyes—

Something learned on battlefields, in the weight of steel, in the sharp regret of victories that cost too much.

“Restraint,” he finally said.

The word hung between us, weighty and sharp.

I leaned forward, letting the firelight catch in my gaze.

"Do you think Odin ever had that?"

Alexey didn't answer immediately.

He sat back, rubbing his temples, his gaze fixed on the table. The firelight flickered over his face, but his expression remained unreadable.

Then, after a long moment, he picked up one of the cards in front of him, flipping it over idly, studying it as if it held the answer instead.

And finally—"Would we be having this conversation if he did?"

I considered that, watching him. "And that's why you stayed by his side."

His jaw clenched. "Because someone had to have it."

The fire crackled. Somewhere down the hall, laughter rang out—carefree, distant.

Here, in the dim glow of the hearth, sat a man who had carried the weight of a kingdom he never wanted—alone, in silence, and without recognition.

And I understood something new.

Alexey hadn't stayed by Odin's side out of blind loyalty.

He had stayed because he knew what Odin lacked.

Because he knew what power did to men without restraint.

Because without him, Odin would have burned the kingdom to the ground long before his crown ever had the chance to slip.

And because—no matter how much he hated it—he had been the only thing standing between Odin and

disaster.
Fascinating.

But also… terrifying.

Because if that's true—if Alexey was the fulcrum, the balance, the thing that kept the kingdom from falling apart—

Then what does that make Odin without him?

And what does that make me?

Had I married the storm, thinking I was the anchor?

Had I been so dazzled by the crown that I missed the hand that held it steady?

I glanced at him again—this brooding man, this living myth, who sat not with grandeur, but with the weariness of someone who had borne too much for too long.

There was no arrogance in him. No hunger for power. No need to be adored.

Only a quiet strength. A deep, bitter knowing.

He hadn't just helped win a war.

He had helped prevent the ruin that might have followed it.

And no one ever thanked him for it.

Not the people.

Not the king.

Not even me.

Until now.

I exhaled, pushing my chair back with a lazy stretch.

"Well, for what it's worth, you would've made a damn good king."

For just a flicker of a moment, something shifted behind his eyes—something unreadable and far too fleeting.

Then, dry as bone, he said, "You married the king you wanted. Don't start collecting spares."

I smirked. "Oh, believe me, Alexey. If I wanted you, you'd know."

His gaze locked with mine. Still. Flat. Dangerous. "I don't respond to summons."

My grin deepened. "That's fine. I don't issue them. I lure."

A pause.

Something in his expression twitched—like he'd just tasted something sharp.

Then he sighed and stood, the scrape of his chair loud in the quiet room.

"Goodnight, Majesty."

I leaned back, unbothered. "Goodnight, Commander."

I didn't expect a reply.

But as he passed, his voice dropped just loud enough for me to catch it:

"I still hate paperwork."

And then he disappeared into the shadows, leaving behind only the soft thud of his boots…

and the unmistakable scent of someone who always walks away just before the fire catches.

A Summer of Delusion and Fire – Arianna

The days did not simply pass—they burned.

Each moment with Odin was an inferno, a divine, all-consuming thing that devoured every breath, every thought, every ounce of me until I was nothing but his.

Our love was not delicate—it did not flutter like the timid wings of spring. It was a roaring blaze, a tempest, an unrelenting force that demanded unwavering devotion.

And I was devoted.

I was going to temper him with my woman heart.

I delighted in the way my fingers tangled in his hair, in the way my lips traced devotion into his skin, in the way I whispered his name into the silence of our bedchambers like a sermon only he was meant to hear.

Every glance was a whispered promise.

Every kiss was an unspoken vow of forever.

Every night was a symphony of desire, each touch composing a melody of longing and devotion so deep it nearly broke me.

Even the briefest of interruptions—a hasty meal, a rushed meeting—became nothing more than echoes in the background, mere shadows against the brilliance of our love.

He was my sun, my storm, my endless, unyielding fire.

And I was his queen.

Even when duty called him away, even when the throne demanded his attention, I did not allow myself to feel his absence.

I refused to be lonely.

Instead, I expanded.

I let my love for him stretch beyond the walls of our palace, spill into the streets, the villages, the farthest reaches of our kingdom.

My love became action.

I built.

Food banks, so that no child would go to bed hungry.

Shelters, so that no soul would suffer the cold alone.

A tradesman's guild, so that the lost and the forgotten would have the tools to rebuild themselves.

And as I watched our kingdom flourish beneath these blessings, I knew—the Gods had chosen me for this.

I was not just existing.

I was becoming.

I had become a force, a legend, a queen whose hands shaped not just policy, but destiny.

And at the center of it all was him.

Odin.

The love of my life.

My husband.

My king.

What more could I ask for?

I had been given everything—the power, the purpose, the means, the opportunity.

And a love so profound it left me breathless.

Surely, no happiness could eclipse this.

Surely, nothing in all the world could rival the fire we had created.

The Gods had blessed me with a love the world would envy.

The First Knight's Gamble – Arianna

Murphy shuffles the deck, the cards whispering as they slip against each other.

We're not playing.

Odin lounged in his chair, boots kicked up on the table, swirling his goblet like a man who hadn't worried about anything—ever. He wore power like a party trick. Careless. Flashy. Completely unconcerned.

Across from me, Murphy flipped a card over with practiced ease, then slipped it back into the deck like it had never existed. His boyish charm filled the space between us—effortless, magnetic. He made the table feel lighter, like the wine was sweeter and the stakes weren't quite so high.

"You're very good at that," I say, tilting my head.

Murphy smirks. "At what?"

"At pretending there's a game when there isn't one."

"Ah." He nods, mischief flickering in his sharp blue-green eyes. "You mean life."

Odin snorts into his wine, but doesn't join the conversation.

Murphy leans forward, elbows resting on the table, still flicking the cards between his fingers. Always moving. Always unreadable. Like a man who's never once let the world know what's actually on his mind.

"You never talk about your past," I say.

Murphy feigns a gasp, pressing a hand to his chest. "My lady, I am a man of mystery. A wandering rogue, an enigma wrapped in a fine velvet cloak—"

"You don't wear a cloak."

"Because I'm practical." He winks. "And devastatingly handsome without one."

I roll my eyes, but the corner of my mouth twitches.

Odin exhales, glancing at Murphy. "Might as well tell her. She's not going to let it go."

Murphy sighs dramatically, tossing the deck onto the table. He leans back, stretching his arms behind his head.

"Fine, fine. Since His Majesty commands it." He waves a hand, mockingly reverent.

I rest my chin in my palm. "I'm listening."

Murphy tilts his head. "You ever hear the tragic tale of the noble-born knight who wanted nothing but pastries?"

I blink. "I can't say I have."

"Well." He grins. "You're in for a treat."

Murphy leans forward and taps his fingers against the table, his usual humor laced through every word.

"My mother baked," he says simply. "Not because she had to. But because she loved it. She could've let the kitchen staff do everything, but no—she was happiest covered in flour, kneading dough, making sweets."

He picks up a card, flipping it between his fingers.

"When I was a kid, I'd sit on the counter and help. She let me roll dough, shape pastries, sneak little bites when no one was looking." His smirk flickers—something real, something close to nostalgia. "I was an excellent baker, by the way."

"I believe it," I say softly.

He lifts a brow. "Do you? Because some people—" he pointedly glances at Odin, "—think it's not very knightly to know how to make a proper crème brûlée."

Odin doesn't react, just swirls his wine.

I ignore him. "What happened?"

Murphy exhales, twirling the card between his fingers. "My mother died when I was sixteen. Fever took her."

I don't say anything.

His smirk is still there, but smaller now, a little sadder. A joke with the teeth filed down.

"After that, my father—Lord Buzzkill"

"Graf Dmitri Voronov," Odin corrected, bored.

Murphy continued. "A very serious man—decided that baking wasn't exactly fitting for the heir to his noble house. He told me I had two choices: join the military or be disinherited."

I frown. "That's a terrible choice."

Murphy shrugs. "Not really. Military came with free food. Wasn't that bad."

I stare at him.

His grin widens. "And, turns out, I was pretty damn good at swinging a sword around too." He leans forward, tapping the deck of cards. "Turns out, fighting is a lot like gambling. If you read the other guy right, you don't even have to swing first."

Odin hums in agreement.

Murphy smirks. "Anyway. I climbed the ranks. Fought well, took orders well. And by some miracle of fate, I ended up under Alexey's command in the civil war."

At that, his smirk softens just a bit.

"I liked serving under Alexey. He took the human cost seriously. Didn't send men into battles he wouldn't fight himself. So, I stuck by him." He rolls his shoulders. "It was alright."

"You followed him," I say.

Murphy shrugs. "It made sense. When the war was over, he was promoted to Commander of the Royal Guard. And me?" He gestures to himself with a flourish. "First Knight of the Guard. A very fancy new title."

Odin chuckles lowly. "Fancy title, but you still drink all the wine like a common bastard."

Murphy places a hand over his heart, feigning offense. "Your Majesty wounds me."

I shake my head. "That still doesn't explain why you dropped your house banner."

Murphy tosses a card onto the table, watching it spin.

"After the war, His Majesty here," he gestures lazily at Odin, "Awarded me the Eastern Isles. Uninhabited lands, and my own title as Baron." His tone is almost careless, like none of it mattered.

"I officially had my own holdings. Which meant I could renounce my father's name and banner. I was a noble in my own right."

He leans back, crossing his arms. "So I did."

I blink. "Just like that?"

"Just like that."

Odin swirls his drink again. "That's when he stopped being Dmitri Voronov's son."

Murphy grins. "And I became Murphy. Just Murphy."

I tilt my head. "So, you—what? Walked away from your noble name, your birthright, because you were angry with your dad? Because you didn't want to play by his rules?"

Murphy nods. "That's exactly right. You understand me perfectly."

"You're absurd," I say flatly.

He winks. "And yet, I have access to all the best food, all the best wine, and all the best comforts, without a single ounce of responsibility and without my dad controlling my life."

I narrow my eyes. "You mean Alexey's food, wine, and comforts."

Murphy grins. "Details. Mere details."

I shake my head, exhaling through my nose. "You are something else, Murphy."

"And you, my queen, are finally catching on."

For all his jokes, all his humor, I see it.

The choice.

Murphy had everything a noble heir should want—lands, a legacy, a name that meant something.

And he threw it all away.

Not because he couldn't handle it.

Not because he was weak.

But because he forged his own path.

He chose a different kind of loyalty.

One not tied to blood or duty.

One he made for himself.

He chose Alexey.

And, by extension, he chose Odin.

Odin sets his goblet down, standing from his chair with a lazy stretch. "Well, this has been fascinating. I'm going to bed."

Murphy smirks. "Always a pleasure, my liege."

I shake my head at their antics, but as Odin steps toward the door, Murphy shuffles the deck again, flicking a card onto the table.

"Queen of Hearts," he muses, tapping the face of it. "Fitting."

I frown. "Why?"

He grins, but there's something too knowing in his eyes.

Something that sees too much.

"Because you, my dear queen, are going to break them all."

Pause.

"One by one. Whether they deserve it or not."

It's still a joke.

Still light.

But beneath it—buried just low enough that you have to feel it, not hear it—

There's a quiet kind of sadness.

A friend's warning.

A soldier's truth.

And when he flicks the card across the table—and it lands square on Alexey's empty chair—

It says everything he never will.

The Night I Grasped at Shadows – Arianna

The days danced by in a dizzying whirlwind of newlywed bliss.

Every stolen moment was laced with passion, every glance a whispered promise, every kiss an unspoken vow of forever.

Odin had returned to me fully, his charm so potent it could bring kingdoms to their knees. His love was a force, a tide I willingly drowned in, washing away the strange, lingering ache of being ignored just the night before.

Tonight, I let it consume me.

The great hall was alight with golden laughter, the flickering glow of candlelight casting shifting patterns over polished wood and gleaming goblets. The air hummed with the low murmur of conversation, the occasional burst of boisterous laughter.

I sat beside Odin at the high table, his hand resting lightly on my thigh as he leaned into me, his breath warm against my ear. "You look exquisite tonight, my love," he murmured, pressing a kiss just beneath my jaw, slow and deliberate. "Like a goddess draped in sunlight."

I shivered, my fingers curling slightly in his tunic. "Flattery will not get you anywhere, husband."

"Flattery?" He feigned offense, eyes glinting with mischief as he traced idle patterns along my wrist. "No, my queen. Just reverence."

I preened beneath the attention, beneath the warmth of his touch, the way his voice dipped just for me.

And yet…

A part of me still bristled.

Because last night, he had forgotten.

Perhaps not forgotten me—but forgotten to look at me the way he always did. Forgotten the weight of his stare, the one he had wrapped around me like a cloak, the one I had begun to wear like a second skin.

I had dismissed it, convinced myself it was nothing.

And yet—here I was, remembering.

My nails traced against the rim of my goblet, my thoughts wandering. And as if the Gods themselves conspired against my peace, my gaze flickered across the room—

And landed on Alexey.

He sat a few places down, composed as ever, watching the card game unfolding before him with detached amusement, a goblet of wine in his hand.

The candlelight played against his features, casting shadows across the sharp angles of his face, the unreadable depths of his gaze.

A legend, Odin had called him.

A man who had shaped the fate of kings.

A man who had saved my husband again and again and again—and yet, never seemed to bask in his own glory.

Intriguing.

He is a walking contradiction.

Slowly, deliberately, I leaned forward, resting my chin in my palm.

"Tell me, Commander Volkov," I mused, voice sweet and edged with something sharper, something deliberately playful.

"Do you ever lose?"

The conversation around the table lulled slightly.

Odin's fingers paused against my thigh.

Alexey, to his credit, did not flinch, did not betray even the faintest flicker of surprise. His gaze lifted, cool and assessing. "At what?"

I smiled, tilting my head. "Anything."

Murphy, already sensing the potential for chaos, grinned. "Oh, Majesty, he's lost plenty. His patience, his sanity—mainly because of us."

Odin barked a laugh, his grip on my thigh relaxing as the moment softened. "That's true. Poor Alexey, cursed with the burden of dealing with fools like us."

Alexey sighed, sipping his wine. "A fate worse than war."

The men laughed.

But I wasn't done with him yet.

I studied him, watching the way he did not lean forward, did not react. He was always measured, always controlled, a blade in its sheath. I wondered what it would take to make his composure crack.

I traced my goblet with a lazy finger. "And if I challenged you to a game? Would you dare risk losing to me?"

Odin turned to me then, grinning. "Careful, love. He's ruthless."

I didn't take my eyes off Alexey. "So am I."

Something flickered in his gaze.

Not shock. Not amusement.

Recognition.

For a breath, the room felt warmer. Smaller.

Then, Alexey exhaled, setting his goblet down with a quiet thud. "I do not play games I cannot afford to lose."

A slow smirk curled at my lips. "And what would you be afraid of losing?"

Murphy all but choked on his drink.

Odin stilled beside me.

The table shifted, ever so slightly, tension creeping in like an unseen fog.

Alexey's gaze did not waver.

"Time," he said simply.

The conversation broke, laughter spilling back in, Odin chuckling as he pressed a kiss to my shoulder, dismissing the moment with ease. "Ah, you see, my love? Our dear Alexey is tragically boring."

I laughed, letting myself be pulled back into Odin's orbit, basking in his attention, his touch, his warmth.

And yet—

My mind lingered.

On Alexey's answer.

On the way his gaze had met mine so deliberately, so unflinching.

Time.

I had asked him what he was afraid to lose.

And that was what he gave me.

Not power.

Not pride.

Not even his legendary reputation.

Time.

What a careful, measured thing to say.

I smiled into my wine, letting the golden hum of the night wash over me.

I had everything I had ever dreamed of. A husband who adored me. A kingdom at my feet. A love story written in the stars.

And yet, I was still reaching.

Grasping at something just beyond my fingers.

Something that would never quite be mine.

The cards were dealt. The night carried on.

And I played my hand as if I did not already know how this game would end.

Evenings by the Channel of Lorna – Arianna

As the sun dipped below the horizon, setting the sky ablaze with streaks of rose and gold, Odin and I rode our horses along the pristine shores of the Sea of Lorna. The waves lapped against the white sand, the turquoise waters glistening under the last light of day. A salty breeze played with my hair, and I threw my head back, laughing as I kicked off my shoes and stepped into the frigid water.

"You're going to freeze," Odin called, reining in his stallion and watching me with a smirk that didn't quite reach his eyes.

I turned to him, grinning. "Am I? Or is this just an elaborate plan to get you to warm me up?"

His eyes darkened with that familiar, practiced heat. In one smooth, theatrical motion, he dismounted. "Oh, is that what this is?" He strode toward me with purpose, boots crunching against the sand. "My clever little wife, always scheming."

I gasped as he scooped me into his arms, cradling me like I weighed nothing at all. "Odin!" I laughed, breathless as he carried me out of the water like some storybook hero.

He pressed a kiss to my forehead—too soft, too lingering—and murmured, "I'll warm you up, alright. But you may not get much sleep tonight."

My heart pounded at the low rasp of his voice. "Good. Sleep is overrated anyway."

We picnicked beside a fire, feasting on bread, cheese, and the sweetest northern berries as twilight crept in. The sea breeze curled around us, stirring my hair, bringing with it the scent of salt and pine. Crabs scuttled around our blanket, gulls cawed overhead, and Odin—Gods, Odin—was glowing in the firelight like something divine.

It was all so perfect. Too perfect.

He was radiant. Attentive. Effortless.

And yet—I felt his performance.

Every kiss. Every touch. Every carefully chosen line.

He was being everything I had once longed for. Everything I had quietly mourned not receiving. It was… overwhelming. Dazzling.

Almost suspiciously so.

Still, I smiled through it, resting my chin in my hand as I admired him. "It's unfair, really."

He glanced up from the fire he was tending, one brow arching in question. "What is?"

"That a man so devastatingly handsome belongs to me alone."

He chuckled—rich, deep, and just a little too well-timed. "Jealous, my love? I assure you, no one else could handle me." He took my hand, brushing a kiss across my knuckles with reverent precision. "Not the way you do."

I shivered—not from the cold, but from the way the warmth in his voice felt like it had been carefully measured out in advance. As though he'd prepared this moment. Rehearsed it.

Still, I clung to it. To him.

I wanted to believe it was real.

Because when he looked at me like that, when he said those things, I felt powerful again. Beautiful again. His again.

And maybe… maybe that was the point.

My thoughts flickered—just for a breath—to a certain stare across a banquet table. To the way another man had said "Time," and meant it.

But I buried it. Deep.

I was head over heels, completely, utterly, blissfully lost in Odin.

And as I gazed out at the sea, waves crashing in their endless rhythm, I let myself believe it.

Let myself believe our love was as boundless as the horizon.

Let myself believe he still meant it.

Let myself believe I hadn't almost slipped.

The Gods had blessed me beyond measure.

And I would not question the gift.

Not tonight.

A Dangerous Game – Arianna

The evening hummed with heat and golden indulgence, the great hall alive with flickering candlelight, the symphony of laughter and clinking goblets weaving through the air like the final notes of some grand orchestral piece.

This was my life now.

And I loved it.

I loved the power and the pageantry, the way courtiers whispered my name with reverence, the game of politics that played out in every well-placed compliment, every knowing glance, every subtle power move.

But most of all, I loved my husband.

When I had his attention.

Odin, radiant and utterly magnetic, lounged in his chair, his smile reckless and easy, his presence commanding the room without effort. A half-full goblet of mead dangled from his fingertips, his copper hair catching the candlelight like fire spun into silk.

"Fools, the lot of you," he declared, voice rich with amusement. "You couldn't bluff your way through a market game, much less best me in cards."

I tilted my head, watching him with playful challenge. "Says the man who just lost two rounds in a row."

Odin clutched his chest as if I had stabbed him, his signature smirk deepening. "My dear wife, you wound me. You know I am merely lulling you all into a false sense of security before I strike."

"Is that what we're calling it?" Velkar Petyr Orlov, High Steward of the Crown, smirked, flicking his cards onto the table.

Odin tossed a peanut at him.

The table erupted in laughter, and I sighed, basking in the warmth of it all.

For all his bravado, Odin had made me feel like a queen—not just in title, but in spirit.

I was adored.

I was cherished.

I was happy.

And then—

The doors swung open.

And the air changed.

Every woman in the hall sat up just a little straighter, eyes flickering toward the entrance.

Alexey had arrived.

Tall. Broad-shouldered. Cloak billowing behind him. He looked as though he had stepped out of a legend, a figure carved from something colder, sharper—something untouchable.

The shift was immediate. The air thickened, charged with something raw and unspoken. Goblets paused mid-air. Conversations stuttered, laughter fading into breathless anticipation.

Hunger.

Not the polite admiration reserved for a nobleman.

Not the fluttering glances meant to flatter.

No—this was something primal.

The women watched him like starved creatures, their gazes dragging over him like fingers, drinking in the sheer power he carried so effortlessly.

Chests up.

Spines arched.

Lips parted.

Dresses adjusted.

A flick of a fan.

A slow cross of the legs.

A delicate tilt of the throat, as if offering.

Their desire hung so heavy in the air, I was half-convinced I could taste it.

And Alexey?

He ignored all of them.

He always did.

His sharp blue gaze swept across the room, not seeking, not searching—simply absorbing.

And then, for the briefest flicker of a second, his eyes found mine.

Something inside me tightened.

It was a fleeting moment, there and gone so quickly I almost convinced myself I had imagined it.

And yet—

I felt it.

A shift.

A spark.

A disturbance in the careful order of things.

"Alexey!" Odin's voice boomed through the hall, his grin wide and wolfish. "Finally, you emerge from whatever Gods-forsaken meeting you've buried yourself in!"

Alexey approached the table, his expression unreadable. Ever the dutiful knight. Ever the shadow at Odin's side.

"Your Majesty," he greeted smoothly.

Odin clapped him on the back, pulling him into the golden glow of the revelry. "Come, take a load off! Have some mead, play a few rounds."

Alexey hesitated.

For just a breath.

And then—his gaze flickered to mine.

Just a flicker.

But it was a pause that was not necessary.
A glance that was not required.

I felt it again.

That strange, unnameable tension.

Then—gone.

Alexey turned back to Odin and nodded. "If you insist, my king."

Odin beamed like he had won something. "Good! I need another worthy opponent to destroy. Arianna here has been humiliating me all evening."

I took a slow sip of my wine, eyes never leaving Alexey's. "I'm simply better than you," I said sweetly.

Odin groaned dramatically. "She wounds me again!"

Murphy raised his goblet. "I support this entirely."

Velkar Orlov chimed in, laughing. "Your Majesty, you don't stand a chance."

Odin tossed another peanut at him. "Silence, Petyr."

Alexey turned toward me next.

His movements were deliberate, precise, controlled.

He bowed slightly. "My queen."

And then—his fingers closed over mine.

I wasn't expecting it.

The warmth of his skin.

The callouses on his palm.

The way his grip was firm but careful—like he could break me if he wished, but wouldn't.

And then—

The spark.

It shot up my arm, lighting up every nerve ending, pooling low in my belly.

It wasn't real, I told myself.

It was nothing.

Just the heat of the moment, the surprise of it, the way he lowered his head and pressed his lips to my skin with perfect, military grade precision.

But I knew better.

This was not a simple formality.

This was not deference.

This was a power shift.

And I had lost.

Because I had been pushing, teasing, poking at his walls for weeks.

And he had never once acknowledged me directly.

Until now.

Until this.

Until the moment he chose to remind me that he had been watching me, too.

Not the way men watch women.

Not the way Odin devoured me with his gaze, like I was something to be owned, to be adored.

No—Alexey truly looked.

He saw what was hiding behind the gold, behind the silk, behind the legend I had crafted so carefully.

And now, with one simple touch, he had taken back the power.

And in that single glance, I knew—I wasn't playing him.

He was letting me play.

To the outside world, it was nothing.

A knight honoring his queen.

A mere courtly gesture.

But between us?

It was a warning.

I let out a slow breath, schooling my features into something serene, something unaffected.

Because if Alexey Volkov wanted to play this game,

I would not be the one to fold first.

"Gods, Alexey, do you always have to look like a brooding statue?" Odin tossed a deck of cards onto the table, his grin wide and careless. "Smile. You might like it."

Alexey barely spared him a glance, flipping through the deck with an infuriating slowness. "I'm quite content as I am, Your Majesty."

"Of course you are." Odin poured him a goblet of mead, shaking his head. "You wouldn't know fun if it slapped you across the face."

Alexey arched a brow. "And yet, I have somehow survived."

"Barely."

Velkar Orlov leaned in, smirking. "So, Graf Volkov, do you actually know how to play, or will we need to explain the rules in small words?"

Alexey tilted his head slightly, as if assessing the question's worth. "Explain them to yourself, if you must.

"Do you know how to win?" I asked Alexey, watching him carefully.

His gaze flicked to mine, unreadable.

Then—so slowly it was almost cruel—a smirk curved the corner of his mouth.

"Would you like to find out?"

Oh.

A slow ripple of heat curled through my chest.

I took a deliberate sip of my wine, letting the moment stretch.

"Yes, actually. I would."

Odin groaned, throwing himself back in his chair. "That's it. I'm out. You two can have your ridiculous battle of wits. I'm going to drink until I forget this is happening."

Murphy, silent up until now, raised his goblet. "It's probably for the best.

Odin turned to him, grasping his shoulder dramatically. "Thank you, my one true friend."

Alexey sighed in my direction. " Deal the cards, Majesty, before you say something you'll regret."

I gave him a wicked smile. "Oh, I will deal them, Alexey. And when I take all your coin, I will use it to buy something truly obnoxious, just to spite you."

Alexey's lips barely twitched. "I have no doubt."

The game was on.

The nobles were already half-drunk, eager to throw away their coin in the name of sport. The air was thick with mead and candlewax, and I could feel the weight of watchful eyes—some entertained, some dismissive, all of them expecting me to lose.

They did not yet know what kind of queen I was.

I glanced at my hand and barely concealed a smirk.

"Well?" Odin grinned at me over his goblet. "Are you feeling lucky, my love?"

"Luck has nothing to do with it," I replied smoothly, stacking my coins in perfect, taunting piles.

Murphy let out a low chuckle. "Gods help us. She's confident."

Velkar Petyr Orlov snorted. "Your Majesty, I say this with the utmost respect—if you think you can win against Graf Volkov, you're more delusional than we thought."

I didn't even look at him as I placed my bet. "I'm sorry, are you still here? I thought you were out of coin last round."

Petyr sputtered. Odin howled with laughter. Murphy clapped Petyr on the back in mock sympathy.

But my real target?

Stone-faced. Unreadable.

Typical.

"Are you planning to fold before we even begin, Alexey?" I teased, tilting my head.

His blue eyes met mine, slow and deliberate.

"No, Majesty," he said in that smooth, unimpressed tone. "I am simply waiting for you to stop talking."

Odin let out a delighted whoop, slamming his goblet on the table. "GODS, I missed this. Someone get me another drink! No—actually, bring the whole bottle! This is far too good to waste!"

I scoffed, narrowing my eyes. "Oh, forgive me for assuming you had a sense of humor, Alexey. It's just so hard to tell sometimes."

"It's there," he said flatly, shuffling his cards with practiced ease. "Buried beneath my will to survive this conversation."

Murphy snorted into his drink. Odin howled with laughter, shaking his head. "I love this. You two should spar more often."

"That's the spirit!" Odin declared, waving at a servant for more mead.

Murphy chuckled into his goblet. "I think this is the most entertainment Alexey has had in a decade."

"At least," Alexey muttered.

I narrowed my eyes playfully. "That is a terrible thing to admit, Alexey."

"And yet," he said, placing his bet without hesitation, "I continue to live with it."

I pressed my lips together to keep from smiling.

Oh, this was going to be fun.

One by one, the nobles fell.

Petyr, his face an absolute tragedy, bemoaning his luck.

Murphy, wise enough to fold early and sip his drink while the bloodbath unfolded.

And Odin—who played cards the way he fought battles: wildly, recklessly, with no real strategy. When I won the round against him, he stared at his cards like they had personally betrayed him.

"I don't understand. I had a great hand," he muttered.

"You had two eights," Murphy pointed out, barely holding in a laugh.

"That's almost three eights," Odin argued.

"It's exactly two eights," Alexey deadpanned.

I smiled sweetly and gathered my winnings.

"Perhaps next time, my love," I said, patting Odin's hand like one would soothe a particularly stubborn child.

Odin groaned and shoved away from the table. "I am never playing cards with you again. You're ruthless."

"You married me," I reminded him.

"Yes, and now I see the error of my ways."

"You were warned," Murphy said.

"You did not."

"I absolutely did."

"Lies and slander!"

Murphy ignored him, turning his attention back to the table.

Only two players remained.

Me and Alexey.

I tapped my nails against the wood, studying him.

He had barely spoken during the last few rounds, playing with cold precision, his face an unshakable mask of boredom.

But I knew better.

He was watching me. Calculating. Waiting.

So was I.

"Well, Alexey," I mused, placing my final bet with a deliberate flourish, "it appears we are the last ones standing."

"A pity," he said dryly, matching my bet with effortless confidence. "I was enjoying the background noise."

I smirked. "Admit it—you're having fun."

He didn't move. Didn't blink.

"You're imagining things, Majesty," he said, flipping his cards over.

And then—

I lost.

For the first time all night.

Silence.

Odin, who had been brooding dramatically in the corner, bolted upright.

"Oh my Gods."

Murphy let out a low whistle. "Well, well."

Velkar Orlov, grinning like a cat, muttered, "I have never been so happy to see someone lose."

I turned to Alexey.

He wasn't gloating.

He wasn't smug.

He was simply existing in the realm of victory.

And I hated it.

"You played me," I accused.

Alexey calmly stacked his winnings.

"I played the game, Majesty, as commanded."

"You let me think I was winning."

"You were winning."

"Until I wasn't."

A flicker of something—amusement, maybe—ghosted across his face.

"And yet here we are."

I exhaled sharply, fighting the urge to smile.

Unbelievable.

Odin raised his goblet. "Well, this is the best night of my life."

Alexey stood, bowing slightly, his blue eyes gleaming with something dangerously close to satisfaction.

"Your Majesty," he murmured.

"Commander," I replied, smirking.

And just like that, the game was over.
I was left with nothing but the echoing reverberation of my own defeat.

The Weight Alexey Carries – Arianna

Alexey was not a man who spoke unless he had something to say. He never spoke to fill the silence.

Most men—especially warriors, especially those who had seen war, who had killed for their kingdom—wore their stories like a badge of honor.

But Alexey?

Alexey wore his like a chain.

I watched him in the weeks after we first met, curious in a way I could not yet explain.

Where Odin drank and laughed and reveled in his victory, Alexey stood at the edges, always watching, always assessing, as if the war had never ended for him.

Where Murphy joked about their past, making light of the horrors they endured, Alexey never indulged in nostalgia. He never told stories of their victories, never reminisced about the battles they had won, never boasted about the enemies he had slain.

He had done his duty. That was all.

And yet, sometimes… in the moments between moments…

I saw it.

The way his hand hovered too long over the hilt of his sword when he heard a sound that didn't belong.

The way he never stood with his back to a door.

The way his shoulders tensed—not visibly, but just enough—whenever a servant dropped a tray, whenever a horse whinnied too sharply, whenever a man laughed too loudly from across the hall.

The way his gaze flicked toward every exit when he entered a room.

The way he controlled his breathing—so measured, so steady, so careful—like a man who had spent too many nights forcing his own heartbeat to slow.

The way his jaw tightened when Odin spoke about the war as if it had been a great adventure and not a graveyard of men.

Yes.

Alexey carried something.

Something he did not speak of.
Something he refused to name.

Trauma.
The weight of war, sewn into the fabric of his being.
The ghost of every man who had died under his command.

Odin had left the battlefield. But Alexey never had.

The war still lived inside him.

It had changed him.
Carved him into something cold and unmovable.

And yet…

I found myself wondering—

If Alexey had been a different man, in a different time, in a different life…

Would he have been warm?

Would he have laughed freely, like Murphy?

Would he have known love, softness, peace?

Would he have been happy?

I didn't know.

But I suspected that even he didn't know either.

And that?

That was the real tragedy of it all.

He was a magnificent thing to behold—
all sharp edges and haunted silence,
like a blade still humming from the last war it survived.
And I, foolish girl that I was,
wanted to trace every crack with tenderness.
To kiss the ruin and call it healing.
To make him smile, just once.
To be the woman he needed,
even if he didn't want to admit it.

The Hunt – Arianna

I should not be here.

The murmurs have made that clear from the moment I mounted my horse. The courtiers think they are subtle, but I hear every word—the soft tuts of disapproval, the half-whispered jests about where a woman ought to be.

"A queen at a boar hunt—how modern."

"What's next? Will she take up arms alongside the men?"

"Perhaps she simply doesn't trust His Majesty to return in one piece."

That last one is closer to the truth than I care to admit.

Odin insisted I come. Insisted. As if my presence here were a necessity rather than a novelty. He was eager when he asked—no, demanded—that I be here, as though he needed me to witness this display of strength. Of dominance.

I've begun to recognize that about him. He thrives under the weight of eyes upon him, feeds off admiration like a man starved for it.

And the court gives it freely.

Now, they cheer as he charges through the trees, golden and reckless, a war god reborn, his laughter cutting through the crisp morning air like a blade. The hounds are baying, the beaters calling out signals, but Odin is already ahead of them all, his sword unsheathed, closing in on the beast.

I sit atop my mare at the edge of the hunting party, my hands tight on the reins, my expression carefully measured. I am watching Odin—but I am also watching Alexey.

He is not cheering.

He rides several paces behind Odin, his movements controlled, effortless. If Odin is a storm, Alexey is the quiet before it. He is dressed in black, a sharp contrast to Odin's gold, his midnight hair brushing his jawline, his blue eyes narrowed in keen assessment.

Unlike the others, he is not enthralled.

Neither am I.

Odin is too close now. Too reckless. His blade flashes in the light, but he does not strike—he is toying with the beast. Letting it charge, dodging at the last possible second, laughing all the while.

"He should have taken the shot by now," I murmur, voice low.

Murphy, who rides to my right, lets out a breathy chuckle. "Oh, he'll take it. Eventually."

I glance at him. Murphy is relaxed in the saddle, reins loose in his grip, watching with the same amusement one might reserve for a particularly entertaining tavern brawl. Unlike Alexey, he is enjoying this. But then, Murphy enjoys most things.

Odin dodges another lunge, laughing as the boar's tusk scrapes his boot. I barely suppress a sharp inhale.

I shift my gaze back to Alexey.

His fingers tighten on the reins. His jaw clenches.

And then—just barely—he shakes his head.

Not in admiration. Not in awe.

But in disapproval.

Alexey has served Odin long enough to know his every impulse, every dangerous whim.

And yet, Odin still manages to test his patience.

It is a fascinating thing, watching Alexey watch Odin.

Where others see bravery, Alexey sees a man tempting fate. Where others see theatrics, Alexey sees a pattern—a recklessness that does not fade but worsens.

And where I see Odin's golden fire, I see Alexey's shadow waiting behind it. Always watching. Always ready to pull him back from the edge before he falls too far.

"Not this time," I think, watching Odin narrowly avoid a goring.

He is going to get himself killed.

A deep chuckle drags my attention away. To my left, Lord Petyr watches me with a smirk, his horse shifting beside mine. He is older than Odin but younger than Alexey, his features sharp and hawkish, his wealth written in every gilded stitch of his doublet.

"Not the most delicate entertainment for a woman, is it, Your Majesty?"

I keep my gaze on Odin. He is grinning, blood-slick and wild-eyed, reveling in the chaos he has created.

"You're right, Petyr. Watching a man get gutted for sport is hardly entertaining. But by all means, continue clapping like a trained seal."

A sharp intake of breath. A laugh, quickly stifled. Murphy chokes on his own amusement beside me.

Petyr bristles, but before he can snap back, Alexey speaks for the first time.

"Enough."

The word is soft but weighted, more a command than a request.

Petyr obeys without argument.

That, perhaps, is more telling than anything else.

A sharp cry cuts through the air. I turn just in time to see Odin make his final move.

The boar charges.

Odin lets it come.

I inhale sharply, my fingers clenching the reins, but Alexey does not move.

He does not call out.

Does not intervene.

Because he knows.

He knows that if Odin dies here, it will be by his own making.

The moment stretches unbearably—too long, too close—and then Odin's blade comes down.

A sickening crunch. The boar collapses, tusks mere inches from his thigh. A moment later, Odin throws his head back and laughs, blood streaked across his face like war paint.

The nobles erupt in cheers.

I do not.

Odin turns, searching the crowd until his eyes find mine. His chest heaves, his smile is wide—too wide.

He wanted me to see this.

I feel Alexey's gaze shift toward me, quiet and unreadable.

I force my lips into a smile and incline my head, acknowledging my husband's victory. But my stomach coils tight, my fingers digging into the leather reins.

Odin is unscathed.

But for the first time, I wonder if that will always be the case.

"I should not be here," I had told myself.

But watching the blood dry on Odin's face,
I finally understood—
I was the only one who should be.

The King's Glory – Arianna

The hall is alive with the scent of wine and woodsmoke, laughter echoing against stone walls. This is how Odin prefers to celebrate—loud, excessive, triumphant.

He sits at the head of the table, a goblet in one hand, a deck of cards in the other, recounting the hunt for the third time that evening.

"It was inches from my leg—inches—but I knew it wouldn't get me," Odin boasts, slapping his cards down onto the table with the confidence of a man who believes himself immortal. "You see, the beast could smell fear, and I had none. None at all."

Murphy, lounging across from him, raises his goblet. "No fear, just the unmistakable stench of near death."

The others laugh, Odin included.

I do not.

I sit beside Odin but not at the table, a quiet observer to the game, my hands folded delicately in my lap. I had played with them before, but tonight, I feel no desire to touch the cards.

Tonight, I watch.

The cards shuffle, coins change hands, and Petyr plays his role perfectly, nodding along to Odin's tale, laughing at the right moments, feeding my husband's insatiable hunger for admiration.

And then there is Alexey.

He sits with them, but he is not truly there. He has not touched his goblet. His cards sit in his hands, but his expression is distant, unreadable.

I wonder if anyone else notices it—the way his focus is elsewhere, locked in thoughts he does not share.

I take a slow sip of wine, setting the goblet down before speaking. "I must admit, I still don't understand the appeal of it."

Odin turns to me, bemused. "The hunt?"

I tilt my head, feigning curiosity. "Of course. Charging through the woods, swords drawn, risking life and limb for the thrill of it. It must be something only a man can truly understand."

Petyr chuckles. "Hunting is in a man's blood, Your Majesty. You needn't trouble yourself with it."

I flash him a polite smile. "Oh, I don't trouble myself with it at all. But I do wonder why some of you seem to enjoy it more than others."

I let my gaze drift to Alexey.

He does not react immediately. He simply places a card on the table, his movements as measured as ever. "Not all men chase glory, Your Majesty."

Odin scoffs. "That is because not all men deserve it."

Petyr smirks. "No glory in standing at the back of the hunt."

Murphy throws in a lazy drawl. "No glory in getting gored either, but that didn't seem to stop you lot from trying."

Odin tosses a coin at him. "Silence, fool."

Murphy grins, pocketing it without hesitation.

I set my wine down, resting my chin against my knuckles. “So is that it then, Alexey? You do not care for glory?”

Alexey does not look at me, does not meet my eyes. Instead, he watches the cards in his hands, voice level. “Glory is for kings.”

Odin laughs, delighted. He slaps Alexey’s back, nearly knocking over his drink. “You see, this is why I trust him. A man who knows his place!”

Petyr chuckles. Murphy smirks over the rim of his goblet.

But I keep watching Alexey.

His hand flexes slightly against the cards. It is the only indication that Odin’s words mean anything at all.

“A noble sentiment,” I murmur. “And yet, I suspect you have little patience for men who chase glory recklessly.”

He finally looks at me. Just for a breath, just long enough for me to see the warning in his gaze.

Let it go.

But I do not.

“You did not think Odin’s hunt was wise.”

The table quiets slightly, only the clink of coins filling the air.

Odin leans back, amused. “Is my wife questioning my skills?”

“Oh, never.” I tilt my head. “I am simply interested in what Alexey thought of it.”

Alexey takes his time placing another card. His voice is carefully neutral. “The King is bold. That is not always a weakness.”

Odin grins. "See? Alexey has faith in me."

But that is not what Alexey said.

Murphy watches me over his goblet, interested. I press on, tone light.

"But boldness and recklessness are not the same, are they?"

Alexey lifts his gaze to mine again. For a moment, I think he might actually answer.

But he does not. He only gives me the slightest incline of his head, the faintest acknowledgment that I am not wrong.

Odin does not notice.

Of course, he does not notice.

He is already talking again, already moving past the subject, already speaking of his next hunt, his next battle, his next great act of legend.

Because Odin is a wildfire—and Alexey is the only thing standing between him and the people of Lorna.

A Plan for the People – Arianna

The fire burned low in the hearth, casting flickering gold against the polished wood of the study. Outside, the wind howled against the castle walls, but within this room, there was warmth—not just from the fire, but from the quiet determination between us.

I smoothed my hands over the map spread across the desk, my fingers tracing the streets of Elarion. This city, this kingdom—it could be more.

It had to be.

"The winters are the worst for them," I murmured, scanning the districts where the impoverished huddled beneath bridges and in the alleyways of the merchant quarter. "Food is scarce, and even if they could work, there are few places that would hire someone without a home address or proper references."

"An endless cycle," Baroness Yulia Romanova agreed, her dark eyes sharp with understanding. She was a woman of striking elegance, her sharp features softened only by the kind of practiced patience noblewomen were forced to master. "No shelter means no work. No work means no coin. No coin means no food." She tapped a nail against the table. "Even the temple can only take in so many. The rest… they fade into the streets."

I hated that.

I straightened. "Then we build something for them. A place where they can eat, sleep, and train for work—"

"That will take land," Grafina Olga Maximova cut in, ever practical. She was a woman of few words, her demeanor cooler than Yulia's, but not unkind. Her auburn hair was coiled in an elegant bun at the base of her neck, her posture impeccable. "And coin, she did not lack."

I met her gaze. "I know."

A beat of silence.

Then—

"I have a property," Olga said, shifting slightly in her chair. "Just outside the city walls. A fifteen-minute ride, no more."

I stilled. "What kind of property?"

"A manor estate. Or rather, what was a manor estate." She sighed. "It fell into disrepair after my grandfather's passing. The structure itself is unsalvageable, but the land is still good, and the wells are deep. It has enough space to house at least fifty families if the proper shelters are built."

My breath caught.

"Fifty families," I repeated, my mind already spinning, already seeing it.

Warm beds. Hot meals. A place where those who had been forgotten by society could stand again.

"You would give this land for this cause?" I asked carefully.

Olga inclined her head. "The land serves me no purpose. I'd rather see it put to use than waste away in obscurity."

It was perfect.

I turned to Yulia.

The Baroness had been listening with sharp focus, one brow arched, her painted lips pursed in thought.

"I will help," she said, as if she had already made up her mind before I could even ask. "I know the merchant class well—I can work with them to establish donation channels. Food, clothing, supplies." She drummed her fingers against the table. "I can also leverage the guilds—a few have been complaining that they lack skilled workers. Perhaps we can arrange for apprenticeship placements."

Relief swelled in my chest.

This was happening.

I exhaled, pressing a hand over my heart, feeling the weight of it—the weight of possibility, of change.

"The people will remember this," I said quietly. "Not the nobles. Not the lords in their halls. But the people who need it most."

Yulia's lips curled. "Good. It's about time they were remembered."

Olga nodded once. "Then it is decided."

It wasn't much, not yet.

But it was a beginning.

A small flame in the cold.

And I would make sure it never went out.

Banquet Scene – Arianna

The hall was alive with warmth and laughter, candlelight flickering across polished silver goblets and golden platters piled high with roasted game and spiced wine. The scent of citrus and cloves hung in the air, weaving through the low hum of conversation.

And then there was Alexey—a shadow among firelight.

Unmistakable.

Dark hair, sharp blue eyes. A lone storm among a sea of redheads.

Even in formal attire, he looked like he belonged on a battlefield, not at a banquet table. Not born to a noble name. Not raised in a court of whispers and silk. Just discipline, control, and quiet command.

I tapped my goblet, tilting my head toward him. "You do know you stick out like a Zavrosian merchant at a winter festival, don't you?"

Alexey barely glanced my way. "Majesty?"

I gestured toward the room with my goblet. "The hair. The eyes. The perpetual brooding. Among a court of redheads, you're practically exotic."

A sharp exhale—not quite a laugh, but enough to amuse me. "My apologies. I had not realized my presence was so disruptive."

"Oh, but it is." I leaned in slightly, voice edged with mock gravity. "A scandal, really. The brooding southern knight who lurks in the background, speaking only when absolutely necessary. The ladies at court find him terribly mysterious."

His gaze flicked toward me, cool but knowing. "Mysterious, Majesty? Or just bored?

I grinned. "A little of both, I think."

He shook his head slightly but didn't argue.

I took a slow sip of wine before pressing further. "Tell me, Alexey—I'm dying to know. What is a man like you doing so far from the warmth of the south? You don't seem the type to enjoy the cold."

He set his goblet down, his movements precise, measured. I saw his features acquiesce, and then—finally—he spoke.

"I was born in the south. My family were citrus farmers." A pause. "I had no desire to be one."

I arched a brow. "So you traded oranges for swords?"

A barely perceptible nod. "Something like that. I enlisted. I was sent north for training and here I am."

"Mm." I studied him over the rim of my goblet. "I imagine you were quite the disappointment to your family."

His jaw tightened—not much, just a flicker. But I caught it. His voice remained even.

"My parents understood."

Something in the way he said it told me they were gone.

I softened my tone, just a little. "And do you ever miss it? The orchards, the warmth? The lack of redheads?"

A beat of silence.

"I do not think of it often."

I took a slow sip of wine, watching him carefully, then smirked. "Liar."

The corner of his mouth twitched—not quite a smile, but dangerously close.

"Would my queen prefer I tell her what she wishes to hear?"

"Oh, absolutely." I leaned in, voice light, teasing. "I prefer my truths dressed up and entertaining."

He considered me for a moment. Then, slowly, deliberately, he leaned forward—just enough.

"I left the south in search of something greater than myself. Something more meaningful." He said with a glimmer of sarcasm in his voice.

I blinked, genuinely intrigued. "And what did you find?"

He took a slow sip of his wine. "Snow."

I laughed, tipping my goblet toward him. "A tragic tale."

"I manage."

I shook my head, still grinning. "So, you're a man who walks away from what doesn't suit him."

His expression remained unreadable, but I caught it—that flicker of something deeper.

"Would Her Majesty prefer I had stayed among the orange trees?" His voice was smooth, even. "Does Her Majesty wish I were not here?"

I smirked, lifting my goblet to my lips. "Not at all. I quite enjoy your grumpy presence at court."

A pause. A slight tilt of his head. "Then I am honored, Majesty."

His voice didn't sound like a man who was honored. It sounded like a man who had learned how to say the right thing, at the right time, without ever truly meaning it.

I was watching him.

And he knew I was watching.

And then, before I could press further—he turned the conversation.

"And what about you?" he said, tilting his head slightly. "Why is a priestess so far from the temple?"

And just like that, the game shifted.

Alexey's past—still intact. His layers unraveled only so far.

For now.

The Future He Sees – Arianna

The chill of the night air had long since been chased away by the warmth of the furs tangled around us, our limbs still entwined from earlier.

Odin lay beside me, broad and flushed with heat, his golden hair tousled against the pillows. He was grinning—that boyish, reckless grin that had unraveled me from the start. His fingers trailed idly along my bare shoulder, tracing invisible patterns on my skin.

"You know," he murmured, voice still thick with sleep and satisfaction, "I've decided I want at least five."

I blinked, amused. "Five what?"

He smirked, lips brushing against my temple. "Babies, of course."

I laughed, shifting onto my side to face him. "Five? Do you intend to keep me pregnant for the rest of my life?"

His hand slid down to rest against my hip, squeezing. "Now there's an idea."

I rolled my eyes, swatting his chest. "Odin."

"What?" He grinned, unrepentant. "You'll make beautiful children, Ari. Strong sons, fierce daughters. Heirs worthy of a king."

My amusement dimmed, just slightly. "And how many do you think I want?"

He hummed thoughtfully, tucking a stray curl behind my ear. "I assume you want what I want."

Assume.

I swallowed, forcing my voice to remain light. "I was thinking two. Maybe three."

"Three is a good start," he mused, pressing a lazy kiss to my shoulder. "But we'll see how you feel after the first. Maybe you'll surprise yourself."

I smirked, arching a brow. "Maybe I'll decide one is enough."

Odin scoffed, propping himself up on one elbow. "Nonsense. You're a queen, love. Your duty is to give me an heir."

A small chill crept down my spine.

Give him an heir.

Not raise one. Not have one.

Give him one.

The distinction sat heavy on my tongue.

But before I could dwell on it, Odin's grin widened, charming, disarming, unstoppable. He shifted closer, brushing his nose against mine.

"Besides," he murmured, voice low, coaxing, "you love me too much to deny me, don't you?"

I sighed, exasperated, but my lips curled in spite of myself. "You are impossible."

He grinned. "And yet, you adore me."

I rolled onto my back, staring up at the ceiling, feigning deep contemplation. "Hmm. That remains to be seen."

Odin gasped, dramatic as ever. "Cruel woman."

I smirked. "Maybe I just need more convincing."

His eyes darkened with mischief, fingers already sliding lower beneath the furs. "Then I suppose I'll have to spend the rest of my life doing exactly that."

I laughed as he kissed me again, all warmth and worship, all golden promises spun in the dark.

I let myself believe them.

The Ice and the Fire – Arianna

The evening hung lazy and golden, the last remnants of sunlight spilling through the castle windows in thick streaks of honey. The hall pulsed with the warmth of wine and candlelight, the low hum of conversation, the occasional burst of laughter from a table of drunken nobles.

At the center of it all was Odin.

My husband. My king.

Radiant. Reckless. Endlessly magnetic.

He lounged in his chair, one arm slung over the back, his second goblet of mead already in hand. He was grinning—that wild, unshakable grin that could convince anyone of anything.

"Where the hell is Alexey?" he groaned, shuffling the deck of cards. "Murphy, go find him and drag him here by his brooding little soul if you have to."

Murphy, lazily stretched out in his seat, raised a single brow. "I think you mean his brooding giant soul," he corrected. "And why am I the one fetching him? He hates this game."

"He hates fun," Odin declared, throwing his hands up. "The war ended two years ago, and he still walks around like we're knee-deep in battle. What was the point of fighting if not for nights like this?"

Before Murphy could answer, a dry, measured voice cut through the chatter.

"I am perfectly capable of walking in on my own, thank you."

Alexey had arrived.

And judging by the sheer irritation on his face, he had heard all of it.

Alexey moved through the room like a shadow that refused to blend in.

The nobles noticed him immediately—well, the women.

They always did.

Spines arched. Chests out. A slow cross of the legs, feigning innocent modesty.

Every woman in the hall undressed him with their eyes.

His broad shoulders were ripe for the gentle slope of a woman's caress.

His dark hair was windswept from the evening air, and his movements held the calculated ease of a man who had seen far too much battle to be impressed by a room full of nobles.

His apathy poured out of his being.

One woman, Lady Evelyne, decided to test her luck.

"Graf Volkov," she purred, sidling up beside him. "Surely a man as disciplined as you must have a softer side. A… more enjoyable one?"

Alexey barely spared her a glance.

"No."

Her smile faltered. "No… to which part?"

"Yes."

"That's not—"

"Deal," Alexey said, sliding into his chair with all the enthusiasm of a man awaiting execution.

Lady Evelyne looked deeply offended, but no one else seemed surprised.

Odin, grinning like a devil, shook his head.

"You really need to stop wasting time, Alexey. Find yourself a woman, settle down. They don't wait around forever, you know."

Alexey barely looked up. "Then they were never mine to begin with."

Odin poured himself another drink, undeterred.

"You could use some fire in those ice-cold veins of yours. You need a woman to warm your bed."

Alexey exhaled sharply through his nose.

"The temperature of my bed is not your concern. Just deal."

I smirked.

Murphy, tapping his goblet thoughtfully against the table, smirked.

"You know, Odin, maybe Alexey just isn't interested in fleeting warmth. Maybe he's holding out for the real thing."

Odin scoffed. "Oh, please. That man wouldn't know love if it stabbed him in the chest."

Murphy tilted his head, eyes twinkling with mischief.

"Wouldn't he? Seems to me, if Alexey ever did decide to let someone in, they'd never get rid of him."

Alexey didn't respond.

Didn't look up.

Didn't even acknowledge it.

Which, to Murphy, meant he'd hit something very, very real.

He grinned into his drink, victorious.

The first few rounds were predictable.

The nobles lost quickly, drunk and overconfident.

Murphy folded after three hands, never one to waste coin in excess.

Odin was Odin—bold, reckless, and entirely winging it.

Soon, it was just Alexey and me.

Again.

I leaned forward, resting my chin on my hand. "So tell me, Alexey—what exactly do you plan to do with your life beyond looming in doorways and terrifying noblewomen?"

He didn't look up from his cards. "That is my life. The looming is free. The terror is simply a side effect."

Murphy whistled low. "Gods, he even says it like a villain. No wonder the ladies are obsessed."

"Obsessed?" Odin scoffed, throwing back a swig of mead. "They're terrified. The poor things can't decide if they want to kiss him or flee the room."

Murphy grinned. "Sounds like a personal problem."

"Gods, you're hopeless," I sighed, shaking my head with mock disappointment. "You mean to tell me you'll spend the rest of your life skulking in corridors and frowning at people? That's not a career, Alexey. That's a public service."

Odin barked a laugh. "A noble sacrifice, truly. Keeping the court on edge, one glare at a time."

Alexey remained unmoved. "It is a thankless job."

Murphy clapped a hand over his chest. "Tragic, really. A life devoted to lurking. So much wasted potential."

I tapped a finger against my goblet. "All that discipline, all that control… wasted on looming. What a tragic misuse of natural talent."

Odin nearly choked on his drink. "HA! You know what he should do? Become a bard. Imagine him reciting poetry in that terrifying deadpan voice of his."

Murphy snorted. "Or a matchmaker. Can you imagine? 'The two of you are compatible. Proceed.'"

I bit back a smile. "Alexey, you'd scare the love right out of them."

"Fortunately," Alexey said dryly, flicking a card onto the table, "I have no dreams of matchmaking."

"Then what do you dream of?" I challenged, watching him closely.

For the first time, he glanced at me. Just a flicker. Just a brief moment of acknowledgment.

"I dream," he said smoothly, "of a quiet game of cards, Majesty."

I smirked. "And yet you continue to show up for them."

"Because he knows I'll hunt him down if he doesn't," Odin declared.

Alexey exhaled sharply. "And because I am weak."

Murphy leaned forward, grinning. "But the queen has a point. You've been the Commander of the Royal Guard for years. You have no other ambitions?"

Alexey considered for a long moment before speaking.

"I am good at what I do," he said simply. "And so, I will continue doing it."

"That is the most uninspired answer I have ever heard," I said, shaking my head.

"What answer would Her Majesty, prefer?" He never looked up. "I'd be delighted to oblige."

"Oh, I don't know," I mused, watching him carefully. "Maybe something with more feeling. More passion. Surely there's something in this world you want?"

Alexey placed his next bet without hesitation.

"I want," he said, "to win this game."

I narrowed my eyes.

"You're insufferable," I told him.

"And yet," he replied, "you continue playing."

Odin laughed so hard he nearly knocked over his goblet. "Oh, she walked right into that one!"

I ignored him, refocusing on the game.

I wasn't going to let Alexey win.

The last hand was played.

I turned over my cards.

Alexey turned over his.

Silence.

A tie.

Odin exhaled dramatically, stretching his arms behind his head. "Well, that's disappointing."

Murphy let out a low whistle, shaking his head. "What are the odds of that?"

Alexey simply collected his cards, calm as ever, his expression a fortress of unreadable precision.

I tapped my fingers against the table, watching him with narrowed eyes. "How convenient," I mused, tilting my head. "Perhaps you let me win half out of pity."

Alexey didn't even blink. "I don't deal in pity, Majesty."

"Then perhaps I let you win half," I countered, lifting my goblet to my lips.

For the first time all evening, he looked at me. Really looked at me. That gaze was sharp, measuring—like he was assessing something I hadn't meant to reveal.

"Then it seems," he murmured, voice smooth as cut glass, "we will never know."

And just like that—

He stood.

No fanfare. No dramatics. No lingering moment of false chivalry. Just the quiet certainty of a man who had already decided the conversation was over.

He left.

And for the first time…

I wanted to chase him.

"Unbelievable," I muttered under my breath, watching his broad frame disappear into the corridor.

Odin chuckled, shaking his head. "He's impossible."

Murphy smirked into his goblet. "You like it."

I scoffed. "I like a challenge."

Murphy's grin widened. "Same thing, really."

Odin waved a dismissive hand. "Don't bother, love. Alexey isn't the type to be intrigued by court games."

No.

He wasn't.

Which made me wonder—

What would intrigue him?

And why, for the first time since stepping into this world, did I suddenly accept it as a dare to find out?

The King Takes What He Wants – Arianna

The plans were coming together.

I prepared my notes for the meeting I would have with Yulia and Olga this afternoon. I was beside myself with happiness and purpose.

I traced my fingers over the blueprints, smoothing out the parchment as I studied the layout. This would be the start of something real.

A shelter for the poor.

A training site for work.

A food bank for those who had nothing.

It was happening.

I was making it happen.

I barely noticed the sound of the door opening behind me—until I felt it.

The shift in the air.

The warmth of his presence.

The way the room itself seemed to shrink beneath the weight of his attention.

And then—his hands.

Familiar. Strong. Sliding around my waist, molding to my body like he had every right.

I sighed, melting into his touch before I could stop myself.

"Gods, look at you," Odin murmured, his lips grazing my ear, his voice thick with indulgence. "My queen, locked away in here, working so hard… when she should be in bed with her husband."

I smirked, not looking up. "I should be, should I?"

"You should." His lips trailed down the column of my throat, sending a delicious shiver down my spine.

"It's a tragedy, really. I've been suffering."

I laughed softly, shaking my head.

"You'll live. I'm busy, Odin. I'll make it up to you tonight, I promise."

I expected a pout, maybe a whine about being neglected.

What I didn't expect—was the soft click of the door locking.

I turned just as Odin pinned me with a look—one I knew too well.

Hunger.

Possession.

Victory, before the battle had even begun.

"Sweetheart," he crooned, tilting his head, wolfish and utterly devastating, "that's not how this works."

A heat flooded through me, traitorous and immediate.

I tried—Gods, I tried—to be strong, to push back.

"Odin, I really—"

"Shhh."

His fingers curled around my wrists, peeling me away from my plans, his hands hot, firm, and insistent.

"As your king," he murmured, smirking against my skin, "I command you to stop thinking for just one moment."

I exhaled sharply. "That's not how this works."

His lips curved against my throat.

"It is," he murmured, "when you're mine."

Then—he lifted me onto the table.

My breath hitched as my back hit the cool parchment, plans crinkling beneath me, forgotten.

His hands were already on my thighs, pushing my skirts up, parting me beneath him.

I gasped, instinctively gripping his arms. "Odin, we can't—"

"We can." His voice was low, thick with certainty, with promise.

"And we will."

He spread my legs wider, sliding his hand against my femininity, his mouth claiming mine with fierce, dizzying need.

And I let him.

Gods, I let him.

Because I was thirsty for his love.

Odin's love was a wildfire, a tidal wave, a riptide that dragged me under before I could think to resist.

He did not wait.

He did not ask.

He took.

And I craved it.

His fingers slid higher, teasing, tormenting, until I was arching into him, desperate, my breath coming faster.

"That's better," he murmured, watching me with a knowing, satisfied smirk. "I knew my queen would see reason."

A traitorous moan escaped my lips.

And Odin devoured it.

His kiss was hungry, his body pressing me into the table, his hands branding me with possession.

"Odin," I gasped.

"Shhh, love," he whispered, not listening, never listening.

"Let me remind you who you belong to."

And then he did.

He pushed inside me.

Right there.

On top of everything I had been building.

And I let him.

Because Odin always got what he wanted.

And in this moment, he wanted me.

Who am I to deny him?

The Mystery of Alexander Volkov – Arianna

The meeting had gone well.

Olga and Yulia had been enthusiastic, hopeful, eager to move into the next stage of building the shelter.

I should have felt triumphant.

Instead, my body still ached—not from passion, but from submission.

Odin.

My heart filled with an aching I wasn't ready to embrace.

I shook the thought away.

Odin loved me. He showed it in the way he knew how. He had always been like this—a wildfire, a force that consumed, never asked, only took.

I had chosen this. I had chosen him.

Hadn't I?

I exhaled, stacking the last of my notes. There were bigger things to focus on.

And then—

I felt a presence at the threshold.

I glanced up.

And there he was.

Alexey.

He had a way of entering a room without making a sound—yet the moment he was there, it was impossible to ignore him.

The flickering candlelight cast deep shadows across his sharp features, highlighting the angles of his cheekbones, the disciplined set of his jaw.

His gaze was the same as always—cool, assessing, as if nothing escaped his notice.

Including me.

I inhaled, a slow smile curling at my lips. “What a surprise,” I said, setting my quill aside. “To what do I owe the honor, Alexey?”

To my delight, his mouth twitched—just barely, almost imperceptibly.

He stepped inside, composed as ever, his movements precise, like a soldier who had long since trained himself out of hesitation.

"I came to bring a donation," he said simply.

I arched a brow. "A donation?"

He nodded once and extended a leather pouch, heavy with coin.

"My men put it together," he continued, his voice even, measured, perfectly controlled. "They heard about your work and wished to contribute."

I took the pouch, feeling the weight of it.

More than generous.

I lifted my gaze back to his, studying him.

Alexey was many things. A warrior. A strategist. A man who did not waste words.

But a liar?

Not a good one.

Ah.

I let the silence stretch between us, watching him, waiting.

His expression did not change.

But his jaw tensed.

Caught.

I smiled. Slow. Amused. Intrigued.

"How very thoughtful," I said lightly, tapping my fingers against the pouch. "Please tell your men that I deeply appreciate their generosity."

His eyes flickered. Just for a second.

He knew that I knew.

And I knew that he knew that I knew.

But neither of us said it.

Instead, he gave a single nod—a retreat, a silent acknowledgment.

"I will inform them," he murmured.

Then, just as quickly as he had come, he turned to leave.

I should have let him go.

But instead—

"Alexey."

He stilled.

It was the first time I had ever seen him hesitate.

Slowly, he turned back to me. Those impossibly blue eyes locked onto mine.

I tilted my head, letting my gaze drift over him, lingering just a little too long.

"You are very kind," I murmured, voice light, teasing. "More than I expected."

His expression didn't change. But his fingers flexed at his sides.

"I do what is necessary."

I smirked. "Do you?"

A pause.

His eyes flicked to mine again—just a flicker, just a breath—before he inclined his head.

And then he was gone.

The door shut softly behind him, leaving me alone in the quiet.

I exhaled, staring down at the pouch of coin, my fingers tightening around it.

Alexey was not an easy man to decipher.

But he was an easy man to admire.

And that—

That was a dangerous thing.

I let out a slow breath, pressing my palm lightly against my chest, as if I could steady the flutter beneath it.

A spark.

That was what it had been.

The first flicker of something dangerous, something new.

I exhaled, leaning back against the table, letting myself fully admit what I had already known.

His beauty was not in the way of vain, pampered lords who spent their days in perfumed baths and their nights whispering honeyed lies into the ears of noblewomen.

No.

His beauty was cruel.

A weapon, rather than an adornment.

A snare disguised as steel.

His face was carved from something unforgiving—all hard angles and sharp lines, a thing of brutal perfection. High cheekbones, a strong jaw, a mouth that seemed permanently set into something unreadable.

And those eyes.

Blue like the frozen depths of the northern sea—cold, endless, a place you could drown in and never be found.

They saw everything.

Even the parts of me I had long since learned to hide.

And his hands—

Gods.

I had never noticed a man's hands before. Not really.

But Alexey's?

Caught between good deeds and what must be done.

They were calloused, veined, impossibly strong. The kind of hands that had known war, had gripped steel and felled men—and yet could be gentle, too, if they chose.

And I hated that I wondered—

What would it feel like if they touched me?

What would it feel like to be held by him?

Would he be careful? Would he restrain himself, hold back his strength, his control?

Or would he let it slip—just for a moment—would he let himself break?

Would he take me to bed like Odin—hungry, insatiable, careless?

Or would he make it a slow, unraveling thing?

Would he kiss me deeply, reverently, his restraint slipping with every passing breath, until he was shaking, whispering my name like a prayer?

Would he pin me beneath him, not to claim—but to surrender?

What would it take to make a man like Alexey to fall apart?

I inhaled sharply, crossing my legs, as if that could banish the thought.

I should have been unnerved.

Instead—

I was ruined.

And Gods help me—

I wanted to ruin him, too.

The Black Swan – Arianna

The air in the ballroom was thick with incense and candle smoke, the scent of mulled wine clinging to every breath. Laughter swelled beneath the music, cascading like silver over the gilded revelry.

And yet—beneath it all, something lurked. A tension so sharp it could carve through silk.

I saw it in the way Murphy's fingers curled tighter around the stem of his goblet.

In the way Alexey's gaze sharpened, his expression unreadable, but his posture too still.

And I felt it. A shiver of something unspoken, something wrong.

Odin's smile was crooked.

And that was never a good thing.

He was in a mood.

His charm fractured under the weight of the crown.

"Come now, Lady Verena," he purred, swirling the wine in his glass. "Surely you wouldn't deny your king a simple request?"

Lady Verena was startlingly beautiful, all ivory skin and dark, sparkling eyes, the kind of beauty that made men stupid and women sharpen their claws. But it was not her beauty that made her notable.

It was her feet.

A dancer of The Aurelia Conservatory, classically trained in the most prestigious academy in Lorna. A legend on the ballroom floor. Her movements had once enthralled the court, a tapestry of grace and artistry woven into every step.

And yet, now—she hesitated.

Verena laughed lightly, the sound hollow, forced. "Your Majesty, surely my skills are best reserved for the stage," she said smoothly, tucking a loose strand of hair behind her ear. "This is not the setting for such—"

Odin set down his goblet with a sharp clink.

Her words died in her throat.

Odin did not like being told no. Not by anyone.

And especially not by a woman.

"A shame," he said, tilting his head. "I had hoped to see what all of Elarion so often brags about."

He let the silence stretch, letting it become uncomfortable. Letting Verena feel the weight of defiance pressing down on her like an iron collar.

When she didn't move, he smiled. A slow, knowing smile.

Then, with an exhale, he turned—casual, dismissive, as if she had already faded from his attention.

Instead, he let his gaze settle on Alexey.

Alexey, who had spent the better half of the evening doing exactly what he did best—avoiding attention. He sat beside Murphy, his posture deceptively relaxed, his fingers idly tracing the rim of his goblet.

But his jaw was tight. His shoulders, coiled with something unreadable.

Verena, taking his silence as an invitation, turned toward him. A safer alternative.

She leaned in, voice light, teasing. "And you, my lord?" she murmured. "Would you not dance with me? Perhaps a simple waltz?"

Alexey exhaled through his nose—not quite a sigh, not quite a refusal.

"I am not a dancer," he said simply.

Verena grinned. "That can be remedied."

Murphy snorted into his wine. "Gods, don't bother. He's about as easy to move as a marble statue."

A flicker of amusement crossed Alexey's face, but he remained as he was. Still. Steady. Unmoved.

Verena, undeterred, leaned closer. "Perhaps I'd like to be the one to carve the marble."

Odin chuckled. A low, quiet sound.

"Ah," he mused, tilting his goblet to watch the wine swirl. "So, the lady does dance—just not for her king."

The words were smooth. Dangerously smooth.

Verena stiffened.

The shift was slight—a twitch of her fingers, a moment of stillness where there should have been none. But I saw it.

Everyone at the table did.

Odin lifted his goblet, taking a slow sip.

Then, so effortlessly, so casually, he spoke:

"You know, Verena, I once heard a man say that a woman who denies a dance has simply never been asked the right way."

Silence.

It was subtle—so subtle that the weight of it did not register at first. But then, slowly, it spread. A growing, unspoken demand.

Verena's lips parted.

Murphy's grip tightened on his goblet.

Alexey—motionless. Expressionless. But something simmered in his gaze.

I felt it again—that prickle of something dark. The slow, suffocating realization that this was no longer about a dance.

It was about power.

About control.

About teaching a woman her place.

Odin did not ask again.

He simply leaned back, waiting.

Letting the moment press in.

Letting Verena feel the pressure settle on her skin.

And I watched as her pride began to fold beneath it.

Watched as she exhaled too sharply, her gaze darting from Odin to the others.

Murphy, tense, his usual humor absent.

Alexey, unreadable—but his jaw clenched just slightly.

I felt it then—a strange, quiet horror.

Because this was not a request.

It never had been.

Verena knew it.

And so, she rose.

A polite, placating smile on her lips.

A surrender.

Odin's grin sharpened.

The orchestra, sensing the shift, swelled into something soft, expectant.

Verena stepped onto the floor.

And then, she danced.

Her movements were as graceful as ever—fluid, practiced, a masterwork of discipline and talent. But there was no joy in it.

Only the stiff, mechanical execution of a command obeyed.

I watched as Odin smiled.

Watched as he sipped his wine, victorious.

I could not explain the feeling that settled in my gut. A slow, twisting unease.

Because he had not yelled.

Had not raised a hand.

Had not forced her.

And yet, he had broken her anyway.

I glanced at Murphy.

His usual smirk was gone. His knuckles white around his goblet.

I turned to Alexey.

He was watching Verena. Not like the other men, who admired the dance.

He was watching the cage close around her.

I swallowed.

And when Verena finally finished, the room erupted into applause.

Everyone clapped.

Everyone smiled.

Everyone except the ones who had truly seen.

Odin turned to Verena, lifting his goblet.

"Lovely," he praised, his voice rich with amusement. "And to think—you almost denied us."

Verena, ever the performer, managed a tight, forced smile.

She sank into a bow.

And then, before the next song could begin—she vanished.

I did not see where she went.

But I knew what I had seen.

I knew what Odin had done.

And judging by the look on Alexey's face—

So did he.

Shattered Dreams – Arianna

The first thing I felt was warmth.

Odin's arm was heavy over my waist, his body solid and familiar against my back.

Then—a sleepy chuckle. Lips brushing against my bare shoulder. A slow, teasing drag of fingers down my spine.

"Morning, my queen."

I smiled sleepily, stretching. "Mmm."

He rolled me onto my back, his eyes dark, unreadable, but his mouth curled into something lazy and dangerous.

A thrill shot through me.

He dipped down, lips barely grazing mine.

Not a kiss. Not quite.

Just close enough to make me ache for it.

I arched into him, my hands sliding over his chest, tracing every hard line, every scar.

He grinned against my jaw, his breath warm as he whispered,

"What would I do without you?"

The words melted into my skin like honey.

This. This was what I had wanted. This was what I had fought for.

I tangled my fingers in his hair, guiding his lips back to mine. This time, he let me.

And Gods—he kissed me like he meant it.

Deep. Slow. Possessive.

I felt it everywhere.

My head spun. My body lit up.

He kissed me like he couldn't bear to leave this bed.

Then—just as quickly as he had claimed me—he was gone.

Odin pulled back, exhaling sharply, like he had to catch himself.

His thumb brushed over my lower lip. His eyes flicked between mine.

Then, that smirk.

That devastating, careless smirk.

"Fuck, you're beautiful, Arianna."

I grinned, already reaching for him again. "Then stay."

He chuckled.

Then—he rolled off of me.

Just like that.

The warmth vanished.

The moment was over.

I caught myself on my palms, staring up at him in disbelief. "Odin—"

"I said no."

His voice was light. Careless. Like it didn't matter.

Like I didn't matter.

He rose from the bed without another glance, reaching for his tunic.

"You're insatiable, Arianna," he said, chuckling as he pulled it over his head.

A joke.

To him, this was a joke.

I sat up, blinking. "Where are you going?"

"Hunting."

I stared at him. "Now?"

He shot me a boyish grin. "It's a perfect morning for it."

My stomach twisted.

I slid to the edge of the bed, letting the sheet slip down my bare legs.

"Odin."

He barely glanced at me as he pulled on his shirt.

I crossed the room, slipping behind him, pressing my chest against his back, my lips trailing along his neck. "Stay."

Odin sighed.

But not the good kind.

Not the I'm breaking for you kind.

The indulgent, but ultimately indifferent kind.

Like I was a mild distraction.

Like he had already made up his mind.

I tightened my arms around his waist, pressing a kiss to the sensitive spot below his ear. "Odin…"

His breath hitched.

I smirked against his skin.

I had him.

Then—his hand caught mine.

And he peeled my arms off him.

Gently. Effortlessly.

Like I was nothing.

I froze.

Odin turned, pressing one last, fleeting kiss to my forehead.

"Tempting, love."

I forced a smile. "Then be tempted."

His lips twitched.

And then—he walked away.

No hesitation. No second glance.

Like it was easy.

I watched as he dressed, moving about the room with effortless confidence, already thinking about something—someone—else.

I folded my arms. “You’re really leaving?”

Odin fastened his belt, grinning over his shoulder.

That same easy, boyish charm.

But something was missing.

Or maybe… something had never been there at all.

“Don’t wait up, love.”

And just like that—he was gone.

I almost called out to him.

Almost.

But the door had already shut.

And I was alone.

Half-naked, tangled in sheets, and stewing in a regret I wasn’t ready to name.

I lay back against the pillows, staring up at the canopy.

The warmth he’d left behind was already fading.

The sheets smelled like him. Like us.

Like what we used to be.

I had never begged before.

Never had to.

But today, I had.

And he had walked away.

I curled my fingers into the sheets, my breath coming too fast, too uneven.

Was this what I had chosen?

Was this what love was supposed to feel like?

Because the newness was wearing off.

And for the first time… I wondered if it had ever been real at all.

And still, I clung to the echo of his kiss like it meant something. Like I still did.

But even echoes fade, eventually.

A Game of Fire – Arianna

I was still reeling because Odin had dismissed me again.

I had surprised him in his study earlier, leaning against the doorway with a teasing smile, hoping for a moment of his attention.

A moment of us.

But he barely looked up from his papers.

Barely acknowledged me at all.

"Not now, love. Later."

Later.

Always later.

And I hated how it stung.

Hated the way I smiled through it, as if I hadn't felt the dismissal like a slap dressed in silk.

Hated how I turned away, craving something I knew I wouldn't find—

not from him.

Not anymore.

I should have gone back to my chambers.

Should have returned to my work, to something useful, something mine.

But instead—

I wandered.

Wine warm in my veins, my steps light with defiance, or maybe desperation.

The castle blurred at the edges, the stone halls softening beneath candlelight and blurred thoughts.

The ache in my chest dulled just enough to breathe.

Just enough to pretend.

And with every sip, I lost a little more of my caution.
Let go of restraint.
Let myself float—reckless, untethered—
chasing the illusion of something that might feel like love.

Or at the very least,
might feel like forgetting.

And that was when I found him.

Alexey.

A fortress of a man.
Steel-walled, battle-worn, impenetrable.

I have never met a man more disciplined, more frustratingly composed—
or more fascinating.

So I test him.

Because I want to.
Because I can.
Because someone should.

Because who will stop me?

Him?

So when I find him alone in the hallway—walking too straight, too controlled, too unreadable—
I decide to poke at the cracks.

Just a little.
Just to see.

"Tell me something, Graf Alexander Volkov," I say smoothly, knowing full well that using his full name and noble title will irritate him.

It does.

I see it in the way his jaw tightens.
I smile.

"You've been drinking," he says, instead of answering.

And that?

That is exactly why I hate him.

Because Alexey sees everything.

My flushed cheeks.

The wine on my breath.

The slow, lazy sway in my stance.

He doesn't ask.

He doesn't accuse.

He just knows.

And it makes me want to burn something to the ground.

I take a slow, deliberate step closer.

"Mm. A little."

He does not move.

Interesting.

"Tell me," I repeat, my voice dropping just enough to test the waters,

"Do you ever stop being so serious, or is it a permanent medical condition?"

He doesn't answer.

Of course he doesn't.

Alexey never gives away more than he has to.

So I do something reckless.

I reach up, my fingers brushing the front of his uniform—

barely a touch at all—

but I feel it.

His breath hitches.
His pulse stutters.
His heart slams against his ribs.

And oh.

Oh.

Now that's interesting.

I hesitate—just briefly—but the moment has already passed.

Because when I look up at him again—
really look at him—
his eyes are sharp, focused, dangerous.

Not angry.
Not irritated.
Just aware.

And I?

I like it.

I like that he notices me.
I like that he's fighting it.

I feel excitement pool low in my belly.

My heart—unpredictable thing that it is—beats too fast for comfort.

So I do what I do best.

I recover first.

"Ah," I murmur, tilting my head, watching him like I've just learned something I shouldn't have.

I let a smirk creep into my voice.

"Not quite so unreadable after all, are you, Alexey?"

A muscle ticks in his jaw.

Good.

Very good.

I let my fingers trail lower—slowly. Just the hint of a whisper against his uniform.

And for the first time, his hand snaps up.

Not rough. Not forceful.

But firm. Unyielding.

He grips my wrist.

Oh.

Now this is new.

I look up at him, meeting his icy blue stare, my pulse thundering.

Challenge glints in my gaze.

His grip is tight—but not tight enough to hurt. Not tight enough to stop me.

I can feel the heat of his palm, the callouses against my skin.

And I wonder—

if I pressed my lips to the inside of his wrist, would he let me?

Would he pull away?

Or would I finally see him break?

What would it take?

I part my lips—just slightly. Just enough to let him see it.

And for a split second—just one—

Alexey hesitates.

His fingers flex around my wrist.

Once.

A small, betraying movement.

And then—

He lets go.

His fingers peel away from my skin, his hand falling back to his side like nothing happened.

But I felt it.

And so did he.

I exhale a quiet, knowing laugh.

"Relax, Alexey, it's no big deal," I say lightly, tossing him one last smirk before turning away. " You act like I was going to bite."

As if my heart isn't still kicking against my ribs.

As if I'm not already thinking about the next time.

And I don't look back.

Because if I did—

If I saw whatever was in his eyes just then—

I might not be able to walk away at all.

The Truth I Don't Want to See – Arianna

Odin is reckless.

Impulsive, unpredictable, ruled by whatever whim grips him in the moment.

And yet, he is charming.

People love him. They always have.

There is a fire in him, an untamed spirit that draws people in, makes them believe in him, follow him, cheer his name.

And when the throne was empty, when the blood of the royal family soaked the stones, it was Odin they turned to.

Not because he was the most qualified.

Not because he was the most disciplined.

But because he made them feel something.

Because he was bold.

Because he was fearless.

Because he could stand in the ashes of a fallen kingdom and laugh, declaring that the future belonged to those willing to seize it.

He has the kind of presence that makes men stand taller, fight harder, believe they can be more.

And I—like everyone else—was drawn to him.

I was pulled into his orbit, consumed by his energy, by his reckless joy and wild confidence.

He looked at me and told me that I was beautiful, powerful, untouchable.

He told me I was his.

And I believed him.

I leapt.

Without thinking, without pausing, without questioning whether I truly knew him.

And now… I am beginning to wonder if I ever did.

Because Odin is not measured.

He is not strategic.

He does not stop to think before he moves, before he speaks, before he acts.

He is a man who leaps first and deals with the consequences later.

And I am beginning to wonder if that is a dangerous trait for a king.

Alexey once told me that power does not change men—it reveals them.

And I see the truth of it now.

Odin, the soldier, the war hero, the man people loved so easily—he was reckless even then.

But when he held a sword in his hand, when he was fighting alongside his men, his flaws were hidden beneath the shine of glory, the thrill of victory.

But a kingdom is not a battlefield.

And a crown is not a weapon.

And now, with absolute power at his fingertips, Odin is still the same man.

Still reckless. Still impulsive.

Still leaping without looking.

The only difference now is that his mistakes do not cost him alone.

They cost us all.

And I…

I do not know what that means.

I do not know what it says about the future of this kingdom.

Or about my own.

Because I thought I was choosing love.
I thought I was choosing passion, adventure, a man who would keep me laughing even in the darkest of times.

But was I choosing a husband—
or a wild, untamed thing that was never meant to be caught?

Did I marry a man—
or did I fall in love with a fire that was never meant to last?

Did I leap into the flames, thinking I could dance through them, only to realize too late that I was burning?

Because Odin was never one to slow down, to think, to build something steady.

And I—I should have known that.

And for the first time, I wonder…

Was I reckless, too?
Did I leap without looking?
And will I spend the rest of my life paying for it?

Uncovering the Wool – Arianna

Odin was laughing.

His voice boomed through the great hall, bouncing off the stone walls, full of wild, unchecked joy.

And I was the only one not smiling.

The gathered nobles chuckled uneasily, stealing glances at one another, their hands tightening on goblets of wine as if unsure whether to celebrate or brace for impact.

Because Odin was in one of his moods.

The kind that swept through a room like a storm—exhilarating at first, thrilling even—
but soon enough, leaving ruin in its wake.

And I saw it now.

I truly saw it.

"Your Majesty, surely you don't mean to commit our forces to such a risk without consulting—"

Odin's chair scraped loudly against the floor as he pushed himself to stand, cutting off the trembling noble before he could finish.

I didn't miss how the man's face paled.

Odin grinned.

"What risk? We have fought greater battles before! What's the point of having an army if we do not use it?"

A cold prickle ran down my spine.

Use it for what, Odin?
Against your own people?

I had not even heard the full conversation—too caught in my own head, too distracted by Alexey's words lingering in my mind—but I didn't need to.

The room had shifted.

The air was different.

Odin was making one of his decisions.

And like always, no one dared challenge him.

I placed my goblet down carefully, pushing back from the table.

"Perhaps we should discuss this further, my love."

Odin's eyes snapped to mine.

They were still bright, still full of that fire that had once enchanted me.

But now, I was beginning to realize—

it wasn't the fire of a ruler.

It was the fire of a man who had never learned to temper his own flame.

He grinned at me, oblivious to the weight in my voice, or just didn't care.

"Come now, Ari. You're not going soft on me, are you?"

The way he said it—

the teasing, the playfulness in his tone—

used to make me feel special.

Now it made me feel small.

I forced a smile.

"And you're not going mad on me, are you?"

Some of the nobles shifted in their seats.

Odin threw his head back and laughed again, as if I had said something amusing.

As if the very suggestion that he could ever be wrong was unthinkable.

Something inside me twisted.

And when he laughed, it hit me—he wasn't even listening.

He never had been.

I felt Alexey's words like a slow, creeping poison in my mind.

Power doesn't change men.

It reveals them.

And now, I could see him.

Not just the man I had fallen for.

Not just the man who had once held my face in his hands and promised me the world.

But the restless soldier who had never learned restraint.

The spoiled man-child who couldn't handle the word 'no'.

The man who had never stopped to consider what came next.

And neither had I.

I had leapt blindly into this fire, and only now—only too late—

did I realize I was already burning.

I had not married a king.

I had married a storm.

And I had no idea how to stop it.

I made a huge mistake.

I leapt into the fire thinking I could tame it. But fire doesn't fall in love. It consumes.

Crown in Freefall - Arianna

Somewhere beneath the warmth of the sun,
beneath the golden sky and his golden touch,
I knew.

From the moment Odin woke me with kisses—too many, too eager—
from the way he whispered love like a performance,
like a man trying to remind himself of something—
I knew.

He was too affectionate today.
Too present.
Too aware of me.

It should have made me feel cherished.
But instead, it made me feel caged.

"You are my fire in the darkest night," he murmured into my neck,
his voice syrup-smooth, soaked in warmth and want,
the kind of thing that used to make me ache with joy.
The kind of thing I used to believe.

But today, it tasted like sugar poured over something rotten.

I laughed—light, breathy, careful.
Let him believe the mask.

"Surely you don't believe that," I said softly.

"Nonsense," he replied, his arms like iron beneath velvet,
his breath teasing my ear.
"And every day, I'll remind you where you belong."

Where I belong.

The words slid over my skin like silk soaked in vinegar.
Sweet. Sour. Possessive.

I smiled.
The kind of smile you wear when the alternative is crying in front of the guards.
The kind of smile you give when you know the moment you stop smiling,
you're admitting too much.

Because it sounded less like devotion…
and more like desperation.
Like a man gripping too tightly to something slipping through his hands.

And I—
I wasn't ready to admit I was already halfway gone.
Not to him.
Not to myself.

So I tilted my head.
Laughed the right way.
Told myself this was still love.

Because the truth?

The truth was clawing at the edges of me—
wild, panicked, unwelcome.
And I wasn't ready to let it in.

Not yet.

The shoreline unraveled before me, endless and wild, the wind tugging at my hair like it remembered who I used to be.
The waves whispered their old, salt-laced secrets—those that belong only to the sea and the women who come here trying to forget.

It had been months since I'd stood here.
Since we'd escaped to the cliffside beaches along the Channel of Lorna.
My favorite place in the kingdom—because it didn't belong to the court, or the crown, or even to Odin.

It belonged to the wind.
To the water.
To me.

The sea stretched out like a promise—so blue it hurt to look at,
so vast it made the palace feel like a cage I had built around myself.

And for one fragile moment, I could breathe.
Because out there…
was everything for which I still dreamed.

Because this was what I had chosen—this wildfire of a man, this reckless, all-consuming thing that burned through me with no regard for consequence.

And Gods help me, I wanted it to be enough.

I arched beneath him, fingers curling into his hair, lips parting on a breathless moan that didn't sound like mine.
Not quite.
Not anymore.

He kissed me like I was already his.
Like I had always been his.
Like he could carve his name into my bones and that would make it real.

And I let him.
Again.
And again.

Because this was love, wasn't it?
This giving.
This losing.
This soft erasure of self in exchange for a man who never learned how to ask.

"You're everything," he whispered, breath hot against my collarbone.

And I almost believed him.

But the ocean kept roaring behind us—
a distant, crashing reminder that there was still something bigger than him.
Bigger than me.
Something vast and free and untouched by fire.

And in that fleeting moment, as his mouth found mine again, I realized—

I didn't want to be burned anymore.

I wanted to be water.
I wanted to be wind.
I wanted to belong to no one.

He pressed me into the dunes,
his mouth greedy against mine,
his weight anchoring me to the sand like a man claiming territory.
His breath dragged rough along my throat,
his hands slid down my thighs,
parting them like a door he already owned the key to.

"I can't wait to eat you alive," he growled, voice thick with hunger—
with the absolute certainty that I was his.

I gasped.

Arched.

Played my part.

Pretended—lied—

to him,

to myself,

that I was fully here.

But then—

a shift.

A flicker in my periphery.

I stilled.

Just beyond the dunes…

Alexey.

Not watching.

Not moving.

But there.

Back turned, posture rigid, shoulders drawn like a man at attention.

A man who saw nothing.

And everything.

The realization coiled through me like smoke.

Dark. Dangerous.

Uninvited.

And then it came—

the thought.

The betrayal.

What would it take to make him love me?

He wasn't even looking at me.

He was just doing his job.

And still—

The treason of it was unforgivable.

It was so wrong.

But the thought had already taken root—and I didn't know how to pull it out.

Gods, what is wrong with me?

And yet—

I didn't stop it.

My breath caught—sharp, involuntary.

Odin groaned, mistaking it for pleasure.

Of course he did.

But I was no longer here.

Not really.

If Alexey ever touched me—

if he ever let the walls drop, even once—

I would have to be the one to pull him apart.

I would have to be the one to unravel that control.

To make him want enough to lose it.

And the thought—

the treason of it—

sent a slow, molten ache curling low in my belly.

"Tell me you're mine," Odin demanded,

his grip tightening like a noose around my waist.

I nodded.

Forced the lie past my lips.

"Yes," I breathed.

But something in me had already cracked.

And when it was over—

when Odin stood, flushed with triumph, smiling like a boy who'd won—

I stood too.

Smiling. Composed.

A queen again.

But inside?

All I felt was the echo of a question
I would never be able to unthink.
And the weight of a truth
I didn't dare name.

We rode along the cliffs, the wind rushing wild through my hair, the Channel of Lorna gleaming gold beneath the late afternoon sun.
The sea stretched out like a promise.
Endless. Dazzling. Deceitful.

Odin was laughing.

Gods, he was laughing—head thrown back, sunlight in his hair, larger than life.
As if the world could never touch him.
As if nothing ever could.

And then it happened.

A crab.

A wretched, insignificant little crab—
scuttling across the sand like a joke no one told.

Odin's stallion saw it.

The great beast reared high, a scream splitting from its throat, hooves clawing the sky.

Odin didn't stand a chance.

One moment—he was light.

The next—he was falling.

Everything broke.

Time. Sound. Breath.
I reached for him, hand outstretched, grasping for air.

"Odin!"

The sky twisted sideways.
The cliffs reeled.
And then—

Crack.

The sound tore through me.
Final. Terrible. Unforgiving.

His skull met the stone.
The rocks drank his blood like it was owed.

I dismounted without thinking. My knees hit the sand. My voice—raw and shrill—ripped from my throat.
"ALEXEY!"

I didn't see him arrive.
But suddenly—he was there.
A shadow at my side, all black leather and clenched fury, falling to his knees beside Odin with the precision of a soldier and the eyes of a man unraveling.

He didn't blink.
Didn't breathe.
His hands moved on instinct—ripping fabric, pressing it to the wound, already soaked in red.

But I saw it.
The crack in his armor.

This wasn't strategy.
This was terror.

"Tell me what to do," I begged, pressing my hands to Odin's blood-slick face, my voice a ragged whisper.
"Please, Alexey, tell me what to do—I'll do anything."

His jaw was locked so tight I could see the tremor in it.
He didn't look at me.

"It's only you and I," he said flatly. Sharply. "We have to move. Now."

Together, we lifted Odin's limp body—his limbs boneless, his breath shallow.

The warmth was already fading from his skin.

I climbed onto the saddle behind him, cradling him against me, holding him like I could stitch his soul back in place if I just stayed close enough.

"Stay with me," I whispered, voice shaking.

"Please, Odin. Please."

He didn't answer.

His head lolled against my chest.

The hooves beat against the earth like war drums.

The sea crashed beneath us, a cruel witness to what had been broken.

And in that moment, as the blood soaked into my gown and the wind screamed past my ears—

I knew.

The life I had built was cracking open.

And nothing would ever be the same again.

The Six-Week Nightmare – Arianna

No one thought Odin would survive.

For six agonizing weeks, he lay in his chambers, as still as a corpse, caught in that cruel limbo between this world and whatever lay beyond the veil.

The finest court physicians hovered over him like vultures, their once-hopeful hands growing clumsy with exhaustion, their faces lined with failure. They applied salves that did nothing, let his blood in a desperate bid to cleanse what no mortal hand could mend, and murmured prayers to Gods who either could not hear us or simply did not care.

And I—

I barely left his side.

By night, I sat beside his bed, watching the slow, torturous rise and fall of his ragged breath, each one a battle waged against the darkness threatening to claim him. His skin, once kissed by the sun, turned waxen and pale. His lips, which had once whispered secrets against my skin, cracked and dried. His once-mighty hands, which had held me so fiercely, now lay motionless, as lifeless as stone.

By day, I whispered to him, my voice hoarse with grief.

"Do you remember the first time we raced along the shoreline?"

"You swore you'd never leave me."

"Please, Odin. Please. Don't go."

I held his hand, willing warmth into it, pressing my lips against his knuckles as if my love alone could call him back. But my words fell into the void between us.

And he did not answer.

And through it all, Alexey was there.

He was my anchor when the weight of despair threatened to pull me under.

He ensured I ate, ensured I slept—though sleep was fleeting and cruel. When the grief became too unbearable, when the walls of Odin's chamber felt like a tomb swallowing me whole, he simply sat beside me in silence.

A silent sentinel.

A pillar of strength for a Queen on the verge of breaking.

It was not love. Not the kind I held for Odin.

But it was something—something forged in suffering, something neither of us had asked for. A bond we could not ignore.

Alexey was not just loyal to Odin. He was loyal to me.

He saw my grief—truly saw it—the way my body trembled under the weight of my sorrow, the dark circles etched beneath my eyes from too many sleepless nights. He saw the way I clenched my hands to keep them from shaking, how I bit my lip to keep the sobs at bay.

And he never turned away.

In the quiet, stolen moments between desperation and waiting, I began to understand why Odin loved this man like a brother.

Because he was everything I was not in those weeks.

Where I was fragile, he was unyielding.

Where I wavered, he stood steady.

Where I despaired, he endured.

He held me together when I was coming apart at the seams.

And I hated myself for needing him.

What a weak, pathetic creature I had become.

I despised the way my fingers would brush against his when he handed me a cup of wine, and I would linger—just a moment too long.

I loathed the way my mind betrayed me, conjuring fantasies of his hands, his touch, his lips—fevered dreams that left me breathless in the dead of night.

Most of all, I hated the way his voice, deep and certain, had the power to pull me back from the abyss when my thoughts wandered to places too dark to return from alone.

And then, one night—just one night—

I broke.

The weight of my sorrow was too great, the loneliness too unbearable. My resolve shattered like fragile glass, and before I could stop myself, I turned to him.

I collapsed into his arms.

His body tensed for only a moment before his arms enveloped me—strong and unwavering.

His warmth was intoxicating.

Grounding.

Dangerous.

My fingers curled into the fabric of his tunic as I buried my face against his chest, breathing in the scent of leather, steel, and something distinctly him.

For the briefest moment,

I forgot.

I forgot my grief.

I forgot my pain.

I forgot the man lying in that bed, struggling for breath.

I only knew the way it felt to be held.

Alexey exhaled sharply, his chest rising and falling beneath my cheek. I could feel his restraint.

In the way his hands hovered at my back before finally settling there—lightly, carefully, as though afraid to grip too tightly.

"Arianna," he murmured, his voice thick with something dangerous. "My Queen."

The way he said it—it was not a reminder of rank or duty.

It was reverence.

Something close to worship.

I squeezed my eyes shut, my fingers tightening around the fabric at his chest. I could not lift my head.

Because if I did, if I saw what I knew would be in his eyes—

I would shatter beyond repair.

And then—

His grip tightened.

Just for a second.

A fraction too long.

A moment of hesitation.

A choice neither of us should have made.

And then, as swiftly as it came—

It was gone.

Alexey pushed back, his hands falling away from me like I burned. His jaw was clenched, his breath ragged.

"This cannot continue," he said, his voice raw, strained. "I am but a man, Arianna. I can break."

His words struck something deep, something terrifyingly real.

Because I wanted to see him break.

I wanted to be the one who made him break.

But not like this.

Never like this.

I turned away before he could see the fresh wave of tears spilling down my face.

Then.

A breath—ragged, shallow—shattered the silence.

A flicker of movement.

I froze.

Odin's fingers twitched against the satin sheets.

A moment later, his eyes fluttered open—unfocused, irises clouded with sleep and something distant, something fragile.

My chest tightened so violently I thought I might shatter.

I reached for him, desperate, relieved, horrified all at once.

But behind me—

A sharp inhale.

I had forgotten Alexey was still there.

Slowly, I turned.

And our eyes met—

Just for a fraction of a second.

Just long enough to see the relief warring with something else.

Something darker.
Something we could never name.
Something that would never go away.

The Stranger in My Husband's Skin – Arianna

The news of the king's recovery spread like wildfire.

The court rejoiced. The people celebrated. Bells tolled in triumph, and the streets swelled with song. Their beloved king had returned to them, plucked from the brink of death by the mercy of the Gods.

Even I, after six weeks of agony, dared to breathe a sigh of relief.

But something was wrong.

At first, I dismissed it as disorientation. No man could sleep for six weeks and wake unchanged. His body was weak, his voice hoarse from disuse. I showered him with love, mustering every ounce of grace and compassion within me. I whispered sweet reassurances, held his hands in mine, kissed his brow as though my touch alone could anchor him back to himself.

But as the days bled into weeks, the truth became undeniable.

This man was not the Odin I had married.

Gone was the warmth in his golden eyes, the boyish mischief that had once set my heart alight.

Gone was the reckless joy, the teasing grin, the effortless charm.

In its place was something cold. Something calculating.

At first, I refused to see it. I convinced myself it was simply the weight of his recovery, the burden of returning to life after dancing so closely with death. I reminded myself that Odin had always been strong, always been resilient.

He would come back to me. He had to.

But the servants whispered.

They whispered of his temper.
Of his cruelty.
Of the way his charm, once boundless, had withered into something sharp-edged and venomous.

Where once he had ruled with recklessness, he now wielded fear like an overt blade.

I heard it in the way the staff flinched when he spoke.
I saw it in the way noblemen's eyes darted toward the door before answering his questions.

And then, the first time he raised his voice at me, I told myself it was stress.
The second time, I feared it was something more.
The third time, I knew.

King Odin—my husband—the man who had made the stars seem closer, the man who had once kissed every freckle on my skin—

Had died on that beach after all.

And somehow, somehow, I was trapped, married to a monster.

How could the Gods lead me, a devout follower, to this fate?

Why would they do this to me?
Why would they let this happen?

The First Time I Truly Feared Him

It was late. The castle halls were silent, the kind of suffocating quiet that came only when too many people were afraid to breathe too loudly.

I lay beside him, staring at the ceiling, listening to his ragged breath in the darkness.

I had stopped touching him in his sleep.
I had stopped pressing close the way I once did, seeking warmth in the depths of the night.

Tonight, I felt his gaze settle on me.

A slow, creeping chill coiled in my gut.

I turned, heart pounding, searching for the man I had married in those golden eyes.

But there was nothing.

No warmth.
No love.
No Odin.

Just a void—endless and hollow.

Something soulless.

Something hungry.

For the first time since Odin woke from his coma—

I knew true, unshakable fear.

Private Eyes – Alexey

The last of the guards filed out, their boots striking the stone floor like the ticking of a deathwatch beetle. The heavy door swung shut behind them with a dull thud, sealing Murphy and me inside the war room's suffocating silence.

I exhaled, slow and measured, forcing the tension from my shoulders. Meetings like this used to be straightforward. Now? Every order was a gamble. Every strategy session a test of endurance. Odin's mood dictated everything. Would he approve? Would he lash out? Would he even remember his own command by morning?

Murphy was watching me, arms crossed, his usual smirk nowhere to be found. The silence stretched between us.

I didn't waste time. "Tell me you've seen it too."

He tilted his head. "Seen what?"

I leveled a stare at him.

Murphy let out a sharp breath, shaking his head. "Of course I've seen it. I was just hoping you'd say it first."

I dragged a hand through my hair before bracing both palms against the table. "Odin has always been reckless. He's always been manipulative. But this?" I shook my head. "This is different."

Murphy let out a dry, humorless chuckle. "You mean like accusing a servant of espionage because the poor bastard sneezed?"

I looked up. "He was ready to have the man executed." My voice was sharper than I intended. "It took three of us to talk him down. And only because Arianna stepped in first."

Murphy's face darkened. "She won't be able to talk him down forever."

I glanced at the door, ensuring it was still shut. Then, quieter, "That's what worries me."

Murphy shifted, his body tensing in a way I didn't like. I pressed forward.

"He's growing impatient with her." The words came out heavy, laced with something dangerously close to fury. "The way he looks at her now. The way he speaks to her."

I swallowed. "I fear one day, he'll strike her."

Murphy went still. Then, ever so slowly, he let out a breath and forced a smirk. "Well, that's the fastest way to turn you against him."

I didn't laugh. I didn't even blink.

His smirk faded. "You're serious."

"Of course I'm serious." I met his gaze, unyielding. "We both knew what he was before. But this?" I exhaled sharply, shaking my head. "This is something else. The injury—" I stopped myself, jaw tightening. "He isn't the same. He doesn't think the same."

Murphy's easy manner was gone, replaced with something sharper. Something bordering on alarm.

"You're not wrong." He ran a hand over his jaw, his gaze flicking to the closed door before lowering his voice. "I saw him humiliate Baron Lev Antonov from the Iskavelle Coast. Called him up front and center at court, asked him a question he knew the man couldn't answer, then had him hauled off to the dungeon for 24 hours. The whole thing was a game to him."

My stomach twisted. Odin had always enjoyed power. But before, he'd at least had the sense to calculate his victories. Now, he was reckless. Sloppy. Unstable.

A danger to himself. A danger to Arianna.

I straightened, my decision already made. "We'll watch him."

Murphy met my gaze. No quip. No smirk. Just a single, solemn nod. "We'll watch him."

The sound of muffled voices drifted through the thick stone walls. The palace was still Odin's.

For now.

I'll Handle It – Alexey

The ink wasn't dry before the first man came to me—splinters in his palms, callouses thick, desperation bleeding through every word.

Odin had doubled the lumber tax.

Not for profit.

Not for war.

Not for strategy.

As punishment.

Because Ivan Babikov had dared to question him. Because a man with sawdust in his beard and truth on his tongue had asked, "Why are you bleeding us dry?"

Odin hadn't answered.

He had smiled.

And then he signed the decree.

The nobles laughed like it was clever.

I did not.

This wasn't ruling. It wasn't even cruelty anymore.

It was volatility—raw, unchecked, and dangerous.

A man with a crown and no discipline.

A king playing god, blind to the fire licking at the base of his own throne.

The Odin I knew was reckless.

He used to mask his cruelty with charm—make people thank him for the wound.

Now? He didn't even bother hiding the knife.

He made enemies out of men he couldn't afford to lose.

And he was dragging us all into the fire.

The Sunfire River Valley was mine—earned, not gifted.

Its loyalty was hard-won. Its peace, harder.

And I'd be damned if I let him reduce it to ash.

I left for the valley before the ink on the decree could dry.

The order burned in my satchel like a wound that refused to close.

When I reached Ivan's homestead, the air smelled of pine and sawdust.

Of labor. Of life.

Things Odin had never understood.

Ivan stood at his workbench, carving more use from wood than Odin had ever carved from war.

He looked up when I dismounted.

Said nothing at first.

Just nodded. "You already know."

I nodded back. "I do."

He wiped his hands, jaw tightening. "I built this with my own hands. Paid my dues. Fed my men. Paid every damn coin on time."

A pause.

"And now my wife will go hungry for speaking a truth the king didn't like."

I stepped forward, pulled a leather pouch from my coat, and pressed it into his calloused hand.

He opened it. Froze.

"Graf Volkov—"

"I'll cover your taxes. Quietly."

His eyes lifted. "My lord, I—"

"You won't lose what you built because the king wants a new toy to break." My voice was iron. Low. Steady. "Let him play his games. You'll survive this. Because I said so."

He stared at me for a long moment, eyes shining not with tears, but fury held back by pride.

Then he said it.

The words I had heard whispered too many times by men who wanted to believe in something better.

"You should have been king."

And for the first time—I didn't flinch.

I had never wanted the crown.

Never craved its weight or the spectacle that came with it.

But I had carried its burden in silence,

in every decision made to keep this kingdom from devouring itself.

And in that moment, I faced the truth I had long buried:

I wouldn't have razed Lorna to ash.

I wouldn't have ruled by whim and whimsy.

And Gods help me—

I couldn't have done worse than the man wearing the crown now.

I nodded once.

Not in agreement.

In acceptance.

It was a regret I live with everyday.

"You take care of your family," I said. "I'll take care of the rest."

I turned and mounted my horse, the pouch of decree still sealed in my saddlebag. Odin's signature, still fresh.

The road home was long.

But not long enough to quiet the truth.

I helped put the crown on his head.

And if he turned his madness outward—

if he bled Lorna to feed his ego—

then I’d be the one to take it back.
He’d rue the day he met me.
Because that would be the day he learned
what it meant to face a king without a crown.

The Fire Between Us – Arianna

The firelight flickered and sputtered, casting long, ghostly shadows along the walls of my parlor. The embers crackled, crying out into the silence, as though mourning something unseen.

I sat motionless.

My hands clenched in my lap.

My body wrapped in the suffocating weight of grief.

I was tired.

Bone-weary, soul-crushed, tired.

And I wasn't sure I was strong enough to carry this any longer.

Behind me, footsteps—steady, measured, yet burdened.

I didn't turn. I didn't need to.

I already knew who they belonged to.

Alexey.

He hovered just beyond the threshold, reluctant to enter, hesitant to speak. As if by stepping closer, by acknowledging the truth of what we had both come to realize, he would somehow make it real.

"What do we do?" I whispered, more to myself than to him.

My voice was hollow, lost somewhere between exhaustion and desperation.

The flames quivered in response, casting twisted shadows that clawed at the walls, stretching and curling like wraiths, devouring the light.

Alexey exhaled heavily, rubbing his temples, his composure—the unwavering strength he had always carried—cracking at the edges.

"I—" He faltered, his voice betraying him. "I don't know."

Silence swallowed the room whole.

Odin had once ruled with reckless abandon. Now, he ruled with fear and iron.

His advisors—the same men who had once adored him, trusted him, revered him—dared not speak against him.

His subjects—the same people who had wept with joy at his reign—now whispered in hushed voices behind locked doors.

Lorna had become a kingdom on edge, walking on eggshells, holding its breath, waiting.

Waiting for the next cruel decree.

The next unforgiving judgment.

The next glimpse of fury where there had once been a semblance of peace.

And for the first time in my life—

I feared my husband.

He terrified me.

The man I had married, the man who had once traced constellations onto my skin and promised me the world, had died on that beach.

And the thing that had returned—

I did not recognize it.

My breath shuddered as I finally stood and turned to Alexey, my throat tightening at the sight of him.

He was tense, his jaw locked, his hands balled into fists at his sides as if he were restraining the urge to break something.

This was breaking him like it was breaking me.

Odin had known Alexey for years. Had been brothers in arms on battlefields, had watched him stand steadfast through storms that would have broken lesser men.

But this?

This was unraveling him at a dangerous speed.

His loyalty to Odin—was carved into the very essence of his being.

But I wondered how long it would hold.

Here he stood, helpless, watching as that same friend twisted into something monstrous before his eyes.

"I don't know what to do, Arianna," he admitted, his voice raw, heavy with the weight of his failure.

His familiar address, while unconscious for him, was like an arrow to the heart for me.

It left me wanting.

I swallowed hard, my fingers curling into the silk of my gown.

"I don't think it can be fixed," I whispered, the truth like broken glass in my throat.

He flinched.

Just barely, but I saw it.

Neither of us wanted to say it.

Odin was gone.

What stood in his place was something dark, something twisted, something that carried his face but none of his soul.

A sharp, shuddering breath left me as I turned away, staring into the fire as if it held the answers I desperately sought.

Alexey remained behind me, unmoving—but I felt him.

Felt the heat of his presence.

Felt the storm brewing beneath his skin.

A shiver crawled down my spine, though the room was warm.

I knew that feeling.

Restraint.

He had been holding it in for weeks.

The guilt.

The rage.

The grief.

And something else.

Something far more dangerous.

Something unexpected.

Something I refused to name.

Slowly, cautiously, I turned back to him.

His gaze locked onto mine.

For a moment, neither of us spoke.

There was no need.

The air between us crackled, thick with something neither of us had the strength to extinguish.

I stood and took a step toward his form, hovering in the doorway.

We had spent too many nights drowning in the same silent misery.

Too many stolen moments where our grief bled into each other, where the only comfort left in this forsaken castle was each other.

I knew the feel of his arms around me.

I knew the sound of his voice, low and steady, whispering that I was not alone.

I knew the way his touch lingered just a second too long when he draped a blanket over my shoulders, as I desperately tried to warm my soul by his fire.

And Gods help me—

I knew the way my body responded to it.

He took a slow, measured step forward.

I did not move away.

"Arianna…"

His voice was a whisper—my name a confession, a plea, a sin waiting to happen.

I exhaled sharply, my hands trembling at my sides.

I should step away.

I should not do this.

I should think about the consequences.

But I didn't.

I couldn't.

My fingers curled into the fabric of my gown, my breath shallow as I stared up at him—this man who had held me together while I fell apart.

He was so close.

Too close.

Not enough.

I wanted him closer.

"Alexey…"

I didn't even know what I was asking for.

Only that I needed something, anything—because I was unraveling, and he was the only thing in this Gods-forsaken world that still felt solid.

I reached for him.

For the briefest of moments—he let me.

His breath hitched, his fingers flexed, his restraint cracked just enough for me to see what lay beneath—the raw, desperate, forbidden thing we never spoke of.

And then—

His hands gripped my arms, not rough, not forceful—but firm.

"Arianna," he said, and this time, his voice was wrecked.

"This cannot happen."

The words slammed into me, sharper than any blade, heavier than any crown.

I flinched, but he didn't let go.

His grip tightened just enough to make me feel it—the restraint, the breaking point, the battle he was fighting with himself.

"Why not?" I whispered.

His jaw clenched. Hard.

"You know why," he said, and there was agony in it.

I shook my head. I didn't know. I didn't care.

"I don't," I breathed, searching his face.

"Then you're lying to yourself."

His words were a quiet, brutal thing.

My fingers trembled against his tunic. "Alexey, please—"

A sharp inhale. A flicker of something dangerously close to surrender.

His gaze dropped to my lips.

And for one, shattering moment—

I thought he might break.

I thought he might pull me in.

I thought I might finally know what his lips tasted like.

Then—he was gone.

He stepped back so fast it felt like a slap.

I was cold.

I was breathless.

I was alone.

His hands flexed at his sides, like he wanted to clench them into fists.

His entire body was a battlefield—one I had no hope of winning.

And then—he exhaled.

A deep, steadying breath.

His voice changed.

Stronger. Harder.

Like he had just reforged himself in fire, sealing every crack I had nearly broken open.

"I will not take advantage of my friend's illness to bed his wife. I will not take advantage of your state of mind."

The words were a slap to the face—cold, sharp, deliberate.

"I will not betray my oath as the Commander of the Royal Guard to have my way with the Queen. This is treason."

“Gods forgive me,” he whispered, not to me—but to himself.

Like saying it aloud might silence the part of him that wanted to stay.

I flinched.

Because that was not what this was.

That was not what I had asked for.

But he had to frame it that way—he had to make it sound crude, selfish, dishonorable—because if he didn’t, if he admitted what this truly was, then he would have to admit that he wanted it too.

The words cut through me like ice.

His gaze lifted—fierce, unyielding.

"This is not who I am."

"This is not who you are."

Something inside me shattered.

Shame.

Humiliation.

Aching, unbearable want.

I turned away first.

I couldn’t let him see the tears burning behind my eyes.

"I’m sorry," I whispered. Lying.

Because I wasn’t sorry.

Because I wanted him.

If he had let me feel something other than this unbearable emptiness—

And yet, if he had kissed me… if he had said my name one more time like that… I would’ve let it happen. I would’ve burned for it.

I wouldn't have stopped him.

And we both knew it.

I squeezed my eyes shut, willing away the burn of unshed tears.

"Gods, why did he have to change?" My voice cracked, raw and broken.

Alexey let out a bitter, humorless laugh. "I don't know."

His voice was hoarse, wrecked with too many emotions to name.

I opened my eyes.

His were still locked onto mine.

Haunted. Wanting. Desperate.

I knew I needed to look away.

I had to.

But I didn't.

I stepped closer.

So did he.

A breath between us. That was all.

A single breath away from something we could never undo.

His fingers twitched again, hovering near his sword hilt—a man at war with himself.

And then—

A loud crash from the corridor outside shattered the moment, sending us both recoiling like we had been burned.

Alexey stepped back first, running a hand through his hair, exhaling shakily.

"I should go."

I nodded. "Yes."

But neither of us moved.

He swallowed hard.

Then, with a look I could not decipher—one of longing, regret, and something else that made my stomach clench—he turned and strode out of the room.

And I was left alone.

With the fire.

With the ghosts of what was.

And the nightmare of what now remained.

The Unraveling – Alexey

I was the Commander of the Royal Guard.

A man of order. Discipline. Control.

I had fought in wars, led armies, made impossible choices in the name of duty.

I had seen my kingdom fall. Men crumble. Blood stain the very soil they swore to protect.

But this?

This was the first battle I could not win.

Because the war was Odin.

And Odin was losing.

The death of a King still living

I remembered him before the fall.

He thought himself a king worthy of legends.

Bold. Reckless. Golden with charm and fire.

A man who could rally an army with a grin, who could lead men to their deaths and make them feel like it was worth it.

He had been my brother once.

My king.

My friend.

And now?

Now I hated him.

I hated the way he spoke to her—
like she was a servant. A pawn. A woman he'd won and forgotten how to cherish.
I hated the way he drowned in mead and delusion, watching his kingdom wither while he laughed into the bottom of his cup.
He didn't just drink it—he marinated in it. Let it rot him from the inside out.
I hated the man he had become.
Small. Petty. Vicious.
And worse—willfully blind.

I had never hated him before.
Not on the battlefield.
Not when blood soaked our armor and we bled side by side for a future we both believed in.
Not even when he crowned himself king.

But I hated him now.

Because he was supposed to protect her.
Because she deserved better.
Because his name was Odin—
And Odin was supposed to be better than this.

I had promised myself I would never be the man who wanted what Odin had."
And yet… here we are.

She didn't complain.
Didn't fight back.
Didn't argue.
Didn't scream.

She did what she had always done—she smiled, she endured, she bore the weight of her suffering in silence.

And it killed me.

She had been so full of life once.
Sharp. Radiant. Untouchable.

Now?

Now, she was withering under the weight of a crown that should have made her powerful.

And I—the man sworn to protect this kingdom, sworn to protect its queen—could do nothing.

I had spent years of my life fixing Odin's messes.
Shielding him from the consequences of his recklessness.
Pulling him back from the ledge when he leapt without looking.
Cleaning up the chaos he left in his wake.

But this?
This was a mess too great, too deep, too broken.

I could not fix this.
I could not fix her.

And Gods help me—
I wanted to.

It wasn't lust.
It wasn't greed.
It wasn't betrayal.

It wasn't some dishonorable urge to steal what wasn't mine.

It was the unbearable weight of watching her suffer and wanting—needing—to take it away.

I wanted to be the shield Odin refused to be.
I wanted to make her smile again.

To hear her laugh the way she had in the golden days before everything had gone to ruin.

I wanted to stand between her and the world and take every sharp edge, every cruel word, every injustice for her.

I wanted to fix it.

Why couldn't I fix it?

I closed my eyes, and I saw before.

Before the fall.

Before the madness.

Before she had learned what it meant to suffer in silence.

I saw the summer evenings, the golden light flickering over goblets of wine, the laughter that once filled this castle.

I saw her.

Arianna.

Smirking over a game of cards.

Rolling her eyes at Odin's dramatics.

Teasing me, poking at the edges of my armor, trying to find the cracks.

I had never let her in.

Because back then, there had been no need to.

Because back then, she had been happy.

Because back then, she had been loved.

Because back then—

Odin had still been Odin.

The man who sat on the throne was not the man I had sworn my loyalty to.

He was a ghost of his former self, a cruel shadow of the king he once was.

And she was breaking because of it.

And I was breaking with her.

Because for the first time in my life, I wanted something I could not have.
For the first time in my life, I had lost a battle before it had even begun.

Because no matter how much I wanted to take her suffering away—
She would never be mine to save.

The Hunting Parties – Alexey

The training grounds echoed with the clash of steel and the steady rhythm of boots striking packed earth. The sun hung low in the afternoon sky, casting long shadows over the men drilling below.

Murphy and I walked along the perimeter, our boots kicking up dust as we looked down on the training yard below. We passed clusters of men locked in sparring bouts. The air smelled of sweat, leather, and the metallic tang of weapons sharpened to lethal precision.

It should have been a routine day. It should have felt like every other afternoon we had spent watching the men hone their craft.

But nothing had felt routine since Odin woke from that coma.

Murphy rolled his shoulders, letting out a slow exhale. "You ever think about how much simpler this job used to be?"

I didn't answer right away, scanning the men below. The clatter of practice swords, the rhythmic bark of commands—this was the kind of order I understood.

I finally glanced at him. "Before or after we became glorified babysitters for a king who wouldn't remember the order he gave the night before?"

Murphy barked a dry laugh. "Before, obviously. Back when the royal guard was mostly for show. Stand around, look menacing, maybe escort some noble from a banquet. Now?" He sighed. "Now, it's like we're trying to keep a rabid dog from biting the wrong people. Innocent people."

I didn't disagree.

Odin's moods shifted too fast, too violently. His paranoia bled into every decision, and his temper—Gods help the poor fool caught in its path.

And then, there was the hunting.

I glanced at Murphy, lowering my voice. "He's taken to hunting. More than usual."

Murphy shrugged. "Hunting keeps him out of the castle. I say let the bastard chase deer through the woods if it means we get some peace."

That was the difference between us. Murphy saw a brief reprieve. I saw something else.

"He doesn't play cards anymore," I said, watching the way Murphy's brow furrowed.

"No, he doesn't," he admitted. "Not since the coma. Not since—" He waved vaguely, as if not saying it would make it less real. "But I don't see the issue. So he prefers hunting over gambling. Let him."

I shook my head. "It doesn't sit right with me."

Murphy exhaled sharply. "Of course it doesn't. Because you can't let anything sit right if it smells like trouble."

He wasn't wrong. But I wasn't wrong either.

"He's been taking men with him," I continued. "Men who shouldn't be anywhere near him."

Murphy's expression sharpened.

I nodded. "Dishonorably discharged soldiers."

He frowned. "You're sure?"

"I confirmed it with the army commander," I said. "These aren't just washed-up veterans. These are men who were kicked out for insubordination, brutality, war crimes."

I met his gaze. "Why would the king—our king—surround himself with men like that?"

This wasn't Odin forgetting himself. This was Odin preparing.

Murphy didn't answer right away. For once, there was no joke, no sharp quip to soften the weight of the conversation.

Finally, he sighed, rubbing a hand over his face. "So what? You think he's—what? Building himself a war band?"

I didn't say yes. I didn't need to.

Murphy cursed under his breath, folding his arms across his chest. "I hate that that actually makes sense."

I turned my attention back to the training grounds. The men below us fought with discipline, with control. The men Odin took with him? They were something else entirely.

"We can't move yet," I said. "Not until we know more."

Murphy exhaled through his nose. "I hate that."

"We focus on the castle," I continued. "We focus on keeping Arianna safe."

Murphy dragged a hand through his hair. "Yeah. That part hasn't changed."

I glanced toward the horizon. "He'll be back tonight."

Murphy stilled.

This wasn't paranoia. This wasn't politics.
This was turning into something else.

A nightmare.

Because everything had changed.

And we both knew it.

The Feral Dove – Arianna

The bedroom was dim, the candlelight flickering weakly against the stone walls. Odin shut the door behind him, rolling his shoulders like he was shaking off something heavy.

His movements weren't as smooth as they once were. No effortless grace, no magnetic pull.

But the intent was still there.

I felt it before I saw it.

Something clung to him tonight—coiled beneath his skin, thrumming like an aftershock, like something unleashed and not yet leashed again.

"Odin," I murmured, glancing up from the pillows. "You're back from your hunt. How was it?"

He exhaled slowly, deeply. Satisfied.

"Mm. It was… eventful."

A pause. A smirk. Something unreadable in his expression, like he was savoring the taste of something only he could still feel.

"The prey put up a fight. More than expected."

A strange chill spread through my chest.

His tunic hit the floor, discarded in a careless heap before he slid into bed beside me. His palm found my hip—a slow, familiar touch, his lips brushing against my shoulder.

It should have felt the same.

It didn't.

Something lingered in him tonight. Something too alive. Too close to the surface.

And then I saw it.

A shadow of bruising along his left cheekbone, just beneath the sharp ridge. Dark. Swollen. Fresh.

My fingers moved before I could stop them, brushing the tender skin.

A mistake.

"You're hurt," I murmured. "What happened?"

Odin stilled.

Just for a breath.

Then—

A chuckle. Low. Leisurely.

His hand covered mine, pressing my palm to his jaw like he meant to keep it there.

"A feral dove got to me."

I frowned.

"A dove?"

His smile was slow. Amused. As if we were sharing a private joke—one only he understood.

"Mm." His thumb ghosted over my wrist, his voice smooth, lazy. "Pretty little thing. But she broke. They always do."

Something cold slid through me.

I didn't know why.

Not entirely.

But I knew—instinctively, in that marrow-deep place where warnings lived—that he wasn't talking about a bird.

Not a dove. Not anything with feathers or wings.

The bruising beneath my fingertips felt suddenly sharp.

I withdrew my hand. Too fast.

His eyes caught it. Tracked the movement.

Slowly, deliberately, he let his own fingers drift over the bruise, a low hum vibrating from his throat.

"The dove had fire," he murmured, tracing the tender skin with something almost… indulgent.

A hum. Low. Satisfied.

Like a man remembering the taste of something rare.

"But the ones that burn the brightest always collapse the fastest."

The air in my lungs turned to glass.

His smirk deepened, slow and lazy, curling like smoke.

"And I do so love to watch them go out."

I let him kiss me.

Because I had to.

Because if I pulled away—if I hesitated—

I might finally learn what happens to doves.

And if I learned that—

I might finally learn what happens to me.

He Didn't Let Me Go That Night.

I had expected him to pull me closer.

But not like this.

Not with this kind of slow, measured control.

Odin had always been passionate. Fierce in his affections, reckless in his desires. But tonight—

Tonight, he was something else.

"You're tense, my love." His breath was warm against my skin. "Why is that?"

I swallowed. "I—I'm not."

A lie. A weak one.

He hummed, dragging his lips along my collarbone, painfully slow.

"You think too much."

His fingers traced down my spine, featherlight.

"You do that often, don’t you? Get lost in your thoughts when I’m right in front of you."

He shifted above me, and I caught the glint of his eyes—dark, knowing.

"That’s not what I want."

My pulse stuttered.

"No more thoughts tonight, Arianna."

His words curled against my skin, warm and quiet, but they didn't feel like comfort.

"I want you soft." A kiss to my throat. "I want you quiet." A touch against my hip. "I want you to just… be mine."

There was something new in his voice.

Something absent of love but full of ownership.

I tried. I really did.

But something about the way he touched me felt… different.

There was no urgency.

No hunger.

Only deliberate, languid possession.

Like he was savoring something.

Like he had already tasted something sweeter that night—and now, he was letting himself indulge.

My stomach turned.

"You’re so quiet." His lips hovered over mine. "Tell me what you’re thinking."

I forced a breath, shaking my head. "Nothing."

Another lie.

He smirked, tracing my jaw with his knuckles. "Good."

And then, softly—almost reverently—

"I prefer you that way."

I shivered.

He felt it.

And he liked it.

He didn't let me go that night.

He held me long after it was over, stroking my hair, watching me with the same quiet, satisfied amusement.

And as I drifted into uneasy sleep, I felt it—

The shape of his fingers, brushing absently over his bruised cheek.

As if remembering.

As if reliving.

As if savoring.

I didn't ask.

I didn't dare.

The Cracks in the Illusion – Arianna

I tell myself it's nothing.

That I'm overthinking. That every marriage has its growing pains especially when overcoming an injury like the one he sustained. That this is simply the weight of responsibility settling in.

But the things I used to brush off… I can't ignore them anymore.

Like last night.

Like what Odin said.

"A feral dove got to me."

The words won't leave me alone. They sit in the back of my mind, curling at the edges of my thoughts, refusing to let go.

It was just a joke.

Just Odin being Odin.

And yet—

The way he said it. The way he lingered on it, rolled it over his tongue like something meant to be savored. Like he found it delicious.

The way he looked at me after, as if he were waiting for me to understand.

And I did.

Something claws at my chest.

I don't know what it is exactly.

I don't want to know.

I shove the thought away.

Odin is my husband. He loves me.

Doesn't he?

I need to focus on something else.

Something I can control.

He keeps questionable company. Men I wouldn't have entertained before, men who laugh too loudly, drink too much, whisper things in his ear that I'm not meant to hear.

We don't play cards with Alexey and Murphy anymore. Not that Odin seems to mind. But I do. I miss it—the sharp wit, the easy laughter, the way it felt like we were equals. Life was lighter.

I used to believe Odin and I were a partnership. That I was his queen in more than just name.

But it's becoming painfully clear that it's only ever about what he wants.

I'm at his beck and call, always. A dutiful wife. A perfect queen. A fixture by his side when it's convenient for him—when it benefits him.

Yet, when I need him? When I want his support? When I tell him about my charity efforts, my goals, my plans?

He dismisses them.

Brushes them off like they don't matter.

Like I don't matter.

And I hate that it stings.

Because I made this choice. I walked into this with my eyes wide open.

Didn't I?

Maybe the truth is simpler. Maybe the truth is uglier.

Maybe the newness is wearing off.

And maybe, deep down, I was never in love with Odin.

Maybe I was in love with the idea of him.

The fairy tale.

The power.

The illusion.

The charisma that had everyone else charmed, too.

I moved through the corridor on unsteady feet.

Another long evening. Another empty seat where my husband should have been.

Where was he?

I told myself I didn't care.

I refused to care.

I turned a corner too fast and walked straight into a wall of muscle.

Alexey.

Of course.

This is exactly what I need right now.

His hands caught me effortlessly, fingers curling around my arms—steady, firm, grounding.

A rush of heat spread under my skin.

I hated that I noticed.

His grip lingered just a second too long before he let go, taking a slow step back.

"Majesty," he murmured, voice smooth, unreadable.

I exhaled, gathering myself, lifting my chin just slightly.

"Do you always appear out of thin air, or am I just special?"

His gaze flicked over my face—assessing, calculating, taking me apart piece by piece without ever touching me.

I hated that too.

"I had no idea how seriously you took your looming duties." I snapped.

Something almost resembling a smirk flickered at the corner of his mouth.

"Would you prefer I announce myself?"

I huffed. "It would be a nice change."

Alexey exhaled slowly. "Noted."

My stomach tightened.

Damn him.

How does he keep doing this?

I tilted my chin. "As much as I'd love to verbally spar with you right now, I'm tired."

His expression didn't shift. "Then get some rest."

I narrowed my eyes. "Is that supposed to mean something?"

A pause.

Then—"Only that you said you were tired."

A sharp prickle ran down my spine.

I folded my arms. "You always say less than you mean."

A beat of silence.

Alexey's gaze flicked to the window, unreadable. "And you always hear more than I say."

The words were careful, measured—an answer that wasn't an answer at all.

My stomach dropped.

Because he was right.

And we both knew it.

A pulse thundered in my ears—anger tangled with something I refused to name.

I held my ground. "You think I made a mistake."

Alexey's expression didn't shift.

"Majesty?"

"You think I made a mistake, marrying Odin?"

A pause.

Then—"I think you made a choice."

I inhaled sharply. Damn him.

I scoffed, shaking my head. "I followed my heart, Alexey."

His jaw tightened—just barely.

He didn't respond.

I hated that more than if he had.

I hated that he let me hear the silence.

"Say something."

Alexey watched me for a long moment.

Then—"I'd be happy to oblige. What would you like me to say?"

I hated him. I hated how careful he was. How he let me do all the talking, all the unraveling, all the thinking.

My chest tightened.

"You are always judging me with your eyes."

His gaze remained calm, steady, unaffected.

"Am I?"

I hated him.

I hated him for not saying what I wanted him to say.

Because he wanted me to say it first.

I swallowed, throat tight.

"You're an ass."

His lips twitched.

But it wasn't amusement.

It was something closer to pity.

And that?

That was unbearable.

I turned abruptly, suddenly needing to be anywhere but here.

"I should go," I muttered. "Odin is waiting for me."

A lie.

Alexey didn't stop me.

He didn't correct me.

But he didn't agree, either.

Instead, he let the silence settle—long, heavy, unbearable.

Like he was waiting for me to take it back.

Like he already knew I wouldn't.

My feet froze.

Heat clawed up my throat, my breath catching.

Slowly, I turned back to him, my heart slamming against my ribs.

His face was calm, steady.

But there was something in his eyes—something deep, something knowing, something utterly devastating.

He knew.

He knew.

And worse?

I did too.

I forced my spine straight, my expression cold, practiced, unshaken.

"I am happy, Alexey, over the moon happy."

Alexey said nothing.

But he didn't need to.

Because the silence itself was damning.

I turned again, walking away with measured, purposeful steps.

I didn't look back.

I refused to look back.

Because if I did…

If I saw the truth in his eyes one more time…

I might break.

Arianna's Lament – Arianna

The candle flickers beside me, casting shadows that stretch and recoil like specters across the open texts strewn before me. The ink is dark, the words crisp, but they do not hold the answers I seek.

They never have.

I blink, willing my exhausted eyes to focus, but the letters blur together, weaving a cruel tapestry of conclusions I do not wish to accept.

Trauma.

Brain swelling.

Cognitive decline.

Mood instability.

I have read these texts a hundred times, searching—pleading—for something more than cold observations. For something more than detached medical theories that diagnose but do not heal.

But the words remain the same.

And the man I love remains lost to me.

I press my fingers against my temples, willing away the dull ache that has become a companion in these endless nights of study. Odin's injury should have been a tragedy overcome. A battle won, another story of resilience to be told.

But it is not.

It is a wound that festers. A sickness that infects not just him—but everything he touches.

The firebrand I married is gone.

What remains is not a man, but embers. Smoldering, waiting—not to warm, but to consume.

I swallow hard, gripping the edges of the tome before me, my knuckles white.

The physicians say that head wounds can change a man. That an injury such as his can turn the gentlest heart to stone, the sharpest mind to ruin. That the pieces of a man do not always come back together as they were before.

But Odin was never gentle.

His mind was never stable.

What, then, has this injury done? Has it damaged him? Or has it merely stripped away the last of his charm and inhibition?

I stare at the pages before me, willing them to shift, to offer a cure hidden between the lines.

Something to bring him back to me.

I have tried to reason with him. To guide him. To remind him of the man he once was.

But Odin does not listen.

He snaps. He rages. He forgets.

One day, he calls me his salvation. The next, he looks at me as if I am his enemy.

I tell myself it is the injury. That his anger, his paranoia, his thirst for control—it is all a sickness.

But deep down, I fear I am lying to myself.

I fear that this is not a sickness.

I fear that this is who he has always been.

That the Odin I loved was nothing more than an illusion—a man who could only play at being noble until the weight of a crown, the weight of power, crushed him into something unrecognizable.

A hollow sound echoes through the chamber as I slam the medical tome shut.

The ache in my chest is unbearable. A wound that refuses to heal.

I have been patient. I have endured. I have prayed.

But how much longer can I wait for a ghost to return?

My eyes drift to the small, ornate box resting at the edge of my desk.

The Eternum Relic.

I reach for it without thinking, my fingers tracing the delicate carvings.

With this, I could see.

One glimpse beyond the veil.

I could know if the man I love is ever coming back to me. If the Gods will restore him, or if I am doomed to spend the rest of my days loving a ghost.

I hesitate, my thumb grazing the cool surface of the relic.

One glimpse. That is all it would take.

A coward's act. To demand certainty from the divine when I have already chosen to believe.

And yet—

I am so tired of believing.

My throat tightens. My grip on the relic falters.

What if I look and see nothing?

What if the Gods have already turned their backs?

What if they led me here not to guide me, but to watch me break?

I close my eyes, inhaling sharply.

No.

With trembling fingers, I shove the relic back into its box and snap the lid shut.

If I cannot trust the man beside me, if I cannot trust myself—then I will trust them.

Because I must.

There can be no other answer.

The alternative is too unbearable to face.

I press my forehead against my folded hands, whispering a prayer that I am no longer sure the Gods hear.

Or worse—

That they do, and simply do not answer.

Ashes in the North – Arianna

The fire crackled in the hearth, sending warm flickers of light across the heavy oak table. A spread of parchment, ledgers, and ink pots lay between us, but I found myself staring at the flame instead—watching the way it curled and flickered, consuming everything it touched.

"We're seeing more displaced souls than ever before," Olga murmured, flipping through her notes. "The food banks are holding, but just barely. The shelters are over capacity. Families are arriving with nothing but the clothes on their backs."

I nodded absently, pressing my fingers against the cool surface of my teacup.

"Do we know where they're coming from?"

Olga hesitated. "They don't seem to know themselves. Some from the west, some from the borders… but the only thing anyone agrees on is that it's raiders."

Raiders.

A vague, nameless threat, lurking in the shadows of my kingdom.

I gripped the handle of my cup a little tighter. "Who?"

"That's just it," Olga sighed. "No one knows. No one has seen them. No one has survived long enough to say if they are Lorinian or Zavrosian. Just that they come, take, and vanish."

Yulia, who had been quiet until now, shifted in her chair. She looked hesitant, almost reluctant, but when she spoke, her voice was steady.

"I overheard something troubling at the market this morning," she said.

Olga and I both turned to her.

"There are whispers about a town in the far north. O'Akla. In the Myroska Tundra."

The name sent a faint prickle of familiarity through me. I frowned, waiting.

"They say it was burned to the ground."

Something inside me went still.

"Nothing left but scorched earth and ruin," she continued. "The chief was slain, and his daughters…"

Yulia's voice faltered.

"What happened to them?" I pressed.

Her throat bobbed. "They were found huddled together. Hiding in the cellar of their home."

A strange pressure built behind my ribs.

"Slaughtered mercilessly," she added quietly.

The room felt too warm.

"I can't even imagine their terror. No survivors?" I asked, though I already knew the answer.

Yulia shook her head.

I swallowed, the taste of my tea suddenly bitter.

A town wiped from existence.

A chief murdered.

His daughters, slain in the dark—huddled together in a place they must have believed was safe. I placed myself in their shoes. My heart ached for their final moments. They must have been terrified.

I let out a slow breath, willing the tightness in my chest to ease.

"No one knows who did it?"

“No one," Olga said, eyes wide. "O’Akla’s so far north it’s practically a ghost town in the snow. You don’t raid places like that. There’s no strategic value. Villages like that—you forget they exist. Just snow, ice, and resilience. Defiance against the elements. Nothing worth burning.”

A shiver coiled at the base of my spine.

I forced myself to sit up straighter, to focus.

"Then we’ll do what we can," I said firmly. "More supplies, more shelters, more resources. Whatever it takes."

Olga nodded, already reaching for her quill.

Yulia exhaled softly. "A tragedy," she murmured, shaking her head. "To be wiped away like that, with no reason at all."

I didn’t answer.

Because reason or not, no one had stopped it.

And I had the sinking feeling that this was bigger than it seemed.

Ashes and Embers – Arianna

I heard him before I saw him.

The heavy creak of the chamber door. The quiet rustle of discarded clothing. The clink of his belt hitting the floor.

He moved through the dimly lit room like a shadow—not the golden king I married, but something dimmer, something unraveling thread by thread.

I kept my eyes closed, my breath steady, pretending to sleep.

Maybe he would slip into bed and say nothing.

Maybe I could pretend I didn't feel the weight of his absence, even when he was here.

But then—

"You're awake."

His voice was different. Not soft. Not teasing. Not the voice that once whispered devotion into my skin.

I opened my eyes, forcing a small smile. "Barely."

He exhaled, sliding onto the bed beside me, his body warm against mine.

"Long day?" I murmured.

"Mm."

That was it. No elaboration. No detail.

Just that single, empty sound.

I turned my head on the pillow, studying him in the dim candlelight.

Odin had always carried exhaustion well. Even in the early days of our marriage, when ruling had only just begun to weigh on him, he had never let it steal his charm—never let it strip away his irresistible, endless magnetism.

But now—

Now, he looked… worn.

His face was sharper somehow. Hollowed.

His eyes darker. Restless.

The golden boy who once lit up every room he entered was dulling by the day.

"I spoke with Olga and Yulia today," I said carefully. "The food banks are overwhelmed. There's been an increase in displaced families, and—"

"Arianna," he sighed, dragging a hand down his face.

I hesitated.

"What?"

"Nothing." His jaw tensed. "Just—nothing. Continue."

I chewed on the inside of my cheek but went on, watching him carefully.

"Yulia mentioned something about O'Akla."

He stilled.

I swallowed.

"It was burned down. No survivors. The chief and his daughters were slaughtered."

Silence.

I could hear the fire crackling. The wind howling beyond the castle walls.

But Odin said nothing.

"Are you going to do something about it?" I asked finally.

His fingers curled into the sheets.

"What exactly do you expect me to do?"

I blinked. "Find out who did it? Protect the rest of the kingdom?"

His jaw twitched.

"Odin—"

"Gods, Arianna, do you think you're the only one who hears these things?"

I froze.

His voice was sharp, edged with something uglier than frustration.

"Do you think I don't have enough to deal with? That I don't hear every pathetic rumor about every village that gets wiped off the map?"

"Pathetic—?"

"O'Akla is gone." His fingers dug into the sheets. "Burned, erased, finished. And I will not waste my time chasing ghosts."

The words struck harder than they should have.

"They weren't ghosts, Odin. They were people. Our people."

He barked a laugh—short, bitter, almost amused.

"Our people? Gods, you're naive." He finally turned to look at me. And I hated it.

I hated the way his eyes held nothing but exhaustion.

Nothing but resentment.

"You still think like a priestess," he muttered.

The words landed like an insult.

"That's not—"

"That's exactly it, Arianna. You have a weak, tender heart." His lips curled slightly. "You think you can save them all? You can't. You think crying over some burnt-down backwater town will bring them back? It won't."

He exhaled sharply, shaking his head.

"You think I should march soldiers into the woods and dig through ashes for a tragedy that has already happened?" His voice dropped lower, sharper. "The dead cannot be saved. Learn that now."

I stared at him.

"You've changed," I said before I could stop myself.

Silence.

Odin didn't move, didn't sigh, didn't even breathe for a moment.

Then—he laughed.

Quiet. Low. Like I had just said something tragically amusing.

"You always say that," he murmured, shaking his head slightly. "Every time you don't get your way."

I blinked. "That's not what I—"

"It is."

His fingers traced a slow line down my arm, deliberate, indulgent.

"You think I don't notice?" His voice softened, dropping into something soothing, patient, dangerous. "How you pout when I don't do exactly as you wish? How your love turns cold the moment I disappoint you?"

A slow breath. His hand curled around mine, bringing it to his lips in mock reverence.

"How selfish of me," he murmured, lips brushing my knuckles. "For thinking my wife would understand the burdens I carry."

My stomach twisted.

"That's not fair."

"Isn't it?" He turned my hand over, palm facing up, studying it like it held the answer to something only he could see.

"I am drowning in responsibility, in war, in the weight of a kingdom that will crush me if I misstep. And my queen—" His thumb brushed my wrist, just over my pulse. "The one who swore to stand beside me—"

A pause.

"Spends her days worrying over beggars."

A lump formed in my throat.

"Odin—"

"Tell me, Arianna." His fingers tightened, just slightly. "What is it you want from me?"

"I want you to protect your people."

A sharp inhale, like I had cut him. Like I had wounded him.

"Oh, I see." A humorless chuckle. "So I am failing you."

I froze.

"That's what you think, isn't it?" His eyes flickered, sharp and piercing. "That I'm not good enough. That I should do more. That if only you were ruling instead of me, things would be better."

"That's not what I—"

"But it is." He leaned in, breath brushing my ear, his voice so soft, so intimate, I barely registered the edge beneath it.

"Tell me, my love. Have you convinced yourself you are the only one who cares for this kingdom?"

My heart slammed against my ribs.

"That's not what I—"

"Because it certainly sounds like it."

His fingers moved to my jaw, tilting my face up to meet his.

"You have always been too soft. Too tender. It was charming, at first."

His thumb brushed over my lips, mocking, gentle.

"But now?" A soft hum. "Now, it's a distraction."

I tried to pull away.

He didn't let me.

"You run around the city like a street healer, wasting your days with the poor, listening to the cries of peasants instead of fulfilling your duty as my wife."

"You let them fill your head with sorrow, with stories, with weakness."

His other hand slid to the back of my neck.

"And you let it make you ungrateful."

A sick feeling clawed at my stomach.

"I'm not—"

"No?" His grip tightened—just barely. Enough to hold me there. Enough to remind me who he was.

"Then tell me." His lips ghosted over my forehead.

"What have I done to deserve a wife who doubts me?"

The words curled around my throat like silk and steel.

"I haven't changed, Arianna." His breath ghosted against my skin.

"But maybe you have."

Silence.

Cold. Unyielding.

The silence after his words was worse than the cruelty itself. Because it left room for me to believe them.

I couldn't breathe.

"Perhaps," he murmured, pulling away, his voice dropping to a hum of cruel amusement, "I should have married a woman with a stronger heart."

The candlelight stretched his shadow across the wall—too long, too dark, swallowing everything in its reach.

"You should stop wasting your time with your little food banks," he murmured, brushing his fingers through my hair like he was soothing a restless child. "If you want something to cry over, cry over that."

My stomach turned.

"Odin—"

"No, you will listen to me." His hand curled around the back of my neck—not harsh, but not gentle. "You spend your days running around the city, pretending to be a moral heroine, playing savior to people who will never repay you."

His breath was warm against my skin.

"And for what? To feel righteous? To feel important?" He pulled back just enough to meet my eyes.

"Your place is here, beside me. That is your duty. Not feeding beggars."

My heart pounded in my ears.

"I won't stop my work," I said quietly.

Odin studied me for a moment.

Then—he smirked.

"I could put an end to it, you know."

The words sent an icy ripple through my spine.

"But I won't."

His fingers traced my jaw, slow, almost indulgent.

"You may keep playing the little heroine for now."

He released me, exhaling like this conversation had exhausted him.

"Just stay out of my affairs, and I will stay out of yours."

And then, just like that—he rolled onto his back. Conversation over.

Like he hadn't just ripped something out of me.

Like I wasn't lying there, staring at the ceiling, wondering if I really was the problem.

But the unease coiled deep in my chest, refusing to leave.

Odin had always been passionate. Reckless.

But now…

Now, he was something else. Something I was afraid to name.

S.O.S. Declined – Arianna

The torches burned low in the grand council chamber, their flickering light casting eerie, distorted shadows against the cold stone walls. The scent of burning wax thickened the air, mingling with something stale. Something rotting.

It took me a moment to name it.

Fear.

Not mine. Theirs.

I stood at the head of the long oak table, hands pressed flat against the carved wood, as if grounding myself would keep the world from tilting. Five men sat before me—Artyom, Boris, Nikolai, Konstantin, and Zakhar—the most powerful lords of the realm. The ones who had the power to stop a tyrant. The ones who, for a fleeting moment, I had believed would help me.

But I should have known the moment I entered the room.

They weren't concerned. They weren't anxious. They weren't even listening.

They were waiting.

Waiting to be entertained.

Waiting for me to beg.

Artyom, slouched in his chair, smirked behind his goblet. Boris exchanged a glance with Konstantin, something amused flickering between them. Nikolai, lazy and uninterested, tapped his fingers against the wood in a slow, rhythmic beat, as if counting down the moments until this would be over.

Only Zakhar watched me closely, his reptilian gaze half-lidded, calculating. Measuring.

My stomach turned.

This was not a meeting. This was an execution.

But I didn't let them see my doubt. My fear. I kept my voice steady.

"Gentlemen," I began, my tone sharp as a blade, "I have asked you here today because we are facing a crisis. My husband, our King, is not himself. You have seen it. The cruelty. The paranoia. The erratic temper." My fingers curled into the table's edge. "You cannot deny it."

Silence.

And then—

A chuckle. Low. Amused.

I turned sharply. Nikolai shook his head, his smirk widening. "Men change when faced with hardship, Your Majesty. Perhaps the King is merely… adapting."

A slow prickle crawled down my spine.

Adapting.

The word twisted in my gut like something poisonous.

Adapting was learning to walk again.
Adapting was struggling with memory.
Adapting was not executing a man for spilling wine.
Adapting was not letting raiders burn an entire village and slaughtering innocent women.
Adapting was not becoming something unrecognizable.

Something monstrous.

I inhaled sharply. "Adapting?" I echoed, my fury igniting like flame to oil.

Nikolai averted his gaze.

Boris sighed, waving a dismissive hand. "With all due respect, Your Majesty, you are his wife." He dragged out the word as though it was an inconvenience. A burden. "You are emotional about this. Give him time. Surely, he will return to his senses."

Emotional.

The word struck deep.

They thought I was hysterical.

A soft laugh rippled through the chamber.

Konstantin leaned forward, his smile carved from cruelty. "Perhaps, my Queen, you should focus your energy on something more productive. A new embroidery project, perhaps?"

Laughter.

Laughter at my expense.

Laughter, when my husband was slipping further into madness by the day.

Laughter, when people were dying.

Laughter, when I had come here as a Queen pleading for the kingdom, and they saw nothing but a stupid, emotional woman.

The room tilted.

I gripped the table, my nails biting into the wood. A slow, terrible realization slithered through me, cold and suffocating.

This isn't ignorance.

This is complicity.

They had already decided.

They would do nothing.

I swallowed the bile rising in my throat. "Do not patronize me." My voice was low, deadly. It cut through the room, through their laughter, through their arrogance. "I am not some court lady prattling about frivolous gossip. I am telling you that this kingdom is in danger."

Zakhar studied me. Unblinking. Waiting.

And then he tilted his head, exhaling slowly.

"And what would you have us do, Your Majesty?" he murmured. "Strip him of his crown? Place you on the throne in his stead?"

The words slammed into me.

I didn't want his crown. I wanted the man who had once worn it with honor.

It felt like a noose tightening. A blade at my throat.

A trap.

They thought I wanted the throne.

They thought I was the problem.

Not Odin.

Not the blood on his hands.

Not the way he was ripping the kingdom apart at its seams.

They thought I was the threat.

A new kind of horror seeped into my bones.

I was not dealing with men who were too blind to see Odin's decline.

I was dealing with men who would let him burn everything before they would ever challenge his rule.

Artyom rubbed his temples, sighing as though this had been an unfortunate inconvenience. "The King is fine," he muttered. "He needs time to adjust to his new reality."

And then his eyes locked onto mine. Cold. Unyielding.

"Go home, Your Majesty. Tend to your husband as a good wife should."

The air left my lungs.

That was it.

That was all they had to say.

I had come here begging for help. Pleading for my husband's soul. For my kingdom's survival.

And they had laughed in my face.

A terrible, crushing silence filled the chamber.

The walls closed in.

I had no allies.

No protection.

No hope.

I was alone.

Utterly. Completely. Alone.

My pulse pounded in my ears, loud enough to drown out the crackling torches, loud enough to mask the sound of my own breaking heart.

Slowly, I pushed back my chair, the scrape of wood against stone the only sound in the vast chamber.

I did not bow. I did not thank them.

I only stared.

And when I spoke, my voice was hollow.

"You are all blind."

No one moved.

No one spoke.

I let my gaze sweep over them, memorizing their faces. These men who could have stopped a tyrant but chose cowardice instead.

"Your ignorance," I whispered, "will doom us all."

And then, without another word, I turned and walked out.

I did not run.

I did not cry.

I did not let them see me falter.

But inside, something cracked.

Something broke.

And as the chamber doors slammed shut behind me, I knew—

There was no saving Odin.

There was no saving this kingdom.

There was only survival.

And I would have to find it somewhere else.

A Widow to a Living Man – Arianna

I barely made it down the corridor before a pair of steel-clad guards stepped into my path.

The Royal Guard.

Alexey's men.

The best of the best—handpicked, battle-hardened, trained for unwavering discipline.

The men sworn to protect the kingdom—not just the king.

But their loyalty?

That was the dangerous part.

They were sworn to Odin.

But they followed Alexey.

And in the moments where the king's orders clashed with their commander's judgment…

Some of them hesitated.

My breath caught.

This wasn't a coincidence.

Something was wrong.

One of them took a measured step forward, his polished gauntlet pressed against his breastplate in salute.

"The King has requested your presence, Your Majesty."

The world tilted.

He knows what I have done.

The realization struck like a slap across the face.

I knew the council would betrayed me but the speed of the betrayal left me reeling.

I had felt it in the air, in their cowardly silence, in the way their gazes darted away when I pleaded for them to act.

They had fed into Odin's paranoia, let it fester unchecked. And now…

Now the axe had fallen on me.

I forced my shoulders back, my chin high, willing my voice to remain steady.

"Then I will not keep my husband waiting."

The guards exchanged a glance.

It was the barest flicker—just a fraction of hesitation—but I saw it.

They knew.

Perhaps they had heard the rage seething behind the doors of the council chamber, had caught the whispers that slithered through the halls like snakes in the dark.

Perhaps Alexey had sent them to ensure I was not taken by rougher hands.

Either way, they would not speak.

They would not warn me.

Because they were soldiers first.

And Odin was still their king.

I followed them, my feet moving mechanically, my mind barely registering the gilded halls as they blurred past me. My hands, trembling, had somehow found themselves clenched into white-knuckled fists at the front of my skirts.

The throne room doors slammed open with a force that sent a violent shudder through my ribs.

I knew before I even stepped inside that this was different.

This was not Odin's usual anger. This was not one of his infamous moods, the storms I had learned to endure, to weather, to soothe.

This was something else.

Something final.

The air was thick—poisoned.

I barely made it two steps before the doors slammed shut behind me and bounced back open.

The sound rang through the cavernous hall like the swing of an executioner's axe.

I inhaled slowly, my fingers tightening in the folds of my gown as I lifted my chin.

Odin stood in the center of the room, bathed in the flickering light of the torches. The fire turned his golden hair into something molten, something unnatural.

He did not look like my husband.

He looked like a man preparing for war.

And I was his enemy.

His lips curled in something that was not a smile.

"My treacherous little wife," he murmured.

The words sent an icy prickle down my spine.

I kept my voice even. "What have I done to anger you so?"

His laugh was cold, sharp as shattered glass.

"You tell me," he said. "Tell me what you've done, Arianna. Tell me why I have councilmen whispering in my ear that my queen—the woman I plucked from the temple and placed beside me—is plotting against me."

A sick feeling curdled in my stomach.

"I have done no such thing, Odin."

Odin took a slow, measured step forward.

"Liar. You're nothing but a lying bitch."

My breath caught. I flinched at the insult.

"You went behind my back," he seethed. "You sought my counsel—my men—to challenge my rule. To paint me as weak. To turn them against me."

His voice was escalating. Uncontrolled. Erratic.

"You," he spat, "the woman I gave everything to. The woman who should be kneeling at my feet in gratitude."

The words hit like a slap, but the true blow came next.

"You wanted power," he sneered. "You married me for it. You latched onto me, like a greedy little leech, hungry for a throne you do not deserve."

I stepped back before I could stop myself.

Odin's eyes gleamed. He saw it. He liked it.

I swallowed hard, forcing myself to hold his gaze. "That is not true."

His lips curled. "Isn't it?"

I shook my head. "No. I married you because I love you. I only want what is best for you. For us. For Lorna."

Something flickered in his eyes.

And then—he laughed.

A deep, cruel laugh, thick with contempt.

"You loved me?"

The way he said it made my stomach twist.

"Do not insult me," he hissed. "You were a foolish little priestess, blinded by your own arrogance. You thought you could mold me into something divine—into a god in your image. The perfect husband. The perfect king."

His lip curled, his golden eyes burning with something rotten and monstrous.

"But I was never enough for you, was I? Not even a king could reach the heights of your expectations."

His voice dropped lower, crueler.

"Not even a god."

His smirk widened, mockery curling at the edges.

"But the Gods don't favor you anymore, do they, Arianna?"

I inhaled sharply. "Odin—"

"They don't hear you," he cut me off. "They don't see you. You were meant to be my queen. Fated to be mine."

He leaned in, lowering his voice to something slow and merciless.

"And you ruined it."

My chest caved inward.

I felt it then—the last vestiges of the man I loved slipping away.

This wasn't Odin.

This was something darker.

Something rotting beneath the skin.

He now stood so close to me I could smell the wine on rolling off his being.

"You were supposed to stand beside me. You were supposed to be my equal. And what do you do?"

His breath was warm on my face, his voice vicious, venomous.

"You waste your days feeding beggars."

My stomach turned.

"You think the poor matter?" he sneered. "You think the weak deserve your mercy? You coddle them like children, as if that will change anything."

His expression twisted.

"You want to play saint, Arianna?" he whispered. "Then do it somewhere else. I warned you to stay out of my affairs and I would stay out of yours."

A pause. A smirk.

"You are no longer permitted to run your little charity projects."

The words took a moment to sink in.

I stared at him, my lips parting, the weight of his decree pressing down like an iron brand.

"What?"

"You heard me," he said smoothly. "It ends today. The food banks. The shelters. The gold you squander on them. Consider it my punishment for your betrayal."

I took a step forward before I could stop myself. "No, please, Odin. You can't—"

His hand shot out.

Fingers wrapped around my throat.

I froze.

The silence roared.

"Do not tell me what I can and cannot do. You have no say in this," he whispered.

The room was spinning.

"Do you hear that?" he murmured, tilting his head slightly, his fingers still crushing.

I gasped. "Odin—"

"Shh," he whispered. "Listen."

His grip tightened. My hands clawed at his instinctually.

The edges of my vision darkened.

And then—he released me.

I stumbled, choking on air.

Odin exhaled slowly, watching me.

"Now do you understand?" he asked softly. "You are nothing without me."

I lifted my trembling hand to my throat.

Tears blurred my vision.

My voice was a rasp, barely there. "You don't love me anymore, do you?"

I hadn't meant to say it outloud.

Odin's golden eyes flickered.

For a moment, I thought—hoped—he might hesitate.

He didn't.

He smiled.

"No."

I hurled myself into his arms like a prayer cast into a storm.

Clung to him—tight, desperate—like my embrace could drag his soul back from the edge.

Like warmth alone could banish the devil already seated in his chest.

But he didn't reach for me.

He didn't even flinch.

And that's when I knew—

I was hugging a ghost,

and the man I loved was already gone.

Then—

He struck me.

The world fractured with the sound.

My vision splintered.

My breath caught.

The floor rose up to meet me like a wave crashing through glass.

I tasted copper.

Salt.

Shock.

I didn't cry out.

Didn't scream.

Didn't move.

I just lay there—

cold stone beneath me,

the echo of his hand still burning in my skin like a brand.

And when I looked up—

he was already turning away.

No apology.

No horror.

No hesitation.

Just silence.

And in that silence,

I understood.

The man I loved was gone.

What stood in his place

was something else entirely.

Something I would never reach again.

"You disgust me," he whispered.

"Get out of my sight."

I didn't move.

I couldn't.

My body wasn't mine.

My thoughts were snowblind.

But then—

a shift in the air.

A shadow in the doorway.
A figure limned in firelight.
Alexey.
Stillness wrapped him like armor.
But I saw it—
the tension in his jaw,
the coiled restraint in his stance,
the way his men—
his men, not Odin's—
began to move.
One stepped toward the door.
A barrier.
A quiet rebellion.
A line in the sand.
Odin didn't notice.
Too lost in his victory.
Too busy basking in the wreckage of me.
But Alexey saw.
He always saw.
And then—
he stepped forward.
"King Odin," he said, smooth as steel.
"I'll take care of this."
Detached. Controlled. Lethal in his calm.
Odin waved him off like a servant.
"Yes, yes—get her out of my sight."
He had no idea.
No idea what he'd just lost.
I saw the loyalty die in Alexey's ice cold eyes.

Alexey's men moved like clockwork.
One knelt beside me—
hands careful, reverent, not rough.
And as they lifted me—
as the room spun and my limbs betrayed me—
Alexey picked me up to carry me.
Then I realized something.
I had not fallen.
I had been caught.
I did not look back.
I couldn't.
If I saw him again, I might shatter completely.
But Alexey did.
And the look he gave Odin—
cold, fathomless, final—
Was the beginning of the end.

As I curled against Alexey's chest as he flew through the corridors, I could feel the magnificent, restrained power crackling beneath layers of muscle. I knew nothing would ever be the same again.

To Shield a Queen – Alexey

Arianna is in my arms.

Too light. Too fragile. Too still.

Her body folds against my chest, weightless—thinner than she should be, thinner than I remember. She was always delicate, but never like this. Never frail. She used to carry herself like a queen in every sense of the word, with a spine of iron and a gaze that could shatter a man's composure. But now—now she is something lesser.

A ghost of herself.

A woman being consumed.

Odin did this to her.

The thought curdles like bile in my stomach, but I shove it down, my arms tightening around her as I storm through the castle halls.

The servants see us.

They gasp. They scatter. They jump out of my way as if I am a storm about to break over them—and maybe I am.

Maybe the cracks are showing.

They do not ask what happened.

Because they already know.

I feel their eyes, their hushed whispers nipping at my heels like scavengers circling fresh kill. But I do not stop. I do not slow.

I cannot.

Because if I do—if I let myself feel too much—I might lose my mind.

She does not sob.

She does not rage.

She does not fight me.

And that is somehow so much worse.

The Arianna I knew was made of fire, of unshakable will, of too-bright eyes and sharp words and laughter that could cut through the darkest night. She was a force—wild, untamed, alive.

But this Arianna?

She is silent.

She is empty.

And I cannot fix it.

The words tear through me like a blade. I have spent my life fixing Odin's mistakes. I have pulled him from battlefields, cleaned up the wreckage of his recklessness, buried his sins so deep no one would ever find them.

But this?

This, I cannot fix.

And for a man like me—a man who builds, who repairs, who protects—that is unbearable.

We reach her chambers. I shove the door open, step inside, and kick it closed behind me, the heavy thud echoing like a gavel in a silent court.

She does not flinch.

She does not look at me.

And it is that—not Odin, not the slap, not the goddamn madness unraveling the kingdom at the seams—that nearly breaks me.

I do not let her go.

I should.

Gods, I should.

But I cannot.

I can feel her warmth through the thin silk of her gown, feel the tremble in her fingers, the way her breath is shallow, barely there.

A memory slams into me—her laughter, sharp and wicked, teasing me across the card table that first summer at court. The way she tilted her head, all amusement and challenge, as if she could pick me apart just for the fun of it.

That woman is gone.

And Odin did not just kill her—he buried her beneath his crown.

"Sit," I say, my voice rough. Low. A command. A plea.

She obeys.

Not because I told her to.

Because she has nothing left.

I watch her sink onto the edge of the bed, her shoulders slumping, her hands folding into her lap like she is trying to disappear into herself.

She is still staring at the floor, as if she cannot bear to look at me.

I inhale slowly, force myself to move. The washbasin in the corner of the room is filled with clean water, a fresh cloth draped over the edge.

I cross the room, soak the cloth, squeeze it out, and kneel before her.

She does not react.

Not when I lift the damp cloth to her bruised cheek, not when I gently dab at the reddened skin, not even when my fingers brush against her jaw, tilting her face toward me.

Her breath hitches—just slightly.

I should be careful.

I should pull away.

But I don't—not while she leans like this.

Because I can feel her pulse hammering beneath my fingertips.

Because I can see her lips part just slightly, her gaze locked onto mine, searching. Needing.

Her breath trembles against my skin.

She is not mine to touch.

Not mine to protect.

Not mine to love.

And yet—

I want her.

I want her more than I have ever wanted anything.

I should pull away.

But I don't.

Not yet.

Because she is leaning toward me—barely, but enough.

Just enough to make the air between us like the breath between a spark and the blaze.

And for one dangerous, reckless second—

I think I'm going to kiss her.

Gods, I want to.

Just once.

To feel what it's like.

To taste the curve of a fate I was never meant to have.

To press my mouth to hers and pretend—for the span of a breath—that none of this is real.

That she is not a queen.

That I am not sworn to her husband.
That we are just a man and a woman standing in the space between ruin and something that might have been love.

But I don't move.

Because if I do—if I touch her—I don't know if I'll be able to let go.
And I will not be the one to break her.
Not when she's already unraveling.
Not when I'm fraying at the edges with her.

I pull away.

Too fast.

Too harsh.

Like tearing myself from flame.

She flinches at the loss of my touch.

My entire body is rigid, trembling, burning.

If I do not leave now, I will not leave at all.

"You should rest," I say, my voice rough, broken.

Her lips part, like she wants to say something—my name, maybe, or something softer, something that will ruin me completely—

And for half a heartbeat—

I think I will go back to her.

That I will touch her again.

That I will let myself fall.

But instead—

"Don't."

It comes out harsher than I mean it to.

A warning.

A plea.

A line in the sand that I cannot not cross.

Because if I do—

I will never come back.

I force myself to turn on my heel and leave, the door closing behind me—

Locking her away from me.

Or maybe—

Locking me away from her.

A Commander's Sin – Alexey

Odin is gone.

Not dead.

But gone.

And I am tired of mourning him.

Tired of holding space for a ghost.

Tired of watching his shadow swallow everything in its path.

Tired of pretending I don't want what he abandoned.

I close my eyes, and all I see is her.

The way she whispered my name, soft and breathless, like she wasn't sure if she was allowed to want this.

To want me.

But Gods, she is allowed.

Because I am hers.

I have always been hers.

And tonight, I am done pretending otherwise.

To hell with it.

To hell with all of it.

I return to her.

I don't walk to her.

I stalk to her.

Arianna stands before me, bathed in firelight, the silk of her gown slipping from her shoulders, barely clinging to her curves.

She is already mine.

Her hair is a wildfire, spilling down her back in untamed waves, catching the light like molten copper, auburn, gold—every shade of the fire incarnate.

Barefoot, breathless, burning.

Her gown slips down one shoulder—soft silk, too fragile for her fire. Her eyes catch mine, shimmering green and gold like a forest at dusk, like home.

She doesn't speak. She doesn't need to.

I feel her in every part of me.

Every breath.

Every scar.

Every wound I never let heal.

I step forward, slow, deliberate. Like a man approaching something sacred.

Because she is sacred.

She is a prayer I was never meant to speak out loud.

And yet I've already damned myself by loving her.

I want to taste every part of her until she is written into my bones.

"Arianna," I whisper.

My voice is hoarse. Wrecked.

Like I've been carrying her name in my mouth for too long.

She doesn't answer with words. Just a slow step forward. A soft, fragile inhale.

Her lips part.

Her eyes drop to my chest.

Her hands rise—hesitant, trembling—and press flat against my heart.

I cover them with mine. Not to hold her in place.

To show her she is safe.

Always safe with me.

She looks up.

The wall between us fractures. Shatters.

And when she leans in—just slightly, just enough—

I catch her.

I tilt her chin and kiss her like she's the only thing that matters in this broken world.

And she kisses me back like she's afraid I'll vanish.

There's no hunger in it. No taking.

Only giving.

Only knowing.

My hands trace the arch of her back, the line of her waist. I press my lips to the inside of her wrist.

To her palm.

To the pulse at her throat.

"I will never hurt you," I breathe.

She trembles.

Her eyes glisten—but she doesn't look away.

And when I carry her to the bed, I do it like a vow.

Like every step is a promise I will not break her.

I lay her down carefully.

Gently.

Like she's something I'm trying to rebuild from ash.

She lets me take her gown.

She lets me undress her inch by inch, not because I demand it—but because she trusts me to see her.

The Gods took their time creating her—and I will take mine worshiping her.

She is glorious.

Every freckle.

Every curve.

The softness of her belly.

The dip of her hips.

The strong, elegant legs that have walked through fire and still haven't buckled.

I don't rush.

I trace my fingertips along her ribs.

Bury my face in the curve of her neck.

Whisper her name into her skin like absolution.

I kiss down her sternum.

Over her stomach.

Across the inside of her thigh.

She gasps when my tongue meets her center—soft, careful, reverent.

She moans my name—breathless, broken.

I do not stop until she's shaking in my arms.

Until her fingers twist in the sheets.

Until she comes with a cry so raw it shatters me.

I gather her into my lap like she belongs nowhere else.

She touches my face. My jaw. My scars.

I let her.

I want her to see all of me.

"Alexey," she whispers.

Her voice cracks.

I enter her slowly—achingly slow—so she can feel every inch, every part of me that has only ever belonged to her.

She gasps.

I still.

She nods, pulling me closer.

"Don't hold back," she whispers. "Not with me."

So I give her everything.

Every slow, reverent thrust.

Every kiss pressed into her throat, her collarbone, her lips.

Every whispered vow I'm not allowed to make.

I worship her body.

Her strength.

Her fire.

Her softness.

And when she falls apart in my arms again, I follow her into the dark.

Because for once—I am not a commander.

Not a soldier.

Not a fixer.

I am just a man in love.

And—I get to love her right.

The way she was made to be loved.

I hold her after.

Bury my face in her hair.

I breathe in the scent of her so deeply the scent lodges in my bones.

I feel her heartbeat against mine.

For one perfect, stolen moment—

I have her

I can be selfish, just this once—

I have fought the wars.

I have buried my brothers.

I have bled for a kingdom that will never bleed for me.

I have honored my duty.

I have suffered in silence.

I have given everything that I have to give.

The Gods let me have this one thing.

Just this one thing.
Just this once.

Then—
A violent jolt.
The world shatters.
The firelight is gone.
The warmth is gone.
She is gone.

I wake up gasping, drenched in sweat, painfully hard, my heart slamming against my ribs like a caged animal.

For half a second, I am still there.
Still inside her.
Still home.

And then—
Reality comes crashing down.
The cold of my chambers.
The empty bed.
The hollow ache in my chest.

It wasn't real.
It will never be real.
And yet—
I can still feel her.

I wake up wrecked.
Ruined.
Unmade.

Because for one perfect, impossible moment—
I had her.
And now?
Now I have nothing.

I bite back a sound—half a growl, half a groan—and sit up, running both hands through my hair.

The taste of her still lingers on my tongue. The scent of her still clings to my skin.

But it wasn't real.

It will never be real.

Loving Arianna is treason against my King.

But not loving her is treason against my heart.

And I do not know which betrayal is worse.

I throw the sheets off and force myself to stand, to move, to breathe.

Because if I stay in this bed, if I let myself close my eyes again—

I will go right back to her.

And I cannot survive that a second time.

The Training Yard – Alexey

I needed to hit something.

Hard.

Again. And again.

Until my arms gave out.

Until my muscles burned.

Until my mind—traitorous, unruly thing that it was—stopped betraying me.

Because this?

This was unbearable.

The dream still clung to me like smoke, the phantom of her touch searing my skin, burning through my veins like a sickness.

Every gasp.

Every whispered plea.

The way she had come undone beneath me—it had felt real.

Too real.

I gritted my teeth and drove my fist into the training dummy, the impact rattling up my arm.

Again.

And again.

Faster.

Harder.

I would sweat it out.

I would beat it out.

I would bleed it out if I had to.

Because if I didn't—

If I let myself think of her—

"Alexey, you absolute mess of a man."

I didn't stop.

Didn't turn.

Didn't acknowledge him.

But Murphy?

Murphy was not a man who took a hint.

"Oh-ho. We are in rare form today," he mused, stepping onto the training yard, arms crossed, eyes far too smug. "Does the dummy owe you money? Or did it seduce your wife in a dream?"

My punch landed so hard the wooden post splintered.

Murphy whistled low. "That bad, huh?"

I exhaled sharply, wiped the sweat from my brow, and turned away.

Murphy, however, was already circling me like a predator who had just sniffed out fresh blood.

"You're never out here this early unless you're trying to work through something." He rubbed his chin, mock thoughtful. "And considering you look like a man who just committed treason against his own damn soul, I'm going to take a wild guess and say…"

I slammed my fist into the post again, splintering it further.

Murphy didn't even flinch.

"It's about Arianna, isn't it?"

The dummy snapped in half.

Murphy let out a low whistle.

"Ohhh, it's worse than I thought."

I glared at him. "Murphy—"

"You kissed her, didn't you?"

I froze.

That was all he needed.

Murphy's grin turned downright feral.

"Oh, you did. You finally—"

"I didn't kiss her," I bit out.

Murphy blinked.

"Oh? Then it was something worse, wasn't it?"

I stiffened.

Gods, he was perceptive.

I could dodge a blade. I could outmaneuver an opponent.

But I could never lie to Murphy.

And damn him, he was enjoying this.

"Gods above," Murphy muttered, almost impressed. "You are a legend. You actually did it, didn't you?"

"Murphy—"

"You slept with her."

I snapped my head toward him, scowling.

"I did no such thing."

Murphy studied me.

Too closely.

And then—

I lunged at him.

Murphy dodged gracefully, laughing as he grabbed a training sword off the rack.

"Temper, temper," he chided. "You're usually much more disciplined than this, Alexey. Could it be that our fearless, untouchable knight has finally—"

I swung.

Murphy blocked—still grinning—until I finally snapped.

"How dare you question my honor?"

The words ripped from my throat, raw, furious, breaking through my restraint like a dam bursting.

Murphy's amusement flickered.

I slammed my sword into the training dummy again, splitting the wood completely in half.

"I would never violate my oath as Commander of the Royal Guard," I bit out. "I would never take advantage of her. Do you think so little of me?"

Murphy's grin faded. Just a little.

Then came something quieter—something more knowing.

"That's not what I meant," he said, rolling his shoulders.

"I know you wouldn't. But, Alexey—" He let out a slow exhale, watching me carefully.

"You love her," he said quietly. Not smug. Not teasing. Just… true.

I said nothing.

Because that was the problem, wasn't it?

I hadn't kissed her.

I hadn't taken her.

I hadn't acted on anything.

But Gods help me, I wanted to.

Murphy knew it.

And then—

Silence.

The truth sat between us, unspoken, unbearable.

And Murphy, being Murphy, had the audacity to smirk.

"Yeah," he murmured. "That's what I thought."

I turned back to the splintered remains of the dummy, grabbed my sword, and took out my frustration the only way I could.

Murphy sighed—exasperated, but still thoroughly entertained.

"Gods, if only Arianna knew what she was doing to you."

That was it. This conversation was over.

I drove forward, pushing him back, our swords clashing in the crisp morning air.

Murphy's expression shifted.

Still amused—

But also intrigued.

"There he is," he murmured, adjusting his stance. "That's what I'm talking about. Welcome back."

We sparred in silence, our movements automatic, practiced, rhythmic.

And for a brief, blessed second—

My mind was clear.

No thoughts.

No longing.

No fire beneath my skin.

Just the sound of steel against steel.

"You know," Murphy mused, ducking away from a swing, "you could just talk to her. That's a thing people do, Alexey. You could always use your words."

I didn't respond.

"Or—" he twisted, narrowly avoiding my next strike, "—you could keep doing… this. Brooding. Torturing yourself for no reason. Pretending you're fine when you're very, very not fine."

I finally landed a hit, slamming my blade against his, knocking him off balance.

"I AM fine."

Murphy laughed.

"Yeah? Tell that to your bleeding fists."

I exhaled sharply, stepping back, lowering my sword.

This was pointless.

Murphy knew it.

I knew it.

"Look," Murphy sighed, raking a hand through his damp hair. "I'll leave it alone—"

I knew he would not.

"—but at least admit it to yourself, Alexey."

I crossed my arms. "Admit what?"

"That you want her."

I clenched my jaw.

Murphy sighed dramatically.

"Fine. Be difficult. But one day—maybe tomorrow, maybe a month from now, maybe years down the line—"

He was enjoying this too much.

"—you are going to snap. And I am going to be there to say I told you so."

I rolled my eyes. "Can't wait."

Murphy clapped a hand on my shoulder. Mock sympathy.

"Try not to suffer too much today, my friend."

And then—

"Oh, and Alexey?"

I turned.

"If you ever need to get her out of your system—"

"Murphy."

"—try something colder than guilt."

Queen's Gambit Declined – Alexey

I stared at the wall.

The candlelight flickered against the evidence of my service—the gilded medals, the awards of honor, the relics of battles I had fought and won.

Proof that I was a man of discipline.

A man of restraint.

A man of honor.

And yet—

My jaw tightened.

Where was the honor in this?

Because it had blurred—no, it had shattered—the moment she looked at me like she did last night.

The moment I dreamed of her—felt her in my arms, in my bed, breathless beneath me.

I had always been a man of control.

But control was slipping through my fingers.

Then—

A knock.

I knew before I opened it.

I should have turned her away.

I should have told her no.

But I didn't.

The air left my lungs.

Arianna stood in the dim candlelight, her auburn hair loose, cascading over her shoulders like fire licking its way through the darkness.

A warning. A reckoning. A wildfire that burned through snow and flesh alike.

The silk of her gown clung to her, delicate straps slipping down her shoulders as if they were daring me to touch.

She was breathtaking.

She was my damnation.

I clenched my jaw.

"Your Majesty." My voice was clipped. Controlled. A warning.

She arched a perfect brow.

"So formal," she mused, stepping inside without invitation. Without hesitation. Without fear.

She moved like she belonged here, in my space. Like she belonged to me.

I stepped back, jaw tight, arms folded over my chest. "What do you want?"

Arianna shut the door behind her, slow and deliberate, sealing us inside. She leaned against it, blocking my escape like a cat cornering its prey.

"You've been avoiding me," she said simply.

I exhaled sharply, forcing myself to look at anything that wasn't her.

"I have been busy."

She let out a quiet, almost amused hum, tilting her head. Assessing me. Studying me.

Like she always did—like she could peel back the layers of my restraint and sift through the wreckage beneath.

"Liar," she murmured.

I remained still. Unmoving.

She took a step forward.

"I think we should talk."

"There is nothing to talk about."

She huffed a soft laugh, shaking her head.

"You never were a good liar, Alexey. At least, not with me."

I clenched my jaw and turned away.

She followed.

"You won't even look at me," she pressed. "Is it because of last night?"

I exhaled through my nose.

Last night.

She thought I was avoiding her because we had almost kissed.

If only she knew the truth.

If only she knew I was one whispered plea from ruin.

"You regret it, don't you?"

I stared at the ground, exhaling sharply. "You are married, Arianna."

Silence.

Then—

A scoff. Soft. Bitter.

"Married?" she repeated, and there was something cold and cruel in her laughter.

She stepped forward, voice sharpened with something dangerous.

"Do you think that means something anymore?"

My entire body locked.

"He said it himself, Alexey." Her voice dropped lower, thick with something I didn't want to name. "He doesn't love me anymore."

Her eyes flickered up to mine, burning, pleading.

"He took everything from me. My work. My purpose. My faith. My—" Her breath hitched. "Everything."

A step closer.

"He is dead to me. He doesn't want me, Alexey."

Another step.

"But you do."

I exhaled sharply, my chest rising and falling too fast. "Stop."

She ignored me.

Another step.

Too close.

"Odin said I was a disappointment to the Gods," she whispered, her voice shaking, but her hands? Steady.

She reached for me.

Fingertips ghosting over my forearm.

A brush of warmth.

Soft. Barely there.

But it might as well have been a dagger to my throat,

I flinched.

She should have pulled away. Gods, I should have.

"Tell me, Alexey." Her breath was a ghost over my lips, warm and laced with something devastating. "If I have already fallen from grace, why shouldn't I fall into you?"

Gods.

I grabbed her wrist before I could stop myself, my grip tight, shaking.

She gasped.

Not in fear.

In triumph.

Because she knew.

She saw it.

The crack in my composure.

The ruin beneath my restraint.

She tilted her head, lips parting, eyes searching, drinking me in, devouring every inch of my undoing.

"You're shaking," she murmured, voice barely above a whisper. "Why is that?"

I exhaled sharply, releasing her like she burned me.

"Go," I said, my voice hoarse, raw, ruined.

She didn't move.

She should have.

She should have run.

But instead—

She leaned in.

So close I could feel the heat of her body against mine.

"No one would ever have to know, Alexey."

Her lips—too close, too soft, too much.

She was trying to destroy me.

And Gods help me, I wanted to let her.

Then—

She was gone.

And I—

I was left to burn.

Willowbrook or Will I Break – Alexey

I needed to leave.

Not tomorrow.

Not in a few days.

Now.

Before I lost the last of my restraint.

Before she sought me out again with those pleading eyes and quiet justifications, wearing sin and desperation like a second skin.

Before I made the biggest mistake of my life.

My hands still trembled as I stormed through the halls, every muscle wound tight, every nerve thrumming. I could still feel her.

The ghost of her fingertips on my jaw.

The way her breath mingled with mine when she whispered—

"No one would ever have to know, Alexey."

I gritted my teeth, shoving the thought out of my mind.

Murphy.

Murphy would understand.

Murphy would know what to do.

I barely knocked before I was shoving my way into his quarters, locking the door behind me.

Murphy looked up from his seat—saw my face—

And immediately dropped the dagger he'd been sharpening.

"Damn it, Alexey."

He sat up straighter, his usual smugness erased in an instant.

"Shit. What happened?"

I exhaled sharply. My throat was tight. My pulse still thrummed with adrenaline.

"Arianna came to my chambers tonight."

Silence.

Murphy's eyes widened—for the first time in a long time, he actually looked unsettled.

"The queen came to your chambers?"

I nodded.

Murphy ran a hand down his face. "Tell me everything."

I hesitated. Then—

"She said Odin is dead."

Murphy blinked. "He's not."

"She meant it in spirit." I met his gaze, my voice hollow. "She said that he doesn't love her anymore—"

I exhaled sharply.

Murphy's expression darkened. "Alexey. Tell me she didn't—"

"She begged me to cross the line."

Murphy's jaw locked. His grip on the dagger tightened.

"And?"

I forced my shoulders to stay loose, to stop shaking.

She said she had already fallen from grace," I continued. "Why couldn't she fall into me?

Murphy stilled.

His usual amusement was gone.

His voice came quieter now, measured. "And then?"

I let out a bitter laugh. "And then she told me no one had to ever know."

Murphy let out a long, slow breath through his nose, dragging a hand through his hair.

I shook my head, my throat tight. "She actually tried to goad me into it."

Silence.

Murphy swore under his breath. "And?"

I met his gaze.

"I told her to go, of course."

A beat.

Then—Murphy relaxed. Just slightly.

He let out a breath, gripping the back of his neck. "Good."

I exhaled sharply, my hands clenching into fists. “Murphy, you know what this means. This is not just about two consenting adults."

Murphy nodded grimly. "No. It’s treason. And if anyone finds out—"

My voice dropped.

"We both die."

Murphy didn’t say anything. He didn’t have to. We both knew the weight of it.

The moment stretched, heavy. Unspoken truths lingering between us.

Then, finally—Murphy sighed, rubbing a hand over his face.

"So what’s the plan?"

I swallowed. Then, finally, I said—

“I’m leaving for a week. I’ll be at Willowbrook.”

Murphy’s brows shot up. “You’re leaving?”

I nodded.

"If I stay, she’ll keep pressing. And I—”

I exhaled, raking a hand through my hair.

"Murphy, I can't let one night with her be the reason we never make it out of this castle alive."

Murphy's expression shifted.

Because we both knew—this wasn't just about one night.

One night would be enough to die for treason. One night would never be enough for love.

Murphy studied me, his mouth pressing into a thin line.

"And you think running is going to solve that?"

"No." I looked away. "But it will buy me time to get my head straight."

Murphy sighed, rubbing his temples.

"Alright. You know what? I respect it."

Then, after a beat—

"But if you come back still looking like a man on the brink of total self-destruction, I'm dragging you to the tavern myself, and we're finding you a nice, uncomplicated woman who doesn't know what a royal scandal is."

I shot him a glare. "Murphy—"

"I mean it." Murphy pointed at me. "You need to get this woman out of your system before she gets you killed."

I shook my head, pinching the bridge of my nose. "I'll be fine."

Murphy's eyes narrowed.

"Yeah? Tell that to the vein in your forehead. It's about to explode."

I let out a slow breath, pushing past him toward the door.

I needed to go.

Now.

But Murphy wasn't finished.

He sighed, running a hand through his hair.

"Alright. But Alexey?"

I glanced at him.

Murphy's usual mirth was gone. Instead, his voice was deadly serious.

He stepped closer. Lowered his voice.

"When you come back?"

His grip on my shoulder tightened.

"Be very, very careful."

Something about the way he said it unnerved me.

I didn't need to ask what he meant.

I already knew.

Because this wasn't going to stop.

Not in a week.

Not ever.

I clenched my jaw, stepping away from his grip, my mind already racing ahead to the ride to Willowbrook.

I would clear my head.

I would get her out of my system.

I had to.

Because if I didn't—

It would spell catastrophe for me

Catastrophe for her.

Wistless Amongst the Willows – Alexey

I came here to forget.

To scrub her from my mind like blood from a blade.

To burn her from my system with cold air, hard labor, and discipline so brutal it bordered on punishment.

But no matter how much I try—

No matter how much I fight—

I cannot rid myself of her.

Arianna.

Queen of Lorna.

Wife of my king.

The woman who will be the death of me.

I don't know if she understands what she's doing.

If she knows she is playing with fire.

If she knows she is playing with our lives.

Or if she just delights in control over something—over someone—anyone—because everything else in her world is spiraling beyond her grasp.

Maybe that's it.

Maybe it's not me she wants.

Maybe it's just the power.

Because I have never denied her.

Not her orders.

Not her wishes.

Not her safety.

But I denied her this.

And for the first time in her life—

Arianna did not get what she wanted from me.

I don't know if that should make me feel proud or terrified.

I tell myself she will cool down in my absence. That when I return, she will have come to her senses. That this is temporary.

But I know her too well.

Arianna does not surrender. She is a woman who takes what she wants. A force of nature too stubborn, too reckless, too damn relentless to let go of a challenge once she's set her mind to it.

And that's what I am to her now. A challenge. A game. Something she is determined to win.

But this isn't a game. This is treason.

And if she keeps pushing— If she keeps playing— We will both lose.

Gods, she will be the end of me and make it look easy doing it.

The cold, lifeless, empty halls of Willowbrook bring me solace, but little comfort.

I take pleasure in the things I always have— Early mornings by the river. The stillness of the woods. The crisp bite of the air before sunrise.

The act of fishing, patient and methodical, gives me a reprieve. A quiet ritual of waiting.

Of stillness.

Of control.

Here, I am just a man.

Not a knight.

Not a lord.

Not the Commander of the Royal Guard.

There is no crown here.

No duty.

No queen with wildfire hair and emerald eyes ruining me.

And yet—

Even here, she lingers.

Even as I cast my line into the water.

Even as I gut and clean the fish.

Even as I walk the vast stretch of land that is mine.

I feel her.

The ghost of her fingertips on my jaw.

The way her lips hovered over mine, waiting—asking—before I tore myself away.

The way she said my name.

Not as my queen.

Not as a lover.

But as a dare.

A challenge I was never meant to survive.

Gods.

I squeeze my eyes shut, pressing the heels of my palms against them—

as if I can force the memory away.

But I can't.

It comes back in pieces, visceral and unrelenting.

I stalked toward her—
The way a man who has already lost does—
Driven.

Desperate.

Knowing there was no salvation beyond the ruins.

She was waiting for me there.
Firelight flickering over her bare shoulders.
The silk of her gown slipping from her body, pooling around her feet like spilled ink.

She was perfect.
A goddess.
A fever dream made of flesh and blood.

Her hair, a living flame, spilled down her back, catching the light like molten copper.
Her skin—Gods, her skin.
Soft.
Fair.
Freckled—each mark a kiss from the sun, scattered across her shoulders, her collarbone, the delicate curve of her hip.

The Gods had taken their time crafting her—
And I intended to paint her with my hands with the same reverence.

I do not hesitate.
I do not wait.
I claim.

She gasped—
But not in protest.
In relief.

Like she had been waiting for this as long as I had.

Her hands trembled as she dragged her fingers over every ridged muscle and scar.

Learning me.

Mapping me.

Her lips—soft and sinful—parted against mine, and I drank from them like a dying man.

Desperate.

Starved.

Insatiable.

Like she was mine.

Like she had always been mine.

Gods.

I lost myself when she shattered beneath me—

And for a moment—

Just a moment—

She was mine.

And then—

I woke up.

Alone.

Broken.

My body burning with something I will never have.

A week should have been enough.

I should have been able to clear my mind—to focus—

To return as if nothing had happened.

But I wake in the night, gasping.

Sweating.

My body aching with need.

I spar until my arms shake.

I run until my legs give out.

I drown myself in ice-cold water, trying to freeze the fire of her out of me.

But none of it works.

She is still there.
Lodged inside me like a blade I cannot remove.
Tomorrow, I go back to the castle.
Back to her.
And I am not ready.

So I do what I must.
I pull myself up from my knees.
I stand in the freezing river one last time—
Letting the cold burn through me, forcing my body into submission.
Then—
I go to the armory.
I strip off my shirt, standing before the cold steel of my own reflection.
My face is gaunt.
The shadows under my eyes linger.
But I do not look weak.
I look sharper.
Lean.
Tense.
A man who has cut out the part of himself that wanted her.
I grab my sword.
I train until dawn.
Every strike.
Every movement.
Every breath.
I rebuild myself.
By the time the sun rises,
I am no longer the man she left ruined.

I am Alexey Volkov.

I do not kneel.

I do not break.

And I do not lose.

And if Queen Arianna dares to test me again?

I will remind her exactly who she is dealing with.

Because I am not her game.

I am not her pawn.

And I will not fall.

Back into the Fire – Alexey

The moment I stepped through the gates of Elarion Castle, I knew.

Something was wrong.

The air was different—thicker.

Heavier.

Tense, like a storm waiting to break.

The weight of it pressed against my chest, familiar and foreboding, a sensation I knew far too well.

I had expected anger. I had expected resentment. I had expected hellfire in the shape of Arianna.

But this?

This was worse.

I didn't even make it to my chambers before Murphy materialized at my side. No smirk. No quip. No easy, lopsided grin that usually signaled mild amusement at my suffering.

Just a sharp hand clapping down on my shoulder as he all but steered me into the nearest empty corridor.

Oh. This was going to be bad.

Murphy didn't even wait for me to ask before muttering, "Good. You're back."

I shot him a dry look. "I see that. What, no quip about my emotional pilgrimage?"

Murphy let out a breath. Not a laugh.

And that was when I knew.

This was really, really bad.

I stilled. "What happened?"

Murphy gave me a look. The look. The kind he only used before dropping catastrophic, life-altering news.

"What happened?" he repeated, incredulous. Then, with barely contained exasperation, "You left for a week, and she lost her Gods-damned mind is what happened."

My stomach dropped.

My pulse kicked up, sharp and angry.

Murphy crossed his arms. “She came looking for you the day after you left.”

Of course she did.

"And?"

"And I told her all I knew—that you had urgent personal business at your estate."

I exhaled sharply, already knowing where this was going. “That must have gone over well.”

Murphy’s flat, humorless stare could have peeled paint from the walls. "Oh, yeah. She was thrilled. Really took it in stride. Handled it like a proper queen."

My jaw locked.

Murphy sighed and dragged a hand down his face. "Alexey, she tried to shake the truth out of me."

I blinked. "Shake—?"

" Physically, Alexey. Like I’m a damn tree she could shake the truth out of. Like I haven’t killed men for less. Like she didn’t realize I could snap her like a twig if I wanted to. The woman is crazy, my friend. She is a lunatic. Emotionally and mentally unhinged. The Queen of Cray Cray. And I—" he placed a dramatic hand over his heart, "—I am so sorry, brother."

I clenched my fists at my sides.

Murphy held up a hand. "But wait! It gets better."

I sincerely doubted that.

"She's been on one all week. Reckless. Wild. Pissing off everyone she possibly can." He let out a humorless chuckle. "It's actually impressive, in a holy-shit-she's-going-to-get-herself-killed kind of way. The way she is committed to suicide by Odin is unmatched."

A slow, dangerous heat crept up my spine.

"What do you mean, reckless?"

Murphy ran a hand through his hair. "Drinking."

I exhaled. "Drinking, or… drinking?"

Murphy's grim expression was all the answer I needed.

"Slurred speech, couldn't walk, couldn't think. Just pissed off. At everyone. I mean everyone."

Oh, no, Arianna.

"She was openly flirting with men at court. Picking fights with the wrong women."

I went still.

Flirting with men all the men.

That was new. That was deliberate.

That was a very, very stupid game she was playing.

With Odin—unpredictable, volatile, prone to violent whims—she was placing her life on whatever mood he happened to be in at the time.

Murphy wasn't done. "Court has been total chaos. I had to station five more guys near her just to keep her somewhat in line. To keep her from going off the edge completely. Five guys, Alexey!"

I clenched my jaw so hard it hurt.

"And yesterday, she wasn't feeling well. She went to the doctor and then locked herself in her chambers and hasn't come out since."

My pulse quickened.

"Locked herself in?"

Murphy nodded. "Hasn't taken meals. Hasn't spoken to anyone. Not even her handmaidens. She won't open the door for anyone. I'm pretty sure she didn't off herself—" He hesitated. Only half joking.

"—because every once in a while, one of the guys hears her screaming at the walls…or whatever the fuck she's doing in there."

The unease twisting in my gut turned into something colder.

I had expected anger. I had expected resentment.

But this?

This wasn't anger. She was spiraling out of control. This was self-destruction.

And if Arianna was self-destructing—

She was going to make sure she took everyone down with her.

Murphy pushed off the wall, his usual levity nowhere to be found.

"You're the only one she listens to, Alexey." His voice was quieter now. More serious. Dangerously serious.

"If anyone can talk sense into her, it's you. Maybe you can get her to stop before she gets herself killed. I'm surprised Odin hasn't done it already, with the way she's been acting. Odin's been in rare form. Unusually quiet himself. Is it a full moon or something?"

I swallowed.

I wasn't sure if that was true.

I wasn't sure if I even wanted that to be true.

But it didn't matter.

Arianna was my queen.

And if she had spent the past week spiraling out of control because of me—

I had to fix it.

Even if it meant walking straight into the fire.

Even if it meant burning alive.

Красивую ложь не переживает никто.
No one survives a beautiful lie.

— Lorinian Proverb

No More Games – Alexey

I should have left.

I should have turned around the moment I stepped through the door.

But I didn't.

Because I have a habit of walking straight into my own ruin.

And Arianna?

She was ruin incarnate.

A walking red flag, blazing with warning. I should have heeded the red hair as the red flag warning it was. She was the kind of beautiful that ruined men, that burned through lives like wildfire and left nothing but smoldering wreckage in her wake.

And tonight—she was coming apart at the seams.

For a long time, I told myself I understood her. I gave her grace, even when she didn't deserve it. I had watched her make one catastrophic decision after another—and now, now she stood before me, trembling under the weight of her own choices.

But I was not a magician.

I could not move her chess piece for her.

She had led herself here.

Not the Gods.

Not Odin.

Not me.

She had done this to herself.

She leaned against the wall near the fire, wearing nothing but a deep green silk robe, the fabric pooling around her feet, her auburn hair, a disheveled mess.

She looked terrible.

Pale. Unsteady. Hollowed out.

A week ago, she was a queen with purpose, something to fight for, something to believe in.

But Odin had stripped her of that.

No love.

No passion.

No purpose.

Just emptiness.

And now? Now she was looking at me like I was the only thing left to hold onto.

She was spiraling.

Drowning.

And she wanted to drag me down with her.

I wouldn't let her.

"I see you couldn't stay away."

Her voice was a sneer. Sharp. Bitter.

A week-old bruise painted her cheek—faded now, the swelling gone. She would recover from the bruise on her face.

I wasn't sure about the bruise on her soul.

I exhaled sharply. "Arianna—"

"You look well-rested."

She cut me off, her voice clipped. Mocking.

Then—she smirked.

Slow. Calculated.

"Are you ready, then?" Her voice dropped lower. "Are you ready to fuck me senseless, Alexey?"

My name had always sounded like a sin on her tongue.

I didn't react.

Not this time.

She stepped closer. Slowly. Like a predator. Like she could hunt me.

"Did I make you uncomfortable?" she murmured, tilting her head.

"Did I… shake you?"

She was baiting me.

And I was so damn tired of this game.

I had spent a week away from her. Away from the suffocating heat of her presence, away from the way she played with fire like it wouldn't consume us both.

I would not let her pull me back in.

"I came back to talk," I said evenly.

Arianna laughed.

A bitter, cruel laugh.

"What a waste."

Another step.

Too close.

Her scent—amber and something darker, something sinful—wrapped around me like a noose.

She lifted a hand. Grazed her thumb over my jaw.

And that was it.

Enough.

I slammed my palm against the wall beside her head.

Hard.

The sconces rattled. The fire flickered.

Arianna flinched.

For the first time—she flinched.

Her lips parted, her eyes slamming shut, a sharp breath catching in her throat.

I leaned in, my breath warm against her cheek. My voice—low. Lethal.

"You think you hold the power here, My Queen?"

Silence.

Her body stayed taut, rigid.

Good.

Let her think.

Let her feel. L

et her learn.

Then, softer—but no less dangerous—

"Look at me, Arianna."

She obeyed.

Her gaze lifted—uncertain. Unsteady.

And for a moment—for a single, shattering moment—I saw something I was never supposed to see.

Fear.

She hated it.

Hated that I saw it.

So, she did what she always did.

She flipped the script.

She stepped back, feigning modesty.

"So," she murmured, her voice light, too light. "Did you enjoy your little retreat, Graf Alexander Volkov?"

I went still.

She was trying to get under my skin.

Wielding my full name, my title—like a blade, smooth as silk, sharp as sin.

"You must have," she continued, her tone turning sharper. "A whole week to yourself. No responsibilities. No kingdom to protect. No queen to be a thorn in your side."

I didn't react.

Not this time.

"I imagine the countryside must have been very peaceful," she mused. "The rivers run wild with the melting snow… much like the man who abandoned his post."

I clenched my jaw.

"Funny. I thought the Commander of the Royal Guard didn't run."

A beat.

"But maybe I overestimated you."

There it was.

Her first real attack.

She smiled at my silence.

Then—her voice dipped, soft.

Dangerous.

"Because while you were off clearing your head..."

She held my gaze, unblinking.

"I found out that I am with child."

Everything inside me went still.

A pause.

Then, calmly, "Congratulations, Your Majesty."

I kept my tone polite. Cold.

"You'll make a great mother."

Arianna stilled.

And then I saw it.

Something flickered behind her eyes.

Something unnerving.

Arianna didn't like when she wasn't in control.

So—she took it back.

She turned, walking away, slow and deliberate, like she had already won.

Then—over her shoulder—

"Careful, Alexey."

She let the silence stretch taut.

"It would be a shame if the court thought you put this baby in me."

Silence.

For a long, breathless moment, I just stared at her.

Not as my queen.

Not as the woman I swore to protect.

Not as the wildfire that had burned me to my very bones.

But as a stranger.

It broke my heart.

Not the threat.

Not the consequences.

But her.

Her.

Because I would have given her anything.

Everything.
And this was how she repaid me.
With a lie.
With a weapon.
With betrayal.
I didn't deserve this.
I had kept my honor.
I hadn't touched her.
I hadn't crossed the line.
But she was willing to lie about me.
To ruin me.
To destroy me.

I exhaled slowly.
Then, quietly—deadly quiet—
"Arianna."
She stopped.
"We both know I never touched you."
She flinched.
Good.
Let her feel the weight of truth.
Let her feel the weight of what she had just done.

I stepped closer.
"How far are you willing to take this?"
She didn't answer.
Didn't smirk. Didn't taunt.
She just stared at me.
So I pressed deeper.
"Until I'm in the grave beside you?"
Her throat bobbed as she swallowed.

For the first time, real fear flickered in her eyes.

"Be careful, My Queen."

My voice was quiet now.

Dangerous.

"You may survive Odin. But if you keep playing this game—" I leaned in, my breath a whisper against her skin.

"You will not survive me."

Then—I turned.

I shut the door behind me.

A second later—

A teacup shattered against the wood.

I would never trust her again.

That realization broke something inside me.

I stared at the splintered porcelain that had slid under the door for a long moment.

Then exhaled slowly.

The encounter could have gone worse, I suppose.

Narrow Escape – Alexey

The teacup shattered against the door.

I didn't flinch.

I just stood there, staring at the fractured porcelain at my feet, letting the silence settle around me.

Arianna.

I should have known. I should have expected it.

And yet—hearing her say it, watching her twist the knife with that cruel little taunt—it still made my blood run cold.

"Careful, Alexey. It would be a shame if the court thought you put this baby in me."

As if I had anything to do with it.

With her.

With her madness.

As if she hadn't just tried to pull me into a grave alongside her.

I dragged a hand through my hair, exhaling sharply.

Arianna was reckless, but this?

This was something else entirely.

This was a woman who had nothing left to lose.

The Arianna I had met a year ago had been careful, calculated—a queen with fire in her heart but discipline in her mind, believing—naïve as it was—that the Gods had a plan for her.

She had married Odin of her own free will.

And suddenly, she thought she could be, do, have anything.

She learned quickly that wasn't true.

And now—now, she was like a dying flame, licking at the edges of a world that would not let her burn free.

I could feel it, the weight of her actions shifting in the air, a storm brewing just beyond the horizon.

Because word was already making its way through court.

It always did.

The queen—Odin's queen—had been reckless this week.

And thank the Gods I hadn't been around to witness it firsthand.

Her lingering touches. Her teasing words. Her playful flirtations.

No doubt, the whispers had already begun.

But at least I hadn't been here.

At least no one could place me in the castle when she had been parading around like a reckless fool, without any regard for her life or anyone else's.

I had left for Willowbrook just in time.

And that absence—the perfect alibi—was the only thing keeping my name out of their mouths.

Had I stayed—had I been within arm's reach of her every time she batted her lashes, every time she put a little too much sweetness in her tone—they would have assumed the worst.

And then—then I really would have had something to worry about.

Because the court never needed the truth.

They only needed a whisper.

And that whisper alone could kill me.

I had spent a lifetime ensuring that I was above suspicion.

Above reproach.

And now?

Now, she had threatened all of it.

And for what?

For power over me?

For a fleeting moment of control over something—anything—in the mess of a life she had built?

Or had she truly lost herself so completely?

I didn't know which answer was worse.

But the question still remained.

What would Odin do?

If he even cared to notice.

If he still had the capacity to care about anything beyond his own misery.

He might do nothing.

He might do too much.

Either would be dangerous.

Arianna should have known that.

But instead, she had gambled both our lives like I meant nothing.

I should be furious.

I was.

But more than that—I was grateful.

Because I had not given in.

Not to her fire.

Not to the temptation of something so utterly wrong, but so devastatingly right.

No matter how much I had wanted her.

And Gods, how I had wanted her.

But the difference between us—the thing that separated me from her reckless abandon—

Was that I understood the cost.

Because if I had given in—if I had let myself have just one night of pleasure—if I had indulged—

It would have cost me my life.

And Arianna?

She might have walked away unscathed.

Or she might have burned right alongside me.

And I wasn't willing to find out.

I turned from the shattered porcelain and kept walking.

Because I had survived Arianna's fire.

And I was not about to get burned now.

The Weight of a Crown – Alexey

The world smelled of oranges and salt water.

The sky stretched out before me in a beautiful hue of blue.

The orchard was sun-warmed, bright, thick with the scent of ripened fruit hanging heavy from the branches. The soft hum of bees filled the air, the leaves rustling lazily in the breeze, golden light spilling long across the earth.

I ran through the orchard, bare feet kicking up dust, small hands sticky with juice, laughter echoing between the trees. The sun burned hot against my skin, but the shade beneath the heavy branches was cool, safe, home.

"Alexey!"

I turned, breathless, chest rising and falling with exhilaration.

I loved it here.

My mother stood at the edge of the grove, her dark braid falling over one shoulder, her apron dusted with flour, hands on her hips in that way that meant I had been gone too long.

"Dinner is ready, my little wolf cub."

I grinned, heart pounding, turning to run toward her—

And then—

The scent of oranges turned to smoke.

The golden light bled into red.

The orchard withered, blackened, burned.

A scream—distant, unfamiliar—tore through the air.

I gasped—

And woke.

Not the south.
Not my mother.
Not home.

Smoke. Thick. Choking. Burning the back of my throat.

My body lurched before my mind could catch up, heart hammering against my ribs, reaching—for what?—for something that wasn't there.

Not again.

Not this.

Not now.

The battlefield clung to me like rot. The scent of mud, blood, and sweat filled my lungs. The fire crackled in the makeshift camp, the dim glow casting shadows over the men lying in the dirt—some breathing, some not.

A sword rested against my leg, heavy, familiar. My armor was spattered with grime, my hands stiff with dried blood.

Not orchards.
Not home.
The battlefield.

I blinked against the dim light, adjusting to where I was.

And then—

A voice, easy, unbothered, cutting through the quiet.

"What a day, huh?"

Odin.

He was grinning like we hadn't just spent hours in the dirt, tempting death. Like this was all some great camping adventure among friends.

"We're going to be legends, you know." He stretched his arms behind his head, looking up at the stars as if he had not just killed men beneath them.
"History will talk about how we saved this kingdom."

Murphy snorted beside me, sprawled on the ground, arms behind his head.

"History can wait. I want a feast. I want fresh pastries."

Another soldier groaned. "Feast? I just want a bed that isn't the ground."

A chuckle passed between them, light, easy, oblivious.

I said nothing.

Because something was wrong.

The night was too still.
Too quiet.

I had a bad feeling.

My feelings are never wrong.

I sat up slowly, listening, above the light chatter of the battalion.

My eyes scanned the woods.
Sharp.
Piercing.

Suddenly—

A shift.
A rustle.
A breath.

The whisper of movement where there should have been none.

We were not alone.

I knew it.

I didn't hesitate.

I stood, turning sharply, my body already moving before my mind could catch up.

A signal. A wordless command. Half the men to Odin, half to me.

We would flank where the sound came from.

Odin grinned, rolling his shoulders, his fingers twitching with excitement.

"Finally."

I became one with the shadows of the tall evergreen trees.

The world was silent at this hour. Still. Frozen.

I inhaled carefully, exhaling in barely-there wisps, forcing my breath to dissipate before it could rise. One wrong breath, one careless plume of fog in the crisp Lorinian night air, and I'd give away our position.

I could not afford a mistake.

The forest stretched ahead—dark, vast, endless.

A battlefield disguised as wilderness.

I moved soundlessly, every step measured, every breath controlled, listening, waiting.

And then—

A shadow.

A flicker of movement just beyond the trees.

I stilled, every muscle locked, my fingers tightening around my hilt.

Not an animal.

Too quiet.

Too deliberate.

A shape emerged from the darkness—lean, armed, moving with purpose.

A rebel.

He passed within arm's reach, oblivious.

He placed a hand against the tree in front of me, adjusting the strap of his weapon, muttering something under his breath.

Checkmate.

I struck.

Quick.

Precise.

My blade found his throat before he could even gasp, the steel pressing just enough to make him go still.

His breath hitched. His pulse throbbed beneath my grip.

I leaned in, voice low, controlled.

"How many of you?"

No answer.

I pressed harder.

"How many?"

A tremor ran through him. Then, barely a whisper—

"Sixteen. Scouting ahead."

I exhaled, nodding once.

"Unfortunate."

I ran my blade along his throat, ending his life quickly and efficiently.

And then—

The night exploded.

Steel clashed in the dark, the quiet shattered by the sound of chaos.

Murphy was already moving, fast, efficient, brutal.

Odin laughed—a wild, reckless sound—as he threw himself into the fight.

A rebel lunged at me. I caught his wrist, twisted, drove my dagger between his ribs.

One.

Another came from the side—I dodged, countered, opened his throat before he could scream.

Two.

Three.

Four.

Bodies fell.

I caught a glimpse of Murphy.

Five.

Six.

I kept going.

Seven.

Eight.

Counting my kills.

Nine.

Ten.

Counting the kills of my comrades.

Eleven.

Twelve.

Thirteen.

Fourteen.

Fifteen.

My vision darted around looking for the last man.

I only count 15.

By the time the fight died down, we were standing among a field of the dead.

Then I saw Odin had captured the leader, a man kneeling in the dirt, bloodied but unbroken.

"We did it," Odin exhaled, chest heaving, exhilarated.

I wiped my blade clean, stepping toward them.

"Keep him alive." I said breathlessly.

Odin scoffed. "Why?"

I met his gaze, calm, unwavering.

"To ensure this is all they have left. We need to question him."

Odin studied me.

And then—

He smiled.

And slit the man's throat anyway.

The body collapsed.

Sixteen.

And something inside me snapped.

The first red flag.

It was the first warning sign.

And I had ignored it.

And years later, as I stood before a broken kingdom, watching it crumble beneath Odin's hands—

I would remember this moment.

The moment I could have stopped it.

But I didn't.

I let him have the throne.

I let him tell his stories.

I let him believe in his own legend.

And now?

Now, the kingdom bleeds for it.

The Storm Before the Storm – Alexey

Odin welcomed me back as if I had never left, his usual boisterous nature a well-worn mask, his grin easy, his voice warm with camaraderie.

Like we were still brothers-in-arms, still young men standing in the dirt, staring down the weight of a kingdom we had yet to realize would crush us both.

He clapped a hand on my shoulder, his grip just a little too firm. Testing. Measuring.

"Alexey," he said, voice thick with something I could not name. "It's good to have you back. The castle's been dull without you."

A lie.

The castle had been anything but dull in my absence.

And then—the shift.

Odin's expression darkened, his fingers twitching at his side. His next words sent a jolt down my spine.

"Tell me—have you heard the rumors about Arianna?"

Oh, fuck me.

I kept my breathing even. My expression unreadable. But beneath it? My heart slammed against my ribs.

Not this.

Not now.

Rumors.

I already knew what they were.

But Odin wasn't just asking if I had heard them.

He was asking whether I believed them.

I kept my voice calm, smooth, carefully controlled.

"I've been away from court, Your Majesty. I wouldn't know."

A beat.

Odin studied me. Weighing. Measuring.

I forced my posture into something easy, something familiar, despite the way my every muscle was wound too tight.

Tread carefully.

"She's been awfully friendly," Odin murmured, rolling the thought over his tongue. "Too friendly, if you ask me. The nobles are talking."

He was testing the waters.

Feeling for weakness.

And Gods help me, I was already running interference. For a woman who had just tried to burn me alive.

I didn't flinch.

"Arianna has always been friendly," I said smoothly. Not defensive. Not too quick. Just easy. Measured. "Someone was likely jealous and twisted her words."

Silence.

Odin grunted, jaw tight.

I saw it happening—the battle in his mind.

He wanted to believe me.

Because if I was right, if the rumors were nothing—then he had nothing to worry about.

But if I was wrong—if Arianna had betrayed him—

There would be no stopping him.

Then—relief.

Odin exhaled sharply, rolling his shoulders, letting out a forced, brittle chuckle.

"You're probably right."

No, I was definitely right.

Because if Odin got it in his head that Arianna had been unfaithful—even if she hadn't—

It would be disastrous.

For her.

For the court.

For the kingdom.

For me.

He dismissed me, and I exited the chamber, every muscle still locked tight, my mind already bracing for what came next.

Because the castle wasn't dull.

It was on fire.

And Odin was about to realize it.

It started slow. Subtle. Easy to miss if you weren't paying attention.

But I was always paying attention.

The nobles were leaving.

One by one, they retreated to their estates—not in a rush, not in a panic, but in that quiet, calculating way that sent ice through my veins.

Like rats abandoning a sinking ship.

They could feel it.

The shift in the air.

The weight of the gathering storm.

The silent but undeniable promise of ruin.

They weren't stupid.

Odin's paranoia was growing. His patience was thinning. And Arianna—the woman he had once adored beyond reason—was no longer untouchable.

And she had no idea.

I hated that I understood why she had done it.

I hated that a part of me ached for the loneliness, the desperation that had driven her to this.

But it didn't mean I could excuse it.

It didn't mean I could save her.

Not this time.

I stepped into the training yard, where Murphy was effortlessly swinging a practice sword, his expression unreadable but his eyes too knowing.

I knew exactly who I needed to talk to.

Because if anyone would tell me exactly how fucked we were—it was him.

The Conversation with Murphy – Alexey

Murphy barely glanced up as I approached, slamming his blade into a wooden post like it owed him dinner.

"You look like a man who's about to drop a very interesting problem into my lap," he mused.

I didn't waste time.

"Arianna told me she was with child."

Murphy's sword stopped mid-swing. He turned to me slowly.

"Odin's?"

I shot him a flat look. "Obviously."

His relief was immediate. Short-lived. Fickle.

"…Then why do you look like you just got handed your own death warrant?"

I exhaled sharply.

"Because she told me, 'It would be a shame if the court thought it was my doing."

Murphy blinked. Once. Twice.

Then—

"I'm sorry. What?"

His lips parted slightly, his brows pulling together like his brain needed a moment to catch up to the absolute bullshit he had just heard.

I empathized.

Then he let out a long, slow whistle.

"She's been promoted to Queen Psycho. My condolences." He shook his head. "Well, the plot thickens. Continue, Milord."

I dragged a hand down my face.
"I will never trust her again," I said flatly. "She lost it on me when I walked away."

Murphy arched a brow. "Lost it like how?"

I hesitated. Then, flatly—
"She threw a teacup at me."

Silence.

Murphy just stared at me. I stared back.

Then—

He laughed.
Hard.

He doubled over, one hand on his knee, the other over his heart, laughing like I had just told the greatest joke of my career.
"Oh, for fuck's sake, Alexey." He wiped his eyes. "A teacup?"

I sighed, folding my arms across my chest.
"Apparently, I wasn't reacting appropriately."

Murphy wheezed. "I knew she was a little unhinged, but damn. Of all the rich bitch things I have heard—"

My jaw ticked. "If Odin finds out—"

"He won't. Her credibility is shot after the week she's had," Murphy interrupted, his laughter vanishing as fast as it had come. He met my gaze, his voice dead serious.

I studied him for a beat. Then nodded.

Murphy exhaled, rubbing a hand down his face.

"You really sidestepped an executioner's axe, Alexey."

I scoffed. "No kidding."

He let out a slow breath. “You know what you should do?”

I sighed. “What?”

Murphy smirked.

"Go to bed. Get some actual rest. And lock your fucking doors this time."

I huffed a dry laugh. "Noted."

And as I turned to leave, one thought lingered—

Whatever Arianna was planning next?

I would be ready.

The Letter Under the Door – Alexey

I knew before I even picked it up.

The envelope lay just inside my door, the edges curled slightly where it had been shoved beneath the frame. A small thing. Innocuous. To anyone else, it would seem like nothing at all.

But I knew.

The weight of it in my hands, the delicate scrawl of my name on the front—

Arianna.

A slow, sharp exhale left me.

I should have left it there. I should have tossed it into the fire, let the flames devour whatever she thought she needed to say.

But I didn't.

Because I am a man who walks straight into the fire, even when I know it will burn.

I broke the seal.

Her scent still clung to the parchment. Faint. A whisper of something lingering, like an afterthought.

My eyes flicked over the words, scanning them with the same precision I would a battle plan—calculating, wary, already bracing for impact.

Alexey,

I don't expect you to respond.

I don't expect you to forgive me.

But I need to say this anyway.

I used to be a priestess. I used to be a lot like you. I was very controlled and methodical. Did you know that? I think you did. I think you saw the remnants of it in me, even when I had long since buried that part of myself.

I left that path behind because I got caught up in the legend of Odin. In the fire of it, the sheer momentum of something too large to stop, too wild to ignore.

I thought I could control it.

I thought I could wield it.

Instead, it wielded me.

This isn't something I can undo.

I am trapped in this gilded cage, married to a stranger wearing my husband's skin and now, I carry life.

I am drowning in the consequences of my own choices.

It is bitter and unforgiving.

What I did to you—what I said—was unforgivable.

I know that. And I won't insult you by pretending otherwise.

I wasn't trying to get you killed. I wasn't even thinking about you when I said it.

I just wanted to feel something. Anything.

Something that wasn't regret. Something that wasn't grief.

I'll admit, it was nice to imagine that it could have been true.

In another life perhaps.

But that's not an excuse. And it's not enough.

Losing you as a friend has been sobering.

I am sorry.

I would take it back if I could. But words, once spoken, can never be unspoken.

I am sorry.

For all of it.

—Arianna

I read it twice.

Then a third time.

My pulse remained steady. My breath even. The only sign of anything at all was the slow, deliberate tightening of my grip on the parchment, the crinkle of delicate fibers bending under my fingers.

She was right about one thing.

Words, once spoken, can never be unspoken.

And she had spoken too many.

A bitter breath left me.

It should have meant something—this apology. This admission. This letter written in careful, regret-laced ink.

Maybe it did.

Maybe it didn't.

Either way, it changed nothing.

Because I knew Arianna.

And if I had learned anything, it was that she only ever reached for someone after she had already let them fall.

I folded the letter with practiced precision.

Then, without hesitation, I fed it to the flames.

And as her words curled into ash, I felt nothing at all.

Control. Alt. Delete. – Alexey

Odin left before sunrise.

No warning. No strategy meeting. No council session.

Just a loud declaration echoing through the eastern corridor:

"I'm going hunting."

A moment later—laughter. Boots. Steel clanking against steel as a handful of his favorite war dogs barked and jeered in drunken camaraderie. I recognized the voices. Soldiers more loyal to Odin's legend than the laws of Lorna. A few had names. Most didn't. And I didn't care to learn them.

By the time I stepped onto the balcony that overlooked the courtyard, they were already mounted, Odin at the center of the pack, grinning like a boy on his birthday.

He was clean-shaven for the first time in weeks. Hair slicked back. Armor polished.

He looked… present. Almost regal.

And that was what worried me most.

"How long do you think he'll be gone?" Murphy asked beside me, arms crossed as he watched them disappear beyond the gates.

I didn't take my eyes off the treeline. "Long enough to make a mess."

Murphy grunted. "Think he's actually hunting?"

"No," I said flatly. "He's brooding with weapons."

He snorted, then fell into step beside me as we turned and reentered the war chamber. The scent of parchment and iron greeted us like an old friend. Familiar. Grounding.

Routine.

"Alright," Murphy said, rolling his shoulders. "We're down four men in the west corridor, and there's talk of moving some of the newer recruits from the outer posts into the city guard."

"Too green," I said, scanning the updated rotation lists. "They'll fold the second someone calls them 'pretty.' Put Malenkov in charge of the transition teams. He can make hard decisions without whining about feelings."

Murphy nodded. "And the roster for Arianna's personal guard?"

I hesitated.

Then I set the quill down. "Keep it lean. Just two men on rotation. Don't make a show of it. She's quiet now, but that won't last."

Murphy eyed me for a beat. "You gonna check in on her?"

"No," I said. "I'm done checking on people who set fire to the house and then cry about the smoke."

He gave a short laugh. "Fair."

We went back to work.

Maps. Schedules. Reassigned patrol routes. A dozen fires that needed putting out, none of which Odin had even acknowledged.

That was the thing about kings like him—when they weren't raging, they were vanishing. And when they weren't vanishing, they were making someone else clean up the aftermath.

I didn’t have the luxury of disappearing. Not anymore.

A knock came at the door. A courier entered, flustered, holding a hastily scribbled note.

"From His Majesty," he said, bowing awkwardly.

I took it, opened it.

Three words.

“Don’t wait up.”

Murphy peered over my shoulder. "Classy."

I crumpled the note and tossed it onto the fire.

"I wasn’t planning on it."

Then I picked up the next report.

Because the world didn’t stop when Odin went hunting.

The Snake Pit – Alexey

The council chamber reeked of stale wine and bad intentions.

I heard them before I even stepped inside.

Voices low. Conspiratorial.

Schemes whispered between sips of their overpriced vintages, tongues sharpened by the taste of power they had not yet seized.

They didn't expect me.

They never did.

I stepped inside.

Silence.

Fifteen nobles.

All seated around the long oak table, hands folded, eyes gleaming with something smug, something eager.

I let the door slam shut behind me.

Not a single man spoke.

I took my time.

Let the silence stretch.

Let them feel it. Let them choke on it.

I wasn't just the Commander of the Guard.

I wasn't just the Graf of the Sunfire River Valley.

I wasn't just the man who had Odin's ear all these years.

I was the only thing standing between them and the throne.

And they hated it.

Hated me.

Good.

"Commander Graf Volkov," one of them greeted smoothly, lifting his goblet in mock welcome. "We were just discussing the matter of the queen."

The queen.

I already knew where this was going.

Still, I let them speak.

Let them dig their own graves before I buried them in them.

"Her Majesty is in a fragile state," another noble said. "With the king absent for such… extended periods of time, we feel it is our duty to ensure the stability of the realm in his place."

A third noble leaned forward, voice honeyed, eyes sharp.

I knew that look.

A man trying to sell poison as perfume.

"We believe," he said carefully, "that Queen Arianna should appoint a regent to assist her in matters of state."

A regent.

A puppet.

One of them.

The realization filled my lungs like smoke.

They wanted to strip Arianna of her authority. Reduce her to a figurehead.
A grieving, vulnerable, powerless pawn in their game.

And they had waited until Odin was gone to do it.

Cowards.

I let them have their moment.

Let them speak their rehearsed little lines, let them believe for one second longer that they had already won.

Then—

I laughed.

Low. Slow. Amused.

It spread through the room like a crack in the ice.

The lords stiffened, shifting uncomfortably in their seats.

The man who had spoken first forced a thin smile. "Commander Graf Volkov—"

I moved.

Not fast.

Not loud.

Just enough.

Enough to place both hands on the table.

Enough to lean forward.

Enough to watch their confidence curdle into unease.

I let the moment linger, let the tension coil tighter, let them sit in the silence they had earned.

And then—

I smiled.

"Tell me," I murmured, letting my voice drop into something dark, something razor-sharp, something that cut, "what kind of men would seek to strip power from a queen—while she carries the future of the throne?"

A visible flinch.

A flicker of panic behind their eyes.

I tilted my head, voice deceptively calm.

"That is what you're doing, isn't it?" I mused. "You waited until the king was gone to prey on a mother-to-be. To push her into a position of reliance while she secures the line of succession."

I let my gaze drift over each of them.

One by one.

Every last one of the snakes.

Poison boiling beneath their skin.

"How unfortunate," I murmured, standing straight again. "How unfortunate that the king will not take kindly to such… treachery upon his return."

Silence.

A charged, suffocating, trapped silence.

I could see it—the fear behind their eyes.

Odin was unpredictable at best.

We all knew it.

But one thing was certain.

He would not take kindly to perceived threats to his wife and heir.

And he would react severely.

I would make sure they all understood that.

"Her Majesty requires no assistance," I continued, my voice a quiet promise of violence.

"She rules in the king's absence, and she will continue to do so.

You will not move against her.

You will not pressure her.

And you will not—" my gaze flicked over the noble who had first suggested the regency, "—whisper treason into her ear in the hopes that she might bend to your whims."

I let my hand rest lightly on the hilt of my sword.

Not a threat.

A reminder.

"You will respect the queen," I said, letting my voice fill the room.

"You will remember your place."

"And if you ever seek to undermine her again—"

I smiled.

"Well." I tilted my head. "I would hate to be you when the king finds out his wife and heir were threatened."

Another long pause.

Then, finally, a noble cleared his throat.

"Of course, Graf Volkov," he murmured, his voice less confident than before. "We were merely… ensuring the stability of the kingdom."

"A noble effort," I said dryly. "One that will not be repeated."

No one argued.

No one pushed back.

They knew.

They had tried to play their hand too soon.

And I had called their bluff.

I turned on my heel, striding toward the doors.

I didn't look back.

I didn't need to.

I reached the threshold then, at the last moment, I stilled.

Not quite a pause.

Just long enough.

Long enough for them to wonder.

Long enough for them to squirm.

I let the silence settle. Let them choke on the weight of it.

Then, without a word, I left.

The council had just learned a valuable lesson.

They were not the ones pulling the strings.

And as long as I was here—
They never would be.

Intruder Alert – Alexey

The night was too quiet.

Not the kind of quiet that meant peace. The kind that wasn't real. The kind that made your instincts bristle, your pulse slow, your mind sharpen.

The castle was never truly silent. There were always footsteps, whispers, movement—the living pulse of a kingdom that never slept.

But tonight?

Tonight, something was wrong.

I knew the feeling.

I had lived in it, fought in it, bled in it.

I moved through the corridors without a sound, my hand resting lightly on the hilt of my sword.

Following the quiet.

Following the feeling.

Following the nagging instinct that had never once steered me wrong.

Then I heard it.

A shuffle.

The barely-there sound of movement.

Too heavy for a servant.

Too wrong to be a guard.

Near her chambers.

I drew my blade.

Then I saw the shadow.

A figure—hooded, careful, slipping through the dim torchlight like he belonged there.

He didn't.

I was on him in two strides.

The first strike came fast.

He was skilled.

Not just some common hired blade. His stance was too precise. His movements, too controlled.

Trained.

Disciplined.

I parried, driving him back.

His eyes flicked to the queen's door—measuring. Calculating.

He's still trying to get to her.

Unbelievable.

I didn't give him the chance.

Steel met steel, ringing out against the stone halls as we clashed, neither of us yielding.

A clean fight would have been preferable.

But there was nothing clean about this.

He was fast.

I was faster.

He was skilled.

I was better.

But he was desperate.

And desperation made men dangerous.

He feinted left.

I saw the strike coming—

But not fast enough.

His blade sliced through my side.

Pain flared, sharp and hot.

I gritted my teeth.

Not now.

Not here.

Not on my watch.

I was the only thing standing between this man and Arianna.

I didn’t slow.

Didn’t stumble.

Didn’t let him see that he’d drawn blood.

His plan will not come to fruition.

Instead, I drove my sword through his ribs, mercilessly.

He choked—a wet, gasping sound.

His fingers twitched, like he might try one last strike.

I twisted the blade.

He slumped.

I watched the light fade from his cold eyes.

It was over.

Murphy found me first.

"Shit, Alexey." That was his greeting.

Not "Are you okay?"

Not "Do you need help?"

Just a deadpan curse like I had personally inconvenienced him by almost bleeding out in the hallway.

“You really need to stop throwing yourself into death matches, Alexey.”

I exhaled slowly, pressing a hand to my ribs.

“Would you rather I let him win?”

“Obviously not,” Murphy muttered, already tearing a strip of fabric off his uniform. “But I’m really not in the mood to stitch you up again.”

Neither was I.

But I let him.

As soon as Murphy had restored me to a functional condition, I returned to the scene of the crime.

How dare you bring war to my doorstep.

Who do you think you are?

This is my castle.

I examined the corridor thoroughly.

Trying to figure out how he got in here.

How he got so close.

Then I turned—

And saw her.

She stood at the end of the corridor, wrapped in a thick robe.

Expression unreadable.

She had heard everything.

Had seen everything.

I expected sharp words. A quip. Something cutting and clever to mask whatever she was feeling.

But there was none.

She just—

Looked at me.

And for the first time in months, I saw something else in her eyes.

Something like relief.

Something like trust.

Something like the realization that no matter what had happened between us—

No matter how reckless she was.
No matter how broken.
No matter how much we fought.

I would always protect her.

I swallowed, forcing my voice to stay even.

"Are you all right?"

Arianna exhaled, pressing a hand to her swollen belly.

Then—

She nodded.

Good.

She hesitated.

Just for a second.

Just long enough for me to see it.

To feel the weight of whatever unspoken thing still lived between us.

But I didn't acknowledge it.

Didn't let it breathe.

Didn't let it matter.

I kept my voice calm. Formal. Unshakable.

"Return to your chambers, Your Majesty. This is beneath your concern."

Her lips parted slightly—like she wanted to argue.

But she didn't.

She just nodded.

And without another word—

She turned.

And disappeared back into her room.

And I—

I stood there.

Bleeding.

Waiting for the sting of it to fade.

It didn't.

Bridges of Ash – Arianna

I had thought I knew loneliness.

I had spent my childhood in books, in duty, in solitude. I had chosen a man who made me feel seen for the first time, a man who set my world alight with promises of more, of everything.

And now, I was alone in a way I had never imagined.

Alone in my chambers.

Alone in my thoughts.

Alone in a marriage that felt more like a coffin than a kingdom.

Odin was gone.

He had been gone for weeks.

Out doing whatever pleased him, while I rotted in this castle, swollen with his child, drowning in a future I had not been prepared for.

I had tried to reach out.

To my mother.

"Honor your husband, Arianna. That is what a queen does."

To my father.

"I love you, but you chose this. Now you must live with it."

To my sisters.

Anastasia. Alisa. Anya.

They smiled as they spoke, their words laced with the venom of women who had spent their whole lives overshadowed by me.

"I suppose you aren't as lucky as you thought you were, Arianna."

"You always did like to win. Maybe this time you lost."

"It's a shame, really. You could have had anything. And yet, you chose… him."

I should have known.

I should have known there was no help coming.

There was no rescue waiting.

I had made my choice, and now I had to endure it.

Odin's absence had given me the gift of clarity.

And I had not liked what I saw.

I had wanted to break Alexey.

I had wanted to shatter him because I had needed something—

Something I could control.

Something I could win.

And I had broken him.

I had watched his composure crack.

I had seen the torment in his eyes when I whispered taunts in the darkness, when I leaned in, when I tested the limits of his resolve.

But I had taken no joy in it.

There had been no triumph in his suffering.

Because the truth was, I had not wanted to break him.

Not really.

I had wanted him to hold me together.

I had wanted someone to carry the burden with me.

I had wanted—Gods help me—

I had wanted him to carry it.

Because this child inside me—this thing that bound me to Odin forever—

Was my cross to bear alone.

What have I done?

Odin would never share in its weight. Odin would never carry anything. Odin had left me here.

And Alexey—

Alexey, in all his impossible self-control—

Had done what I could not.

He had resisted. He had held the line. He had denied me.

And I had hated him for it.

And I had admired him for it.

The alcohol had loosened my tongue.

The suffocating regret had made me reckless.

"Careful, Alexey. It would be a shame if the court thought you put this baby in me."

As if he had anything to do with it.

As if he has been anything but honorable.

As if I could twist fate itself and remake my child into something other than what it was.

As if I could claim Alexey's honor for myself and pretend this life inside me had been created by love instead of blind, foolish, selfish desperation.

It was a beautiful dream.

I had lashed out because— I wished it were true.

I wished Alexey was the father. I wished Odin had never touched me. I wished I had been smarter.

But I wasn't.

And Alexey had known it.

"We are the sum of our choices."

I heard him say once in passing.

Not to me, but now his words reverberate in my mind.
His voice.
Without malice.
Without judgment.

But the words had felt like a blade, cleaving through the last illusions I had been clinging to.

And yet—

For all his anger, for all his frustration with me—

He had still protected me.

The assassin had almost made it to my chambers.

I had known something was wrong when I heard the clash of steel, the shouts, the thunder of boots in the corridor.

And then—

Alexey.

He had come for me.

Like he always did.

The devotion in his blue eyes had weakened me in ways I could not name.

It had stirred something inside me that I was too afraid to examine.

But I knew what it was.

I knew.

I had found out later that he was injured.

Another scar.

Another wound.
Another mark on his perfect body on my account.

I can't seem to stop hurting him.

The guilt was overwhelming.

I should not care.

But I did.

And I did not know what to do with that.

I did not know what to do with any of this.

Because Alexey was everything I had convinced myself did not exist.

A man of unwavering discipline.

A man of duty.

A man who, despite everything, still came when I needed him.

I had played with his honor.

Toyed with his restraint.

Tried to pull him into my ruin, to make him suffer because I was suffering.

And he had paid for it.

With his silence.

With his rejection.

With his blood.

And I would never forgive myself.

I looked down at my hands, at the swell of my stomach, at the gilded prison of my own making.

And for the first time, I whispered aloud the words I had been too afraid to speak.

"I made a huge mistake."

I did not cry.

There was no use in crying now.

I had already drowned.

And no one was coming to pull me from the water.

The Slow Burn to Nothing – Alexey

The court settled into an uneasy rhythm over the next four months, like a fire that had burned too hot and left only embers in its wake.

Odin was gone more often than not, taking “hunting trips” and “military inspections” with a group of men who thrived on his chaos. He left me behind.

"Hold down the fort, Alexey."

And I did.

I attended council meetings. Oversaw patrols. Reviewed trade reports. Ensured the castle didn’t fall into complete disarray while our king sought his amusements elsewhere.

It wasn’t that I trusted his judgment.

I just didn’t care.

Not anymore.

Odin would do as Odin pleased. He always had. No amount of reasoning, no amount of restraint, no amount of caution would ever change that.

So I did my job.

And I kept my distance.

I spent my free time alone, save for the occasional exchange with Murphy. Even then, I barely spoke of anything beyond logistics.

It was better that way.

Safer.

For everyone.

The garden was quiet, save for the rustling of spring time flowers rustling in the breeze. The scent of earth and fading flowers lingered in the crisp air.

Arianna sat with her hands resting lightly on the swell of her belly, her auburn hair tucked behind her ears, her face calmer than it had been in weeks.

The sharp, desperate edge to her had dulled. Odin's absence had helped.

She wasn't playing games. She wasn't testing boundaries. She wasn't trying to see how close she could drag me to the fire just to watch me burn.

I exhaled slowly, rolling the tension out of my shoulders, feeling the weight of it settle right back in place. My body ached—not from battle, not from wounds, but from something heavier. A kind of tiredness that lived in the bones.

I should have kept walking.

I should have left her to her solitude.

But against my better judgment, I sank onto the bench beside her. Not close. Not comfortable. But beside her, nonetheless.

I didn't look at her.

Didn't offer anything beyond my presence.

And for a long time, neither of us spoke.

The late afternoon light slanted through the branches, catching in the copper strands of her hair. I glanced at her out of the corner of my eye.

Her belly was bigger now.

Noticeably so.

The last time I had seen her up close, the change had been subtle—easy to overlook if you weren't paying attention.

Now, there was no mistaking it.

No hiding it beneath the folds of a gown.

No denying the weight of the life she now carried.

Odin's child.

The future of the kingdom.

She exhaled softly, her fingers tracing the embroidery on her dress absently.

"I wish I was still like you," she murmured.

I arched a brow. "Like me?"

"Disciplined," she clarified. "I wish I hadn't… gambled my life on Odin before getting to know him."

A humorless chuckle left me before I could stop it.

"That's one way to put it."

She huffed a breath of laughter herself, though there was no humor in it.

"It's the only way to put it."

I didn't argue.

She exhaled, tilting her head back, staring up at the sky as if looking for answers she already knew she wouldn't find.

"I thought the Gods held my fate in their hands. That if I followed them, if I served them, they would guide me to what was meant for me."

A pause.

"I thought Odin was meant for me. A gift from the Gods."

There was no bitterness in her voice. No anger. Just regret.

"I was so sure."

She let out a slow, tired breath.

"And now, I don't even know who I am anymore."

I didn’t sugarcoat my response.

"You are the sum of your choices."

She stiffened slightly, like my words had struck something raw.

"You may regret your choices," I continued, "but that does not mean you were powerless in making them."

Arianna let out a small, breathy laugh—half amusement, half self-loathing.

"Spoken like a man who never makes mistakes."

I turned to her then, my expression unreadable.

"I have made plenty of mistakes, Majesty."

Her gaze flickered to mine.

" And yet, fate always seems to favor you."

I exhaled through my nose.

" No. I just don’t jump off cliffs and pretend I can fly.”

Arianna’s lips curled slightly—almost a smirk.

"And yet, you sit beside the woman who fell headfirst into the abyss."

"Against my better judgment." I admitted.

She laughed. It was breathy and real.

Silence stretched between us, heavy but not uncomfortable.

For the first time in a long time, she didn’t argue.

She didn’t reach for a blade.

She didn’t try to make me feel anything at all.

Instead, she just sat there.

She looked down at her hands, flexing her fingers slightly before smoothing them over the curve of her stomach.

"Do you think there is a way back?" she asked quietly.

"From what?"

She hesitated.

"From this. From what I've become."

I studied her for a long moment.

"That depends. Do you want to go back? Or do you want to move forward?"

Her fingers curled into the folds of her dress.

"And what do you think moving forward looks like?"

"Making better choices."

Arianna let out a slow breath, nodding slightly.

She did not argue.

Did not fight me on it.

For the first time in a long time—she simply listened.

She looked out over the courtyard, something unreadable crossing her features.

"I was so sure of Odin," she whispered again.

I let out a slow breath of my own.

"So was I." I admitted.

She glanced at me then, her expression unreadable.

"And yet, here we are."

"Here we are."

The garden was silent. The air was crisp.

And for the first time in a long time, I did not feel like I was at war with her.

Just two people.

Two ruined people.

Trying to find their way through the wreckage.

The Weight of a Kingdom – Alexey

The castle always felt lighter when Odin was gone.

Not truly safe. Not truly at peace. But lighter.

Like the air had loosened its grip, like the walls themselves had exhaled in relief.

Odin came and went as he pleased.

Hunting trips.

Banquets in the countryside.

Women who weren't his wife.

As long as he was distracted, the castle could breathe.

And I—

I could almost pretend Lorna wasn't burning.

But I knew better.

The nobles were starting to poke at the edges of power. Testing the seams. Searching for the weak points.

They weren't bold enough to make their move—not yet.

Not while I was here.

Not while Odin still had some grip on his throne.

But I saw it.

In the way they whispered just a little too long.

In the way letters passed between hands like secrets meant to stay buried.

In the way some had started leaving court entirely, as if they wanted no part in what was coming.

They could smell the blood in the air.

And they were waiting.

Waiting for Odin to get himself killed on one of his reckless excursions.

Waiting for the queen to give birth.
Waiting for their moment.

I had made sure they didn't find one.

I held the line.

Not through grand gestures or public threats—but in the way I watched them.

I saw them.

And they knew it.

The queen was really showing now.

The delicate beginnings of a pregnancy had turned into something undeniable.

A swelling stomach, the weight of a future heir growing with every passing day.

It wouldn't be long now.

Soon, there would be a child to keep the castle on its toes.

A child that would shift everything.

A child that Odin would lay claim to without ever carrying the burden.

A child that Arianna would love, fiercely and without question—
Even if it was the chain that bound her here forever.

I had nothing to say to her.

She kept to herself.

And I kept to my duty.

Lorna still stood.

Odin still reigned.

The castle still breathed, for now.

And I—

I would keep it that way.

Until I couldn't.

Until the fire reached the gates.

Until the moment they finally made their move.

And then—

Then, I would be ready.

The Price of Charm – Arianna

Something is wrong.

I know it before anyone speaks it aloud.

The pain comes in waves, sharp and unrelenting, but there is no progress.

No relief.

No sign that this child wants to enter the world.

My body is torn between life and death.

Twelve hours.

That's how long I have labored, each contraction stealing more of my strength.

And Odin?

He returned halfway through.

I heard the clamor of his hunting party in the courtyard.

The laughter.

The revelry.

He had not asked for me.

Had not sent for news of my condition.

He had not come.

Because he didn't care.

This was his child, and he could not be bothered to see if I survived bringing it into the world.

I should have known.

The pain is unbearable.

I feel myself slipping, the edges of my vision growing hazy.

I hear the midwives whispering.

Too much blood.

The baby isn't coming.

I know what that means.

It means I will die here.

In this empty bed, beneath these suffocating sheets, surrounded by people who do not love me.

And I do not care.

What is left for me in this world?

My husband is dead to me.

My child will not survive.

And Alexey—

Alexey is lost to me.

What a complete and utter mess I have made.

I don't remember when he arrives.

I only know that suddenly, he is here.

A voice at the edge of my fading world, rough and desperate.

Someone must have told him. Someone must have whispered the truth in his ear—

The queen is bleeding out. She won't survive the night.

And now, he is kneeling beside me.

Alexey.

My anchor.

My greatest shield.

His hand finds mine, and for the first time since this nightmare began, I feel something solid.

Something real.

Something alive.

"Arianna," he breathes. His voice is wrong. Unsteady. Raw.

I blink sluggishly, my head tilting toward him.

He is gripping my hand too tightly.

His face is drawn, his jaw clenched, his perfect composure fracturing before my eyes.

Alexey.

Always so calm.

Always so controlled.

But not now.

Not for me.

For me, he breaks.

I try to smile. It doesn't work.

I watch as unshed tears pool in his icy blue eyes.

He cries for me.

I don't deserve it.

Any of it.

Any of him.

He shakes his head, his fingers tightening around mine.

"Stay with me, Arianna."

His voice is low, rough, desperate.

I want to look at him—really look at him.

To memorize the sharp lines of his face, the unwavering blue of his eyes.

To hold onto the one thing that has ever truly been mine.

But I am so tired.

So heavy.

And I see it now—what I have done.

I have shattered him.

Just like I wanted to.

But it is nothing like I thought it would be.

There is no satisfaction.

No victory.
Only this.

The pain.

The unbearable weight of what I have destroyed.

I told myself I wanted to break him. To watch his composure crack, to see if there was a man beneath all that restraint who could bleed like the rest of us.

And now, here he is.

Bleeding.

And I feel nothing but shame.

I took an honorable man and crushed him in my palms because I could.

Because I wanted to feel power in a world where I had none.

And he didn't deserve it.

Any of it.

We women complain about how chivalry is dead. We pine for good men, wondering where they have gone.

But the truth is, more often than not, we have buried them beneath the delicate weight of our own cruelty.

We test them, push them, wound them—just to see if they will still stand.

And when they do, we find new ways to cut them down.

I thought I would enjoy this.

That breaking Alexey would give me back some piece of myself.

But it only leaves me hollow.

Ashamed.

"I lost them," I whisper, my voice barely a breath. "Both of them. I have no reason to stay."

Alexey flinches.
Like the words physically wound him.
His fingers tighten around mine, his breath ragged.

"This is the sum of my choices, Alexey," I murmur. "Don't act surprised. You know that."

I do not have much time left.
I can feel it.
The world tilts, the candlelight flickers, the voices around me begin to fade.

I think of another life.
A life where I chose him.
A life where I wasn't blind, wasn't foolish, wasn't cruel.
A life where he was mine, and I was his.

I see it, just for a moment—
A quiet home, far from court and its poison.
His arms around me at night, strong and steady.
His lips pressed to my temple in the early morning light.
A child—our child—with his blue eyes, his quiet strength, his unshakable heart.

It would have been beautiful.
And it will never be mine.

I pray that he finds such a dream.

He deserves love and happiness.
That some woman, some better woman, will give him the life I should have.

Her hands will not be careless.
She will know exactly how to handle a man like Alexey.
She won't pick at his restraint, she'll honor it.
She won't wield his goodness, his honor, as a dagger against him.

She'll stare down those cool blue eyes, witness his beautiful soul, and make him understand what a treasure he is.

She will match his wit, his love, his devotion, with admiration, not cruelty.

What a fearsome woman I will never get to behold. She will be the anti-me.

Where my hands harmed, her hands will soothe. Alexey deserves nothing less.

My fingers move.
Just barely.
I reach for him.
The only man I have ever truly loved.
The only man I will ever love.

"Alexey," I whisper.

His breath catches.
He knows.
He sees it.
He knows what I am saying, even if I do not have the strength to speak it.

This is my final truth.
It was always him.

The midwife's voice cuts through the haze—
Something about pushing.
Something about trying.

I do.
And for a moment—hope.

But then—
Silence.

I know before they say it.
I know by the way the midwife lowers the bundle in her

arms.
By the way the priest grips his holy symbol too tightly.
By the way the room—so full of frantic voices only moments ago—
Falls into suffocating stillness.

I know because I cannot hear my child cry.

A breath shudders from my lips.
Stillborn.
A daughter who never took a breath.
A princess who never got to be.
A queen who never rose.

The grief is distant at first, buried beneath the fire in my veins, beneath the unbearable pull of my body tearing itself apart.
Blood soaks the sheets beneath me.
Too much.
Too fast.

I am slipping.

Somewhere above me, Alexey is shouting.
I don't hear the words at first.
His voice is all wrong—
Unsteady.
Broken.

He is still gripping my hand.
Still begging me to stay.
Still trying to be my unshakable knight.

And yet I have broken him.

And I do not want to fight anymore.

Alexey, please, just let me go.

The warmth is fading.
The world is tilting, slipping away from me.

Alexey leans in.
I feel his breath against my skin.
His voice is low.
"Arianna, please."
I close my eyes.
I exhale slowly.
The world softens.
And I let go.

The Human Cost of My Mistake – Alexey

Arianna is dead.

The baby is dead.

And yet—

The castle is alive.

Laughter spills through the halls.

Music plays.

Goblets clink in careless, drunken toasts.

I stand outside her chambers, where the scent of spilled blood still lingers.

I do not move.

It should be me in there.

Cleaning it up.

Staring at what's left of my failure.

I press my fingers against my brow, willing the pressure in my skull to ease.

But it only grows.

I should have protected her.

I should have seen this coming.

Arianna was too bright.

Too warm.

Odin loved her—but he also consumed her.

And I let him.

I was his right hand.

The man who pulled him from the fire, steadied him, cleaned up his messes.

How many times did I excuse his recklessness?

How many times did I stand beside him, thinking it was my job to keep him upright—when in truth, I was only holding him up long enough to do more damage?

I didn't stop him.

I held him up.

And now, the woman he loved is gone.

A sharp commotion cuts through my spiraling thoughts.

I hear my name.

Urgent.

Desperate.

I turn as one of my men rushes toward me, breath heavy with exertion.

"Commander—there's a woman demanding to see the King. She says she doesn't have time to come back later."

The words barely register.

I can't handle more.

Not now.

Not tonight.

Not after this.

Not after her.

I grit my teeth.

"What woman?"

"She's pregnant, sir."

He hesitates, gaze flicking downward. Avoiding eye contact.

"And she says… the child is the King's. She is from O'Akla. The village that was burned down."

The realization hits me instantly.

I felt the color drain from my face.

If true, this wasn't just a rumor.

It was confirmation.

The stories Arianna heard.

The whispers in the court.
I had dismissed them as gossip.
And if this is true, I would be wrong.
I would be so terribly and unbelievably wrong.
The weight of it settles in my chest.
My body locks.
I move before I think.

The entrance hall is dimly lit, torches flickering against stone.

She stands in the middle of it.
A young woman.
Very, very young.
Barely eighteen if I had to guess.
She is small but unyielding.
Her hair—
Strawberry blonde. It catches the firelight like spun gold.

She is beautiful. The kind of beautiful that just is without trying. Freckles fray across the delicate curves of her cheeks.

But her eyes—
Her eyes are what stop me.
Piercing teal blue.
Too sharp.
Too steady.
Too aware.
She is aware—but empty.

Like the humanity has already been siphoned out of her.

Like she has nothing left to give.
And I see it instantly.

As she stands here,
She is in labor.

And she is right—time is not on her side.
Her arms cradle her belly, breath shallow.
But she does not shake.
She does not cry.
She is past fear.
Past suffering.
Past the cruelest four-letter word of all.
Hope.

Her voice is flat. Unapologetic. Over it.

"I am from O'Akla. I was left without a village, without a home, without a family—and-“ She pauses momentarily as if considering the weight of her next words. “With a child in my belly. The King's child." She punctuates.

I don't speak. I just listen in silent horror.

She does not flinch under my stare.
She does not wilt.
She does not break.

"And I cannot care for the baby."

She shrugs, a movement so small it barely registers.

"Since I have nothing with which to care for a child, I have come to ask His Majesty to do so in my stead."

Her throat bobs—
But her stare never wavers.

"Put me to death, do it. I won't protest. I will gladly accept my fate. Just—"
A breath. A sharp inhale.

"Just—take care of the baby, please. The baby didn't do anything wrong."

She sways.

I move before I think, catching her arm just as her knees threaten to buckle.

"What is your name?" My voice is quiet. Cautious.

She exhales sharply.

A flicker of hesitation.

"Mari—" A sharp wince. "Marigold."

Marigold.

The name sounds like the first peek of sun after a blizzard.

The name lodges itself in my chest like a blade.

I don't know why.

I hold her upright.

"Alright," I say. "I've got you."

My voice is different now.

Steadier.

As gentle as I can manage.

"Come with me, Marigold."

And I take her to Odin.

A Fate Worse Than War – Alexey

Odin is drinking when we arrive.

Celebrating.

Arianna isn't even cold in her grave.
The child either.

My stomach churns.
Disgust floods through me, bitter as bile.

He is laughing, throwing back goblets of mead, surrounded by the worst kind of men—the ones who cheer too loudly for their king, no matter what he does.

The ones who have never told him 'no.'

And then we step into the great hall.

His gaze lands on her.

Marigold.

The laughter dies in his throat, the light in his eyes curdling into something uglier.

Recognition.
Disgust.

"You?" he scoffs, lip curling. "You have the gall to show your face here, whore?"

I don't move.
I don't breathe.

He doesn't deny it.

He doesn't ask who she is.
He doesn't ask why she's here.

He already knows.

And that's when I know.

It's all true.

Every word that she spoke is fucking true!

I am paralyzed with horror.

Marigold does not flinch.

She stands before him, straight-backed and poised, unshaken in the face of the man who stole everything from her.

She is beautiful.

Too beautiful for this place, for this moment, for him.

She should have been created by gentler hands than the ones that put her here, at the mercy of this monster.

She speaks.

Calm. Measured.

A voice sharpened down to the blade of survival.

"I have come bearing you the gift of a child."

Her voice does not shake.

Odin snorts. "And?"

And?

And not a single protest.

And not one denial.

I feel my lungs collapse.

Oh, Gods.

The rumors. The whispers.

The stories of O'Akla.

I heard them at court—

Odin was responsible.

A tax dispute.

One house short.

A necessary punishment.

My thought was, Odin doesn't collect taxes.

It must be a tall tale.

Noble speak nonsense.

I never questioned it.

I never looked deeper.

And now, she stands here.

A lone survivor.

And that means—

There were no survivors because Odin made sure there weren't.

Because Odin had already taken what he wanted.

The weight of it crushes me.

Odin didn't just burn a village.

He didn't just wipe out a town over coin, so he says.

Like he is a beggar hard up for cash.

He did this.

He did this to his own people.

He did this to a young woman whose life had barely begun.

And I let him.

The King of Lorna burned a village to the ground, murdering every man, woman, and child except for one.

One woman.

Her.

A woman he chose—not to spare.

Not out of mercy.

But to take.

He could have ended her after he had taken what he wanted from her, yet he did not.

The weight of it presses down on her, yet she stands as if she does not feel it.

As if she will not allow herself to feel it.

She sways—just barely.

I reach for her. A small instinct, an impulse—
But she pulls away before I can steady her.

She steps forward instead.

"His Majesty has made sure I would have no means to care for this child," she says coolly, her voice like steel wrapped in silk. "What else could be concluded, other than that His Majesty would intend to raise His child in a manner to which he is accustomed?"

Sharp. Smooth. Calculated.
Wise far beyond her eighteen years.

Her strength is unbearable to watch.

"Please."

A soft plea.
A codicil.

A blade sheathed in quiet dignity.

All she has left.

And for the first time in my life, I feel guilt settle in my bones like an all consuming sickness.

Because I knew.
I knew Odin was getting worse.
I knew his cruelty had grown, unchecked, since his injury.
I heard the rumors. I heard the pleas.

And yet, this woman is the first undeniable proof.

The first glue holding together everything I tried to ignore.

Everything I tried to excuse.

Odin is not just cruel.
Odin is a monster.

And I did not stop him.

The whole reason I stayed behind in Elarion was to temper Odin's worst tendencies, and I couldn't even do that.

I'm an utter failure.

Odin smirks.

Like a cat catching a mouse.

"I'll consider it." He muses with a smirk. "On. Your. Knees."

I feel it in my bones—the moment something inside me snaps.

Something shifts.

Irreversible.

Final.

Nothing will ever be the same again.

If I don't stop this, I will never be able to look at myself in the mirror ever again.

She doesn't hesitate.

She kneels.

Pressing her hands to the cold stone.

But she does not cry.

She bows her head before the man who took everything from her.

And this—this is worse than war.

Because in war, there is resistance.

A fight.

A struggle.

A battle to be won or lost.

Even in the trenches, there is hope.

Even in the bloodshed, there is a reason to keep going.

But this?

This is what survival looks like when you have no choices left.

There is no war here.
No power struggle.
No push and pull.

She has nothing left to lose.
Because Odin has already taken everything.

There is nothing left to mourn.
Because mourning requires the belief that something was ever yours to hold.

And she does not even believe her life belongs to her at all.

She kneels before him—
Not in reverence.
Not in defiance.
But in resignation.

And it is the saddest thing I have ever seen.

A pain so sharp slashes through my chest, I have to look down—
Half-expecting to see myself split open, filleted cleanly by the sheer cruelty of it.

I take a step forward before I even realize I'm moving.

The final stroke of midnight.
The moment the glass slipper shatters.
The moment I see what my inaction has done.

What my inaction has cost her.

And Odin—

Odin laughs.

As if this is funny.
As if this is a joke.

It grates against my skin.
It burns.

His laughter settles into something low, self-satisfied.
He leans back in his chair, a cruel smirk playing at the edges of his mouth.

"The Gods favor me still."

The room stills.

Odin exhales, shaking his head as if in awe.

"Arianna's child failed me. A useless, dead thing. A weak thing." His lip curls. "That loss nearly cost me Zavros. But this?"

He gestures vaguely toward Marigold—toward the life slipping free from her body.

"This is proof. A sign. The Gods have righted their wrongs."

He shifts forward, resting his elbows on the table. His gaze flicks to Marigold.

"You will raise the child for me.

In the castle.
This child will be my new heir instead."

A pause. A slow smirk.

"And you?"
His fingers drum lazily against the armrest. Amused. Detached. Cruel.

"Death will have to wait for you, little dove.
I'm not finished with you yet."

His voice is almost bored, as if this decision means nothing to him.
As if she means nothing.

"You'll stay where I put you.
Tend to what I leave behind.
And when it grows, it'll never know who you are."

A pause. A flicker of satisfaction.

"You won't be it's mother, little dove.
You'll be its shadow."

A slow breath leaves me.
My fingers twitch.
My control wavers.

Marigold does not move.

His gaze sweeps the hall, sharp. Deadly.

"If word spreads—"

A pause.
A shift.
A warning.

"If a single whisper of its true maternal parentage reaches Zavros, the treaty I made with Zavros falls through."

And then—

"I will kill everyone in this room."

Silence.

Gods.

His cruelty knocks the wind from my lungs.

Then, he moves.

He stumbles from his chair.

His hand rises.

To strike her.

She is already kneeling.

Yielding.
In labor with a child she did not consent to.

And that is the moment I break.

He will touch her again over my dead rotting body.

I move.

Faster than I ever have.

I don't think.

I don't hesitate.

I don't question.

I stop him.

My fingers close around his wrist.

The room freezes.

Silence.

Every eye on me.

For the first time—

Odin looks surprised.

Like a man who forgot he could be challenged.

I don't let go.

I don't speak right away.

I hold his gaze.

I let the weight of this moment settle.

And then—I say it.

Even.

Calm.

Measured.

"There's no need to excite yourself over this woman, Your Majesty."

Odin hears the shift in my voice.

The room feels it.

Everyone feels it.

I am not excusing him.

I am not helping him.

I am not standing beside him.

Not anymore.

I look at him—

Really look at him.

And for the first time, I see him for what he truly is.

A man who will destroy everything.

A man who has already begun.

A man I will have to stop.

One day.

But not here.

Not now.

Not yet.

I cannot save her from what he has already done.

But I can save her from this.

I will not let him strike her down while she is already kneeling in submission.

I let my grip tighten.

Just enough.

Enough to make him feel it. Enough to make sure he understands.

NO MORE.

Not this time.

And then, I speak.

"I will handle it."

I say it in a way that tells him he is done here.

I say it in a way that leaves no room for argument.

I say it in a way that ensures—this will never happen again in my presence.

"Go enjoy your party."

And just like that—

Everything changes.

Culpability – Alexey

I don't speak as I carry her through the halls.

She doesn't fight me.

She doesn't cry.

She doesn't beg.

She does nothing.

Her body is tense, rigid, hollow.

Not trembling.

Not resisting.

Just—waiting.

And then—

She flinches.

So sharply.

So instinctively.

Like a wounded animal expecting the next strike.

It stops me cold.

For a second, my grip nearly falters.

For a second, I almost let go.

Her breath catches—just barely—

Just long enough for me to see it.

The unfiltered terror that she tries to swallow down.

A reflex.

A survival instinct.

A woman who has known unbearable pain at a man's hands.

She is painfully aware of every place my hands touch her.

Every contact point.

Every inch of space between us.

And I feel it.

How she recoils.

How she braces for something I will never do.

Like I am poison.

Like Odin.

Oh, Odin.

What have you done?

I am a knight.

I was supposed to slay the dragon.

I was supposed to protect.

I was supposed to stop this.

Instead—

I fed the flames.

I stood by.

I let this happen.

I let this kingdom fall under the rule of a monster, and I watched.

And now—

The fire has consumed everything.

It has all but consumed her.

And I was the one who made sure of it.

I swore an oath to protect this kingdom.

I thought that meant protecting its king.

But I was wrong.

Gods, I was so wrong.

I should have protected the kingdom from its king.

I should have burned him down before he ever had the chance to light the match.

But now, it is too late.

It's entirely too late.

And the proof of my failure lies motionless in my arms, afraid to breathe.

I bring her to a small chamber.

Not a grand birthing suite.

Not a place of comfort or honor.

Just a room.

A hidden space.

A quiet exile.

Somewhere she can have a moment of peace.

It is all I can offer her.

It is not enough.

I do not speak as I set her down on the small bed.

She does not fight.

She does not flinch.

She does not look at me.

Like she has already left her body behind.

My mind is still ringing.

Still processing.

Still trying to piece together how the hell I let things get this far.

This night is too much to bear for this knight.

The weight of it presses down.

Illuminating every crack in my composure.

And then—

"You're staying, Alexey."

Gretchen, the midwife's voice slices through my thoughts like a blade.

I exhale sharply. "I don't think that's nec—"

"I need help."

Her tone is steel.
Unyielding. Unquestionable.

"My team is dealing with the Queen. You hold her hand. You talk her through this—just like you would talk an injured soldier through an injury on the battlefield. Just like I just watched you do for Arianna."

Arianna.
Gods.

That—
That, I understand.

I stay.

Marigold never screams.
Not once.

She grips the sheets, her breaths ragged, but she does not cry out.
She does not give this world the satisfaction of bearing witness to her pain.
She will not let this cruel world see her break.

She endures.

Not when the contractions wrack through her body like tremors.
Not when her fingers clench so tightly her knuckles turn white.
Not even when the pain must be unbearable.

Ripping her apart.
Tearing her open.
Making room for the child of the man who stole everything from her.

Her silence cuts deeper than any scream ever could.

It is equally sad and beautiful.

I kneel beside her, pressing a cool cloth to her forehead.

It feels like a pathetic offering.

A meaningless mercy.

But it is all I can give.

"Breathe," I say quietly.

She exhales sharply.

Her body locks up.

Another contraction.

I offer her my hand.

To my surprise—

She takes it.

I rub my thumb against her temple, soothing.

She jumps—just slightly.

A flicker of instinct.

But—

She does not pull away.

"You're doing well," I tell her.

The words feel hollow.

Like throwing a bucket of water on a house already burned to ash.

She does not look at me.

She does not acknowledge me.

But—

She does not let go.

And so, I hold on.

Tight.

Unwavering.

Like maybe—

Maybe if I just hold on long enough, I can stop the world from collapsing around her further.

Another breath.

Another contraction.

Another ripple of pain across her face.

I tighten my grip on her hand.

"Almost there."

"The baby is almost out."

Still—

She does not cry out.

She does not give in.

Doesn't yield.

She endures.

And then—

A final push.

A sound cuts through the room.

Not Marigold's.

A wail.

Sharp.

Piercing.

Alive.

The room stills.

A breath.

A pause.

"A girl," Gretchen murmurs.

Her voice is almost reverent.

Tiny.

Red-haired.

Perfect.

I watch as Marigold stares at her child.

Chest heaving.

Expression empty.

She does not reach for her.
She does not weep.
She does not react.

Nothing.

Because the world has already taken everything from her.
Because she has nothing left to give.

And I don't know why I say it.
But I do.

"I'm going to make this right, Marigold."
"I promise."

She finally looks at me.

Not with gratitude.
Not with hope.

But with something hollow.

Like a woman who has heard too many promises before.
And seen every one of them broken.

Her gaze lingers—steady, unblinking.
Not searching.
Not questioning.
Just watching.

Waiting.

For what, I don't know.
For me to take it back?
For me to choke on my own words?

For me to realize—

There is nothing to be made right.

The silence stretches—vast and merciless.

And I swear I can feel it.

It presses against my ribs, thick and suffocating, wrapping around my throat like a noose—like it's daring me to fill it.

I don't.

I can't.

Because there is nothing to say.

I have seen men die on the battlefield. Watched the light leave their eyes. Held their hands as the life drained from them.

I have seen grief.

I have seen rage.

But I have never seen anything like this.

Like a woman who has already died standing.

I expected defiance.

I expected fury.

I expected anything but this.

This emptiness.

This quiet, unbearable absence.

I force myself to swallow, but the weight of it stays lodged in my throat, bitter and unyielding.

I turn away before it undoes me completely.

Because if I stay in this silence any longer—

I might have to admit what I already know.

I let this happen. And there is no making it right.

The Line in the Sand – Alexey

I brace my hands against the basin, watching as water drips from my face, pooling into the cracks of the stone.

The candlelight flickers.

The walls breathe in shadows.

The room is silent—too silent.

But I can still hear it.

The echoes of laughter from the great hall.

The clinking of goblets. The revelry.

Odin's voice, drunk and triumphant, ringing through the castle like a war drum.

I squeeze my eyes shut.

How is this real?

How can a man rejoice when his wife—his queen—lies dead?

How can he raise a goblet when his child—his own blood—never even took a breath?

How can he stand beneath the same roof where a woman he brutalized has just given birth to a child she never asked for?

And yet—

He drinks.

He laughs.

He celebrates.

The realization sits like poison in my gut.

I open my eyes and stare at my reflection in the water.

But the man staring back at me—

I do not know him.

There is no knight in that reflection.
No soldier.
No protector.

Only something else.
Something hollow.
Something dangerous.
Something broken.

A man who built a throne out of his own blind devotion—
And watched the monster he put there burn the world down.

Gods help me.

I could have taken the crown.
I should have.
I let fear dictate my decision.

I told myself I did not want power.
That I had no interest in ruling.
That Odin was better suited, and my place was beside him, not in front of him.

I told myself I was doing the right thing.
That the crown would make me something I did not want to become.
That I would fail.
That I would be no better than him.

But I was wrong.

Because I could not have done worse.

Odin was reckless before.
Wild. Unruly. Dangerous in ways that I could temper.
Ways that I thought I could contain.

But then—

Then the head injury took the last of his humanity.

Then, the fire in him turned to rot.

And I should have acted.

I should have faced it sooner.

I should have stopped this before it ever began.

I should have seen what was happening—

Not the rumors.

Not the whispers.

The truth.

I should have seen the kingdom catching fire before the flames reached the throne.

I clutch the edge of the basin, my knuckles going white.

I have fought in wars.

I have stood on battlefields soaked in blood.

I have watched men die in agony.

I have killed with my own hands.

And yet, this is the first time I have ever been truly afraid.

Because this is my fault.

I didn't want the crown because I was afraid of the harm I would cause.

That decision aged well; didn't it?

I held Odin up when he faltered.

I shielded him from the worst of himself.

I made excuses for him.

I let him take the throne.

I let him rule.

And now—

Arianna is dead.

Her child is dead.
And Odin—the monster I armed—laughs.
I did this.
I built this.
I made him untouchable.
And now—
I have to be the one to undo it.
A slow, deep breath.
I cannot undo this.
I cannot bring back the dead.
I cannot wash the blood from my hands.
But I can end this.
I can draw the line.
I can bury my loyalty.
I can burn my oath to ash.
Because I will not stand by and watch this kingdom burn beneath his rule.
I will not allow another woman to suffer what Marigold has suffered.
I will not be passive.
I will not be careful.
I will not make this mistake again.
I wipe the water from my face.
Turn on my heel.
And walk out.
Because tonight—
I bury my loyalty.
And tomorrow—
I start a war.

The Devil's Bargain – Alexey

Odin lounges in his chair when I find him.

A goblet in hand.

One leg draped over the armrest.

Reclined, comfortable. Untouched.

A dead wife.

A dead heir.

And he drinks.

He grins when he sees me, unbothered, unburdened, untouched by the grief that chokes this castle.

There is no mourning here.

Only revelry.

Only a king too drunk on his own power to realize that he is already rotting.

"There he is."

Odin lifts his cup lazily, as if greeting an old friend at a tavern.

"I was wondering if you had gotten lost."

I step forward, my face unreadable. Controlled.

Dangerous.

I will not show him my disgust.

Not yet.

"You have a daughter," I say evenly.

Odin blinks.

Then scoffs.

"Hells, I had a feeling that wench would spit out a girl, just to spite me." He rolls his eyes and takes a long drink.

Not even a pause.

No flicker of hesitation.
No shame.

He does not care.

"Well, no matter." He waves a hand carelessly, already dismissing her existence. "It doesn't change the arrangement. She will be known as Arianna's child, and I will preserve my treaty with Zavros."

His smirk curves like a blade.

"The Gods smile favorably on me, Alexey."

The Gods.

As if the Gods still look at him at all.

I do not answer.

Odin studies me over the rim of his cup.
His instincts should have warned him.
But he is too drunk on power to feel it.

"Something on your mind, old friend?"

Old friend.

The words are an echo of another life.
Another man.
They used to mean something.

Now, they are nothing but a ghost.

I keep my tone neutral.

"I had a thought."

Odin smirks. "That's dangerous."

You have no idea.

I ignore him.

"If the child is to be Arianna's, then she will be of great importance to your treaty, yes? Eyes will be on her if she is left at court. Questions will be asked. The truth may be discovered."

I let the words settle.

Let him think they are his thoughts.

"It would be far easier to keep the truth concealed if someone with absolute loyalty were to monitor the princess at all times. Away from court."

Odin raises a brow.

I tilt my head slightly. Careful. Calculated.

"As a personal favor. From an old friend."

I see it.

The moment he considers it.

The wheels turning.

He thinks I am offering a service.

A kindness.

He leans back, grinning.

"You always were a good man, Alexey."

I want to kill him.

The thought comes too easily.

Too smoothly.

Like a blade sliding between ribs.

Odin gestures vaguely.

"Fine. Take them to your estate." He waves a hand, careless, indifferent. "Just make sure that wench knows her place. She's a nursemaid, nothing more."

His smirk sharpens.

A predator pleased with himself.

"You'll keep her in line, won't you?"

I nod.

A single, precise movement.

"Of course."

My voice does not betray me.

Not yet.

I turn on my heel and leave before the mask cracks.
Before the anger breaks free.
Before I let him see it—
See me.

Because I know the truth now.

I built this monster.
And I am going to tear him down.

The Moment We Knew We Unleashed a Monster – Alexey

The castle halls roar with laughter.

Goblets clink.

A celebration of nothing.

An heir who isn't an heir.

A king who isn't a king.

I move through the corridors like a shadow, unseen, unheard.

There's no reason to be secretive—no one is looking for me.

But they should be.

Because I am no longer one of them.

Because tonight, I made a decision.

Because tonight, I turned my back on my king.

And I don't regret it.

Not even a little.

When I reach Murphy's chamber, I shove the door open without knocking.

He's at his table, half-dressed, a bottle of Zavrosian brandy in front of him.

His boots are kicked off, his tunic loose—

The signs of a man who has drunk himself into something close to peace.

But the second he sees my face—

That peace shatters.

Murphy straightens.

His fingers tighten around the bottle, but he doesn't drink.

"I am so sorry about Arianna, man," he mutters.

His eyes flick over my face, searching.

Whatever he sees there—it makes him go still.

A moment passes.

Then, quietly—

"Wait. What else has happened?"

I don't sit.

I don't waste time.

I plant my hands on the table—

Knuckles white. Breath slow. Measured. Controlled.

Until it isn't.

"We really fucked up, Murphy."

Murphy's humor vanishes.

Just like that.

"Fuck, what happened?"

I exhale sharply, my jaw locking so tightly it aches.

"The rumors were true. The rumors we thought were rumors. They were all true, fucking true, Murphy. O'Akla was burned to the ground—by Odin."

Murphy frowns. "O'Akla? The small mountain town? The fur traders?"

I nod.

His confusion deepens. "But… why? The rumors said taxes? Since when does Odin collect taxes? That makes no damn sense anyway. You can't collect taxes from the dead. Besides, O'akla is so far up north in the Myroska Tundra, what would he have to gain?"

I don't answer.

Because I don't fucking know.

Because maybe—

There was no reason at all.

Murphy studies me.

Waiting.

Then—

I see it.

A flicker of something in his gaze.

Doubt.

Not in me.

In Odin.

Finally.

He is keeping up.

Murphy leans back, gripping the arm of his chair.

"Did you know about this?"

The way he says it—

My gaze snaps to him.

Offended.

Angry.

Finished.

"Of course not. I wouldn't have allowed this savagery."

Silence.

"I – I thought it was idle gossip. I had no idea it was true."

Then Murphy exhales, dragging a shaking hand down his face.

"Shit."

I nod.

"Yeah. Double shit."

Murphy looks up.

His face shadowed.

Something dark settles behind his eyes.

"This happened right under our noses? So, how exactly did you find out?"

I exhale slowly.

Steady.

Controlled.
But it doesn't matter.
The words still hurt.
"He burned the village to the ground. Killed everyone. Except one woman."
Murphy's fingers tighten around the table's edge.
His eyes search my face—
Like he doesn't want to believe what he already knows I am going to say.
My voice catches.
"He left her pregnant and homeless. Her family, her village—gone."
Murphy stiffens.
His jaw locks.
His breath leaves him slow and sharp.
"It can't be true."
But we both know it is.
"She came to court tonight."
My voice is a razor.
"On her hands and knees, Murphy."

I choke back tears and anger as the images come rushing back into my mind.

Murphy's gaze darkens.
"Begging Odin to take the child, to provide for the baby."
The words burn in my throat.
"She didn't even care if he had her executed. She welcomed it. It was one of the first things she said to me, Murphy. So young. Barely 18, if I had to guess. And she willingly walked into this castle, expecting not to leave alive."
I inhale sharply, swallowing the raw ache in my chest.

"Whoa." He mutters.
"I have never seen a person so broken."
I shake my head.
"Not even the men we fought with in the war. Even they had hope. They didn't want to die. They didn't welcome it. Long for it. She had… He left her with nothing to live for."
I force the next words out.
"She was already in labor. That would mean all of this took place 3 months after he woke up from his coma, if we date it back 9 months. This was after the accident."
Murphy's breath catches.
"She waited until she had no other choice," I say, my voice quiet but heavy.
"Until the child was coming—until there was nowhere left to run. Nowhere left to turn… but to him. It must have destroyed her. To swallow her pride and beg for the child's life."
Murphy doesn't speak.
But I see it.
The flicker of sadness.
Guilt.
Regret.
I keep going.
"And Odin laughed at her suffering."
Murphy goes still.

"I am sorry." Murphy sat up straight. "He did what, now?"

And then—
I say the worst of it.
"Now, he's demanding she pretend the baby is Arianna's."
Murphy's fingers dig into the table.

"Come again?"

"He wants her to raise the child as the daughter of a dead queen—to maintain his treaty with Zavros. A treaty he had already made that hung on Arianna's child. With that child gone, he will use this new one as the replacement."

Murphy swears under his breath.

I nod grimly. "If the truth gets out, the deal collapses."

I pause, jaw tightening. "I still don't know what he's getting in return." I admit solemnly.

Murphy is stone still.

Then, slowly, his fingers curl into fists.

When he speaks next, his voice is different.

Cold.

Sharp.

Unforgiving.

"So not only did he burn a town for no reason, violate an innocent woman, and demand she raise his child under his thumb—he also wants her to erase herself from existence completely. He wants to make her nothing. He wants her to become nothing."

His voice is raw with disgust.

"Pretend that her baby is actually Arianna's?" He repeats as if trying to process the insanity of it all.

I nod. Once.

Murphy shakes his head, exhaling through his nose.

His gaze locks onto mine, sharp and cold.

"That's not madness, Alexey. That's calculated. That's cruelty with intent. That's the rawest form of evil. Even war wasn't this brutal. He is unleashing a new level of savagery on her. Like he enjoys it."

I know.

And I let it happen.

I was his right hand.

His war brother.

The one who pulled him from the fire.

The one who kept him standing—long enough to do this.

I fought beside him.

Bled beside him.

Believed in him.

I thought I could temper him.

I thought I could shape him.

I thought I could hold him back.

But I didn't.

I held him up.

And now—

The man I once called brother has burned a village to ash.

Ripped an innocent woman from her life.

Turned her body into his personal playground.

And when she returned, on her knees, with his child in her arms—

He laughed.

He laughed.

Like it was a joke.

Like her suffering was amusing.

Like it was all some grand fucking game.

Like she wasn't a person.

Like she doesn't have human feelings.

I pace like a wolf in a cage.

My voice is a snarl.

"He called her a nursemaid."

The word burns my throat.

"A fucking nursemaid, Murphy. Like she was hired. Like she's just some handmaid who stumbled into the worst moment of her life and—"

I punch the wall.

Stone meets skin. My knuckles split. Blood smears.

I do it again.

I recount the events out loud.

"She begged me to kill her. She welcomed it. She was in labor. And he laughed. He fucking laughed," I repeat.

The horror echoing in my mind.

I whip around. My chest heaves.

"I saved him. Over and over. I dragged him from death like a fool—like a damn fool—and he turned around and did this."

I clench my jaw so tight it aches.

"I should have let him die."

Murphy blinks.

I don't.

"Back then. On the battlefield."

I breathe—sharp and ragged.

"There were so many moments. I had the chance. I hesitated. And then I fucking saved him. No man left behind."

I shove another chair over. It splinters.

"I thought I was saving a good man. I thought I was doing the right thing."

I turn to Murphy.

My voice is wrecked.

"This. This is what he did with my loyalty. He raped an eighteen-year-old woman, killed her family, forced her to carry around his sin and shame, and when she could no longer carry it, she asked him for mercy—for the baby, not even herself—and he laughed in her face. He demanded she erase herself. He broke her. Then told her to smile. To be grateful she was ruined by a king like she should wear it like a badge of honor."

Nausea rolls over me.

Murphy stares at me.

Then—

Slowly—

His fingers tremble.

His throat bobs.

A long, shuddering exhale.

A sound too human.

Too broken.

Too fucking late.

It's entirely too fucking late.

The guilt.

The shame.

Claws at my chest.

Murphy drags a hand down his face, breath shaking as it leaves him.

And then—his voice.

Soft.

Raw.

A blade dragged over an open wound.

"We didn't save him, Alexey."

The words land between us.

Heavy as a war drum's final beat.

His gaze locks onto mine.

The guilt in my chest threatens to split me open.
Murphy doesn't look away.
Doesn't soften the blow.
Doesn't offer comfort.

Because there is none to be had.

He exhales. Slow.
"We unleashed him."

The room is silent.
The words settle—
Sinking.
Festering.
Ripping me apart from the inside out.

Because I know.
I know.
And that makes it worse.

He looks sick.
I swallow.
And then—a quiet, irreversible realization settles between us.

We are no longer Odin's men.
We are not fixing a mistake.
We are betraying the King we swore to protect.

And we don't care.

We did not fight for this.

We wanted to make Lorna better.
Not burn it to the ground.

I inhale, forcing steel into my voice.
"I convinced him to let me take her to Willowbrook."
Murphy looks at me. "And, How'd that go?"
I meet his gaze. "And I'm getting her out."

Understanding dawns.

"I told Odin I'd make sure she obeys," I say. "That I'd keep her under my watch. That it would be easier for me to protect the child's identity, his secret, this way. I made him see the cost benefit to him. Letting me do this means Zavros will never know his scam."

I shake my head.

"I'm not letting him ruin her life any more than he already has. He has already taken far too much. It ends right fucking here. No more."

Murphy exhales, dragging a shaking hand through his hair.

"Shit, Alexey. This is heavy."

"I know." My voice is steady. Cold.

Then, quieter—deadly:

"I need your help."

Murphy looks up at me.

"I can't do this alone. I need a second sword to look after them when I am at court—overseeing the end of Odin Dragunov."

I let the words settle. Let him feel their weight.

"Be my second sword," I continue. "Help me see this through, and when it's done, you'll never have to lift a blade again. I'll make sure you can drink, gamble, and waste your days however you please—without ever worrying about coin."

A pause. The smallest crack in the tension.

I allow myself to smirk, just a little.

"Plus, there's free food and wine in it for you."

Murphy doesn't hesitate.

His fingers curl into a fist against the table, his shoulders squaring.

"I got you, brother."

His voice is steady. No doubt. No hesitation. Just loyalty.

"Anything you need."

A beat. A shift.

Murphy's voice hardens.

"We're not his men anymore, Alexey."

He doesn't say Odin's name with respect.

Not anymore.

His voice is iron.

Absolute.

"We're her royal guard, not his."

And just like that—

Everything changes.

Murphy reaches for the bottle.

Lifts it in the air.

His voice is steady. Unshaken.

"To the future queen."

A slow smirk curls at the edges of his mouth—

But his eyes—

His eyes tell a different story.

Then, for the first time that night—

Something flickers beneath the smirk.

Something real.

Something reverent.

Something unforgiving.

He shifts the bottle just slightly—

Not just a toast.

A vow.

His voice deepens.

Final.

"And the queen's mother."

Not just the woman who bore Lorna's future. The woman who endured. Who bled. Who survived.

She isn't just the vessel. She isn't just the nursemaid. She is the mother of a queen.

And we are her guard.

This is our solemn vow.

The Sound of Silence – Alexey

The castle halls are quiet now.

The revelry has faded.

The nobles and knights are either drunk or asleep, oblivious to the monstrous things that happened under this roof tonight.

Odin's laughter still echoes in my head.

The sound of Marigold's knees hitting the stone floor rings even louder.

I exhale slowly, steadying myself before pushing open the chamber door.

Inside, she sits on the edge of the narrow bed, her hands curled protectively around the child in her arms.

She hasn't named her yet.

The firelight flickers, casting jagged shadows across her face.

Her hair is still damp with sweat, clinging to her temples.

Her skin is bloodless with exhaustion.

She should be asleep.

But she isn't.

She doesn't even look at me when I step inside.

She is awake.

Silent.

Waiting.

I close the door behind me, letting the quiet settle between us before I speak.

"You won't be staying here."

She stiffens.

Slowly, she lifts her head—

And when her gaze meets mine—

Sharp.

Guarded.

Waiting for the next blow.

She doesn't look afraid.

She looks ready.

Not for kindness.

Not for rescue.

For whatever fresh cruelty is coming next.

I feel a violent pain in my chest.

Her voice is hoarse. Empty. Stripped down to the bone.

"...The king commanded that I raise the child here."

"He changed his mind."

The lie comes effortlessly.

Lies always come easy when they serve the right cause.

"He has more important things to concern himself with than the cries of an infant."

She watches me carefully.

She doesn't believe that.

Good.

She shouldn't.

I fold my arms behind my back, keeping my face neutral. Keeping myself together.

"The child is too valuable to be left at court. The castle is filled with nobles and spies—too many eyes, too many risks, too many questions."

I tilt my head slightly.

"It would be far easier to keep the truth concealed if someone with absolute loyalty were to monitor her upbringing closely."

She knows what I'm saying.

She knows this is not a kindness from Odin.

But she does not trust that it is a kindness from me, either.

I wait.

Then, finally, she speaks.

"Where are you taking us?"

Her tone is flat—too flat. Calculated. Measured.
Not the voice of a woman waiting for orders.
But the voice of a woman who has already put the pieces together.

She doesn't ask who made the decision.
She only asks where.

Because she already knows the answer.

She clocks me in record time.

I study her for a moment.

A flicker of something passes through me—something close to admiration.
She isn't broken.
She's watching me as closely as I watch her.
And she saw it first.

The shift. The strategy. The hand behind the curtain.

And she called it for what it was.

She knows it was my call.

Amazing.

"To Willowbrook."

She blinks.

For the first time, uncertainty flickers across her face.

"Willowbrook?"

I nod. "The chateau is isolated in the Sunfire River Valley," I continue, my voice steady, clinical. "Removed from court, well-fortified, and far from prying eyes. It is the perfect place to hide a princess in plain sight."

The words leave my mouth like a report.

Facts. Strategy. Logistics.

Not mercy.

Not salvation.

Just cold, measured practicality.

Her fingers tighten around the child.

I wait.

Then, softer than before—

"Why are you doing this?"

Her voice is quiet. Not cautious. Not hopeful.

Just tired.

I expected the question.

I expected the doubt.

I expected the wariness in her eyes, the sharpness, the bracing for another turn in the trap.

She has no reason to believe this is anything but another command she must obey.

Another move on the board.

Another way the men in power decide her fate for her.

I hold her gaze.

Steady.

Unreadable.

And then, I say it.

I let her know my truth.

"Because the only thing more dangerous than a monster on the throne—"

A pause.

A long, terrible pause.

Her fingers curl tighter around the baby.

My hands curl into fists.

"—is the man who helped put him there."

The truth sits in the air like a curse.

She doesn't flinch.

She doesn't blink.

She just stares at me.

And I can't breathe.

Because this is the first time I've said it aloud.

The first time I've let myself admit—

This kingdom is not just Odin's ruin.

It's mine.

The blood he spilled is on my hands.

The villages he burned? I helped him keep order while he did it.

The people he crushed? I was the one who kept them in line before he ever lifted the hammer.

I built him into this.

I sharpened the blade that he became.

I watched, I justified, I smoothed over, I cleaned up—

And now?

Now, I stand in front of a woman who lost everything because of it.

A woman who had to kneel before the man who violated her, begging for the life of his child.

A woman who should hate me.

A woman who does not even have the luxury of hatred, because she is too fucking tired to carry it.

Her silence guts me.

Because she should spit at me.

She should curse my name.

She should tell me I am no different from him.

But she doesn't.

And somehow, that is worse.

Her breath stills.

A shadow flickers across her face.

But she does not speak.

Her fingers tighten around the baby, her knuckles white with the pressure.

She doesn't cry.

She doesn't plead.

She just breathes.

Slow. Measured. Controlled.

I watch her, waiting.

For what, I don't know.

A reaction?

A sign that she is still human beneath all the devastation?

But there is nothing.

She isn't fighting.

She isn't surrendering.

She is calculating.

And suddenly, I understand.

She isn't just listening to me.

She is studying me.

Dissecting every word, every shift in my expression, every flicker of hesitation.

Not just for answers.
For leverage.

She is brilliant.
Even in ruin, she is brilliant.

I admire her strength.

I resent she had to have it.

I exhale sharply, raking a hand down my face.

"You didn't come here because you wanted to," My voice quieter.
"You came because you had nowhere else to go."

She doesn't confirm it.
She doesn't need to.

I already know.

Because no woman willingly kneels before her rapist.
No woman willingly hands her child over to the man who destroyed her.

Unless she has already exhausted every other option.

My stomach twists violently at the realization.
She was trapped.

Arianna's food banks were shut down.

Arianna's shelters were closed.
The villages would not shelter her.
The temples must have turned her away.

The nobles would never lift a hand for her.

Once they saw she was unmarried and pregnant.
Society would have cast her aside.

No support. No safety. No choice.

And so, she did the only thing a mother could do. She walked into hell's fire.

She faced the devil himself.

And she begged.

Not for her own life. She didn't care about that.

She was already done.

But for the child.

The only thing left in this world worth fighting for.

And Odin laughed.

Gods, I will never forgive myself for this.

I take a slow step back, needing distance, needing air.

The room suddenly feels too small, too heavy.

Her eyes track the movement. Silent.

Still watching.

Not out of trust. Not out of fear.

Just out of habit.

Because she knows better than to stop watching the men who hold her fate in their hands.

I swallow the guilt, pressing it deep into the pit of my stomach where it can fester alongside the rest of my failures.

I force my voice steady.

"Get some rest, Marigold."

She doesn't move.

I nod toward the child.

"You'll need your strength."

She exhales.

Not in relief.

Not in gratitude.

Not in anything I can name.

Just… existence.

Her silence is deafening.

And before I can say anything else—before the grief and rage and regret crack open inside me—

I turn and leave.

Моя боль — моя корона.
My pain is my crown.

Carried with Love – Alexey

The bells toll.

Slow. Steady. Somber.

Arianna is dead.

Her child is dead.

The nation grieves. The people gather. The priests murmur their prayers. The nobles bow their heads in practiced sorrow.

And Odin?

Odin is not here.

He does not stand before her grave. He does not watch as the cooper-haired girl he once claimed to love is lowered into the earth.

He is not here to see the way the people mourn her.

To see the way they loved her.

To see the way their tears shame him.

And I don't know if it is good or bad.

A man who does not mourn his wife, who does not lay her to rest himself, is a man who is either too ashamed to face what he has done—

Or too empty to care.

I do not know which is worse.

Murphy stands beside me. Silent. Watching.

His arms are crossed, his face set in stone, but I see it—the tension in his shoulders, the slight twitch in his jaw.

Odin is his king.

Odin was his friend.

But today, I think Murphy realizes—truly realizes—what we have done.

We put a man on the throne who does not feel.

I say nothing.

I simply watch as the green eyed girl I once knew—the girl who laughed in ballrooms, who twirled on balconies, who thought she had married a man worthy of her love—is swallowed by the earth.

And I think: She is lucky.

She never lived long enough to truly see the kind of monster Odin is.

I did.

And I let it happen.

I feel the weight of it pressing into my ribs, into my skull, into the marrow of my fucking bones.

The weight of my failure.

I fought beside Odin. Bled for him. Killed for him. I held up his banner, his name, his fucking crown.

And now?

Now I know the truth.

I put a monster on the throne.

I swallow hard, staring at the fresh mound of dirt. I try to think of Arianna's laughter, but all I can hear is Marigold's voice.

"You can do whatever you want to me. Just—take care of the baby."

She came to court prepared to die.

Murphy shifts beside me.

I drag a hand down my face. My throat tightens.

I have fought in war. I have seen men impaled, gutted, burned alive. I have heard their screams as they bled out in the snow.

But I have never—never—seen someone so utterly ready to die.

Odin didn't just hurt her.

He erased her.

And still, she carried the child.

She could have abandoned it. She could have left it in the woods, or at a temple, or with a stranger on the road.

But she didn't.

She carried it.

Despite the violence that created it.

Despite the memories that must have haunted her.

Despite knowing that every kick in her belly was a reminder of what had been done to her.

She carried it with love.

Gods.

I exhale sharply, bracing my hands against my knees.

How long did she wander, I wonder?

How many doors did she knock on, hoping someone would give her shelter? How many nights did she go hungry? How many times did she lie awake, terrified of what would happen once the child was born?

She exhausted every option.

And when there was nothing left, when she was truly out of choices—she came to the one place she swore she never would.

To kneel. To beg.

And he laughed.

He laughed.

Murphy exhales sharply beside me.

His head is bowed, his hands clasped in front of him. But I see the way his fingers tighten, the barely restrained tension bleeding through his body.

He feels it too.

The wrongness of all of this.

I force my breath steady.

The bells toll again.

Arianna is gone.

But Lorna remains.

And I am the only thing standing between this kingdom and another war.

I cannot break.

I have no choice but to endure.

But Gods help me—

I am cracking.

A New Beginning in the Ashes – Alexey

The carriage rocks gently over the frost-covered road, the wheels creaking beneath the weight of silence.

It is cold.

Not just in the way the air bites at my skin, but in the heavy quiet that has settled between us—a silence so thick it feels like something I could reach out and strangle.

Murphy sits across from me, his usual humor absent, his gaze fixed out the window.

He hasn't spoken much since we left the castle.

And then there is Marigold.

She sits beside me, holding the baby girl wrapped in thick wool, her fingers curled possessively around the small bundle.

She does not look at me.

She does not look at Murphy.

She stares out the window, her profile illuminated by the faint glow of the rising sun, her expression empty.

But I see it.

The weight of what she has endured.

The unbearable grief of losing everything.

She should not have had to carry this burden.

She should not have had to kneel before the man who stole her dignity and beg for mercy that would never come.

She should not have had to bring a child into the world in silence, choking on her own sorrow.

A sharp, bitter taste rises in my throat.

I watch her for a long moment, studying the delicate slope of her nose, the way her fingers tighten subtly around the child every time the carriage jolts.

She is strong.

Stronger than any woman I have ever known.

And yet—

She should not have had to be.

A single tear slips down the curve of her cheek.

She does not wipe it away.

She does not acknowledge it.

She simply lets it fall.

My chest tightens.

I cannot bear it.

Before I can second-guess myself, I lift my hand and wipe the tear from her face.

Her skin is warm beneath my fingers.

The moment stretches between us.

For the first time, she turns her head and meets my gaze.

Her eyes—so blue, so deep with sorrow—lock onto mine, and for the first time, I see it.

The raw, unbearable exhaustion she has been trying to hide.

She waited.

She waited until the last possible moment.

Until there was no other choice.

She didn't come to court as a mother protecting her child.

She came as a woman resigned to die.

And I—I let that happen.

I helped put the man who broke her on the throne.

The thought burns in my chest, but I force my voice steady.

"The worst is over."

It is not a lie.

It is a vow.

And I will make sure of it.

Something breaks.

Despite her best efforts, her face crumbles.

A shaky, gasping sob escapes her lips, and before she can stop herself, she buries her face against my chest.

I don't think.

I simply hold her.

Her slender shoulders tremble as the grief she has kept locked away finally spills free.

She cries for the first time.

For her family.

For her home.

For the life that was stolen from her.

I tighten my arms around her, murmuring quiet reassurances against her hair, feeling the full weight of my vow settle over me.

I will protect her.

I will protect this child.

I will make this right.

After a long moment, she pulls back, cheeks damp, breaths uneven.

She swallows, then whispers, "Thank you."

I shake my head. "You do not need to thank me."

She searches my face, something unreadable in her expression.

Then, finally, she offers, "For your generosity."

Murphy sniffs loudly from across the carriage.

We both turn toward him as he sighs dramatically, crossing his arms.

"Well, now I feel like an ass. Here I was, ready to make a joke about how we were all gonna die of frostbite before we made it to the chateau, and you two go and have a moment."

Marigold blinks.

Then, to my shock, she laughs.

It is soft—just a small, choked sound—but it is real.

Murphy grins.

"See? I knew I could make her laugh. I have a gift, Alexey."

I exhale, shaking my head.

For the first time in days, I feel something other than anger or grief.

For the first time in a long time, I feel hope.

The Road to Willowbrook

The carriage rolls steadily over the frozen road, the rhythmic crunch of wheels on ice the only sound in the still morning air.

The horizon is painted in muted shades of gray, the kind of quiet, overcast sky that stretches endlessly over the northern hills of Lorna.

Marigold sits next to me, her shoulders squared, her posture straight, always braced for something.

She holds the child—the tiny princess Odin will never deserve—wrapped in thick wool, nestled close to her chest.

She hasn't spoken much.

She hasn't fought, hasn't questioned, hasn't pleaded.

But she hasn't relaxed either.

Not once.

I exhale, adjusting my gloves before breaking the silence.

"Willowbrook is a half-day's ride from here," I tell her, my voice even. "The estate sits beyond the central fields, where the hills open up into the Sunfire River valley."

Marigold's fingers trace absently over the baby's blanket, but she does not lift her gaze from the window.

"In the spring, wildflowers cover the grasslands," I continue, my tone softer now, picturing it in my mind. "The wind carries the scent of lavender and golden heather. There are five willow trees in the courtyard, and a brook runs along the northeast edge of the property."

I pause.

"That's where it gets its name."

Her lips press together faintly, as if she wants to respond but refuses to let herself.

Instead, it's Murphy who huffs, stretching his arms behind his head.

"He's leaving out the best part," he smirks. "The kitchens."

Marigold blinks, caught off guard.

Murphy grins. "The cook at Willowbrook—Margaret—now that's a woman worth fighting for. She makes this roasted duck with caramelized apples that could make a man weep."

Marigold almost smiles.

Almost.

Murphy gasps dramatically. "She is terrifying, too. She once slapped me with a wooden spoon for eating straight out of the pot."

I shake my head. "You deserved it."

"I was starving."

"You had eaten an entire loaf of bread ten minutes prior."

"I was still starving."

Marigold exhales through her nose—not quite a laugh, but close.

Murphy grins in triumph.

For a moment, the tension eases.

For a moment, she isn't a broken woman holding a child that never should have been born from such cruelty.

For a moment, she just is.

But as soon as it comes, the lightness fades.

She turns back to the window. Her shoulders stiffen again.

I don't blame her.

This world has not given her many reasons to trust it.

I tighten my jaw.

I will never let Odin take anything else from her. Not while I draw breath.

Made in the USA
Coppell, TX
09 May 2025

48914331R20308